Praise for ...

The Blue Umbrella

"I've loved all of Mike Mason's writings—his imaginative short stories, his thoughtful essays on vital topics like marriage, children, and joy. Now, here's another side of Mason—*The Blue Umbrella* begins a series of wild and wonderful novels where invention truly takes flight. Here fancied possibilities turn real in characters and events whose dramatic turns of action are anchored in a real place, Five Corners, where Porter's General Store still opens its doors. Reading this magical work makes me wish for my own blue umbrella, makes me hope that this series will join others in the minds of readers who loved Madeleine L'Engle's sci-fi writings. As L'Engle herself insisted, this kind of fiction is not just for children. It's for people. People like you!"

Luci Shaw, author of *The Crime of Living Cautiously*
and writer-in-residence, Regent College

Other fiction by Mike Mason

The Furniture of Heaven

Do you send the lightning bolts on their way?
Do they report to you, "Here we are"?
—*Job 38:35*

Everyone begins as a child by liking Weather …
Not this or that kind of weather, but just Weather …
You learn the art of disliking it as you grow up.
—*C. S. Lewis*

Contents

Chapter 1

FIVE CORNERS

Not many people are killed by lightning.

Zac's mother was.

Zachary Sparks, though small for ten years old, had a look of perpetual astonishment that made him seem larger than life. His eyes were nearly the biggest part of him, round and wide, and his eyebrows had a natural arch as if held up with invisible strings. His voice was high and excitable and his whole body seemed full of little springs. Even his hair, fiery red and frizzy, looked as if *he* was the one hit by lightning. Everything about Zac Sparks was up, up, up.

Until his mother died and everything changed.

Zac lived with his mother beside a golf course. Every day after school he picked up balls from his backyard to sell for fifty cents apiece. He was happy and carefree and his mother was good to him. He had no father. At least, he'd never known his father.

At night, when there were no golfers, Zac's mother liked to go walking across the wide, rolling lawns of the course. To her it was like a big park. She never met anyone else out there. This was a small town and it was quite safe (except for lightning). She liked being in nature and she loved all kinds of weather, especially weather that had what she called *character*, the kind you could feel on your skin: wind, cold, hail, pelting rain, thunder, and lightning.

Whenever a good electrical storm happened in the middle of the night, Zac's mother would wake him up and they'd sit on the veranda listening to the long, almost articulate rumbles and watching the lightning illuminate the great treed corridors of grass. The two wouldn't say much. They didn't have to. The sky did the talking for them. Some of Zac's happiest memories were of sitting up with his mother at night to revel silently in storms.

The irony was that Zac's mother was killed by something she loved. It happened one night when she went walking in the pouring rain, carrying, as usual, her umbrella. Of course, she knew better than to go walking on a golf course with an umbrella in a thunderstorm. But this was not a thunderstorm. On this night there just happened to be one stray bolt of lightning.

One was all it took. Her crumpled body was found the next morning in the center of a fairway. The canopy of her umbrella had been completely consumed, leaving nothing but the skeletal metal frame.

It was the first day of December, just weeks before Christmas, and Zac Sparks was an orphan.

That day and the next were a blur. Even the funeral, on the third day, Zac scarcely remembered—except for the moment when the coffin was being carried outside through the church

12

doors. The weather was unseasonably mild; instead of snow a light drizzle fell. As the coffin moved down the steps and was loaded into the hearse, the rain turned to sleet, then to hail. Small white pellets of ice filled the air and bounced all around like popcorn—one bounce, then still—as though the ground were alive. The clatter, especially loud on open umbrellas and on the wood of the coffin, was like applause.

Then Zac saw something he'd never seen before: a *hailbow*. Though he didn't know to call it that, he knew it was special. It was one of those days when about five kinds of weather were in the sky at once. There were towering clouds, black ones very black and white ones very white and fierce-looking. Between the two the sun came out and brilliantly illuminated the hail. It was like being inside a living diamond. Then the ice wall began to move away and against its glitter he saw the hailbow. It was like a rainbow but pale, almost white, with just the loveliest hint of ghostly hue. The whole scene was so dramatic—huge clouds, falling ice, sunshine, the bow—and in a few minutes it was all over. But it stayed in Zac's memory, just as if his mind's eye had snapped a photograph.

After that, everything was swallowed up by the Aunties. Zac didn't know them; they lived far away in a place called Five Corners. When he first met them at the funeral reception in his home, he began to understand why his mother had never mentioned them. They were horrible.

They were very, very old. Auntie Esmeralda, especially, was so ancient she looked ready to crumble away like a frail piece of lace. Her skin, where not obscured by a thick paste of makeup, was an unnatural, papery white, and she was draped in a long white fur coat. Very tall, she carried a cane, held herself rigid as a ruler, and wore her gray hair long and straight like a girl's.

As Zac stood bewildered in the midst of the reception crowd, that gray curtain brushed his face and a thin, metallic voice rasped in his ear, "You poor, dear boy. How tragic to lose your mother. And in such a horrid way." Auntie Esmeralda sounded as if she had a file stuck in her throat, scraping the human warmth off every word. "But don't you worry. You're coming home with us, isn't he, Pris?"

Home with them? Zac's home was here. With his mother gone, Mrs. Pottinger from next door had been staying with him, just as she had every evening when his mother went walking.

"Dear boy, you have nothing to fear. Your Aunties will take good care of you." This came from Auntie Pris in a voice two octaves lower than Esmeralda's. Much shorter than her sister, Pris seemed almost as wide as the other was tall. More than fat, she was big: squarish, broad-shouldered, solid as a stump. In contrast to Esmeralda's fur, Pris was dressed in a short pink skirt with matching polka-dotted blouse. Perched on top of her blockish head was a pink pillbox hat. Zac was torn between amusement and horror.

Of course, the Aunties were terribly nice to him, hugging him to pieces, patting his extraordinary hair, crooning condolences, and plying him with cookies. Zac hated it all. These strange women were more suffocating than the stiff collar and suit he had to wear.

Sure enough, their tune soon changed. When the reception was over and everyone but the Aunties had left (including even Mrs. Pottinger), they began barking orders: Do this, do that, shut up, stop moping or we'll give you something to mope about. Finally Zac was sent to his room, where he listened restlessly to a fitful wind that developed into driving rain, horrific lightning, and great claps of thunder exploding like bombs. Amidst this clamor, for some reason the most terrible sound was the occasional *tap-tap-tapping* of Esmeralda's cane.

Early the next morning he was roughly awakened as the Aunties, each yanking one of his arms, dragged him from the house and shoved him into the backseat of their big black Cadillac. Throughout that long, stormy day they drove, stopping just once for gas and food. Where did these old women get such energy? It was bizarre—their mysterious vitality combined with an appearance of decrepitude. Throughout the trip Zac sat silent, dozing or staring out the window, his left leg jiggling in a nervous tic.

Only once did the Aunties speak to him. Esmeralda, who was at the wheel, turned to him and glared. "Zachary"—she spoke his name as if it were a dead rat she held at arm's length by its tail—"is a ridiculous name. From now on we'll call you Boy."

And so they did. But his name wasn't all Zac lost that day. He'd had no chance to pack any of his belongings or toys—not his giant monkey, nor his collection of soldiers, nor his box of interesting bits of metal. Not even a toothbrush or his army camouflage pajamas. All he had was the suit on his back and a photograph of his mother that he'd slipped into his pocket.

In this rude fashion was Zachary Sparks uprooted from his childhood home and whisked away to the town of Five Corners to live in a mansion with a plaque by the door that read THE MISSES ESMERALDA AND PRISCILLA HENBOTHER. The Aunties were, it seemed, his only living relatives; there was no one else to take him in. Their house, built of stone—even the floors were marble—had the bleak, dank feel of a castle. No wonder Auntie Esmeralda always wore furs, though Auntie Pris huffed and puffed about in short sleeves, her bright pink skin glistening with sweat.

The place was loaded with china. Hundreds of figurines occupied coffee tables, glass cabinets, windowsills, every available surface. Zac noted a preponderance of elephants, but there were also large vases, luridly painted plates, baskets of swollen fruit. All were made of the most delicate-looking porcelain, as fragile as they were ugly. How did two such large and ancient ladies manage to navigate this glass jungle without breaking anything? All Zac knew was that it was no place for him.

From the moment they arrived, the Aunties bombarded him with warnings: "Don't sit there, Boy … Be careful around that lamp … Do try to keep your leg still …" What was Zac to do? At least the Aunties' silence in the car had left him to sort through his own thoughts. Now every word they spoke froze him tighter until he felt like one of those awful china figurines, condemned to hold one position forever. He was so nervous that, while trying to avoid a row of plates, he backed

16

into a whatnot (a piece of furniture whose only purpose, he decided, was to hold knickknacks in ambush for boys) and broke a small pink elephant.

"*Idiot*! What have you done!" screamed Auntie Esmeralda in a voice itself like breaking glass. Auntie Pris, down on all fours to scoop together the fragments, sobbed as though tears might glue the elephant back together. How strange to see this huge woman crying over a trinket! Meanwhile Auntie Esmeralda, tall as a thunderhead, planted herself directly in front of Zac and croaked, "You … you wicked, clumsy imbecile! Go straight to your room."

Zac didn't move. He didn't breathe.

"You heard me, young man. March!"

Still he didn't move. He'd turned to stone.

"What's wrong with you?" she demanded.

"Auntie," he finally managed, "I don't know where my room is."

Esmeralda's pale head on its long, wrinkled neck turned once to the left and then around to the right, like a bird's, as though examining him with each eye separately. "Well, we'll soon fix that. Pris, escort this boy to his room. Something tells me he'll be spending a lot of time there."

Leaving her precious pile of shattered china, Auntie Pris, with considerable effort, heaved herself to her feet. Drying her eyes with an enormous pink hankie, she growled, "That boy needs a cage, not a room." Spinning him around with surprising force, and poking him in the back with a finger stiff as a billy club, she marched him out of the parlor, up a broad staircase, and along the hall to a door on the right. There, completely filling the door frame, she panted, "You'd better change your ways, Boy, or you won't survive long around here." Thrusting him inside, she shut the door and rattled a key in the lock.

So there he was. The room had a bed, an end table, a wooden chair. Its one window was already claimed by darkness. Though the storm had abated, a wind still blew and tree branches scraped against the pane. Rain drummed steadily.

For a long time Zac sat on the edge of the bed, his mind numb. Eventually he recalled the picture of his mother, still in his suit pocket. He pulled it out, but it was too dark to see and he couldn't find a light. Cold, he climbed under the thin quilt and lay there, stiff as a corpse. He returned the photograph to his pocket but kept his hand on it.

And so concluded Zachary Sparks's first day in Five Corners, the first day of the end of his life. The Aunties might as well have put him in the coffin along with his mother and let the dull rain pound them both into the ground.

Chapter 2

Signs

Zac awoke once during the night. Wrapping himself in the quilt, he crawled from bed to peer out the window. By now the rain had stopped and all was eerily still. It was too dark to see much. He was just about to turn away when he saw a burst of light. It seemed to come from the rooftop of the building across the street. A few seconds later came another bright flare, then another and another, as though someone were up there taking pictures with a big flash camera. Erratic at first, before long the flashes flowed in a flickering stream like the glow from a movie screen. Then came one tremendous blaze so bright that Zac jumped. It was as if the sun had emerged for one split second, filling the sky. In that moment, a long wooden sign hanging over the front of the building was illuminated and its letters burned into Zac's vision. In old-fashioned script, gold on a royal blue background, it read PORTER'S GENERAL STORE.

For a long time Zac waited for something else to happen, but nothing did. He couldn't help but be reminded of lightning, and of the strike that had killed his mother on the golf course. But no thunder accompanied these flashes across the street, and unlike lightning they did not appear to strike the building so much as to flow into it in a smooth current.

What finally distracted Zac from this mystery was his need to pee. But there was no toilet. He was about ready to go out the window when for some reason he thought of looking under the bed. *Aha*: a pot. Though he'd never heard of a chamber pot, he guessed its purpose and awkwardly put it to use, after which adventure he returned to bed and fell fast asleep.

The next thing he knew, it was broad daylight and his door was just opening to admit the oddest person he had ever seen. Very short, hardly taller than Zac himself, it was neither a boy nor a dwarf but a very small man—a midget?—who was very, very old. His face, wrinkled as a raisin, contrasted with a bald, oblong head so fantastically smooth on top as to seem polished. His body, though short, was longish-looking, so that all in all he gave the effect of being reflected in a slightly distorted mirror. Dressed in a dark, funereal suit, this apparition came straight to Zac's bedside and stood there at attention like a little soldier. Zac wondered if he were dreaming. Then the dream spoke, in a thin, nasal voice like an oboe.

"Good morning, Boy. I am Butler, personal servant to the Misses Esmeralda and Priscilla Henbother. The efficient running of this household depends entirely upon myself."

A gap in his teeth lent Butler's speech a continual whistle. A white napkin draped over one arm, he carried a round silver tray that he lowered onto the bedside table. Straightening up and pointing his chin in the air, he pronounced, "I hope you like peanut butter sandwiches. It's all you get until the party tonight."

"Party?"

"Of course. You do know what today is, don't you?"

Zac shook his head.

"Why, it's Auntie Priscilla's birthday! A very grand occasion, catered entirely by yours truly. Now, do you have a present for me?"

A present? How was Zac supposed to come up with a birthday present?

Waggling a finger toward the floor, Butler said impatiently, "A present, Boy, a present!"

Oh. Zac groped beneath the bed for the chamber pot. Butler accepted it with a grimace and, holding it straight out like a ceremonial offering, he turned and processed from the room, his tiny black shoes clicking like a tap dancer's.

For a long time Zac lay perfectly still, pondering this odd little man who seemed to have stepped from the pages of a fairy tale. The tray held one sandwich and a glass of water, as if Zac were a prisoner in a dungeon. Finally he sat up and did what he always did with food: played with it. First he peeled off the crusts and, after some swordplay, swallowed the swords; then he rolled the remainder into a tight ball between his palms and licked and sucked the wad like an ice cream cone. Gazing around as he ate, he considered possibilities of escape. But the door was solid as a coffin lid and the one window offered not so much as a drainpipe to cling to. No crowbar, no matches, not one thing upon which a boy's imagination might seize.

So: He really was a prisoner. *What now?*

His thoughts turned to his father, who had once been a

prisoner of war and had escaped, only to be killed in a mysterious accident. His mother had often told him this story, and many others, but since it all happened before Zac was born, it didn't seem quite real.

More real was Mr. Pottinger, a former neighbor. He enjoyed hiking and he'd promised to take Zac out in the woods and tell him the names of trees and plants. He was a rock hound and he'd promised to take Zac fossil hunting. He'd promised to set up his telescope in the backyard and show Zac the wonders of the universe.

The only problem was that Mr. Pottinger never kept his promises. He seemed to forget them as quickly as he made them. It never occurred to Zac to ask the elderly man *when* they would do all these things. He just waited and waited.

When finally he'd discussed all this with his mother, she explained, "Dear, you mustn't expect too much from poor old Mr. Pottinger. He's an alcoholic."

"A what?"

"He drinks too much liquor. It addles his brain and makes him undependable. He's promised Mrs. Pottinger the moon for years. They aren't a happy couple, I'm afraid."

After this, whenever Mr. Pottinger had called to him over the fence, Zac pretended not to hear and quickly went inside. Unless his mother was there, he avoided his own backyard.

Sitting now before his window at the Aunties' place, Zac pulled out the photograph of his mother. It showed her in a cane rocking chair on the veranda—the same veranda where the two of them had sat at night to watch storms. In the picture, however, the sun shone and her long brown hair gleamed and she held a bouquet of her beloved roses. She seemed just about to say something.

Zac spent the rest of that day sitting on his one chair and looking out his one window like a little old man in a rooming house. This was far from his natural behavior; normally he would have been dancing on the ceiling. But with his mother dead and replaced by two old hags, all of his prodigious animal energy became concentrated in the continual jiggling of his left leg.

The view from his window was not without interest. The Aunties' house was situated at the town's main intersection, where five roads converged like the rays of a star. Naturally Zac was most drawn to the building across the street: Porter's General Store. Even in daylight, though the two-story frame structure appeared normal enough, it seemed somehow alive with mystery. He wished he could see inside but he could not, on account of the big green awnings over the display windows. Yet even the play of shadows on the canvas was intriguing— rich and suggestive as dreams. The large blue and gold sign shone as though illuminated, while smaller signs stenciled in gold along the bottom of the windows read EYEGLASSES, COFFEE, PENNY CANDY, UMBRELLAS REPAIRED.

Catercorner to the Aunties' house, another eye-catching sign announced in childish letters ELDY'S BALLOONS AND FLOWERS. This placard surmounted a rickety wooden vendor's stand with a rainbow-striped awning on an otherwise vacant lot. On the next corner stood a white clapboard church that, with its high steeple, looked unusually narrow. A quaint, highly ornamented sign identified this as THE CHURCH OF ST. HELDRED AND ALL ANGLES. (Zac looked again; yup, *angles*.)

On the fifth corner, between the church and the Aunties' house (Zac could just see this by pressing his cheek to the glass), was another conspicuous sign with tall barber poles at either end, proclaiming WORLD'S SMALLEST BUSINESS ESTABLISHMENT. This boast was actually longer than the building it blazoned, which indeed was the smallest one Zac had ever seen, next to an outhouse.

The one street sign he could read identified the road below his window as HENBOTHER HILL. All day long at the five-cornered intersection, people and cars came and went, the traffic forming an intriguing balletic pattern as drivers took their turns.

Daydreamily immersed in these observations, Zac became aware of a distant *tap-tap-tap* that drew closer and closer until suddenly the door flew open and Auntie Esmeralda invaded the room. Seeing this white-haired specter in a silvery fur coat, palely aglow in the light from the window—it was like one of those nightmares where one is riveted by something horrid and cannot move a muscle to get away.

Practically pinioning Zac's foot with her cane, Esmeralda proceeded to deliver his instructions for the party. He was to remain in his suit (as if he had any choice) and take up a position at the front door, where he would be in charge of greeting guests and collecting their coats. These he was to take upstairs and pile on his bed. After everyone had arrived, he was to report to Butler in the kitchen for further duties.

Throughout this harangue Zac avoided meeting Auntie

Esmeralda's piercing eyes. Instead he watched her hands, especially the one clasping the cane handle. Even for a tall person, she had extraordinarily long and slender fingers with immaculately manicured nails. The skin was oddly smooth, not a wrinkle to be seen, and with no makeup it appeared even whiter than her face.

Now this hand brought the cane right up to Zac's eyes and began waving it slowly back and forth. Though he wanted to look away, he could not.

"That's right, Boy," she intoned. "You have good reason to pay attention to this cane. Because it has two very interesting applications, both of which involve you. Can you guess what those are?"

Zac said nothing.

"Then let me tell you. One has to do with your backside. And the other"—she made a sound that was evidently a laugh but seemed more like a snake's hiss—"has to do with your *inside*. What do you say to that?"

Zac could think of no reply.

"Come, Boy, has a cat got your tongue?"

Zac stared.

"You do know how to talk, don't you?"

He nodded.

"Then say something!"

"Yes, Auntie. What should I say?"

"That will be all. Boys should be seen and not heard."

Chapter 3

The Party

The night of the Aunties' party it snowed—first thin, starved flakes barely identifiable as snow in the gray twilight, then fatter flakes that whirled as the wind picked up. By party time it looked as if a down-quilt factory had exploded.

For a long time Zac sat at his window, mesmerized, until at last Butler came to fetch him. Decked out in a tuxedo and fairly bursting with officiousness, the little man repeated Zac's instructions several times and ran a lint brush over his suit. Then he ushered him downstairs and stationed him at the front door in the shadow of the distressingly buoyant Auntie Pris. Brimming with birthday bubbliness, she wore a pink leather suit with an enormous hat that looked as if it were made from a toilet seat. Esmeralda, now in a white mink stole and silver lamé gown, glittered from head to toe with a dark, electric energy.

Zac was expected to answer the doorbell, bow to guests, and say, "Good evening. May I take your coat?" For some reason he was required to bow with one arm bent behind his back and the other over his stomach. Auntie Pris tried to demonstrate but couldn't quite, on account of being too thick in the middle. Everything about the woman was big, from her bosom to her elephantlike ears to the long, stiff black hair that sprouted from the mole on her chin. Of all the mysteries Zac would encounter in this strange new place, one of the most puzzling was why a person wouldn't bother to pluck such an ugly bristle.

Zac did well with the first few guests. But by this time he was so hungry (in twenty-four hours he'd had nothing but a peanut butter sandwich) that when three ladies arrived and he tried to bow to each one, he keeled over. The next thing he knew, Auntie Pris was yanking him to his feet, saying, "What a clumsy boy! Yesterday he broke one of my precious elephants and now he's trying to break his own head. Get up, Boy, get up!"

After this Zac worked hard at staying alert. The cold air, at least, he found invigorating, as a gust of winter arrived with each of the guests. Stomping their feet on the mat, shaking the white powder from their hats, and blowing vigorously into their fists, they seemed walking incarnations of the cold and the wind, the snow and the night. Esmeralda greeted each one with, "Wretched weather!" while Pris chimed in, "Positively wicked!" Amidst a chorus of "Happy birthdays," the guests piled their bulky garments on top of Zac until he could scarcely see. The coats were so heavy he could take only three or four at a time, and even then he struggled as he labored up the stairs like a small woolly mammoth. Adults were such large creatures, he thought, especially the ones the Aunties knew. And their coats were rank with musty smells:

smoke, sweat, damp fur, creams and perfumes, old age. Mixed with all this was the smell of the weather and the unique odor of each individual. Except for the outdoors smell, which was good, all the others seemed to belong not to human beings but to some alien race.

When the pile of coats, hats, scarves, and gloves on Zac's bed nearly touched the ceiling, still the guests kept coming. Chancing a peek into the parlor, he saw them packed upright from wall to wall, like expensive cigars in a box. Balancing drinks in one hand, plates of *hors d'oeuvres* in the other, they shouted into each other's faces. Their laughter sounded oddly like cries of pain.

Finally, when the doorbell had been quiet for some time, Zac set out to find the kitchen and report to Butler. En route he chanced to overhear a conversation between two middle-aged gentlemen as straight as poles, standing so close together that their waggling beards nearly touched.

"You saw the new houseboy?"

"That runt at the door? A funny-looking creature, isn't he?"

"That hair!"

"Yes, looks like he's had a bad fright."

"Perhaps he just looked in the mirror—"

The men guffawed, nearly choking on their drinks.

"To be fair, I heard he just lost his mother."

"Shame!"

"I'm sure Esmeralda and Priscilla will do him a world of good."

"Yes, if he needs whipping into shape, they're the ones to do it."

A hand touched Zac's shoulder and he turned to see another person his own size, bearing aloft a large tray piled with tiny sandwiches. It was Butler, his long face as grotesquely wrinkled as the rest of his head was gleamingly smooth.

"You, Boy, come with me," he whistled in his reedy voice. He appeared, as much as an extremely small man is capable of doing, to swell with importance. Depositing his tray on a sideboard, he led Zac through a door opening into a pantry and thence to the kitchen, prattling all the way.

"How do you like our little party? Naturally I made all the arrangements. Birthdays, holidays, Valentine's—I handle them all. And everyone who's anyone attends. Of course"—he lowered his voice conspiratorially—"the definition of *anyone* depends on the Aunties. It's very easy to be cut from their list. But then certain steps can be taken to rectify that status. It's really quite difficult to survive in Five Corners without being in Butler's—I mean, the Aunties'—good books."

Zac, finding it odd how this elderly man kept referring to *the Aunties*, ventured to ask, "Are they your aunties too?"

With a withering look Butler replied, "They're everyone's aunties. That's just what they're called."

In the pantry—a narrow room with rows of plank shelves stacked with canisters, cartons, jars—Zac noticed one box larger than anything else, wrapped in foil paper and tied with an enormous pink bow. Patting it delicately, Butler gushed,

"Auntie Pris's birthday present. Naturally I know already what it is. I know everything about the Aunties." Lowering his voice, he confided, "It's a purple porcelain elephant all the way from India! Trust me, Boy, it's an eyepopper. It will be the biggest piece in the entire collection."

Butler went on to explain that ever since childhood the Aunties had exchanged porcelain birthday gifts. "Priscilla fancies elephants; Esmeralda prefers vases and such. And just between you and me"—he added this in a voice so low that his whistle was louder than his words—"you'll find their collections to be extraordinarily large."

A moment later they reached the kitchen, where the first thing Zac saw was a long counter crowded with plates piled high with tiny, triangular, crustless sandwiches. Butler noted with satisfaction Zac's hungry stare.

"Pretty, aren't they? A fine piece of work, if I do say so myself." As Zac reached for one, Butler slapped his hand. "Not for you, Boy. For you I've saved the crusts. You can nibble them while you do these." He pointed to a pile of dirty pots and dishes by the sink. "Pull up a stool, get busy, and I'll be back shortly to check on you."

No sooner had he left than Zac gobbled a few crusts, all the while gazing longingly at the sandwiches. Surely it wouldn't hurt if ... and before he knew it he'd popped one into his mouth. It was delicious, but gone in no time. He took another, then another. However, when he tried to rearrange the plate into its original symmetrical tower, with three sandwiches missing it was noticeably lower than all the others.

Positioned about the kitchen were several step stools, giving Butler (and Zac) ready access to stove, sink, counters, and cupboards. Standing on one of these, Zac was proceeding to transfer the whole plate of sandwiches into a cupboard when he heard the door swing open. Heart pounding, he hugged the plate close to his body, willing it to disappear.

Behind him no one spoke. He waited. Still nothing. Butler was there, all right; Zac could feel his presence. But he wasn't making a sound. Seconds ticked by. The plate was heavy and Zac's hands trembled. Finally, when he could stand it no longer, he peeked over his shoulder. To his surprise, standing by the door was not Butler but a little girl in an apron. Smaller than Zac, probably a couple of years younger, she had short, straight black hair, a pixieish face, and the brightest black eyes Zac had ever seen. She stood perfectly still, gazing at him.

"Hi," said Zac.

She did not react.

"My name's Zac."

She smiled.

"I'm new here." He was getting tired of holding the sandwiches. "I was just, ah, putting these on the counter."

Stepping down from the stool, Zac replaced the plate. Without a word the girl picked up one of the plates herself, turned with it, and vanished through the swinging door.

Quickly Zac fulfilled his plan of stashing the diminished plate of sandwiches in the cupboard. Then he thought he'd better get busy with the dishes. As he worked, he opened the cupboard a crack every once in a while to sneak out a sandwich.

He made a game of tossing them in the air and catching them in his mouth, until before long the plate was empty and he washed it.

Meanwhile the black-eyed little girl kept returning to fetch plate after plate of sandwiches. Each time Zac noticed her pause to smile at him shyly. He tried asking her questions—"What's your name? Do you live here?"—but always she lowered her eyes, picked up a plate, and left without responding.

When Butler eventually returned, Zac watched as he surveyed the now-empty counter, his head cocked like a bird awaiting a worm.

"I was sure I made twenty plates of sandwiches," he murmured. Then he looked directly at Zac. "How, pray tell, can one entire plate of sandwiches vanish into thin air?" He stared so piercingly that Zac was just about to break down and confess, when Butler looked away, shook his head, and said, "That girl. She's always up to some trick."

"Who is she?" asked Zac.

"Why, that's the Cholmondeley girl. Chelsea Cholmondeley." Butler pronounced the last name with just two syllables: *Chum-ly.* "Daughter of the Reverend."

"I tried making conversation," Zac ventured, "but I couldn't get much out of her."

"Much? You won't get *anything* out of that girl. That's the whole trouble."

"What do you mean?"

"You heard for yourself, didn't you?"

"Heard what?"

"Why, nothing! Nothing at all! That's exactly what I'm saying."

"You mean she doesn't speak?"

"Won't speak is more like it. Won't say a word. Hasn't for years."

"You mean she's dumb?"

"She's not dumb at all, she's smart as a whip. But she won't make a sound. Not that she doesn't have a good set of lungs. Oh, she was a yeller, that girl. Used to talk a blue streak. But not now. You could beat her till she's black and blue and she wouldn't say ow!"

"You're not going to beat her, are you?"

"What would be the point of that? No point at all. That girl will go to her grave before she'll 'fess up to those sandwiches." After a pause Butler added, "But a whole plateful! Well, it can't be helped."

As Zac finished washing dishes, Butler bustled about, chattering as he hopped from stool to stool. At one point Chelsea returned, apparently awaiting further orders. Butler, as speechless as she, stood with fists on hips and glared. He worked his lips but all that came out was a low whistle like a kettle on the verge of boil.

"You ... you ..." he finally spluttered, "you're enough to try the patience of an oyster!"

"Butler," said Zac from behind, "I ... I took those sandwiches."

Whirling around, Butler looked genuinely surprised. "You! Here one day and already up to no good?"

"I was so hungry! I didn't think they'd be missed."

"Missed! You won't miss your head either when I chop it off!"

For a moment Zac fully expected to be punished in some horrendous way. But instead the little man deflated and, giving Zac a completely human look, said simply, "Well, there are sandwiches left over anyhow." Quickly recovering his formality, he snapped, "Enough! I've had it with both of you. I'm a butler, not a nanny. Off to bed you go."

Glad to be released, Zac tailed the little girl through the pantry, though by the time he reached the front hall, she had vanished. Where? To her own home? Or was she, too, a prisoner in the Aunties' fortress?

Back in his room Zac sat beside the heap of musty coats and peered out the window as snow piled against the crossbars of the panes. The wind was loud, even louder than the volume of talk downstairs, though from time to time he was aware of the crystalline chime of glasses, like the sound of a spell being woven in an enchanted castle.

Studying the heap of coats, he recalled a story his mother had read to him, in which some children came upon an old wardrobe filled with winter coats. As the children parted the coats and stepped through, the back of the wardrobe opened like a tunnel into another world where all kinds of adventures happened. Zac sighed, longing for such an escape; but surely his room at Five Corners allowed no such possibilities …?

Suddenly a burst of light filled the dark window. He held his breath and pressed his nose to the glass. Seconds later came another flash, then another. At first intermittent, soon they were flowing fast in a flickering stream. Like the ones he'd seen the night before, they seemed to emerge from the rooftop of Porter's General Store, though it was hard to tell through the whirling snow. What could possibly produce such a phenomenon? Fireworks? A drive-in movie? Finally he could stand it no longer—he had to investigate.

Downstairs the party was louder than ever. By now, Zac felt sure, everyone would have forgotten him. It would be the easiest thing in the world for a boy to slip out undetected. But it was a wild night; he would need a coat. What harm could it do to borrow one? He'd be gone but a few minutes, just long enough to have a look around.

Pawing through the pile, he found a soft, silvery ladies' fur with a high collar that might help to disguise him. Anyone would take him for a little old lady leaving the party early. Though relatively small, it was still far too long for Zac, but with the belt he was able to hitch up the lower part around his waist. Emerging into the upstairs hall and catching a glimpse of himself in a full-length mirror, he guessed he looked a good deal like whatever creature the coat was made from.

Waddling partway down the stairs, he crouched on the landing and watched for the coast to clear. A pair of guests stood in the front hall, obviously deep in conversation and not about to budge. Zac was weighing his chances of slipping by them when, through the pantry door, more flashing lights appeared, this time from an enormous pink birthday cake crowded with lit candles, being wheeled in on a cart by the diminutive Butler. Slowly, to the *oohs* and *ahhs* of the chatting couple, the cake floated past, spilling its lambent light over the fantastic road map of Butler's ovoid face. Just outside the parlor door, he paused and signaled. From within came a shrill voice, rising above the others: "Everybody! Everybody! Quiet, please! As you know, we are gathered here to honor a most distinguished lady …"

After more preliminaries another voice was heard, much quieter, barely above a whisper: "My dear sister, how time has flown. And yet, I must say, its ravages have not touched you. You are just as lovely as when I gave you your first elephant. Do you remember—that little plaid one? So many, many years ago."

From his perch on the landing Zac was surprised at how penetrating was Esmeralda's voice. He might have darted for the door right then, had he not felt almost paralyzed by that voice.

"And now, dear Pris," she continued, "it is my pleasure to present you with yet another small token of our great sisterly love."

An audible gasp (apparently over the size of the foil-wrapped gift) was followed by a rustling of paper, and finally by a squealed exclamation that might have been an elephant's mating call. A moment later Butler wheeled the blazing cake into the parlor and the entire assembly erupted into "Happy Birthday."

Here was Zac's chance. Like a silvery weasel he glided down the stairs and across the hall. He knew exactly how the door opened and in a moment he was through. Bracing air filled his lungs and snowflakes swirled around him like confetti. As if waiting with open arms, the whole great dark outdoors rushed to greet him as he practically flew across the porch and down the steps.

And then behind him came a piercing cry—"Stop, thief! Someone's stealing that coat!"—followed by a loud crash.

Chapter 4

The Cane

Instantly the front porch was flooded with light, and people poured out the door. On the sidewalk in his fur coat, an animal caught in headlights, Zac froze.

"Grab him! Don't let him get away!"

A dozen pairs of hands lifted him off his feet and manhandled him up the steps and into the parlor. Surrounded by adults, he felt every face glaring as if he were an ax murderer. The woman from the front hall (who had raised the initial alarm) hauled the fur off him and held it up like a trophy as she darted from person to person, crying, "Mary Cholmondeley's chinchilla coat! He almost got away with it!"

Near Zac's feet Auntie Pris in her toilet-seat hat knelt over a pile of broken china that looked suspiciously like the remains of a large purple pachyderm. She wasn't crying, exactly; rather, what emerged from the pink-lipsticked cave of her mouth was a keening wail so shrill that Zac wanted to plug his ears (though of course he didn't dare).

By now Auntie Esmeralda had recovered enough from shock to screech—albeit in her unearthly *sotto voce* rasp—"You ungrateful wretch! *Do you see what you've done?* You made my sister drop her birthday present."

With improbable suddenness Pris's wailing ceased and her savage face swung toward Zac. "Tell me just one thing: How is it that a china elephant can travel all the way from India but cannot survive for one minute in a house with a small boy?"

A chorus of assenting murmurs went round.

"Do you realize what I paid for that gift?" challenged Esmeralda. "And that coat you had on—do you know what chinchilla is worth?"

"Of course he knows," snorted Pris. "That's why he took it. That coat was a gift from your Aunties to Mary Cholmondeley, the wife of our good Reverend."

Esmeralda aimed a long, bony finger at Zac's chest. "What have you got to say for yourself, young man?"

"I wasn't trying to steal it, Auntie. Honest, I wasn't."

"*Honest!* Why, there's more honesty in my fingernail than in your whole body."

It was certainly the longest fingernail Zac had ever seen.

"Besides," whimpered Pris, "you've ruined my party!" And again she wailed like a siren.

"Come now, Boy," broke in Esmeralda, "just where do you think you were going with that coat?"

"But I wasn't going anywhere!"

"Not going anywhere? I suppose that front door and that sidewalk lead nowhere. And just what were you planning to do when you *got* to nowhere?"

"Nothing, Auntie. I promise!"

"I'll promise you," growled Pris.

"So. Going nowhere and doing nothing," concluded Esmeralda, "and in a chinchilla coat to boot. We'll see about that." Sinking her claw into his shoulder, she parted the crowd and propelled him into the front hall. "Young man, you march up those stairs and go straight to bed. We'll deal with this tomorrow."

As Zac turned to go, Esmeralda called for Butler to remove all the coats from Zac's bed and to sweep up the mess in the parlor.

"If anything's missing from those pockets, Boy, I'll take it out of your hide. You've already got a good thrashing coming."

Head hanging, Zac climbed the wooden hill as heavily as if it led to a gallows. Once in his room he went straight to the window, but no more flashing lights appeared. When Butler arrived, Zac stole a look a him, but his face was set as a mask. He spoke only once, pausing in the doorway with a last armload of coats.

"I hope you realize I'll be telling the Aunties about those sandwiches." Lifting his pointy chin until it aimed almost directly at Zac, the ancient little man backed out the door and locked it behind him.

Instead of going to bed as Esmeralda had ordered, Zac sat for a long time gazing at the rooftop of Porter's General Store. The wind had died down, all was still and dark; nothing moved except the slowly falling snow.

Having fallen asleep in the chair, he awoke suddenly. It was still dark, though not completely. The first gray light of dawn hung in the air like something not so much present as faintly remembered. Zac felt something was about to happen. He sensed it so strongly that, though he was shivering with cold and ought to have crawled into bed, he lingered at the window in the gradually increasing light.

Below him the scene was the same as the day before, yet utterly transformed by a blanket of fresh snow. It was like awakening to a different world, all soft and glistening, changed to a beautiful strangeness. St. Heldred's church, as clean and white as a building could be, looked dingy by comparison with its surrounding glory, while Eldy's balloon and flower stand, festooned with drifts, might have been a fairy palace. Every letter of the Porter's General Store sign wore a stole of radiant white, and every windowsill of every house, every crossbar of every window, was dressed as with an altar cloth from heaven. Telephone poles and fence posts were capped like little bishops with perfect, conical hats and even the delicate icing on the power lines lay untouched in tall, magnificently unbroken rows of holy stillness.

It was all so exquisite that Zac knelt by the window with his hands and nose to the glass, trying to get as close to the beauty as he could. And that's when he saw the man.

He was standing in the doorway of Porter's Store. He wore a white shopkeeper's apron, white as the snow, and he was completely still, as still as the dawn. He seemed perfectly a part of this quiet, perfect morning. At first Zac couldn't quite make him out in the semidarkness, wasn't even sure he was really there. Then, gradually, beneath the white apron appeared denim overalls and a red flannel shirt. One hand rested on his waist while the other held what at first seemed a walking stick, but turned out to be a furled umbrella.

At this point, with the charred skeleton of the umbrella that had killed Zac's mother still vividly etched in his mind, the boy at the window nearly turned away from the man across the street. But something kept him looking.

That something was the man's face, clearer now in the growing light. Right away Zac saw it was not a handsome face, not by a long stretch. No, a plainer face could hardly be imagined. What was striking about it, however, was how full of character and good humor it was. This was a peculiarly happy face, and for that reason, attractive.

Correctly guessing the man to be Mr. Porter, Zac couldn't help staring, as the storekeeper in turn surveyed the silent, snowy morning. Still he had not moved; all that changed was the light. Though Zac himself couldn't see the sunrise, he knew Mr. Porter was seeing it. New-minted light was reflected in the man's countenance, in his eyes, in his smile that was as warm as if his best friend—in the person of the morning—had just arrived at his doorstep.

He was still beaming when he happened to glance up at the window where Zac was watching, and their eyes met.

Embarrassed, Zac drew back behind the curtain, and when he looked again, Mr. Porter had withdrawn into his store.

But Zac stayed at the window. He stayed until the yellow, clanking plow came rumbling along to perform its glorious violence upon the perfect snowdrifts, and he stayed until the first car crept squeakily along the frozen street. He kept staring as other cars arrived to enact their elegant, five-cornered ballet and as the first shovelers began to clear sidewalks in front of houses where smoke rose straight up from the chimneys. And he kept on staring long after, because he just couldn't tear himself away. Moreover, though he wasn't aware of it himself, his left leg was not jiggling. A boy who, until two days ago, had never merely looked out a window for more than five seconds at a time now found himself rooted to one spot, hardly daring to breathe lest he lose hold of …

What?

He didn't know.

But something in Zachary Sparks had changed.

His meditations at the window were interrupted by the chime of the doorbell and by Auntie Pris's heavy tread downstairs, followed by the strange sound of her deep voice squealing, "Edgerton Cholmondeley! How good of you to come! And after your dear wife receiving such vile treatment last night."

"Yes, I'm afraid it's been very hard on her," came a sonorous voice whose aggressively blithe tone seemed at odds with the sentiments expressed. "She found it difficult enough just to attend the party. And then for this to happen …"

"Oh!" bawled Pris as if she'd been shot. "That poor woman!"

"She has been through rather a lot. She would have loved to accompany me today but—"

"Heaven forbid! In her condition? We perfectly understand, don't we, Esmeralda?"

On the flagstones of the front hall came the telltale tapping of the cane.

"Edgerton, what a pleasure to see our good Reverend," said Auntie Esmeralda, "though one does wish for happier circumstances. I'm afraid that boy of ours deserves to be roasted over a good hot fire."

"Roasting's too good for him," grumped Pris. "Skin him alive is what I say."

"I'm not sure I'd go quite that far," chuckled Reverend Cholmondeley. "Perhaps it's best to leave such punishments in the hands of the Lord."

"Spare the rod, spoil the brat," returned Esmeralda. "He's upstairs now, cooling his heels. I've a good mind to put bars on his window and a stouter lock on the door and just leave him there."

"Now, now, Esmeralda. We must consider appearances."

"Truth is, Edgerton, now that we've got him, we don't quite know what to do with him. He's an unruly sort."

"Precisely why I've come: to offer my services. Speak, ladies, for your servant listens …"

The three of them must have moved into the parlor, for Zac could no longer make out their conversation, though its drone penetrated his bones. About ten minutes later he felt the staircase shake as though a small crowd were approaching, whereupon the door flew open to admit (just barely) Auntie Pris. She was so large she had to angle sideways to enter, and as she turned to face Zac, he noticed what big teeth she had, so big they seemed always bared like some grisly animal's. Forever out of breath, she was more so now from the stairs.

"Boy," she wheezed, "you have a job to do. Come with me."

Not the tiniest bit happy about being released from his room, Zac followed her down into the parlor. There, in an enormous pink wingback chair by the fireplace, sat the Reverend Edgerton Cholmondeley of St. Heldred and All Angles Church. He was a man with a fair number of angles himself. Exceedingly thin, he had sharp, bony elbows and knees, a pointy nose, and a long, rectangular face. His look was piercing, like a bird of prey's, and he was dressed in a black morning coat sprinkled with dandruff. To Zac he looked less like a pastor than an undertaker.

When Auntie Esmeralda introduced this eminence to Zac as "the most distinguished man in Five Corners," the Reverend protested, "Please, I'm only a humble servant of the Lord."

"My one wish," continued Esmeralda as though she hadn't heard, "is that our new ward were not so utterly undeserving of receiving a visit from, I repeat, such a distinguished personage."

45

"Give the boy time, Esmeralda. I think we can all expect great things from him. Isn't that so, son?"

"Yes, sir," mumbled Zac.

"There's a good boy."

"But, sir …" Zac began, emboldened by this encouragement.

"You will call him Reverend," said Auntie Esmeralda.

"Reverend, sir," Zac rushed on, "please believe me—I didn't mean to steal your wife's coat. I was only borrowing it, and just for a few minutes."

"Borrowing, my foot," piped up Auntie Pris, who today was dressed in pink shorts and a T-shirt whose floral pattern came close to matching that of the love seat she occupied with her sister.

"No, no," Zac spluttered, "I promise you!"

"Quiet," said Esmeralda in her whispery but commanding voice. "Reverend Cholmondeley did not come to hear explanations. He came to receive an apology. And while you're at it, you can apologize to your Auntie Pris as well, for ruining her birthday. If I were you, Boy, I'd get down on my knees."

Zac chanced one more pleading look to the Reverend.

"You heard your Auntie!" boomed Pris. "On your knees!"

Zac crumpled as if felled by a cannonball.

"Now," instructed Esmeralda, "apologize. First to the Reverend and his wife."

"But please, I didn't do anything," Zac protested. "Cross my heart."

As Zac made the sign of the cross over his heart, Pris screeched, "How dare you be sacrilegious in front of our Reverend!"

"Come, come," coaxed Esmeralda. "You were caught red-handed, outdoors at midnight, wearing Mrs. Cholmondeley's chinchilla coat, and running—actually running—at top speed into the street."

"Well …" Zac stared at the floor.

"Well, what? What exactly were you doing out there?"

"I was just …" For some reason Zac didn't want to mention the extraordinary flashing lights atop Porter's Store. It seemed a matter not to be spoken of casually.

"Yes? We're waiting."

"I was just going for a walk."

"A *walk*!" roared Pris. She struggled ponderously to raise herself from the love seat and then, thinking better of this maneuver, sank back. "I'll just bet you were going for a walk. A nice long one too."

"Now, now," soothed Esmeralda. "Let's get to the point. The boy knows why he's here. Boy?"

Zac drew a blank.

"I'll ask you once more. Why have we brought you into the august presence of Reverend Cholmondeley?"

Zac looked all around the room, as if the answer to this query lay hidden amongst the china knickknacks.

"We're waiting," said Esmeralda. "Three adults with far more important things to do await the response of an urchin."

Staring again at the floor, Zac whispered, "Apologize?"

"What was that word? And look Reverend Cholmondeley in the eye as you say it."

Zac lifted his head, but one glance into those hawklike eyes made him flinch. Scrambling to his feet, he said, "But I didn't do anything. I wasn't stealing the coat. And Auntie Pris, I'm sorry about your birthday present, but I wasn't the one who dropped it."

From the quality of silence that now descended upon the room, Zac knew he had crossed a terrible line. When Auntie Esmeralda finally spoke, her voice was no louder but its tone was frighteningly changed.

"Priscilla, would you like to do the honors?"

"It will be my great pleasure," answered Pris.

Esmeralda, without rising, handed her sister the cane. This time Auntie Pris, leaning her whole weight upon the cane and groaning like a wounded walrus, was successful in heaving herself off the love seat. Zac found himself wondering why Esmeralda, who didn't appear to need a cane, normally carried it instead of Pris.

Planting herself directly behind Zac, the large woman gave the stick one resounding rap on the floor and said, "Bend over, Boy."

"But—" he protested.

"Bend over, I say."

Zac knew what was coming. Bending, and gripping his knees with his hands, he braced himself while recalling the words of Butler about little Chelsea: "You could beat her till she's black and blue and she wouldn't say ow!"

Then Reverend Cholmondeley rose from his pink throne. "Ladies, ladies. May I be so bold as to intervene?"

"Be my guest, Edgerton," said Pris, making an elaborate gesture of proffering him the cane.

"No, no," he replied, throwing up his hands. "It isn't my intention to add to the misery of one of God's small creatures. Indeed I wish to forgive him. Extending forgiveness, as you know, is one of the prerogatives of my office. Boy, will you accept?"

Zac looked up, completely mystified. The Reverend's voice never varied in its quality of being too loud, too public and orotund, as though he imagined himself addressing a large assembly.

"Oh, I understand," he continued, "for one steeped in guilt, the concept of magnanimous pardon is difficult to grasp. And of course, it doesn't free you from the consequences of your sin. In fact"—he here addressed the Aunties—"I have a proposal. You're right that the boy cannot stay in his room forever. Idle hands are the Devil's playground. He needs work, and I have just the job for him."

All eyes watched expectantly while, hands behind his back, the Reverend paced back and forth, then abruptly stopped, jabbed a finger in the air, and declared in a clarion voice, "*What is bent must be straightened.*"

Obviously a man acquainted with dramatic timing, he paused to let his point sink in.

"What is bent, I repeat, must be straightened. I've been thinking, you see, about our plans for the new church hall.

Building requires nails, which I just happen to have. Three big boxes down in the cellar."

Again Reverend Cholmondeley paused theatrically, as if waiting for someone to complete his perfectly transparent line of thought. When no one did, he resumed in a lower voice, "Let me tell you something about those nails. A little secret."

Pause again, then lower still: "They're bent."

One could have heard a bent pin drop in that room.

"Yes, I say, completely bent. But not—and here is my point—not beyond redemption. As you know, redemption is my business. And I'm here to tell you: Those bent nails—behold!—will be made straight. Praise the Lord!"

Beaming all around with supreme satisfaction, but meeting only blank stares, the Reverend tumbled on: "Do you see? I planned for my son to straighten those nails; he's always wanting to earn pocket money. But now I'm thinking: Why not have your boy help him? Without pay, of course, as discipline. Chesterton, you know, is a good, solid lad. Time spent with him could be better than a hundred whacks with the cane. Not that the cane isn't a fine method of …"

Apparently afraid he'd said too much, Reverend Cholmondeley looked flustered. The Aunties, however, took up the slack and heartily congratulated him on a fine idea. And so it was arranged that the next day at noon Auntie Pris would escort Zac to the church rectory, where he'd be set to work straightening nails with Chesterton Cholmondeley.

"I believe you're right, Edgerton," said Esmeralda. "Those two can keep each other in line."

"And if not," added Pris with a meaningful look, "there are other ways." She rapped the cane once sharply. Zac couldn't help staring at it. Made of some darkly lustrous wood, its grain was alive with intricate patterns. The strange thing was, for such a fearsome object it was really quite beautiful.

Chapter 5

The Weight of Clouds

The next morning, according to instructions, Zac met Butler in the kitchen for breakfast. He found the little man perched on a stool, stirring a pot of porridge. Though Zac disliked porridge, he ate three big bowls of it.

"Never saw a boy so fond of porridge," said Butler. "I was afraid you'd expect another plate of dainty sandwiches. Or perhaps some escargots or *pâté de foie gras*?"

Though intent on eating, Zac paused to hazard a look at Butler. The long face was so complexly wrinkled that it was impossible to interpret its expression.

"How many did you get?" Butler asked.

"Pardon me?"

"I asked," he repeated, "how many you got. How many whacks?"

"Whacks?"

"With the cane."

"Oh." Zac had assumed he was asking about the sandwiches. "None."

"None? Lucky boy. I'd have guessed two: one for wrecking Pris's party, and one for stealing that chinchilla coat."

"I wasn't stealing it."

"No, I'm sure you weren't. Just something to wrap up in as you ran away."

"I wasn't running away, either."

"Don't kid me, Boy. I'm not as young as I look. Nor as old." Though Butler's tone was suggestive, his face gave away nothing. "When you do get your whacks," he continued, "just pray it's not from Esmeralda. Pris is big, but … let's just say you don't want to be on the wrong end of Esmeralda's stick. She's got an arm on her and she'll make you beg for more. You have to say, 'Please, Auntie, may I have another?'"

Just then the swinging door opened and who should appear but the white shadow herself. Butler became intent on stirring his pot.

"Too much chatter in here," snapped Esmeralda. "Have you started on that silver, Butler?"

"Just about to, Auntie."

"Good. At noon Pris will take Boy to the Cholmondeleys. I want all that silver polished and put away by then. Understood?"

"Consider it done."

After she left, Butler dragged his stool over beside Zac at the kitchen table. There he opened the lid of a large wooden chest full of gleaming silverware. Selecting a fork and unscrewing a jar of grayish paste, without a word he handed Zac a cloth and demonstrated the art of polishing. To Zac the silver already looked as polished as could be. But he did his best to imitate Butler, and for some time they worked in silence.

Zac had a thousand questions. What was to become of him? Would he be like Butler, a house servant? Glancing at the odd little man, it was easy to imagine the two of them as child slaves in the castle of cruel giantesses. When Zac could stand the quiet no longer, he ventured, "I know you're called Butler, but what's your real name? I mean, if you don't mind my asking?"

This time the look on Butler's face was not hard to interpret. Zac gathered that he did *very much mind* being asked his real name. So the silence resumed, and the polishing went on, hour after hour until Zac felt like his fingers were turning to silverware. Occasional noises from the next room betrayed the proximity of the Aunties.

Finally the swinging door opened and there was Auntie Pris, dressed in a loud Hawaiian frock and a clashing hat that looked like a cushion.

"Time to go, Boy. Let Butler finish here. You go upstairs and change into these."

Mrs. Cholmondeley, she said, had been kind enough to find him some clothes—a warm shirt, cords, a jacket—so at last he was able to climb out of his dumb old suit. As he tossed it in a heap into his closet, however, the thought struck him that he'd worn that suit to his mother's funeral. And then he recalled the two of them in the store the day they had bought it.

"It's for Mr. Pottinger's funeral," she'd said.

"Why do I have to go to some old funeral?" Zac protested.

"Mrs. Pottinger needs us, dear. It's for her sake." She patted his hair as she so often did. Even now he could feel that touch; he could almost see her face …

"Hurry up, Boy!" barked Auntie Pris from downstairs. "What's keeping you?"

"Coming, Auntie."

Carefully he gathered up the suit coat, the pants, and the white shirt and hung them neatly on a hanger. Then he bolted from the room and flew down the stairs two at a time. At the bottom he nearly collided with Auntie Pris, which would have been less fun than running into a stone wall.

"Boy, you march right back up those stairs and take them one at a time like a gentleman. This is a fine old home and I'll not have you treating it like a playground."

Zac did as he was told, and then the two of them emerged into the sunny, snowy brightness of the afternoon. It felt wonderful to be outside. How strange that with Zac's mother gone and his life so changed, the sun still shone gloriously in a sky as blue as the bluest eyes, and the snow sparkled like laughter in a merry face. Zac wanted to pick up a handful and see if it was sticky. He wanted to throw himself down and make snow angels. He wanted to climb the snowbanks and build forts. But of course he did none of this. Instead, like a prisoner on his way to the rock pile, he walked stiffly beside his enormous, silent warden, who moved surprisingly quickly. Auntie Pris may have had trouble getting up off a couch, but once under way she was unstoppable.

Despite the nippy weather, she hadn't bothered to put on a coat. But then, it wasn't far to the rectory where the Cholmondeleys lived, beside St. Heldred's. A grand, white frame house with a broad porch on three sides, it was larger even than the church. The front door alone looked wide enough for Auntie Pris to walk through without turning sideways. Just as she raised her hand to knock, the door opened upon Reverend Cholmondeley, so that she came within an inch of striking him on the nose.

"My, my," said the Reverend, gingerly raising his own hand in defense. "I'm not sure I should let you in, Priscilla. Moses, for striking the rock, was barred from the Promised Land."

"No time for sermons today, Edgerton. I'm just delivering your little nail-straightener."

"Ah, good. How are we today, Boy? Chesterton is so looking forward to meeting you."

He glanced behind him, and following his gaze, Zac saw, sitting at the foot of the staircase, a boy who looked a little like Frankenstein: big, stocky, square-headed, square-shouldered, everything square down to the rims of his tortoiseshell glasses.

"My son, Chesterton," said the Reverend. "He prefers to be called Ches but I think he'll outgrow that. Won't you, son?"

"Not in your lifetime. I hate *Chesterton*." He spat out the word.

"And this," continued the Reverend smoothly, "is, ah …"

"Zac," said Zac. "Zac Sparks."

"We call him Boy," said Pris.

Zac went up to Ches and stuck out his hand, but Ches looked away as if he'd been offered a rotten fish. Abruptly he stood and began climbing the stairs.

"Chesterton!" said his father. "Just where do you think you're going?"

"To my room. What's it to you?"

"Son, I didn't let you stay home from school so you could play in your room."

"I don't *play*," sneered Ches. The square back continued to retreat up the stairs.

"But what about those nails?"

Ches paused. "Oh yeah. How much did you say again?"

"A quarter-cent a nail."

Ches considered. "Half. Make it a half and you're on."

"A half-cent a nail? Well, all right, then. Will you take, ah, Boy here down to the cellar?"

"How much does he get?" asked Ches. "Nothing? I get a half-cent, he gets zip. Right?"

"That's what we talked about, son."

"Good. I just wanted to get it straight."

"Like the nails!" joked the Reverend, laughing heartily. "Good boy."

"Ha ha," said Ches tonelessly. "All right, Bud, let's get started."

The "Bud," Zac realized, was directed at him. Nobody in this town seemed inclined to use his real name.

He followed Ches's lumbering frame through a doorway and down a flight of cellar stairs. Ches walked flat-footed, thumping along with his arms straight at his sides, palms facing back, his whole body stiff as if to keep any part of it from touching any other part. Even after reaching the bottom of the stairs, he kept on with the same heavy tread, as though still going down.

The cellar was unfinished, one bare lightbulb dangling from the ceiling. Occupying the center of the room was a furnace with so many pipes it looked like the invention of a mad scientist. Piled all about were cardboard boxes full of church magazines, mimeographed papers, bundles of receipts. Rags littered the floor; weathered planks were stacked along one wall. Two small windows admitted sunlight that fell mostly on dust, rust, and cobwebs.

"So, you the kid who stole my mom's coat?"

"I wasn't stealing it," Zac began.

"Should've. It's a dumb coat anyway. She'd have thanked you for making off with it."

"I wasn't trying to make off with it."

"What were you doing, then, running around at midnight in a woman's coat? Huh?"

Zac hesitated. He wasn't ready to tell anyone about the flashing lights above Porter's Store. "I just wanted to get outside. It was cold, I needed a coat. That's all."

Ches raised his black eyebrows, thick as moustaches, while his small eyes regarded Zac levelly from behind bottle-glass lenses.

"You're some liar, Bud. But never mind. Let's get to work."

Ches led him to the cellar's only piece of furniture, a long wooden bench heaped with tools that looked as if they hadn't been touched in years. Beneath the bench sat two orange crates chock-full of bent nails.

"Rev's crazy," said Ches.

"Rev?"

"The Reverend, my esteemed old man. Give me a hand here."

Even with Ches's strength it was difficult to budge the crates.

"How in tarnation did he get these things down here?" Ches grunted. "Maybe Auntie Pris. She could lift these with her little pinky. Ha ha."

Ches did not laugh, he just said the words: *ha ha*. Gradually Zac learned that this was how he always laughed, and the closest he came to a smile was a grimace.

When finally they managed to drag the two crates from under the bench, Ches found a couple of hammers and said, "Choose your weapon." Placing the nails one by one on a length of steel I-beam, they began to pound. "I hope Rev's working on a sermon right now. This will drive him nuts. Ha ha."

With the first few nails Zac mostly hit his fingers. It took a while to learn to hold the nail just so and strike it exactly right. For some time the two of them worked without talking.

"Don't say much, do you?" observed Ches. "You're probably scared to death of all the loonies in this town, right?"

"Dunno," Zac answered. "My mom died." He hadn't planned to say this. He wasn't even thinking about his mother.

"So I heard," said Ches. "Tough."

Without looking up, Zac asked, "What are you planning to do with all the money you make?"

"Who, me? Instruments. And they're expensive. I mean, if you want good ones."

"Instruments?" Somehow Zac couldn't imagine Ches enjoying music.

"Weather instruments. Barometers, hygrometers, wind gauges, stuff like that. I'm building me a weather station."

"What for?" As far as Zac was concerned, if you wanted to know the weather you just stuck your nose out the front door.

"I'm aiming to be a meteorologist." Pronouncing this word, Ches swelled with pride.

"You want to study meteors?"

"No, dimwit. A meteorologist is someone who knows all about weather. I practically know it all now. By college I'll know so much they'll probably just hand me my degree on a platter. That's what Rev says."

"And what then?" Zac was still trying to figure out whether or not to be impressed.

"Then I'll study the weather, just like I do now. Only I'll have better instruments and they'll pay me big bucks."

Ches explained that ever since receiving a rain gauge for his sixth birthday, he'd been methodically learning about all aspects of weather. "Right now I'm on nephology." At the predictable blank stare from Zac, he added, "The study of clouds. I've been on them for six months."

"Six months on clouds! Why? I mean, what's to know?"

"Loads. You'd be surprised."

"Like what? Surprise me."

Setting down his hammer, Ches led Zac to one of the cellar windows. Though the pane was small and incredibly dirty, still it showed a patch of sky—mostly clear but with two white, fluffy, midsized clouds afloat in the blue, like Spanish galleons in full sail.

"See that cumulus," said Ches, "the bigger one? How much you think that baby weighs?"

"That cloud there? Nothing. It's just floating in air."

"Wrong. A cumulus like that, about a quarter cubic mile in volume, weighs somewhere around four hundred tons. Maybe even five or six, depending."

"You're kidding."

"Nope. And your typical cumulonimbus—a rain cloud? That can weigh millions."

"Of tons?"

"Tons."

"But how? Why doesn't it come crashing down?"

"It does, dummy, when it rains or snows. But meanwhile it's in the form of water vapor, which happens to be lighter than air. Even a million tons of cloud is lighter than the air under it. That's how heavy air is. You didn't know that, did you?"

"Guess not."

"Right now you're carrying about two tons of air on your shoulders. That's the principle of the barometer, which predicts weather by measuring air pressure."

Just then Reverend Cholmondeley's voice came singing down the stairs. "Why don't I hear any pounding down there? Are you boys cooking up mischief?"

"Just taking a little break," answered Ches.

As they resumed hammering, Ches griped, "If anyone's cooking up mischief, it's Rev. All that religion stuff's wacko. He doesn't even believe it himself."

"But he's a minister."

"Exactly. Brood of vipers. He likes standing up there on Sundays and having everyone worship him. Me—I'm an atheist." Ches pronounced this word with the same pride he'd given to *meteorologist.* "How about you, Bud?"

"My mother believed in God."

"Huh. Look where it got her."

An awkward silence fell between them, until Ches said, "Look, I'm sorry about your mom. I just think religion's for the birds."

For the next couple of hours they worked steadily and Ches kept a running total of how much money he made. At half a cent a nail, he was soon up to two dollars.

"I'll get Rev to pay me for yours, too," he said. "That brings me to four."

"Will he go for that?"

"No problem. He's always trying to get in good with me. Besides, he really wants these nails, the old skinflint."

"Why's a skinflint paying good money to straighten nails?"

"Some tax angle. Rev pays me for stupid jobs like this, then he writes it off on his income tax. And he'll use old nails but bill the church for new ones. Always some angle. That's how the church got its name. Ha ha."

"St. Heldred's?"

"And All Angles. Don't forget the angles. Rev's got more angles than a dodecahedron."

After another hour the boys had had enough. They went upstairs to find Reverend Cholmondeley nodding asleep over a heavy book.

"There's the great preacher," whispered Ches, "preparing another stirring sermon. Poor guy can't even keep himself awake."

Late that night as Zac lay in bed, he thought about his new friend, Chesterton Cholmondeley. At least he guessed Ches was a friend; it was a bit hard to figure him out. Zac had never met any kid who wanted to be a meteorologist. Or who said he was an atheist. Never met anyone named Chesterton, either. Or Cholmondeley. Zac decided that if he had a middle name it would probably be Complicated.

Chesterton Complicated Cholmondeley. A name that suited its bearer well. Ha ha.

Just as he was drifting off, Zac heard the sound of rain.

He was surprised, because the sky had been clear all evening. The midday convection clouds (Ches's term) had cleared well before sunset, and even now Zac could see stars through his window—stars so bright and close they seemed just across the street. Yet the rain persisted and grew louder. Curious, he rose and went to the window. The glass was not wet, nor the outside sill, nor the trees nor the streets. There was not a cloud in the sky.

Listening intently, he realized the rain sound was not directly overhead, on his own rooftop. Rather it seemed concentrated in the area of Porter's Store. But there was no sign of wetness over there, either. Just the sound, the unmistakable thrum of rain, pouring out of a sky studded with stars.

After puzzling and puzzling, Zac returned to bed and let the mysterious rainfall lull him to sleep. So gentle and musical it was, almost like a woman's voice, singing.

Chapter 6

The Cholmondeleys

"Would you boys like some coffee cake?"

Zac and Ches had worked on nails for about three hours the next day, when a voice—not the Reverend's this time, but a woman's—called softly down the stairs. Ches, arching heavy eyebrows, glanced at Zac. "Coffee cake? Well, well. Rev must be out. Let's go." Trudging up the stairs, he added over his shoulder, "You should be honored. Sleeping Beauty doesn't often put in an appearance."

At the top of the stairs he led the way into the kitchen. The room was clean and bright, but bare looking. Nothing on the counters, no small appliances, none of the usual kitchen paraphernalia. One cupboard door stood open, but its shelves were empty. The fridge and stove looked fresh off the salesroom floor. And there was no aroma of warm coffee cake.

Beside the little chrome table in the nook stood a woman who looked as if all the color had been drained out of her. Pale skin, listless eyes, faded sunflower-print dress. Even her hair wasn't white or gray, just colorless. She stood with one hand leaning on the table and the other pressed to her forehead as if nursing a headache.

"Hello, boys," she said. "I've got some coffee cake for you." On the table were three plates, a knife, and a foil package. "Sara Lee."

"Cool," said Ches, touching it. "So—to what do we owe this honor?"

The woman smoothed back her hair and sighed. "Ches, mind your manners. Are you going to introduce me to your friend?"

"Mom, this is Bud; Bud, this is Mom." Ches rhymed it off as if reading from the foil package.

"I'm sorry about the coat," Zac blurted out.

"Coat? Oh, that. It's no problem, really. Do you have a name besides Bud? Ches calls everyone Bud."

"Zac. Zac Sparks."

"Zac Sparks," she said, listening to the sound. "That's nice."

"And you're Mrs. Cholmondeley?"

"Mary. Please call me Mary."

"Can I call you Mary too?" said Ches.

"Only if I can call you Chesterton," said Mary, smiling weakly.

"Ha ha," said Ches.

"Could you find your sister, please?"

"*Chelsea*!" Ches's voice boomed so suddenly that Mary nearly jumped out of her faded dress. "*Mom's up from the dead*!"

Instantly from around the corner appeared the short, shiny black hair and the astonishingly bright black eyes of the little girl Zac had met the night of the Aunties' party.

"Hi," said Zac. The bright eyes slid away from him.

"Come, Chelsea," said Mary. "I've got some coffee cake for you." The three children sat at the table while Mary remained standing. "I believe I'll go upstairs and rest a spell. You children help yourselves."

"What about drinks?" said Ches. "Drinks usually go with a snack."

"Oh, dear. I'd forgotten. I'm sure there's a carton of milk in the church hall."

"Sure, Mom. We'll grab some later."

Just before leaving, Mary paused to say, "Zac, it's so nice to have you with us."

"Thanks for the cake," he replied.

As they started into the snack, Zac commented, "Usually these things are heated up."

"Not around here," said Ches.

Then Zac asked if there might be something to drink in the fridge.

"That thing's empty," said Ches. "Always has been, always will be."

"Empty? Then why have it?"

"Appearances."

"Don't people in your family ever eat?"

"We eat. Just not here in the kitchen."

"In the dining room, then?"

"Oh, no. Far's I know, that dining room's never been used."

"Never?"

"Not in my lifetime. Rev eats in his office at the church. That's where he hangs out. Chelsea and I usually eat in the kitchen at the hall."

"And your mom?"

"Upstairs. In her room. What she eats I have no idea. Mostly crackers, I think. Like a parrot. She lives in that room. That's why I say you should be honored. She even put on a dress. Mostly it's the old bathrobe."

Zac tried to imagine this woman in a chinchilla coat. "That fur coat of hers—does she ever wear it?"

"Only to the Aunties' parties, and she hates those."

"Then why go?"

"Required. It's the one thing Rev makes her do. I guess they have some kind of deal. She doesn't even go to church anymore. Can't stand Rev's sermons. Dunno how anyone can."

Absentmindedly Zac was nibbling his coffee cake into the shape of an airplane. Chelsea ate hers with her head down, but when finished she sat back and gazed at the two boys.

"So tell me," said Ches, "what *were* you doing outside in my mother's coat on the night of the party?"

The question caught Zac by surprise. He glanced over at Chelsea.

"Don't worry," said Ches. "She won't tell. She's not about to tell anyone anything. Are you, sis?"

Chelsea shook her head. Then she made some movements in the air with her fingers.

"That so?" said Ches. "Very interesting."

"Did she say something?" asked Zac.

"Nah. Just a little story about a certain plate of sandwiches. Don't suppose you know anything about it?"

"Oh. I'm sorry, Chelsea. I didn't mean to get you in trouble."

Chelsea made some more gestures.

"No trouble," said Ches. "She thought it was pretty funny. She likes playing tricks on Butler. The old goat. So—back to the question. What were you doing on the night of December the fifth?"

Zac hesitated. He was beginning to feel he had to tell someone.

"Tell you what," Ches said. "I'll pay you for the info. Rev coughed up your share of the dough. So here." He took three one-dollar bills out of his pocket and spread them on the table.

"It's worth that much?" said Zac.

"The money's yours anyway. You earned it fair and square. And there'll be more from today."

"You sure this is okay?"

"Who's to know?"

That did it. Zac felt then that he could trust Ches, and Chelsea, too. So, keeping his voice low, he told them the whole story. He told about his mother's accident and funeral, about coming to live with the Aunties, and about breaking the china elephant and getting on the wrong side of them.

"There's no right side," snorted Ches.

Then Zac told about being in his room with all the coats. It felt good just to be talking. Finally he got to the part about sitting by his window and seeing—for the second time—the strange lights flickering above Porter's Store, and knowing he had to investigate.

Ches made a sound like a whale shooting spray out of its blowhole. Abruptly he stood up and stomped across the room. Swinging around to glare at Zac, he said, "That's it? I paid three bucks for *that*?"

"What's wrong? You asked me to tell you what happened, so I'm telling."

"Listen, Bud. You're not telling me anything new. Everyone in town knows about Porter's Store."

"Knows what?"

"All those funny lights and sounds and weird goings-on. It's ancient history. I knew that stuff in my mother's womb."

Zac stared. Weird goings-on? "Then you can tell me what it's all about?"

"Sure, Bud. I'll put it into one sweet word for you: *haunted*. That place is haunted as a cemetery in Transylvania. Everyone knows that. It ain't no secret."

"Haunted? By what? Or who?"

"Who cares? Haunted's haunted. Best thing to do is just stay clear of there, that's all."

Zac noticed that Chelsea was making hand signals, but Ches ignored her. "What's she saying?"

Ches glared at her. "Says she has to go to the bathroom. Why don't you just go, Chelsea?"

"Wait a minute," Zac persisted. "How can you say to stay away from Porter's? It's a store. People shop there. Doesn't your family shop there?"

Ches harrumphed. "My family doesn't shop. We scrounge. We eat whatever's left over from church suppers. And people bring us stuff. That's about it for shopping. Even if we did shop, we wouldn't go to Porter's. Nobody does."

"If nobody shops there, how do they stay in business?"

"I mean," Ches qualified, "nobody who's anybody. It's an old folks' store. Old fogies hang out there, chewing the fat. That's about it."

"But Mr. Porter's a young man. I've seen him."

"On the outside. Inside he's old."

"How do you mean?"

"Don't you know anything? Some people are just old all their lives. Like they're born that way."

Looking at Chesterton Cholmondeley in his thick glasses, his large, blocky face blank with arrogance, Zac knew just what he meant. "Like you?" he suggested.

"Have it your way, Bud. Yeah, like me. Rev says it's something that happens to an only child."

"But you're not an only child."

"Might as well be." He jerked his head toward Chelsea. "She's enough to make anyone old real fast. She put mom half in the grave."

"You mean by not talking?"

"Exactly. I'd try that trick myself if I had the nerve. But she's the one with nerve."

"Why does she do it? I mean, not talk?" When Ches didn't answer, Zac asked her directly: "Why don't you talk, Chelsea?"

71

Before this Chelsea's fingers had been flying away. Now her hands fell to her lap and she bowed her head. Zac couldn't see her face at all, just the mop of shiny black hair.

After a minute he went on, "Butler said she *can* talk but she won't. Is that right?"

"Of course it's right," retorted Ches. "Listen, Bud, how am I supposed to know what goes on in a little kid's head? She won't talk, that's all there is to it. Maybe she's smarter than all the rest of us put together."

It was quiet for an uncomfortable space. Full of questions, Zac didn't seem to be getting any answers. Ches had his own way of not talking.

"Okay," Zac relented, "but back to Porter's. You're telling me no one ever goes there except old people?"

"And kids," said Ches. "For candy."

"You don't like candy?"

"Can't say I care for it. Certainly not enough to darken Porter's door. Besides, candy's bad for you." After a moment he added, "Oh, yeah, and eyeglasses. And umbrellas. Porter repairs them. Believe it or not, that repair biz keeps him hopping. Without candy and glasses and brollies, he'd go bust."

"But if the place is haunted, why does anyone go there at all?"

"Daylight. Not much happens during the day. Besides, the whole place isn't haunted, just the second story. That's where you saw the lights, right?"

"Yeah. On the roof."

"That's the hot spot, all right. Where the old man hangs out."

"Old man?"

"Old Mr. Porter. The guy who started the store in the beginning."

"He's still alive?"

Ches turned his back and stared out the window. "You tell me," he said.

For a long time no one except Chelsea's fingers said anything. How Zac wished he could understand her!

"Let me get this straight," he said. "You don't know if old Mr. Porter is still alive or not? What is he—some kind of ghost?"

The question was left hanging as they heard the front door open and someone stomping off snow on the mat. A few moments later Reverend Cholmondeley appeared in the kitchen. He was the only man Zac had ever known to wear a cape. Its black shoulders were dusted with white flakes, not all of them snow. With his long, pallid face, ashen hair, and a certain chill he brought into the room, the Reverend might have been a ghost himself.

"Hello, boys," he boomed in his overly cheerful tone. "Having a little snack, are we? Where'd you get the cake?"

"Mom dug it up from somewhere," said Ches.

The Reverend frowned. "Your mother's not well; you shouldn't—"

"We never bothered her," snapped Ches. "You think we would? Know when the last time I bothered her was?"

"Now, Chesterton—"

"About ten years ago, that's when."

Folding his hands, the Reverend mused, "Perhaps the hammering disturbed her."

"Yeah, and one day the Big Hammer's gonna come down on this whole town. Ha ha."

The Reverend frowned more deeply, then brightened and said, "How's the work going?"

"Done for the day," said Ches. "Even slaves punch a clock."

"In that case, why don't you take your friend up to your room? You could show him your barometer."

This suggestion seemed to meet with Ches's approval. "Okay, Bud, let's go."

"Reverend Cholmondeley?" Zac piped up.

"Yes?"

Zac couldn't restrain his curiosity. "Is it true the second story of Porter's Store is haunted?"

Ches and his father exchanged glances. Clearing his throat, the Reverend said, "Ah, I wouldn't call it haunted. Not exactly. No, haunted is a poor term for it."

"Then what goes on there? Everyone seems to know about it but me."

"What goes on? Well … let's just say the Porters, Junior and Senior both, don't fit very well in our community. They're rather odd."

"In what way?"

Reverend Cholmondeley ran a finger underneath his clerical collar. "You know, it's very hard to answer that question, because the Porters are so secretive. That's what it is, you see. They keep to themselves, so no one really knows what all goes on over there. We just know it's odd. Very odd."

"But old Mr. Porter isn't dead?"

"Dead?" This time the finger under the collar almost completely circled his neck. "Again, I'm not sure that's exactly the right word for it. In my business one learns to be very precise with language."

"Then he's alive?"

Reverend Cholmondeley craned his long, stringy neck so high that he appeared to be trying to squirm out of his suit.

"I'm afraid," he said finally, "these are rather delicate questions. I'd prefer you discuss them with your Aunties."

Throughout this time Chelsea had been looking straight at her father, not moving her hands, just gazing, bright-eyed. Zac couldn't help noticing that her father never once looked back at her.

"Now, if you'll excuse me," said the Reverend, "I have a sermon to prepare."

The three children headed upstairs. As the boys entered Ches's room, Zac noticed a closed door farther down the hall that he assumed to be Mrs. Cholmondeley's. Chelsea disappeared into a room beside it.

"How come your dad pays no attention to Chelsea?" Zac whispered. "It's like she's not even there."

"She's not," said Ches. "Not for him. He never talks to her, never looks at her."

"But she's his daughter."

"Tell *him* that. Rev has basically disowned her. If she was older, he'd probably throw her out of the house."

"But why?"

"You have to ask?"

"Because she won't talk?"

"Exactly. Everyone knows she can talk. So Rev says let her talk. Why should he talk to a brick wall? If she talks to him, he'll talk to her, but not until. So that's where it stands."

"He won't learn to read her hand signals?"

"Are you kidding? He wants a daughter, not a trained monkey. That's why he puts up with all my guff. At least I talk."

Ches's room, large and bright, was fronted by a set of sliding doors opening onto a balcony. "Master bedroom," he said proudly. "Rev sleeps in the church hall."

"How come?"

Ches shrugged. "Married to his work."

Dominating the room was a narrow cabinet about four feet tall made of polished mahogany and studded with brass dials and glassed panels.

"My pride and joy," announced Ches. "An Admiral Fitzroy barometer. Fitzroy was the captain of the *HMS Beagle*—you know, with Charles Darwin? On their voyage to the Galapagos, they used a barometer just like this."

While Ches took obvious delight in showing off the workings of this elaborate instrument, Zac kept staring at a large chart over the bed that pictured about thirty different kinds of clouds: cirrus, stratus, cumulus, cirrostratus, on and on. The rest of the room was littered with books and other weather apparatus. Even the balcony was crowded with instruments: thermometers, rain gauges, an anemometer for measuring wind speed, endless gadgets.

"You've got so much weather stuff," Zac said. "What more could you want?"

"Lots. Right now I'm saving up for a nephoscope—an instrument for measuring cloud movement. Plus I want a Galileo thermometer, a sling psychrometer …"

Ches droned on and on. The bigger the words he used, the faster he talked. After a while Zac made the mistake of asking, "Haven't you got any toys?"

"Toys?" Ches's nose wrinkled like a big rabbit's.

"Yeah. Things to play with."

"Like what?"

"How about soldiers?"

"Soldiers? What do you mean?"

"You know, toy soldiers. For playing war and stuff."

"Why would I play war? I'm a pacifist."

Deflated, Zac stood looking out the window at the main intersection of Five Corners. Porter's Store looked smaller from here, and beyond it he could see the whole of the big hill (locals called it a mountain) that loomed over the town. At its peak was a peculiar rock formation, a kind of cloven spire resembling a pair of lifted hands holding between them … what?

"Wind Mountain," said Ches. "And the wind sure whistles through that gap. On a blustery day, or night especially, you'd think some giant was up there blowing on a bottle."

"I'd like to climb it," mused Zac.

"Can't. A little ways up there's a big barricade with a KEEP OUT sign."

"Why?"

"Old mine up there. People say it's dangerous."

"What kind of mine?"

"Bud, you ask too many questions."

At that moment Chelsea appeared in the doorway holding a bouquet of purple flowers.

"Don't bring those things in here," warned Ches.

"The flowers?" said Zac. "Why not?"

"Absolutely *verboten*. She knows it too. I made a deal with Rev. He bought me the Admiral Fitzroy only after I promised to have nothing to do with Eldy. Rev hates flowers and balloons."

"How come?"

"Just because Chelsea loves them. She's always bringing them home. Rev's punished her and punished her and she just keeps doing it. She's one stubborn kid."

"How can anyone hate flowers? Is he allergic or something?"

Chelsea, still standing in the doorway, was making hand signals.

"What's she saying?" Zac asked.

"Has to go potty," said Ches. "Real bad."

"No, really."

Ches considered. Finally he told Chelsea, "Sorry, kid. Can't help you."

Giving up on the hand signals, she looked at Zac and beckoned with her whole arm. But when he made a move to follow, Ches grabbed him.

"Not so fast, Bud. You'll get us in trouble. With the Aunties."

"Where does Chelsea want to take me?"

"Eldy. She wants you to meet him. She's sweet on him. Thinks the whole world revolves around him. She's daft."

"Is she?"

"Well, you know. She's actually quite bright. But Eldy's blind and she's sorry for him. Plus you can't get a word out of him, so they have that in common. I'd like to know what they find to talk about."

Zac tried to imagine a blind, silent old man carrying on a conversation with an unspeaking little girl. Then another question occurred to him. "If Eldy is blind, how does he tell the colors of the flowers he sells?"

"Dunno," said Ches. "Smell?"

"Or the balloons?"

"Beats me. Even if he could see, it wouldn't matter—he's so bent over that all he looks at is the ground. Listen, you don't want to go messing with that old geezer. Trust me. The Aunties hear you're over there, they'll beat your backside into hamburger."

They heard Reverend Cholmondeley talking loudly downstairs. A moment later he called up, "Boy, your Auntie Esmeralda is here for you."

"Speak of the Devil," murmured Ches.

Chapter 7

Essence of Summers Past

Though the day was so warm that most of the snow had already melted, Auntie Esmeralda wore a full-length silver mink coat with matching hat. Her hair was piled high, her pale face plastered with rouge, and she wore so much mascara that her eyes looked drawn on with magic marker. Zac had never seen so much makeup on anyone except a clown.

"There you are, Boy," she crooned. "Reverend Cholmondeley tells me you've done a fine job of straightening nails."

She inclined one elbow toward Zac and reluctantly he took her arm.

"There's my little man," she said.

Stepping with exaggerated daintiness in her high-heeled silver shoes, she let Zac escort her down the front steps of the rectory and into the street. But once there she broke into such long strides that Zac had to trot to keep up with her. Though she carried the cane, clearly she did not need it.

"I've had such a lovely time and I want to tell you all about it."

Niceness dripped from her like slime. What was she up to?

"I've just come from the Big City."

The Big City (Zac would never hear it referred to by any other name) was about an hour away.

"It's so exciting. You'll like it."

So Zac was going to the Big City?

"And can you guess who lives there? Someone very special."

Though the sun shone warmly, Zac shivered inside. He could not guess who the special person was.

"Let me tell you, Boy. It's someone who wants very much to meet you. In fact we were discussing you just today. I wonder if your ears were burning?"

Zac's ears, along with the rest of him, felt like ice.

"Don't worry. Though you haven't met, already he likes you enormously. In fact he loves you."

"Who?" Zac asked.

"Dada. Our father, mine and Auntie Pris's. Next to us, he's your only living relative. Imagine that!"

Zac tried to imagine. The Aunties were so old—was it really possible their father was still alive? And would he be as horrid as they were?

"We've arranged a little visit for this Saturday. Isn't that lovely?"

By now they had entered the stone mansion and Zac was taking off his jacket. Though Auntie Esmeralda did not remove her mink, she opened it to reveal a white satin gown. Zac was struck again by how thin she was, barely more than a skeleton. Bending to his level, she looked him straight in the eye. Even through all the makeup he could almost see her skull.

"I've told Dada what a fine young gentleman you are. I expect your best behavior when you meet him. Is that clear?"

For the first time in this conversation, her veneer of niceness flickered and Zac saw how deadly serious she was. He nodded.

"Repeat after me," she said. "I shall treat Dada …"

"I shall treat Dada …"

"… with utmost respect …"

"… with utmost respect …"

"… because …"

"… because …"

"… Dada loves me …"

Zac balked.

"Dada loves me," repeated Esmeralda.

Zac mumbled, "I haven't met him yet."

Auntie Esmeralda's long fingers with their long nails dug painfully into his arms. "Say it," she demanded.

When Zac still hesitated, she touched the head of her cane to his nose. "Perhaps you need a little help?" She pressed harder, then harder still.

Tears of pain springing in his eyes, Zac said, "Dada loves me."

"Good boy." Esmeralda straightened up. "Now run along to the kitchen. Butler has a job for you."

Every day that week, both before and after straightening nails with Ches, Zac was put to work with Butler. Today his task was to wash every dish in the kitchen cupboards. So shaken was Zac from his encounter with Esmeralda that he worked automatically, not even caring that the dishes were already clean. Finally he looked over at Butler, who was stirring a bowl with a big wooden spoon, and said, "The Aunties are taking me to meet Dada."

Butler stopped stirring.

"Do you know him?" Zac asked.

Butler resumed stirring, but more slowly.

"I know Dada," he answered.

"What's he like?"

Butler stirred and stirred, more and more slowly, until once again he stopped. At the mention of Dada's name it was as if the person himself had entered the room. As if Zac didn't need to ask anything now. As if somehow he knew.

Eventually Butler replied, "The less said about Dada, the better."

Neither of them spoke after that. Butler stirred and chopped and rolled, and Zac washed dishes until finally he was sent to his room.

Butler tended to remain silent with Zac whenever the Aunties were nearby. When it was clear they were out of the house, however, he waxed garrulous.

"That Esmeralda," he'd say, "she forever complains of being cold, and Pris is always hot. Pris turns down the thermostat when Esmeralda's not looking, and then does the fur fly!"

To Zac the house was never warm. But here, he realized, was the reason Esmeralda always wore furs, even indoors, whereas Pris seemed to wear as little as possible (except for her outlandish hats). It turned out that Esmeralda owned a fur store called The Mink's Meow, while her sister ran a hat shop called The Sane Hatter.

"Nothing sane about those hats, if you ask me," said Butler. "But those two shops, no doubt about it, are the toast of the town. Very swank. Even people from the Big City consider Five Corners *the* place to buy furs and hats."

Unfortunately Butler's commentary seldom touched on any subject that Zac was really curious about, and he had a way of deftly deflecting probing questions.

Toward the end of the week Zac was put to work alone, since Butler wasn't well. Indeed the poor man looked quite green and wobbly and had to take to his bed. Zac was reminded how very old Butler was—as ancient as the Aunties, though without their peculiar energy. He was simply old, lonely, worn down. Wondering if Butler had served the Aunties for a very long time, Zac was filled with pity for him.

Once, while working on his own, Zac had to pass through the dining room where he'd never been. It was a dark, windowless chamber with a long table and a massive ebony china cabinet. The dominant feature, however, was a large oil painting illuminated by a small light. The life-sized, half-length portrait showed a boy about Zac's age dressed in old-fashioned clothing: a ruffled shirt, a puffy-sleeved velvet jacket laced across the front, and a soft, shapeless hat. All black. The painting, perhaps of a family ancestor, was obviously very old, its surface webbed with fine cracks. From the moment Zac entered the room, the eyes of the half-smirking boy seemed to fasten on him. In the stark

84

lighting he looked almost alive. Startled, disturbed, Zac quickened his pace.

Just as he reached the opposite door, however, he stopped. He thought he'd heard a voice. It seemed to him—but no; how could it be?—that the boy in the painting had spoken. Half turning, Zac almost said, "What?" But the painted boy, though apparently still watching him, had certainly not moved a muscle. Zac hurried on.

Sometimes Zac was allowed to eat with Butler in the kitchen, but more often a tray was sent up to his room. When confined to quarters, since he had no toys, he often brought out the photograph of his mother. An hour could go by as memories and fantasies flooded him. In the picture she sat on the veranda surrounded by roses—in gardens, in wooden tubs, on trellises. The roses had beautiful names: Paradise Gold, Peace, Crimson Glory, Heavenly Radiance. Zac could almost hear his mother reciting the names. They were like the names of things in a faraway country where everything was perfect.

His other favorite recreation was looking out the window. Automatically each morning he awoke at dawn and went to the window just as Mr. Porter, in his white apron, unfailingly appeared in the doorway of his store to greet the new day. Always he carried his umbrella (a detail Zac tried to overlook), and always he waited for the sun to rise before returning inside. Even on a cloudy day Mr. Porter seemed to sense the precise moment of sunrise, as invariably this information was reflected in his extraordinary smile. Zac never tired of watching him; it was almost like watching the sunrise itself. Every once in a while the man would glance up at Zac's window, but Zac always looked away.

Later in the morning the storekeeper would reemerge to sweep the sidewalk, roll down the big green awning, and carry out some larger items of merchandise: snow shovels, stepladders, toboggans. Always he kept his umbrella with him, crooked over an arm even as he handled heavy articles. Zac found this custom not just troubling but puzzling, since there had not been a drop of rain since the day he'd arrived in Five Corners. Ches had said that Mr. Porter repaired umbrellas, so perhaps he carried one as a sort of trademark. In fact the awning over the front windows, besides bearing the single word PORTER'S, displayed a picture of an open umbrella, bright blue, with a pattern of white, fluffy clouds on the paler blue underside.

After arranging his sidewalk display, Mr. Porter would stroll over to chat with Eldy at the balloon and flower stand. On the way, sometimes he crossed the street to visit someone (presumably the barber) in the World's Smallest Business Establishment. So far Zac had not seen the barber, who seemed to remain in his shop all the time.

As for Eldy, Mr. Porter's manner of greeting him was to place a hand on the old man's bent back, horizontal as a tabletop, and gesture with his umbrella toward different sights, talking all the while, apparently commenting on events in the life of the town. He would also point to the sky and the clouds, as though conjecturing about the weather. At times this overhead pointing was so elaborate that he appeared to be marshaling some great invisible air force. Eldy, gaze fixed on the ground, made no obvious response, even when Mr. Porter occasionally drew with the tip of his umbrella in the dirt right under the old man's eyes. Could Eldy see something after all, or was this just Mr. Porter's mannerism? The umbrella was so much a part of him that it seemed a physical extension of his thoughts.

After these chats the storekeeper would help Eldy unfurl the rainbow-colored awning over his stand and perhaps move some pots or boxes for him before strolling back to Porter's. This ritual took place every day except Sunday, almost as though it were necessary for the continuance of the town itself.

On Friday, Ches and Chelsea accompanied their mother to a doctor's appointment in the Big City, traveling by bus because Mary didn't drive. This left Zac to straighten nails alone; he was even allowed to walk to the rectory by himself. The weather, strangely for December, had turned almost summery; the sun shone brightly, birds sang, and Zac whistled as he walked. It was the best he'd felt for a long time.

With no one to talk to, he worked faster than usual and had soon finished the entire second crate of nails. Then he wandered upstairs to find Reverend Cholmondeley in the living room, head bowed, with a large black book in his lap. Though he appeared deep in study, a snuffling noise told Zac he was asleep. On the verge of waking him, Zac hesitated, feeling a stab of curiosity about Mary Cholmondeley's room upstairs. What did she do up there? Zac couldn't imagine anyone wanting to spend all her time in one room. For him, certainly, this was punishment.

So far gone was Reverend Cholmondeley that his breath came, not quite in snores, but in percussive snorts. No one else was home. Zac was just a few steps from the staircase, which was covered in soft carpet. Before he could stop himself, he was dashing up the stairs two at a time. He would just have a peek. No harm in that.

Passing Ches's room, he headed straight for the closed door he knew must be Mary's. He didn't pause until his hand was on the doorknob, a chunk of many-faceted cut glass like a huge diamond. Why was he doing this? Nosiness, that was all. Besides, he didn't think Mary would mind. Hadn't she told him herself, "Zac, it's so nice to have you with us"?

He opened the door and went in. It was a surprisingly small room, like a child's. One window, one chair, a dresser, and a single bed covered with a woolen afghan. What immediately caught his eye was an object on the tiny bedside table: a squat container made of blue china, like a vase but lidded, its narrow neck perforated by a circle of small holes. Zac knew instantly what this was because his mother had had one much like it. The two articles were even inscribed with the same words: ESSENCE OF SUMMERS PAST.

Zac's mother had loved roses, so much that she couldn't bear to be without them through the winter. So every autumn she collected the last blooms from her garden and hung them upside down to dry. The petals shrank, became brittle, and took on a dark golden patina with rainbow highlights, like mica. When they were fully dry, she detached the petals and placed them in the receptacle on the mantel, which stood beside a picture of Zac's father. These petals were never removed. This year's petals covered last year's, which rested on petals from the year before, and so on. The dried petals retained a musky perfume so that all winter long the fragrance of some twenty years of roses—the essence of summers past—subtly pervaded the room. At least, that's what Zac's mother said; Zac himself never noticed the smell unless he went right up to the mantel and sniffed.

There in Mary Cholmondeley's bedroom, before this object that reminded him vividly of his mother, tears welled in Zac's eyes. It was almost like entering his own home to find his mother in the kitchen, her long brown hair dusted with flour, lifting a pan of his favorite cookies from the oven. Approaching the bedside table, he put his hand on the lid of the vase, raised it, and leaned over to inhale, fully expecting to be met with the rich, dark odor of old roses.

That was not what he found. There was a smell, but it was an odd smell. Stale, rubbery. Peering inside, Zac saw that the vase was filled with small, brightly colored scales that resembled flower petals, but clearly were not. The colors were too bold: red, green, orange, purple. He picked up an orange piece, petal-shaped but pliant, stretchy.

89

Balloons! The vase was filled with fragments of balloons. Taking out a handful, Zac sifted them through his fingers. Why would someone collect old bits of balloon in a beautiful vase?

Just then the doorbell rang. *Oh no—Reverend Cholmondeley would wake up!* Moments later he heard the Reverend's voice in conversation at the front door. Replacing the lid of the vase as carefully as if it were a dynamite cap, then softly closing Mary's door from the inside, Zac crawled under her bed. Surely no one would look for him here. Several minutes passed, during which he heard no sound. His mind raced with plans for escape. But every plan ran smack into Reverend Cholmondeley who would, Zac guessed, be prowling around downstairs, searching for him.

"Boy!"

The inevitable call found Zac still utterly unprepared.

"Hello, Boy! Are you there?"

He couldn't stay where he was. The Reverend would think he'd left the house, and how would he ever explain that? Nothing to do but face the music. Quickly crawling from under the bed, Zac opened the door, closed it again, and tip-toed to the head of the stairs.

"Boy, are you down there? Why don't I hear any hammering?"

The voice was fainter now. The Reverend must be in the kitchen, calling into the cellar. Without thinking, Zac flew down the stairs and across the living room. In seconds he was at the kitchen door, listening to the man's descending steps.

"Reverend Cholmondeley!" he blustered. "I'm up here! I've been looking all over for you!"

A moment later the Reverend's ghostly head peered from the cellar doorway.

"There you are, Boy."

"Reverend Cholmondeley, I've been looking all over for you," Zac repeated.

"Have you now? Well, that's very curious …"

"We must have just missed each other. I heard the doorbell and ran upstairs …"

That was all the explanation Zac could think of. Weak as it was, for some reason the Reverend accepted it. Perhaps he was still not quite awake.

"I see. And how are you coming along with those nails?"

"I've finished, sir," announced Zac triumphantly. "The whole two crates. Completely straight. Come and see." He was practically giddy with relief.

"And have you started on the third?" asked the Reverend.

"The third? The third what?"

"The third crate. You're not done by a long shot if you haven't touched the third one."

"But there were only two, sir. At least, that's all we ever saw under the bench. Do you mean there's another crate somewhere?"

"Right there, in the same place. There were three crates of nails under the bench."

"Well, I'm sure you're right, sir. But you'll have to show me. I would have kept working if I'd known—"

"Come along, Boy."

In the cellar Reverend Cholmondeley inspected the second crate of fully straightened nails and pronounced it a job well done. Then, peering into the shadows beneath the workbench, he scowled. Though anyone could see plainly that no third crate was there, still he got down on all fours to search. As Zac joined him, it felt like they were playing some game, pretending to be animals.

"How strange," muttered the Reverend. "I know there was another crate down here. Are you sure you didn't move it?"

"Oh no, sir. We only saw the two. I swear."

"Well, it must be hiding somewhere."

For the longest time Reverend Cholmondeley (with Zac doing his best to appear helpful) combed every square inch of that cellar, searching for an orange crate of bent nails as if it were the lost treasure of Solomon. Somehow Zac knew it wasn't there. One gets an instinct about such things, and Zac's instinct told him that Reverend Cholmondeley, for all his book learning, could not count to three.

"Well, it's not here," he said finally. "Where would a crate of bent nails go? Nails can't fly, and they wouldn't just get up and walk away, would they?"

That left crawling, though Zac didn't mention that.

Suddenly stiffening, the Reverend looked as if he might have swallowed a bent nail. Slowly he said one word: "Porter."

"I beg your pardon, sir?"

"That man Porter shortchanged me." For some time the Reverend stood quite still, cradling his chin in one hand. In his frayed black suit, with his wispy hair and parchmenty skin, he seemed curiously right at home in the cellar, as though a spider might come along and spin a web between a rafter and his ear.

Finally he sighed. "Well, there's nothing for it. Two crates aren't enough for the new hall. And we need to keep you busy, don't we? I'll just have to go and rattle that man's cage."

Reverend Cholmondeley was halfway up the stairs before he paused to add, "Hold on, Boy. You can't stay here alone. You'll have to come along."

Zac fell in behind and a minute later the two of them were crossing the street, the Reverend's black cape billowing in his haste. Zac was bewildered. Reverend Cholmondeley was taking him to Porter's Store, the haunted place? And they were going to talk to Mr. Porter himself, a man for whom Zac already had strong and somewhat complicated feelings?

"I want you to know," said the Reverend, "that I am not, nor ever will be, a patron of this establishment. However, if a person needs bent nails, this is the place."

Zac couldn't quite believe this was happening. In a moment they were standing beneath the wide green awning in the very spot where Mr. Porter had stood when Zac first saw him. It felt like crossing a boundary into some other world. Touching the door handle, a green metal bar emblazoned with a white 7UP and bubbles of effervescence, the Reverend paused long enough to say, "It's lucky for us that the Aunties are away. If I were you—and even, come to think of it, if I were me—I wouldn't mention this little visit to them. Agreed?"

Zac nodded, and the door swung open.

Chapter 8

An Awful Man

Inside Porter's Store, the first thing Zac noticed was the cloud chart, high on the wall behind the cash register. He'd seen it before. It was the same as the one Ches had in his room, only much older, yellowed and curling at the edges.

The next thing Zac was aware of was the music. Not instruments, but a voice, a woman's voice, high and clear like bells. Far away or near? It was hard to be sure. Hadn't he heard it before? But where? The singing merged, somehow, with the peculiar quality of light in the store, which felt strangely like being outside. It was as though the building were lit not by its two rows of hanging bulbs in green shades, but by the sky. Not a bright, sunny sky but a soft, pewtery one, like twilight. The light in the store was almost like the radiance in a face or a pair of eyes.

So strong and curious was this heightened atmosphere that, as Zac followed Reverend Cholmondeley along an aisle, he seemed to be aware of every article in the store at once. Every last detail, down to the peanut-shaped glass handle on the lid of an antique Planters jar, leapt to life with photographic clarity. The pendant, toffee-colored curls of flypaper; the six-flavor ice-cream chest; the rows of hurricane lanterns; a big glass box with a hinged lid holding a round of pale yellow cheese the size of a hubcap. There were barrels of rice, flour, sugar; canisters of dates and figs; enormous jars of pickles, and smaller jars—like tilted fishbowls with screw-on lids—for candy: gumdrops, humbugs, jujubes, licorice, maple buds. And in tall, narrow jars, thick striped peppermint sticks of all colors.

Not only Zac's eyes but his nostrils widened in wonder at smells that reminded him of his mother's kitchen. Here, too, were racks of spices, bundles of dried herbs, and canisters for raisins, brown sugar, chocolate chips. One side of the store was devoted to foodstuffs and the other to dry goods, both modern and old-fashioned, including everything from shoes and neckties to mops, dishes, fishing gear. Many of the goods in Porter's, Zac would learn, were secondhand, for the proprietor catered to the poor as well as to the rich, and he enjoyed giving a new lease on life to what was broken-down and rejected.

The store was laid out in two narrow aisles divided by a middle set of shelves and flanked by long glass cases. Behind each counter a wheeled ladder on a sliding rail gave access to shelving stacked to the ceiling with merchandise. At the top were the larger items—stovepipes, watering cans, sleds—while the smallest articles were behind glass: buttons, razors, mousetraps, eyeglasses. Above the counters in several places hung spools of thick white string and rolls of brown wrapping paper. In one corner, atop a small barrel, sat a checkerboard made from one dovetailed side of a wooden box. In another corner stood a gramophone, its big golden horn blossoming like an exotic flower.

All of these astoundingly clear impressions registered with Zac in the few seconds it took for him to walk from the front of the store to the back. There, in the hardware department, among tools, cans of paint, small appliances, and nails, were the old men. Clustered around a woodstove, beside a silver five-gallon coffee urn, were several small, round tables, each with a pair of old men seated on spindle-back chairs, gnarled fingers curled into the handles of their coffee mugs as if frozen there for a hundred years. No other customers were in sight. Though Zac and Reverend Cholmondeley had entered to a buzz of conversation, all talk died as they drew near the back. One man who had been reading a newspaper lowered it, adjusted his trifocals, and folded and smoothed the paper elaborately.

"Afternoon, Reverend," he said.

"Afternoon, Abe," replied the Reverend.

"If I may say so, it's a surprise to see you here."

"As you well know, nothing but the Lord's business could bring me here. A mission of mercy for Mother Church. Is the boss around?"

"If I'm not mistaken, he's out back in the umbrella factory. I'd be more than happy to fetch him for you."

"I'm obliged."

Abe lowered his chair, which had been cocked against the wall, and rose with the same meticulous deliberation with which he had straightened his newspaper. Walking as if searching for purchase with each step, he disappeared through a door beside a flight of stairs in the back corner. Meanwhile Reverend Cholmondeley steered Zac to the section of the rear wall where nails were kept in small wooden drawers. Idly the Reverend pulled open a few drawers to finger some tiny finishing nails, some blue-black bolts, some four-inch spikes. He seemed particularly enamored of the spikes.

Finally Abe returned with Mr. Porter. Though Zac heard no one approach, suddenly he heard again the beautiful singing. Had it stopped, or had he just stopped noticing it? And then a voice said, "Hello, Edgerton," as though its owner had just been deposited there by a gust of wind.

Turning to meet the man he'd been watching every morning from across the street, Zac was taken aback. The storekeeper's face, though youngish (about thirty?) and quite plain, was so full of character that all at once Zac understood what a face is, or can be: a clear image of the soul. A perfectly naked, honest portrait of the inner person.

"There you are, Porter," said Reverend Cholmondeley.

"And who have we here?" asked Mr. Porter.

"That? He's the Aunties' new boy."

"Hi," said Zac. "I'm Zac Sparks."

"Zac. Zachary Sparks. What a good name. A name full of life. I'm Sky Porter. Please call me Sky."

Here three remarkable things happened at once. At the sound of Mr. Porter's first name, something like a bolt of electricity rippled down Zac's spine. At the same time, Sky looked straight into Zac's eyes, and Zac looked into his, and they were

97

the deepest, bluest blue Zac had ever seen—truly like the sky itself. The third extraordinary thing happened when the boy took the man's extended hand, and it felt so warm and firm and friendly that suddenly everything seemed completely normal in a way Zac had forgotten it could be. He felt steadied, affirmed, righted. Himself.

"Here, here," Reverend Cholmondeley protested. "Porter, you know the Aunties won't approve."

Mr. Porter—Sky—kept hold of Zac's hand, and of his gaze, too. The moment would have lasted longer if Reverend Cholmondeley hadn't taken both their arms and pulled them apart.

"I'm here on business, Porter," he blustered, "the Lord's business. I shouldn't have brought the boy."

Slowly Sky shifted his attention to the Reverend.

"Those nails for the church hall—you shortchanged me." Reverend Cholmondeley, who always spoke too loudly, delivered this pronouncement as though Mr. Porter were deaf. All the old men were listening, regarding the scene mildly like cows gazing over a fence.

"As you know," proceeded the Reverend, "the church isn't made of money. We need nails—bent ones."

Sky Porter gazed at Reverend Cholmondeley, too long, too deeply. The Reverend tugged at his collar. They were such a contrasting pair: the one man so vibrant, so intriguing, the other frayed as an old lamp shade.

"Edgerton," said Sky gently, "I gave you those nails for free. And you're saying I shortchanged you?"

Reverend Cholmondeley's mouth worked rapidly into a series of different shapes. Finally he spluttered, "Yes! That's exactly what I'm saying."

"Well," said Sky, "I'm happy to give you more bent nails. I'll give you brand-new ones, if you wish."

"No, no, bent is fine. I won't be beholden to you, Porter."

Sky gave him a quizzical look, then indicated a good-sized canvas mailbag slumped on the floor beneath the rows of nail drawers. "I'll need a hand with this."

"Boy," said the Reverend with a stiff nod.

Together Zac and Sky shimmied the heavy sack from under the shelving. Handing the Reverend a metal scoop and Zac an empty peck basket, Sky said, "Help yourself."

Reverend Cholmondeley dug the scoop into the mouth of the sack, drew it out full of bent, rusty, three-inch nails, and dumped the load into Zac's waiting basket. As the first scoopful landed more heavily than Zac expected, he shifted his hold, cradling the basket in his arms rather than gripping the handle.

"So how are you liking our weather, Edgerton?" Sky asked. "All that snow on Monday—marvelous, don't you think?"

"I'm not much of a winter person," replied the Reverend.

"Ah. I suppose you prefer a day like today—warm sunshine, sparkling air, bit of a breeze to blow out the cobwebs? Almost like spring."

"I'm no lover of spring," grunted the Reverend.

"You surprise me! You don't mean you're a summer person? Can't wait to bask in the warm honey of July? Why, I don't recall ever seeing you with a tan."

"Porter," said the Reverend, pausing in his work of ladling nails, "the truth is, I don't much like the outdoors. Give me a book-lined study, a hearth, a cup of tea. I pay no attention to weather."

Zac's basket of nails was nearly full and feeling quite heavy and awkward. He could have used a third hand. Also, he was preoccupied with what Sky was saying—or rather with how he said it. Speaking of the seasons, somehow his voice seemed to take on the very mood and coloring of each one. And those blue eyes: Was Zac imagining it or did they actually change hue? They seemed deepest when he talked of summer, a lighter blue at the mention of spring, and a pale bluish-gray for winter. Indeed the man's whole face changed aspect, from cheeks rosy with cold to a bronzed, summery glow.

So absorbed was Zac in these observations that he must have slightly shifted the basket. The next scoopful of nails landed not quite in the center, unbalancing the load so that it slipped, tipped upside down, and plunged to the floor. Nails flew everywhere. They skated across the linoleum, spewed under shelves, bounced like popcorn around the feet of the old men. More than a few landed in the cuffs of Reverend Cholmondeley's black trousers.

For several long seconds all eyes looked down, then slowly around, taking in the full scope of the disaster. Finally Zac ventured a peek at another face that was now registering a remarkable change of aspect and hue: Reverend Cholmondeley's. With his thin lips working, his skin blotching red and white, his head nearly popping out of the tight clerical collar, the man himself seemed a pressurized canister of nails ready to explode.

And then Sky Porter did something so astonishing, so breathtaking, that Zac almost cheered out loud. Burying both his arms in the original sack of nails, the storekeeper drew out two dripping handfuls and hurled them like lightning bolts onto the floor. And then he did it again! Before Zac could have sneezed, two more fat fistfuls of nails went clattering like metal rain all over the already nail-strewn linoleum.

Then, with a sound that seemed to turn the whole world upside down and shake it free, Sky Porter threw back his head and laughed. The old men joined in, slapping their knees and guffawing, and as for Zac, he erupted into the loudest laughter of all. It gushed out of him like a geyser, releasing not just the tension of his clumsiness and the fear of Reverend Cholmondeley's reaction—no, though he did not realize it, all the repressed grief of his mother's death came bubbling forth in the mysterious form of golden, lighthearted laughter that went on and on, long after the original joke was forgotten, long after every propriety had been breached, laughter that kept coming and coming for the sheer outrageous joy of it.

Everyone laughed, every soul in that room. All except one. Reverend Edgerton Cholmondeley did not laugh. What he did, Zac didn't know, for throughout that glorious spree of laughter, he completely forgot the black-caped, buzzardlike man. He was gone, vanished, an extinct species.

Not until the mirth subsided did Zac notice that all was not well with the Reverend—something about the flashing darkness in his eyes, and a coldness that drifted off him as from a glacier, and the tightness with which he grasped Zac's arm and began marching him off down the aisle. And his silence, his dead silence.

"Edgerton!" called Mr. Porter. "Don't take it so hard. A thousand nails are as easily cleaned up as a hundred."

At the front door Reverend Cholmondeley paused just long enough to turn and face Mr. Porter down the long aisle. He seemed to be working at trying to say something, but all he could do was emit a series of quick pants like a runner out of breath. Finally he pushed open the door and yanked Zac through it.

Covering the distance to the rectory with huge, lunging strides and tugging Zac all the way, not until the Reverend stood on his own front porch did he manage to utter five words punctuated by hyperventilations.

"What … a perfectly … awful … man!"

Chapter 9

Sky

For the rest of that day and night Zac kept thinking about Mr. Porter and his astonishing gesture. Between the man and the boy those nails had formed a bond, which, Zac reflected, was just what nails were for. He thought about Mr. Porter's name, the one he'd told Zac to call him: Sky. Zac kept saying the name to himself, savoring the sound and recalling its wondrous effect on him. And he kept picturing the store, seeing every detail in his mind as lucidly as if he were still there. Though he hadn't looked carefully at the faces of the old men, he could see them, too, each one of them, as if he'd known them all his life.

That night a wind came up. Long after Zac went to bed he lay awake listening to its mysterious sound—*What was wind, anyhow, and where did it come from?*—and to the tree branches tapping and scraping on his windowpane. The sounds seemed intelligent, somehow, the branches like fingers drumming out a code he couldn't quite decipher, and the wind like a person whispering. Zac wasn't disturbed by this, only intrigued, all senses alert. Though he must have slept, he had the sensation of being awake all night long.

Just before dawn, automatically he rose and went to the window. The night's wind had swept Five Corners clean, so clean he could almost see the marks of an invisible broom on the immaculate lawns, streets, gardens, hedgerows. And yes, there he was, right on schedule—Sky Porter—occupying the doorway across the street, waiting, just like Zac. The blood red flannel shirt, the apron white as white, the faded denim coveralls blue as dawn. And that face—so unlike any other face Zac had ever seen, so disarmingly real. When the sun arose and shone full upon it—oh, if Zac had been a bird he would have broken into song! As it was, his heart beat like a bird's and nameless feelings stirred in him.

What else to do? He had to go. He had to go over there and see Mr. Porter again. Sky. Why not now? Now was perfect. The house was all quiet; Five Corners looked deserted. No one stirred but Sky Porter and Zac Sparks. And Sky was obviously not busy. If Zac just ran over for a chat, he could be back almost before he'd left. No one would see him, no one would know.

So out he went. Quiet as a cat's shadow he slipped down the stairs and dashed across the street. The storekeeper was just turning to go inside when Zac called in a loud whisper, "Sky!" The man turned, saw him, smiled broadly, and held out not just one hand this time but two. Two hands, two arms, wide open. Would he wrap Zac in a hug? Suddenly awkward, the boy held back. But the hands stayed out-stretched until finally Zac took them, both his small hands in the bigger ones, and then came something he had never done before: a double handshake. No brisk pump, this one moved in a warm, tremendous rhythm like ocean waves.

"Zac," said Sky, looking him right in the eyes. "How good to see you."

"I had to come," blurted Zac. "I just had to. What you did yesterday with the nails … I can't explain … It did something. It was … amazing."

Zac's words both gushed and stumbled out like a quick-running stream tripping over stones. Throughout, Sky kept hold of the boy's hands, a palpable current passing between them.

"I guess I've always felt—I don't know—like something's missing. I never even knew it till yesterday, in your store, when I felt so different. I mean, it's like no one's ever been *there* for me. Except my mom, of course. But my dad, he wasn't there; I never even met him. And now they're both dead and I have to live with these awful Aunties across the street and they're *horrible.* I mean, lots of people seem to like them but really, honestly, they're *horrible*—"

He saw a shadow fall across Sky Porter's face and against the sunlit door behind him. A tall, thin shadow. Without turning, Zac knew exactly whose shadow it was.

"What, pray tell, is going on here?" said a raspy whisper.

"Why, hello, Esmeralda," said Sky. "Zac and I were just shooting the breeze."

"So I hear. Porter, if any more breeze gets shot around here, I'll do some shooting of my own. Do you understand?"

"I'm not sure I do, Esmeralda."

"Then let me spell it out, Porter. If I ever catch the two of you together again, conspiring behind my back—and if I ever catch you, Boy, anywhere near this man or this store—there will be consequences you do not want to imagine. Is that clear?"

"Aren't you being a little hasty …?" began Sky.

"*Have I made myself clear?*" After an uncomfortable silence Esmeralda continued, "I'll take that as a yes. And I'll hold you, Porter, responsible. Boys will be boys, but you are an adult and I warn you: If you insist on befriending this boy or encouraging him in any way, he will be severely punished. And you'll have no one to blame but yourself."

Throughout this conversation Zac kept hoping—even expecting—Sky Porter somehow to defend him, to stand up to his Auntie, to say or do *something*. But he did nothing. He simply stood there in Esmeralda's shadow and took her abuse. He was a good head shorter than she, and acted it. No throwing nails this time; no devastating comeback. Not until Esmeralda, spinning Zac around and poking her cane in his back like a rifle, began propelling him across the street did the storekeeper call out, "A good day to you, Esmeralda. And don't worry, Zac—everything will be fine."

Without stopping or turning, Esmeralda croaked, "The nerve of that man!"

Fine? Everything would be fine? But there was nothing fine about the way Auntie Pris met them at the door with a look that could have frozen a snake's blood. And there was nothing fine about the way the two of them marched Zac into the parlor and Pris thundered, "Bend over, Boy!"

"But all I did was—"

"*Now!*" Her boom was so loud it rattled the china figurines.

Zac bent over.

Up in his room he collapsed on the bed with his face to the wall. Sunshine poured through the window but he wasn't about to look there. As Butler had predicted, after the first whack Esmeralda had forced him to say, "Please, Auntie, may I have another?" So he got another, and then again he had to ask the awful question. She stopped there, thankfully, though not without giving him a good tongue-lashing for leaving the house without permission, talking to that "horrid clerk," and saying nasty things about his Aunties.

"And today of all days!" exclaimed Pris.

"Do you know what today is?" demanded Esmeralda.

Zac drew a blank.

"Think hard."

Still nothing came.

"Then I'll tell you: Today is Saturday. And what happens on Saturday?"

Zac remembered. And somehow just the memory struck him more painfully than any blow of a cane.

"Come, Boy. What happens today?"

"Dada?" he whispered.

Yes, Dada. Today was the day of the promised visit to the Big City. Nevertheless, as Zac lay on his bed in numb shock, it wasn't Dada he thought about, nor about the Aunties or his beating. No, it was Sky Porter. He thought about their talk and about the storekeeper's interaction with Esmeralda. Why had Zac blurted out all that crazy stuff to a perfect stranger? The man must take him for an idiot. Even without Esmeralda's warning he would never want to talk to Zac again. That's why he hadn't risen to the boy's defense. *Everything will be fine*? What a dumb thing to say! As for throwing those nails on the floor, he hadn't done it because he cared anything for Zac; it was just to please himself. He was strange, eccentric, a character. He was like Mr. Pottinger, a nice man but untrustworthy. Nice men were the worst …

At least with Dada, Zac knew what to expect. He would be as bad as the Aunties, or worse. Zac would find out soon enough. His day had barely begun.

When Auntie Pris fetched him later that morning, Zac could barely stand.

"Don't limp, Boy," was all she said as she bundled him downstairs. "You can walk normally if you try."

Already the big black Cadillac was rumbling like a tank in the driveway, with Esmeralda drumming her fingers on the steering wheel. Just as in his trip to Five Corners (how hard to believe that was only a week ago!), Zac felt very small crawling into the huge backseat and hearing the door slam. Somehow Pris managed to wedge herself into the passenger seat, while Butler, looking like a small child, stood waving from the porch. As the car passed Porter's Store, Eldy's stand, the tiny barbershop, and St. Heldred's Church, Zac wondered vaguely whether he'd ever see Five Corners again.

It didn't matter. He'd had enough of this place.

Chapter 10
Dada

No one talked during the hour-long drive to the Big City. The only sound was Pris breathing heavily through her mouth. Esmeralda drove with both hands on the wheel, upright and stiff, while Pris sat massive and motionless like a big dark cloud herself. She wore a scanty black chiffon dress with a feather boa and matching broad-brimmed hat. Esmeralda was dressed in a slinky black gown with a half-length gray coat that looked covered with little lumps of spilled brains. (Mrs. Pottinger, who'd had one of these, said it came from newborn lambs.)

Zac's leg jiggled the whole way. Though the day was sunny, he noticed a bank of swollen black clouds on the western horizon, apparently hanging over the Big City. (What would Ches's cloud chart call those? Nimbostratus?) Halfway there the clouds swallowed the sun and soon it was raining big splotting drops. At first the drops came sparsely, like blobs from a giant fountain pen. Then the sky unleashed such a downpour that the windshield went opaque and the car rooster-tailed through lakes of water. Other cars were pulling over but Esmeralda, fighting the tug on the steering wheel, drove stolidly on.

Though Zac could see nothing, he knew when they'd reached the Big City. A different feel pervaded the air, like swarms of buzzing insects, though the only sound was the steady drum of rain and the slap-slap of the wipers. They might have been in any city of the world, or in any world of the universe.

Truly the city *was* big; they drove and drove. When Esmeralda finally parked, Zac had no idea where they were. Though the rain had slowed, the sky looked darker than ever and clouds of vapor drifted like smoke from explosions. Only after they'd walked a fair distance along a tree-lined gravel path did the outlines of an enormous, porticoed building loom. Several stories high, it was red brick with white columns and a wide stone staircase. The front doors were guarded by two fierce-looking statues of some creature with wings and scales.

Inside, the Aunties stopped at a front desk to speak to a woman in a crisp white dress with a tiny white hat folded like a newspaper sailboat.

"We're here to see Mr. Henbother," said Esmeralda, signing a book.

"Yes, of course," said the woman. "Room 311."

They walked down a wide terrazzo corridor, up two flights of stairs, down two more corridors. The building seemed even vaster inside than out, and the way was dotted with many more women in white dresses and sailboat hats and at least as many men in white coats. White shoes, too. There were also people not dressed in white. The white ones moved primly, purposefully, while the others sat on benches or shuffled

111

dreamily along the corridors like ghosts. Many of these wore bathrobes and some made noises: gurgles, groans, lip smacks, meaningless chatter. From one section of the third floor came terrible sounds: cries, howls, animal noises, and, worst of all, raucous, empty laughter.

Zac realized he was in a mental hospital. At the end of a corridor they came to a sitting area where Esmeralda instructed Pris to keep an eye on Boy while she conferred with a nurse.

She was gone quite awhile. Auntie Pris, her black chiffon duskily transparent, remained standing, as she could not possibly have squeezed into one of the chrome chairs. Zac, to avoid looking at her, stared out a window. As there was nothing to see but a dense gray drizzle, he studied his own reflection in the dark glass. It didn't seem like him but someone else, not even a boy but a small man who had grown old very fast and was about to fade away. With the pain from his beating, both physical and emotional, and the terrifying atmosphere of the hospital, he felt that whatever spark of life still smoldered within him would not take much to snuff out.

Then he heard Esmeralda say, "Dada will see us now."

Flanked between the Aunties, Zac was steered toward a door bearing the nameplate RUTHERFORD HENBOTHER. On the threshold a wave of panic hit him and he tried to pull back.

"Watch it, Boy," hissed Esmeralda in his ear. "Best behavior, or you'll be sorry."

The door swung open and in they went. There, in a wheelchair by the window, sat a figure completely muffled in glossy black fur. Within the lavish cuffs of a full-length coat his hands were just visible, white and twisted as roots. Puffy black slippers encased his feet, while on his head was a large, round hat with the face of a badgerlike animal poking from its front. Huge earflaps, and the animal's overhanging snout, left the man's face concealed in black shadow. Out of the shadowy hole came a thin, otherworldly voice with a faintly foreign accent.

"Ah, my girls. How lovely to see you."

"Dada!" squealed the Aunties together. "How are you? Are you keeping warm? Are you getting out? Are they feeding you enough?"

The questions tumbled forth as Pris and Esmeralda rushed to attend to Dada, adjusting his furs, patting his arms, changing the position of his chair. The room was excessively warm, causing Zac to wonder why anyone would need all that fur. (Later he learned that Dada, though paralyzed from the neck down, was always cold.)

"Enough," said Dada finally, and the Aunties withdrew a few steps. "My girls. Let me look at you."

An uneasy silence ensued as the Aunties stood at attention to be inspected.

"Priscilla," said Dada.

"Yes, Dada?"

"Get rid of that revolting dress."

"But last time you said—"

"Don't tell me what I said. I'm telling you now that I never want to see that rag again."

"Yes, Dada."

"You know very well you're nothing but a big ugly slug. Am I right?"

Auntie Pris looked too shocked to speak.

"Answer me, girl. What are you? Say the words."

Biting her lips, she looked ready to cry.

"Speak!" Barely raising his voice, Dada somehow gave this command the force of a shout.

Pris blubbered, "I'm a big ... ugly ... slug."

"Louder!"

"I'm a biguglyslug."

"Tell the world!"

Like someone about to plunge into icy water, Pris took a deep breath and roared at the ceiling, "*I'm a big ugly slug!*"

"There," said Dada. "How does that feel?"

"Better," whimpered Pris. She was shaking all over.

"Control yourself, girl. You're a mess."

Unlikely as it seemed, Zac felt sorry for Auntie Pris.

"Now, Esmeralda," said Dada.

Esmeralda stiffened. "Yes, Dada."

"You needn't look so pleased with yourself. Are you forgetting our little talk last week?"

"Yes, Dada. I mean, no, Dada. I haven't forgotten."

"Oh yes, you have. You must have forgotten, or else why haven't you brought me *it*?"

"Dada, you know how hard—"

"Quiet!" Once again Dada's thin, toneless voice, so feeble he could barely raise it, somehow sounded like a yell. After a considerable silence he resumed, "For this time I'll let it go. At least you brought me the cane."

"Yes, Dada."

"You must always bring the cane. You know that, don't you, Esmeralda?"

"Of course, Dada."

"Because the cane is mine, isn't it? It's not yours, it's mine."

"Yes, Dada, I know."

"And you must always keep it with you. Always."

"Always."

"Good girl. Now let me see it."

Laying the cane across her two open palms, Esmeralda brought it near the oval of fur where Dada's face was. From the dark cave protruded a bulbous, mushroom-colored thing. A nose. Dada appeared to be smelling the cane. Then he turned his head slightly and massaged a leprous cheek against it like a cat rubbing its scent on a leg of furniture. Zac gaped. The nose, the cheek, seemed more like tumors than parts of a face.

"That will do," said Dada finally. "Now give it to me."

With a similar show of ceremony, Esmeralda laid the cane across Dada's lap where it rested like a royal scepter. She drew back several steps.

"Now, Esmeralda, tell me why you're so late."

"The weather was terrible, Dada. Heavy rain, in sheets. All the cars were pulling over. And the misconduct of the boy delayed us. We've brought him to meet you."

"Yes, he's right here," said Pris brightly. "Remember we told you all about him?"

"Misconduct?" said Dada.

Esmeralda stepped forward and whispered in Dada's ear. The only word Zac heard clearly was "Porter." Following this exchange, in that wire-thin voice Dada said, "Boy, come here."

Zac didn't move. He couldn't. A terrible weight pressed him to the floor. Though moments before he'd been sweating in the close, stale air, now he felt cold with fear.

"*Boy!*"

Zac jumped. More than just hearing Dada's command, he felt it, like a needle piercing his heart.

"*Come here!*"

Immediately he was at Dada's side, drawn, or sucked, by the weird power of that voice. Standing this close, Zac nearly gagged on the smell—something like camphor, and beneath it a more potent odor that the camphor sought to mask.

"Now," said Dada, "what's this I hear about Mr. Porter?"

"It won't happen again, I assure you," Esmeralda interjected. "I've strictly forbidden the boy ever to talk to Porter."

"Quiet," said Dada. "Let the boy speak for himself. Your Auntie Esmeralda tells me you've made friends with Mr. Porter."

What was Zac to say? It wasn't just that he couldn't talk; he couldn't seem to form words in his mind. Poking out from beneath the badger face, Dada's cancerous nose, nostrils dilating, seemed to be sniffing him.

"Speak up, Boy."

Please don't yell again, Zac thought. He didn't ever again want to feel the needle jab of that unearthly voice.

"Not anymore," he heard himself say.

"Not anymore what?" said Dada.

"Not friends anymore. I'm not friends with Mr. Porter."

"Something's changed?"

"Yes, sir. I thought I liked him, but I don't. I won't be talking to him anymore. I promise."

Zac was gaining courage. It felt good to say this out of conviction, not just because he thought it was what Dada wanted. How bewildering, then, when Dada answered, "I'm sorry to hear that, Boy. Very sorry."

What?

"I'm afraid your Auntie Esmeralda did a bad thing when she warned you to stay away from Mr. Porter."

"But Dada—" began Esmeralda.

"You see, Porter has something I want, something very valuable. I want it, and I intend to get it." Within the dark cave of furs, the head quivered and the nostrils flared. "You know what it is, don't you?"

Dada was right. Zac knew.

"What is it, Boy? What does Dada want?"

"The umbrella," said Zac. "The blue umbrella."

Dada chuckled—a rusty, grating sound. "What a clever boy. You're clever enough to get me that umbrella, aren't you?"

"What?"

117

"You heard me."

Knowing he had to answer, Zac said, "I don't know."

"You lie. You know you can get that umbrella. If you don't know, you will fail. And you don't want to fail, do you?"

"No, sir."

"Then tell me you'll get the umbrella."

"But how, sir?"

"Get close to Porter. Hang around the store. In fact ask him for a job. Go to work for him. Get familiar with all his routines." Dada's voice, working its way under the skin, seemed more and more like Zac's own voice, Zac's own thoughts. "Watch carefully what he does with that umbrella. Wait for your chance then seize it. What could be simpler?"

"But Dada," said Esmeralda.

"Quiet! Do you have a better plan?"

Esmeralda was silent.

"Exactly," said Dada. "All your plans have come to nothing. Now, Boy, you know what to do?"

All at once Zac felt different. He felt challenged by the idea of succeeding where the Aunties had failed. It gave him a sense of power, where before he'd had none.

"Yes, sir," he said.

"You'll get the umbrella?"

"I'll get it."

"And when you get it, bring it straight to Dada. Yes?"

"Yes, sir."

"Good boy. Now come here."

Here? Zac was already so close that he could have sat in Dada's lap. He inched nearer still.

"Now take my hand."

"Pardon me?"

"You heard."

Deep within the fur cuffs Dada's hands lay coiled like nests of bony worms. Zac would no more reach in there than into a snake pit. As he hesitated, he felt that small, decrepit body gathering all its strange energy, and he knew what was coming. *The yell.* He could feel it rising and rising like a volcano, the thin, whispering scream that would sound on the outside like dry leaves rustling but inside would be a dentist's drill in his heart.

Before it could come, Zac stretched out his hand and let it hover just inches from one of those horrid claws.

"Come, Boy, I cannot move. Take my hand and place it on the cane."

Trembling, Zac closed his fingers around Dada's, feeling not skin, not even bone, but stone. Cold, lifeless marble, so cold he nearly recoiled as from fire. Lifting this dead weight, Zac placed it on the crook of the cane—a part worn darker than the rest, almost black. He meant to snatch away his own hand, but as his fingers touched the wood with Dada's, they froze. A shiver of cold stabbed through him like an icicle, even as he heard Dada sigh with satisfaction.

"Good boy!"

The words came to Zac as from a long distance away. Was it just that he was shaking so hard, or was the cane itself

119

trembling? He felt something going out of him, like breath, or life.

And he fainted.

Next thing he knew, he was lying on crisp white sheets that felt like a slab of ice. Though awake, he was in an odd state of mind, as if at the bottom of a well and peering up at the tiny opening, whence sounds swam down muted and echoey, sights dimmed and swirling. Most keenly he was aware of Dada's voice jabbering on and on in an animated, even elated, tone. The only words that came through clearly were "*the umbrella … umbrella … the blue umbrella …*"

Zac felt himself roughly shaken.

"Get up, Boy. Get up!"

"You can't stay here all day."

It was Pris and Esmeralda, hoisting him by the arms and swinging his feet to the floor.

"Stand up. Don't wobble about."

"There's nothing wrong with you."

He felt dizzy, but he was standing.

"Come along. We must go."

He took a few steps. With movement, awareness came rushing back. He was in a room in a mental hospital. Dada's room. He looked at the bed where he'd been lying. It was just a bed. Over by the window, motionless in a wheelchair, sat an old man swaddled in furs. Just an old man. Gone now was any sense of the powerful force that had gripped Zac.

"Esmeralda," croaked Dada, "I don't care for that lipstick. Change it."

"Yes, Dada."

"And Priscilla, see that the boy gets a haircut. He looks like he's on fire."

"Of course, Dada."

"And send me the nurse. I'm hungry."

Just a weak, crotchety old man attended by two fawning biddies. That was all.

But as Zac walked back with his Aunties through the cavernous corridors, down the wide stone staircase and out along the tree-lined path to the car, he knew something was different. Something about him that he couldn't quite put a finger on had changed. Even his body felt unfamiliar, like a different body.

So strong was this sensation that, once ensconced in the backseat of the Cadillac with the streets of the Big City flowing grayly past, he brought his hand right up to his face and stared at it, remembering. Then violently he wiped it on his pants, trying to rub the thing off, the creepiness. But there was no expunging it. Something was on him—something terrible—that wouldn't come off. And something was gone that he couldn't get back.

Chapter 11

Barometer Falling

St. Heldred and All Angles Church was a tall, narrow, white clapboard building with a too-small, purely decorative steeple. No bells hung in the belfry, no stairs led up, no cross adorned the apex. Once there had been a cross but it had blown down. Indeed the whole building might have blown down were it not for a web of black steel struts strung between the rafters, installed years before when winter storms had threatened to collapse the place like a house of cards. Now considered a historic building, it was kept in repair by public funds. A plain little church with bare wooden pews and tall, clear windows, it boasted no statues or paintings, no stained glass, no fine carpeting. There weren't even floral arrangements on the altar (the Aunties, who held considerable sway in church affairs, making sure of that). Plainness, however, was not the immediate impression conveyed to a Sunday morning visitor, for all the church ladies wore fine furs and fancy hats from the Aunties' shops. Looking out over the congregation, one saw a rich tapestry of mink and ermine, sable and chinchilla, and a cornucopia of fruit, flowers, baubles, and bangles burgeoning atop coiffures.

On Zac's first Sunday at St. Heldred's, he still felt vaguely ill—weak, headachy, crampy—from his meeting with Dada the day before. All he wanted was to curl up and sleep, but of course his presence was required at church. Seated between the Aunties in their front-row pew right under the nose of Reverend Cholmondeley, Zac knew he had to feign attention to the service, especially when Pris stood up to sing a gravelly, mawkish solo. Her hat, festooned with a forest of colored metal discs on long stalks, jangled like wind chimes each time she warbled a sustained note.

Following her song, she delivered a lengthy announcement about a pre-Christmas sale at the Sane Hatter. As she droned on and on about styles, fabrics, prices, accessories, several women paraded down the aisle to model her wares. Zac, meanwhile, became absorbed in the sound of tree branches tapping against the tall windows like someone wanting in.

When it came time for the sermon, Reverend Cholmondeley mounted a tiny spiral staircase into the pulpit, a high, narrow structure of polished wood that resembled an upright coffin. Perched there in his black cutaway coat, with his pale face and sharp features, he might have been a buzzard roosting in a dead tree. His text he announced as Psalm 91:16: "With long life will I satisfy him."

"My friends," he began, "in our series on long-livers of the Bible, we come today to the granddaddy of them all. Not Adam, who lived to nine hundred and thirty, nor even Noah, who attained the ripe old age of nine hundred and fifty. No, the champion of all, my dear friends—and I speak his name with a holy hush—is …"

Reverend Cholmondeley leaned far, even dangerously, out over the edge of his pulpit, spread wide his long arms as though indicating an immense measuring stick, and pronounced in a penetrating whisper, "*Methuselah*!" In the following long, dramatic pause, slowly he straightened up, and waggling one finger high in the air, he continued, "Methuselah lived to the astounding age of"—he performed a tremendous flourish as if magically producing a bouquet from his sleeve—"*nine hundred and sixty-nine*!"

A longer, more dramatic pause.

Then: "Think of it, my friends. Imagine seeing the return of spring to the earth no less than nine hundred and sixty-nine times! Imagine nine hundred and sixty-nine candles on a birthday cake! Picture, my friends, the sheer size of that cake! How far would *you* get trying to blow out nine hundred and sixty-nine candles?"

After an extended tribute, the Reverend began to ask what had happened to such longevity in modern times. Why did people today die so young, and was there no remedy? Though Zac could not follow all the medical and scientific data, his ears perked up at these next words.

"We just happen, my friends, to have two ladies in our midst who have attained an unusually impressive age, yet who carry their years with such grace as to be the envy of the young. Dear ladies, stand up, would you, and take a bow."

Esmeralda and Pris, rising majestically to face the congregation, bowed deeply—Pris, at least, attempted this maneuver—as the church filled with applause.

"I won't be so indecorous, ladies," continued the Reverend, "as to ask you to reveal your exact ages. But truly you put the rest of us to shame. We look to you as exemplars of the godly living that secures the biblical promise of long life for the righteous."

The Aunties sat down to another round of applause, which they received with the queenly dignity of two stately trees drinking in the summer rain. Following a lengthy discourse on righteousness, and a final hymn, the Reverend called upon Esmeralda to deliver announcements.

Standing at the front in her full-length ermine coat with matching hat, Esmeralda looked literally like a pillar, as if her tall frame held up the church. Zac could not decide whether she did or did not look her age. Clearly she was old, even ancient, yet her very age shimmered on her like dew. After reciting the usual schedule of teas, bake sales, and committee meetings, she cleared her throat and carefully broached what appeared to be a sensitive topic.

"Old age," she began, "as Reverend Cholmondeley will be the first to agree, is not always a blessing. Sometimes it is a disgrace. Right now, for example, the beauty of our church grounds is being defaced by a presence who can only be described as an eyesore. You all know to whom I refer. How long will we put up with lunacy, beggary, and hucksterism right here on our own property? Does Five Corners not have a perfectly adequate home for the aged? Do we at St. Heldred's wish to keep a diseased, decrepit squatter from finding his rightful place in our community—a place where he can live out his years in comfort and dignity? People of St. Heldred's, I beseech you: Join with Reverend Cholmondeley, Priscilla, and myself in taking action to remove this scandal from our midst."

Esmeralda went on to announce a public meeting, a petition, a phoning committee, and various other means of becoming involved in this cause. Afterwards, as the adults milled about, Zac felt a tap on his shoulder.

"What's wrong with you, Bud?" said Ches. "You look terrible."

"Dunno," shrugged Zac. "Flu or something. Say, what was all that about a scandal?"

Ches rolled his eyes but said nothing. Chelsea, behind him, did a pantomine of smelling flowers.

"Eldy?" Zac guessed.

"You got it, Bud. The one thing I'll say in the old guy's favor is that the Aunties hate his guts."

"Why?"

"Why not? He's a useless old dud."

"But your father just preached a sermon about how good it is to be old."

"Not like Eldy. He's all bent over and everything. Rev says he's like that because he's not upright in heart."

"So the church wants to close down Eldy's stand?"

"Not everyone, but some. Rev's pushing for a new hall on the church parking lot. If that goes through, Eldy's out, since he's basically camping on our lot. Esmeralda's been trying for years to get Eldy thrown off, but it always comes to nothing."

"I get the feeling that whatever Esmeralda wants, she gets."

"Mostly, but not when it comes to Eldy. People think he's good luck or something. And they don't want an old cripple getting shoved around. So there are all these meetings and petitions, but nothing changes. It'd be easier to stop people breathing air than to stop Eldy from selling those wretched balloons."

Chelsea was signing, trying to get their attention.

"What's she saying?" asked Zac.

"Says it's high time the old guy was kicked out. For his own good."

Chelsea put her hands on her hips and glared. Ches glared exaggeratedly back, and Zac decided to drop the subject. He felt weak and dizzy. By now they'd moved outside and the gray heaviness of the day seemed to settle over him like a cloak. All morning it had been trying to rain, the cloud cover low and uniform, the air dense with held moisture like a sponge, or like a person on the point of crying.

"Some weather," Zac commented.

Ches looked at his watch. It was a large, ponderous affair resembling a compass. Studying the brass-encased dial, he reported, "Temperature: 10 degrees Celsius. Relative humidity: 92 percent. Dew point: 10. Barometric pressure: 101.7 kilopascals and falling. Hmm, interesting." Giving Zac one of his perfectly bland stares, he added, "Yes, I suppose you could say that's some weather."

"Ches, what are you talking about?"

"The weather, you dimwit. You made an inane comment and I'm just clarifying with some accurate data. Haven't you ever heard of dew point, kilopascals, isobars?"

"I thought weather was sun, clouds, rain."

"That's kid stuff. If you want to talk real weather, let's hear some numbers."

Zac's head was spinning. "Wait—you said the weather today is interesting. To me it looks pretty dull."

"Not to me. Last night my Admiral Fitzroy read 104.5 kilopascals. Now it's down to 101.7. That's a big drop, and it's still falling."

"So?"

"Means a big change coming. Probably a lot of wind, maybe even a storm."

Hearing a jangle of metal, Zac turned to see Auntie Pris in her preposterous hat. Her heavy hand gripped his shoulder and it was time to go.

On Monday morning, to his surprise, Zac was sent to school. The Aunties said they were tired of trying to occupy him, but Zac sensed they were more concerned about his growing familiarity with Butler. In his crusty way the old man seemed to enjoy Zac's company, and as the Aunties grew wise to this, they took steps to separate them.

Zac didn't mind. Though he'd never liked school before, now it was a welcome escape. Strolling along with Ches that first morning, he felt better and all seemed well. The one-room schoolhouse, approached along a gravel lane lined with tall Lombardy poplars, sat atop a knoll just outside town. According to Ches, the Aunties themselves had once taught here before launching their more lucrative retail businesses.

The present schoolmaster was Mr. Edmund Twitchell, a thin, nervous man who made it clear that his last name was to be pronounced with two syllables, not one. Even so, behind his back the children all called him Mr. Twit, or just The Twit, and the boys referred to school as Twit's Hell. Moreover Mr. Twitchell had a way of wiggling his ears when agitated (which was often), a tic that sparked even more name-related ridicule. As Zac found out soon enough, however, he was not a man to be toyed with.

The class of twenty-five was composed of all ages from grades one through eight. The smallest boy, though not the youngest, was an eight-year-old named Eric White, whom everyone called Little Eric. He sat at a front desk right under the nose of Mr. Twitchell. About halfway through the first period, he shot up his hand to answer a question, but another boy beat him to it. Poor Little Eric got only as far as "Mr. Twit—" before the other boy cut him off.

Ears bright red and flapping, Mr. Twitchell fastened his bulbous eyes on Little Eric. "What did you say, White?"

"Nothing, sir."

"You did so. You said something. What was it?"

"I only wanted to answer your question, sir."

"Well, then, White, answer this question: What did you say? Speak up."

"I was only saying your name, sir, but Andy interrupted and—"

"What is my name, White?"

"Twitchell, sir. I mean, Mr. Twitchell."

"But that isn't what you said, is it?"

"It's what I *meant* to say, sir."

"But it's not what you *actually* said, is it?"

Little Eric had no answer.

"How many syllables does my name have, White?"

"Two, sir."

"Then come up here, because I think you need a way of remembering the number two."

Little Eric sat perfectly still.

"*Move!*"

The boy jumped to his feet and stood trembling before Mr. Twitchell, whose ears were nearly flying off his head. Without taking his eyes off Eric, he opened a drawer of his desk and withdrew a long wooden ruler.

"Bend over, White."

"Please, sir—"

"*Now!*"

No sooner had Little Eric bent over than Mr. Twitchell delivered a sharp blow to his backside. The little boy yelped in pain.

"How many was that, White?"

Straightening up shakily, Eric said, "One, sir."

"What do you say now, lad?"

"Please, sir, may I have another?"

Up to this point the horror of this scene had riveted Zac's attention. But at these words the horror touched not just his mind but his flesh, as he began to shake and sweat. The Aunties themselves, he realized, must have initiated this method of discipline in the school.

"I'm so glad you asked, White," said Mr. Twitchell. "I'm delighted to give you another."

As the boy bent over again, the teacher, more sure now of his aim, dealt an even sharper blow that sounded like a rifle shot. Eric burst into tears.

"Now tell me, lad, how many was that?"

"T-t-two, sir."

"Right you are. What an intelligent lad. Do you think you can remember that number now?"

"Yes, sir."

"And what is it the number of?"

Little Eric looked blank.

"Hurry up, lad. What is this all about?"

Fortunately Eric's mind cleared enough to say, "Your name, sir. It has two syllables."

"Right. Will you remember that now?"

"Yes, sir."

"And what will happen if you do not?"

"More blows, sir. I'll get two more blows."

"*No*! You'll get *four* blows next time, you rascal. And after that it will be eight, then sixteen, and thirty-two. And the same goes for the rest of you."

Glaring out over the class, Mr. Twitchell's searchlight eyes settled on Zac.

"I'll teach you scalawags multiplication on the skin of your bottoms. And after that we'll move on to trigonometry and calculus. What you don't learn with your mind will be beat into your behind."

Zac sat rigidly (except for his violently jiggling left leg) and stared straight ahead. The scene with Little Eric, he saw too clearly, was meant as an example for him.

Chapter 12

The Blue Umbrella

After school that first day Zac again fell in beside Ches, who appeared to have no one else to walk with. Chelsea, too, walked alone, which struck Zac as odd since there were other girls her age. But then he thought of Mary, their mother, all alone in her room. And then there was the Reverend, nodding in his chair over some heavy tome, or maybe opening a can of soup for himself in the church hall. The Cholmondeleys, Zac reflected, were one lonely family.

At first he and Ches didn't talk. Zac, besides being troubled by the scene with Little Eric, was preoccupied with having to ask Sky Porter for a job. Finally he said, "Ches, can I tell you something?"

"Do I want to know?"

"Probably not. But I need to tell someone. I have to do something today that I don't want to."

"That's life, Bud. Get used to it."

Zac wondered what he was doing with this sullen, self-centered bore. He thought about breaking into a run and leaving Ches in the dust of his gloomy thoughts. But Ches was his only friend in Five Corners—or friendlike substitute—so he pressed on with what he needed to say.

"The Aunties want me to get a job at Porter's. I'm going there right now to ask."

Ches stopped walking. His great head swiveled toward Zac like the turret of a tank. "You what?"

Knowing Ches had heard him, Zac didn't respond. Behind those thick, tortoise-shell glasses, Ches's eyes narrowed to glinting points.

"You idiot," he said. "Didn't I warn you to stay away from that place? I'll tell you one thing—you start hanging out with that creep Porter and you won't be walking home from school with me. Not on your life."

Ches walked faster so that Zac had to hustle to keep up. Then Ches stopped again and demanded, "Why? Just tell me why."

"I told you. It's the Aunties. They're making me."

Ches shook his head. "Must be more to it. The Aunties hate Porter's guts. You sure you're not holding out on me?"

Zac bit his lip and looked away. He couldn't tell Ches about Dada. He just couldn't.

"You're not a very good liar, Bud. But okay, have it your way."

They were drawing near the five corners, approaching the back of the stone behemoth of the Aunties' house. The white steeple of St. Heldred's was visible all the way from the schoolhouse, but now they could also see the rectory and the multicolored awning of Eldy's stand. Just as the Porter's sign came into view, Zac heard something. A familiar sound, high and musical. Not instruments but a voice, a

134

woman's voice. Far away, across town somewhere, a woman was singing. It was like the music Zac had noticed upon first entering Porter's Store. Come to think of it, he'd heard this other times since then, at odd moments, without paying it much attention. Now, for some reason, it sounded very clear and gave him a tingly feeling. Suddenly he was curious.

"What's that sound?" he asked.

"What?" Ches listened. "Oh, that. It's just O."

"O?"

"Yeah."

"O who?"

"Just O. That's her name."

"O? Nothing else?"

"Right. If she's got another name, no one knows it. She doesn't know it herself. Doesn't know nothin'. She's just O. Or Zero, if you ask me."

"Who is she?"

"Town drunk. Likes to sing. Roams all over town, lives nowhere. Sleeps in alleys, on benches. Crazy as blazes. Just your typical wino. Every town has one."

"You mean an alcoholic?" Zac thought of his old neighbor, Mr. Pottinger. "But she's a woman."

"They're the worst, Bud."

Zac listened more intently to the singing. Though he couldn't hear words, the tune had an astounding clarity, a purity that touched him.

"It's beautiful," he said.

Ches grunted.

"I'd say that lady can really sing."

"Sometimes," Ches acknowledged. "Other times she sounds like a wounded cat. I never listen. Nobody does."

The singing stopped. The boys were standing in front of the Aunties' place. Staring across at Porter's Store, Zac said, "I guess I have to do this."

"It's your funeral," said Ches.

For about a full minute neither of them moved. The word funeral made Zac think of his mother. Finally, in a rare moment of intuition, Ches said, "Sorry, I didn't mean …"

"It's okay."

Ches went on, "I don't blame you for not wanting to work at Porter's, that's all. That place is enough to give anyone the creeps."

"Yeah. I mean, no, it's not that. I don't know. Maybe I feel different now. Maybe it will be all right."

Ches raised one heavy eyebrow, then turned to cross the street to his house, his broad, implausible back lurching away, arms dangling palms-backward gorillalike. Just once he glanced back to say, "Take it easy, Bud."

Facing Porter's Store, Zac found himself studying the big plate-glass windows, not looking at anything in particular but rather at the glass itself. For the first time in his life, he noticed three distinct aspects of a window. First there were reflections on the surface of the glass. Then there was what you could see through the glass, inside. Finally there was the glass itself, an object in its own right, transparent yet substantial. It occurred to Zac that he was about to pass through this barrier from

136

outside to inside—from the outer world of mere reflections to the inner world where things were real. It was, for him, a strange thought.

All at once he had the feeling of being watched. The Aunties, peering from behind their curtains? Quickly, before either he or they could have a change of mind, Zac crossed the street and put his hand on the green metal 7UP door pull. Then he was inside.

It was quiet. On his first visit he'd been struck by how different everything looked, as if bathed in an ethereal light. Today the store appeared quite ordinary—even faded, dingy, cluttered. But now Zac noticed its aural quality, the acoustics, which felt different somehow from anything he could remember. The air seemed both silent and resonant, both muffled and peculiarly clear, as though he were at the bottom of the sea or inside a great bell that had been struck a long time ago and was still faintly trembling.

He saw Mr. Porter. Perched at the top of a sliding ladder, he was arranging merchandise on an upper shelf. The moment Zac entered, the man stopped, turned, and looked directly at him. That look took Zac by surprise. Already he'd forgotten the amazing quality of this face, how real it was, how singularly present. Zac realized he hadn't seen Mr. Porter all weekend, hadn't watched for him from his bedroom window as he had every other day. Now the boy felt confused. And something else: ashamed. What was he doing here?

"Hi, Zac," Sky sang down. "What brings you here?"

Without thinking, Zac said, "I don't know." It sounded dumb, but at that moment it was the truth.

Slowly Sky backed down the ladder and skirted the counter. Zac hadn't moved, except for his head, which he bowed. As Sky drew near, he reached out one finger and lifted Zac's chin.

"Does Esmeralda know you're here?"

Looking him in the eye now, Zac felt a tremendous desire to tell the truth, the whole truth. But another force held him back. He was about to answer that Esmeralda herself had sent him here, but thinking better of it, he said only, "She knows."

"And she allows you? After what she said the other day?"

"I begged her," Zac lied. After one lie, the rest came more easily. "I told her I get so restless sitting alone in my room or doing housework. I think maybe I'm driving them crazy. So I asked if I could get a job to help pay my way. Please, Mr. Porter, could you hire me? I'm a really good worker. And you wouldn't have to pay me much, or anything. I just like it here …"

Zac was talking so fast, there was no separating the lies from the truth.

"Please, Mr. Porter? Please?"

"Sky," he reminded. "I asked you to call me Sky."

"Right."

"Names are important. There's power in a name. There's power in your name, Zac. It's a good name, bright and lively. If you and I are going to work together, we ought to be on a first-name basis, don't you think?"

What? Had Zac heard right? Swelling with excitement he said, "You mean …?"

"I mean," Sky continued, "how would you like it if I called you Mr. Sparks?"

Zac couldn't help smiling. Certainly no one in his life had ever called him Mr. Sparks.

"Or how about Sir? Would you like to be called Sir?"

Zac's smile widened. The idea was absurd. "But Mr. Porter, does that mean I'm hired? Are you really giving me a job?"

Now it was Sky's turn to smile, and then he threw back his head and laughed—that thrilling, liberating laugh that Zac recalled so well from their first meeting. All this time he'd remained aware of the room's heightened, bell-like acoustics. But now it seemed that all the bells on earth were ringing. Zac couldn't help himself—he laughed too, without even knowing why. Laughing seemed to be something one did in Porter's General Store.

"Let me put it this way," said Sky eventually. "Mr. Porter won't give you a job. But Sky will. Is it a deal?"

"Yes, sir!" Zac exploded.

No laugh this time. "I'm serious, Zac. If you want to work for me, you must call me Sky."

"Okay, Sky!" And as soon as Zac said the name, it all came back to him—exactly how he'd felt when he first heard it: as if hit with a soft bolt of electricity … as if something inside him gave way. And looking up into the depthless transparency of Sky's eyes, he felt calm, steady, safe. He felt as though he'd known this man forever and they were the best of friends, and Zac could say or do anything he wanted. He could just be himself, but himself as he'd never known himself. It was such a strange feeling that Zac couldn't keep gazing into those blue, blue eyes; he had to look away.

As he did so, he saw the umbrella cocked over Sky's arm. And then a very different set of feelings surged through him as he recalled his mother's death, the burnt husk of her umbrella, and then the Aunties and Dada and the charge they'd given him, which was his whole reason for being here in Porter's Store: to steal this very object that now lay just inches from his grasp.

Sky noticed his stare. "She's a beauty, isn't she? Would you like to have a closer look?"

He held out the umbrella, leaving Zac stunned and confused. The object both repelled and fascinated him.

"I don't know if I should," he said.

"Don't worry. It won't explode in your hands."

Still Zac hesitated. Sky's offer seemed too intimate, somehow, as if this near stranger were handing over his wallet. But finally Zac couldn't resist. He reached out and took the umbrella by its furled part, and in the process he unintentionally touched Sky's hand. For a moment they held the umbrella together; then Sky's hand withdrew and Zac was left holding it alone.

It was astonishingly light. He hefted it, joggled it up and down, could not believe how weightless it felt. No wonder Sky could carry it around all day without seeming the least encumbered. It almost did not seem to be a material object, though it did have a definite feel. Running his hand over the fabric, Zac was reminded of his mother's touch, her hand on his forehead, her hair brushing his face. The umbrella was that soft, even warm. It seemed alive, almost breathing.

Then he clasped the wooden handle. It was wondrously smooth. Again and again he slid his hand along its satiny curve; it seemed the most perfect shape imaginable. How many hours—or years?—had Sky Porter's hand rested in exactly this spot?

Embarrassed at this thought, Zac offered the umbrella back to Sky.

"Don't you want to open it?" Sky asked.

The suggestion was startling. No, it hadn't occurred to Zac to open it. A sense of taboo restrained him. It was like daring to snoop in someone's diary. And he thought again of the charred frame of his mother's umbrella.

"Isn't it bad luck to open an umbrella indoors?" he demurred.

"Trust me: No bats will fly out; no bogeyman will get you."

As Zac still balked, Sky reached out and undid the umbrella's strap. With a sumptuous rustle the blue fabric fell loose like the plumage of some large, exotic bird. To Zac's surprise the canopy's undersurface, while the same beautiful blue as the exterior, looked remarkably different. Instead of the flatness of cloth, it gave an appearance of depth, as though one could look into it a long, long way, perhaps even to infinity. Was this impression just a trick of light on the rippling folds? Then Sky said, "Go ahead—open it," and as Zac peered more closely, searching out the release mechanism, the inner fabric seemed more wondrous than ever, like nothing else he'd ever seen. Though it did remind him of something—but what?

Pushing on the spring-loaded catch that released the canopy, he half-expected the umbrella to burst open, but it did not. Instead he had to slide the golden ring all the way up the shaft until it docked with a coupling. The metal spreaders stretched to reveal more and more of the cloth's amazing interior, until finally the entire canopy lay wide open in a taut, scalloped dome. Gazing up in wonder, Zac felt small, but big inside, as though standing on a mountaintop with nothing but sky overhead.

"Hmm," said Sky. "Looks like it might rain after all."

He pointed to the umbrella's farthest fringe. The entire canopy was a deep, diaphanous blue, except in this one place where the fabric seemed discolored by some grayish-black shapes. Zac stared, fascinated.

"Might even be a storm brewing," Sky added.

What was he talking about? The darkish shapes, now that he mentioned it, did have the bruised look of storm clouds. Surely Sky must be joking—as if to suggest it might rain right here in the store! Laughing uneasily, Zac abruptly handed back the umbrella. Sky twirled it a few times like a parasol, then released the catch, slid the ring back down, and fastened the strap around the furled canopy.

"What do you think, Zac?" he asked.

About what? The umbrella? The possibility of rain?

"I don't know," said Zac truthfully.

Sky let some silence rest between them, before saying, "So it's settled. You'll come to work for me. Agreed?"

Zac nodded.

"Good. As it happens, all the shelves in the store need washing. Can you start right away?"

"Sure. Anything."

Sky gave Zac some rags and a pail of soapy water and sent him up the ladder, and for the next couple of hours, he enjoyed being absorbed in a mindless task. He was aware of the storekeeper puttering about, and dimly he recalled that he was supposed to be keeping an eye on the umbrella, watching for a chance to nab it. But mostly he didn't think about that—only about cleaning the shelves, and about Sky, and about the umbrella's strange beauty. He kept seeing it in his mind. The handle was made of some honey-colored wood with a beautiful grain, full of swirls and patterns that almost seemed to mean something or to tell a story.

That first afternoon in Porter's General Store, Zac was the happiest he'd been since coming to Five Corners.

Chapter 13

Eldy

When Zac emerged from Porter's, the sun, as though split in two by a sword, was setting behind the steeple of St. Heldred's. A strong wind had arisen, gusting up Henbother Hill toward the mountain. Glancing at Ches's balcony, Zac saw the vanes on the anemometer spinning wildly. Eddies of dry leaves bustled, vaguely humanoid, along the streets. Crossing toward the Aunties' house, he rejoiced in the smooth, muscular resistance of the wind.

As something brightly colored blew toward him, he stopped. Balloons! Without thinking, he grabbed the long, trailing string, and the big bunch of balloons tugged at his arm like a kite. He let them pull him along, relishing the clean power of the wind pouring through his body. Soon he was skipping, then running up Henbother Hill. He could have stopped—the tug of the balloons wasn't that strong—but he didn't want to. He wanted to give himself to the wind wherever it led. He wanted to fly. Practically laughing with the fun of it, he realized he hadn't run, or played, or done anything really fun since before his mother's death. That thought made him run even faster.

Henbother Hill was long and steep and he was panting hard but loving it. Leaving houses behind, on and on he went, even after the pavement gave way to a narrow dirt path. So intent was he on giving himself to the smooth, beautiful pull of the wind that he barely saw the imposing black-and-yellow-striped billboard with tall letters reading KEEP OUT! Well beyond the town now, his only company was rocks, tall grasses, bushes, sky, when all at once, as he rounded a bend, the full outline of Wind Mountain with its oddly split peak hove into view.

And then he heard it: the voice of the mountain. The wind, funneling between the two towering rock pinnacles, made a sound like someone blowing across the mouth of an enormous bottle. Zac stopped in his tracks, listening. First one note, low and sonorous; then another, a little higher; then a third note, higher still; then back to the first. The mountain was singing! It was singing to Zac! He knew it was for him because he recognized the song. The pitches weren't exact, but they reminded him clearly of a song his mother had sung to him when he was little. Transfixed, he drank in the music with his whole body. And then he began to climb toward it, slowly now, up and up. He forgot he was holding any balloons; he forgot all about Five Corners, Dada, the Aunties; he even forgot his mother was dead and that he'd had to leave home, so immersed was he in this one thing, the windsong. The notes kept coming, tugging at his heart, not always in the same order but still the same three distinct tones—and Zac followed. He was almost there, almost at the music's source, when he saw something startling.

145

A gallows. A tall, wooden scaffold with a heavy, dangling rope. Puzzled, he approached the thing, came right up and put his hands on the wooden railing and peered up at the rusted iron housing from which the rope hung. And then, following the rope, he looked down … down … into a hole. A dark, deep, square hole, walled with planking. A mine shaft!

He recalled Ches telling him about the old, abandoned mine on Wind Mountain. It was dangerous, Ches had said. No one was allowed up here. Nervous, Zac almost turned to go, but the noise stopped him. Noise? Yes. The shaft was full of sound. Not the song of the wind but other sounds: muffled, mysterious, faraway, but big. Deep rumblings, crashes, roarings. Distant peals as of thunder, a pounding like surf, mighty rushings and booms as if train cars the size of hills were being shunted around deep in the earth. And an updraft, too, streamed out of the mine, so strong that Zac almost let go of the balloon string. As he backed away a few steps, the big sounds died away and there was only the moan of the wind through the mountain cleft. Just one note now, one throaty bottle tone.

So close was Zac to the peak that he not only heard that note but felt it, thrumming in the air and within him. Climbing the last few yards up to the towering twin spires, soon he stood in the gap between them, his arms spread, one hand on each of the cool rock walls, in the very mouth of the windsong. Curiously the music here fell silent; all was perfectly still.

Facing back the way he'd come, he had a spectacular vista. From here the sun, instead of being speared by the church steeple, sat just on top of it like a Christmas ornament. Zac laughed aloud: He'd outrun the sun! The five-cornered intersection looked like a star. There was Porter's Store and the Aunties' house; the rectory where Ches and Chelsea lived; the tiny barbershop; and spread out around was the whole town, including The Mink's Meow and The Sane Hatter and the school he'd attended for one day but already hated. In one glance Zac's entire life at Five Corners came into focus. Though he'd been here for just over a week, it seemed forever. Lifting his eyes to the horizon, he could just make out the tops of some tall buildings with a few lights coming on. The Big City.

Dada … the Aunties …

He had to get back and no one must find out he'd been gone. But what about the balloons? He still had them, a big bunch in his fist, and he knew whose they were. They were an old man's livelihood and Zac would have to return them. He must go back down the mountain straight to Eldy and hand over those balloons, hoping to heaven no one saw him. Studying the lay of the land, he noticed a lane that paralleled Henbother Hill, descending through trees and appearing to emerge behind Porter's, just across from Eldy's stand. Perhaps he could take that route without being detected.

To Zac's surprise the same wind that had blown him up the hill now reversed and blew at his back, so that soon he was racing downhill at top speed with the balloons practically lifting him off the ground. He didn't care about falling; he was safe in the sure-footedness that comes with wholehearted abandon.

Not until he stood in the lane across from Eldy's stand did he pause to catch his breath. He could see the old man's bent form behind the counter, the rainbow-colored awning flapping above him like sailcloth. It would be a simple matter to cross the street and hand over the balloons and leave. Eldy couldn't talk, so there would be no conversation, no reason to hang around. With any luck Zac would get back to the Aunties' without their knowing a thing.

All went as planned, until the moment when he tried to give the balloons to Eldy.

"Sir, I think these belong to you."

The old man seemed not to have heard. His back turned, he was busy arranging flowers in a large purple vase on the ground. He wore jeans, a dark blue, fisherman-knit sweater, and white canvas sneakers. Zac marveled at how bent he was, literally at ninety degrees. To him ground level was like a kitchen counter.

"Sir? Your balloons. They got away in the wind."

Still no response. Was Eldy deaf as well as dumb?

"Sir, I have to be going. Maybe I'll just tie your balloons to this post. Okay?"

Slowly the old man turned, until Zac looked down not at his back but upon his round, bald head fringed with white hair. The tanned skin looked like an ancient vellum map. It was freckled with brown age spots, as many, it seemed, as stars in the sky.

Then Zac heard a voice. No—he didn't actually hear anything, but words seemed to form inside him. The words said, *They're yours. I want you to have them.*

He was sure Eldy hadn't said anything. Zac must have imagined the words, only they didn't feel like one of his own thoughts. They sounded not just in his head but in all of him, and they gave him a wistful feeling, as of something long forgotten.

He wanted just to hand over the balloons and be gone. But with the old man doubled over, his hands dangling as if trying to tie his shoelaces, Zac could see no way to give him the string.

"Like I said, sir, I'll just tie your balloons to this post. Will that be okay?"

Again came the feeling of words forming inside him. *You followed the wind. The balloons are yours.*

Again this was a thought Zac would not have had on his own. It surprised and perplexed him. Finally he said, "But I don't want them. I mean, I can't keep them. It wouldn't be right."

It's right, said the interior voice.

"You don't understand—"

I understand, Zachary.

When the voice said that, calling him by name, Zac got a thick, spongy feeling. But wait a minute—what was going on here? He was having a conversation, out loud, with himself!

"Please, I really can't keep these balloons." After all, what would he do with them? There was no way the Aunties would let him have them.

149

As if Eldy, or the interior voice, had heard even Zac's unspoken thoughts, the response came, *You are a wind lover. The Aunties do not know the wind.*

What was that supposed to mean?

"My Aunties would kill me if they knew I was talking to you. Please take your balloons."

One brown wrinkled hand floated up to rest on the counter. Understanding that Eldy was ready to take the balloons, Zac placed the string in the open fingers, which closed around it. Then he turned to walk away.

Wait, said the inner voice.

Zac stopped.

Take one, said the voice.

Zac didn't move.

Just one. This one?

Turning slowly, Zac saw Eldy's two hands waving above the counter. In one was the big bunch of balloons, in the other a single bright red one.

Red. Zac's favorite color.

My gift to you, said Eldy.

By now Zac knew the voice must be Eldy's. He couldn't be imagining all this. He stood there staring at the one red balloon, feeling drawn. For a ten-year-old boy, balloons did not hold great excitement. But at that moment this one appeared so beautiful, so desirable, that Zac felt he wanted it more than anything.

Stepping forward and taking the red balloon, he said, "Thank you."

The reply came swiftly: *A sword will pierce it, but no sword can thwart it.*

Though Zac heard these words clearly, only much later would they register. For now he felt like he'd been given a million dollars. He was so light and free he went off skipping. He could have run up and down Henbother Hill a hundred times. But the sun was down and he knew the Aunties expected him. He reached their porch feeling so happy he nearly waltzed into the house with his red balloon in plain view. But at the last moment he tucked it under his jacket, hiding the bulge as best he could, and gently opened the door. He listened, then darted across the front hall and up the stairs.

"*Boy!*"

Auntie Pris's strident cry struck him in the back like the *thwang* of an arrow.

"Just where do you think you're going?"

"Upstairs, Auntie. To my room."

"You impudent rascal. Come down here."

He didn't move.

"But Auntie—"

"*Come down this instant!*"

His foot was on the top step. He thought of unzipping his jacket and flicking the balloon down the hall out of sight. But he was too alarmed to do anything except turn and trudge down the stairs. Standing before Auntie Pris, he hunched his shoulders and sucked in his gut in a desperate attempt to hide the obvious.

"What have you got there, Boy?"

"Pardon, Auntie?"

"There's something under your jacket. What is it?"

"I don't know, Auntie."

"Of course you know. Open up that jacket."

What could he do? He undid the zipper, just enough to show the top of the red balloon, like a rising sun.

"What's this? I don't believe …"

Swift as a pouncing cat, Pris drew out an enormous pearl-tipped hatpin and plunged the point into Zac's chest. It was a wonder she didn't kill him. As it was, the balloon exploded with a gust of wind in the boy's face and he fell to the floor (mostly from shock). Pris grabbed his jacket collar and yanked him up.

"What was that noise? I heard an explosion." It was Esmeralda, her whispery voice barely controlled. To Zac she had never looked so tall. Meanwhile Pris had turned red as the balloon and likewise looked ready to explode.

"This boy … this *boy* …"

"Yes, yes, spit it out, Priscilla."

"… came home with … a *balloon* …"

"No!"

"… under his jacket …"

"No!"

"He was trying to hide it. One more second and he would have vanished into his room."

"Well, I never …"

"Auntie Esmeralda," Zac piped up, "please—"

"Please, nothing. What have you got to say for yourself, Boy?"

"I'm trying to tell you, Auntie. You see—"

"Yes?"

Zac was thinking fast but nothing was in his brain, nothing at all—until he opened his mouth.

"Auntie," he said breathlessly, "I got the job!"

"What?"

"Mr. Porter gave me a job. Just like Dada wanted. I worked there all afternoon, ever since school."

Both Aunties appeared momentarily confused. If Zac could just keep diverting them …

"Cleaning shelves," he went on wildly. "And I kept my eye on the umbrella the whole time. Just like Dada said. I even held it, and opened it—"

"You what?"

"Yes, he let me hold the umbrella, and open it up—"

"You don't say?"

"Yes. It's wonderful! It's so … beautiful. I understand why Dada wants it."

"You understand nothing!" snapped Esmeralda.

"Yes, Auntie. Nothing."

"Get to the point, Boy," said Pris, jabbing her hatpin in the air. "What were you doing with that balloon?"

Inspired, Zac hurried on. "At the end of the day Mr. Porter asked me to run an errand. To Eldy. You know, the balloon man? He told me to return a bunch of balloons that had gotten away in the wind."

"Yes?"

"What else could I do? I had to go. And then—"

"Then what? You stole one for yourself?"

"No, Eldy gave it to me. He wanted me to take the whole bunch. I wouldn't, but he insisted I have one. Just one, that was all."

"I see," said Esmeralda. "So it's true. You brought a balloon into this house."

"I didn't know—"

"Nonsense. How could you not know? Are you an imbecile?"

"No, Auntie."

"Yes, you are. What's more, you had that umbrella in your hot little hands and you didn't nab it? What a fool! Bend over."

"Auntie, please—"

"Bend over!"

As it turned out, Zac received only one whack with the cane. When he asked for another, Esmeralda replied, "That will do for today. But listen, Boy: If I ever catch you again with that awful old man or his balloons, you'll wish you didn't have a behind. Is that clear?"

"Yes, Auntie."

Dismissed to his room, Zac was halfway up the stairs when Esmeralda added, "And another thing: Bring me that umbrella tomorrow, without fail, or you'll get two strokes with the cane. And three the next day. But there won't be a next day, will there?"

"No, Auntie."

Chapter 14

The Storm

In his room Zac flopped onto the bed and, to his own surprise, burst into tears. Though he'd been dealt only one blow this time, the prospect of more serious beatings to come was terrifying.

So much for Eldy. He seemed like a nice old fellow but he'd gotten Zac into a peck of trouble over one stupid balloon. Surely he knew how the Aunties would feel about it? But then he hadn't exactly said anything, had he? With a shock Zac realized he must have imagined that whole conversation with Eldy. How else to account for it? In any case the old man was trouble.

And then there was the problem of the umbrella. Zac would be caned again tomorrow if he didn't steal it. But he liked Mr. Porter! He didn't want to steal anything from him. Besides, how would he do it? Just grab the thing and run? Then it would be up to the Aunties to answer for him. Zac knew already that Mr. Porter would not stand up to them, so that plan might work. But it was sloppy. Far better if he could nab the umbrella without being seen.

For a long time he lay on his bed going over various schemes, none of which seemed promising. Outside the wind had picked up, even stronger than before, and he heard the familiar sound of tree branches tapping on his windowpane. Through the glass he watched the sky grow dark, not just with evening but with a phalanx of black clouds advancing from the west. *Phalanx:* He recalled the word from a book he'd read on ancient warfare. It was a formation of infantry moving in close ranks with spears and shields overlapping. Zac imagined an army of relentless warriors marching on Five Corners to annihilate the town with all its crazy, terrible inhabitants. That would suit him just fine.

Only when he recalled his run up the mountain did he begin to feel better. Ches had said no one could go up there, but Zac had gone. That, while it lasted, had been fun. And discovering the strange, wild sounds deep in the old mine shaft. And standing between the two tall peaks—he'd felt so peaceful there. That place held a great stillness, so pure it was like a presence. Zac, not used to being still, didn't know quite what to make of it.

With that thought he fell asleep and dreamed of his mother. Such beautiful dreams! There she was, arranging a bouquet of dew-spangled roses ... or sitting by the window, just gazing out, wearing the red cashmere sweater Zac loved (so soft!) ... or aproned in the kitchen, stirring a batch of his favorite cookies (peanut butter chocolate chip with cornflakes) ... or in full flight on a rope swing, laughing, her long hair streaming, holding Zac as a tiny baby on her lap ... (That last image—upon awaking he wondered how he knew about it. He felt sure that, like the other scenes, this one must really have happened, but he was equally sure he'd never even seen such a photograph.)

The most mysterious dream that night involved a stranger. An unknown man came to Zac's bedside right there at Five Corners. It wasn't scary; quite the contrary. Smiling broadly, the man handed him a cardboard shoe box. Zac knew exactly what this was. It was the box in which he kept his collection of soldiers: cowboys and Indians, infantry and cavalry, sailors and desert sheikhs. All about two inches high and molded from bright plastic. At night, when he should have been sleeping, he liked to wage spectacular battles all over the convoluted countryside of his covers. Often his mother took the shoe box away at bedtime. How surprising, then, when the man in Zac's dream brought him his old shoe box, clearly inviting him to play. Zac was just about to open the box when he heard shots—pistols, muskets, cannons—all the noise of a real battle, just as he pretended to hear whenever he played war. Sometimes he even made the shooting sounds out loud: *bang, bang, boom, cheeeowww—*

He awoke, not to shots but to the sound of branches banging against his windowpane. The wind had grown so blustery that the branches clattered like a rain of stones, as if someone in the street below were trying desperately to get his attention. So strong was this impression that Zac sat up in bed and was about to run to the window when the entire pane shattered like a bomb exploding. Flying glass pelted the bedspread but Zac himself was untouched. As he threw the covers aside and stood up, the blast of wind nearly knocked him down. Stumbling to his knees, he had to hang onto the chair to keep from being blown backward. The tree branches were right inside now, like gnarled old hands reaching for him. Strangely, he wasn't frightened. Still under the spell of his beautiful dreams, there on his knees before the wide-open window with that tremendous wind blowing full upon him, face-to-face with the vast, stormy night—it was awesome. And louder even than the wind itself, filling the room as the sea fills a shell, came the deep organ tones of the mountain peak.

Then Zac saw something even more dramatic. Across the street, just above Porter's Store, the most beautiful display of flashing colored lights filled the sky. He had seen northern lights, but these colors were even more vivid. Brilliant streamers trembled in the dark as if a rainbow—or many rainbows—had unwoven to blow like hair in the wild wind. It was fantastic, dreamlike, yet so real. Torn between wonder and incredulity, Zac's mind swam trying to make sense of the spectacle.

Behind him the door flew open so violently he thought it must be the wind. But as he turned, there in the doorway, looming tall as a tower in a billowing, beribboned nightgown, stood Auntie Esmeralda.

Thumping her cane across the floor to where Zac huddled, she hissed, "How dare you disturb our sleep!"

"It was the wind, Auntie—"

"I suppose the wind shattered this window?"

"The branches—when it's windy, they tap against the glass and—"

"Branches, my foot! How would you like me to tap against your skull?"

Zac shrank before the raised cane.

"You little imp—you were trying to escape, weren't you?"

"No, Auntie."

"It's plain as day. Do you think I've forgotten the last time you went running off at night? You're a little night crawler, aren't you?"

"No, Auntie, I promise—"

"That's the last time you play this trick. Come with me."

Pinching Zac's ear, she yanked him to his feet. As she stormed from the room, he had to scamper along sideways to keep his ear from being pulled off. At the end of the hall, she dragged him into a spare bedroom where she flung open a closet door and shoved him inside. The door slammed, a key rattled in the lock, the cane went thumping away, and Zac was left alone in the darkest place he had ever been.

Even when his eyes had adjusted, not a sliver of light crept under the door, not a glimmer showed anywhere. The only light was the phosphorescent squiggles that danced in his eyes when he rubbed them. The only sound was the howl of the wind, more distant here but still wild enough to send shudders through every board in the house. Later came the splatter of heavy raindrops on the roof, and later still the clatter of hail. Crouched on the floor, rocking back and forth, Zac had plenty of time to ponder the night's events, including his dreams and the strange rainbow-colored lights over Porter's Store.

He tried exploring. Groping about, he brushed against a row of coats on hangers. Otherwise the closet was quite empty, except for a knob on the wall that, when he pulled it, opened a small, square hatch into what must have been a laundry chute. The hole was about big enough for Zac to crawl into, but in the total darkness that idea was not appealing.

The closet's only other feature was a protruding section of bricks, no doubt the chimney. It was very warm, and soon Zac had to remove the jacket he'd slept in. As he did so, his hand brushed against something pliant, rubbery ... *Aha!* Still clinging to the lining was the husk of the red balloon that Auntie Pris had popped. Fingering it in the darkness, Zac was reminded of sitting on his mother's lap as a small child and caressing her earlobe. The balloon was that soft and comforting. Though he couldn't see it, he could almost feel its color: a rich, deep red.

Stroking the balloon, he fell asleep and once again had beautiful dreams. This time, however, he had no time to recall them as he awoke abruptly to the sound of a key in the lock. The door burst open and he covered his eyes against the morning light. Expecting the Aunties, he heard instead a voice that sounded like an oboe with a cold.

"Good morning, Boy. Not that there's anything good about it. I trust you've had your beauty rest? Wish I could say the same."

Butler. Dazed by the light and too groggy to reply, Zac eventually opened his fingers just a crack. At least the peculiar little man carried no stick. But as Zac's eyes adjusted, he realized something was wrong. Butler looked, if possible, even smaller and older. Much older. Shrunken, wasted, withered. So striking was the change that Zac was soon wide awake and on his feet.

"Butler, what's wrong?"

"Oh dear … what have you got there?"

Frowning intently, Butler stared at the boy's hand, which Zac realized still held the balloon fragment. Quickly he tucked it in his pocket.

"Nothing," he said.

"A big, fat red nothing, if you ask me. A suspiciously balloony sort of nothing. Am I right?"

Zac didn't reply.

"You'd better not let the Aunties catch you with that."

"They already did."

"Uh-oh. How many did you get?"

"Just one."

"Lucky. Very lucky. But you'd better dispose of the evidence, that's all I can say."

With Butler leading the way, they moved out of the room and down the hallway. The little man was so old and decrepit he hobbled.

"What's wrong?" repeated Zac. "You look like you've been run over by … a *hearse*."

Grimacing, he replied, "I have, Boy, I have. It's what happens when you're old. The hearse passes over and you think you're done for. Then somehow you get on your feet again for another round."

"You mean you nearly died?"

"I've nearly died many times. Getting a bit tired of it."

"But what happened?"

Butler's eyes, normally weak as old tea bags, burned with intensity. "Don't ask! I'll thank you not to ask." Then, the fire fading, he added, "I'm just under the weather, that's all."

Shuffling down the hall, Butler led Zac to his old room. It was a disaster. Broken glass, twigs, bits of window frame were strewn all over the floor and everything was soaking wet. Though the wind had died down, outside a steady rain still fell. Branches and a few large limbs littered lawns and sidewalks. Ghostly rags of cloud brushed the rooftops. Zac stared at Porter's Store, but of course there was no sign now of the strange phenomenon he'd witnessed in the night.

His room held some new items: a red metal toolbox, a large sheet of plywood, and a broom, mop, and pail. Butler said the Aunties had told him to board up the window.

"I wasn't trying to escape," Zac protested. "It was the wind coming in, not me trying to get out!"

"Whoever was coming or going, it won't happen again. Not through this window."

Sad and frustrated, feeling more than ever a prisoner, Zac set to work with Butler to clean up the mess. Before long, however, it became clear that every movement was agony for the little man. He was having trouble just standing, let alone pushing a broom or swinging a hammer.

"I'm sorry," he sighed, slumping onto the bed. "I just can't do this. I must rest. Just a few minutes …"

In no time he was sound asleep. He looked so pale that he had Zac worried, though his breath and pulse were even. Old as Butler was, asleep in Zac's bed he looked more than ever like a little boy. Pulling up a blanket around the sleeper's chin, Zac returned to the task of nailing up the plywood. It felt strange to be boarding up his own window, but he knew there was no arguing with the Aunties. As luck would have it, however, the plywood had a knothole in one corner, with a round plug that slid nicely in and out.

This job finished, Zac crept downstairs to find himself some breakfast. There was no sign of the Aunties. He realized he just had time to get to school. In the rain he could have used an umbrella, but according to Butler the Aunties didn't believe in them. So he ran all the way with a newspaper over his head.

As he arrived at school, he met just the person he wanted to see: Chelsea. But before he could talk to her, a meaty hand clapped his shoulder and a bearish voice growled, "Hey, Bud. How's the little shopkeeper? Did you have fun playing store?"

Staring at Ches Cholmondeley's big, blockish face, Zac had no clue what to say. So much had happened since he'd last seen Ches—only yesterday, was it? How could Zac tell about his time with Sky, or the experience of handling the umbrella, or catching the balloons and running up the mountain, or what he'd heard in the mine shaft, or his meeting with Eldy, or his beautiful dreams, or the rainbow-colored lights atop Porter's Store?

The bell rang and Zac gave Ches a vague answer as they moved off to class. For the rest of that day he kept looking for a chance to talk to Chelsea. Not sure what he would say, or how he would interpret her hand signals, he knew only that he had to communicate with her and it had to be alone. This was awkward. Chelsea was always alone, but for Zac, an older boy, to be seen with a younger girl would look odd.

Last period that afternoon they had art, the one subject the whole class did together. The desks were pushed into groups of four and Zac managed to sit next to Chelsea. Feeling shy, and not wanting to draw attention, at first he pretended to be completely absorbed in his potato-print project. But all the while he was struggling with what to say, or how, or even why. Finally, reaching into his pocket, he took out the scrap of red balloon and passed it to her under the desks. Chelsea's bright eyes lit up and she started making hand signals.

Of course this wasn't allowed; it was "talking" in class. But even sign language could be done clandestinely, like whispering. Zac whispered back, saying he wasn't sure of all she'd said, but yes, the balloon had come from Eldy. She made more signs, ending with her palms together in the posture of prayer, then laying her head on them as on a pillow. Her eyes closed and she smiled radiantly. Zac was about to whisper back when a voice barked, "*You! Boy!* Come up here this instant!"

Zac groaned. He knew what was coming. Bleakly he trudged to the front, bent over, and received two smart whacks with the ruler. Mr. Twitchell didn't pack nearly the same punch as Esmeralda, but the beating still left Zac with black thoughts.

Walking home from school with Ches, he didn't say one word. He decided Chelsea wasn't the only person in the world who could dish out the silent treatment. Ches, used to it from her, didn't seem to mind. Zac almost felt understood.

The next day he slipped Chelsea a note with a long list of questions. A day later the note she passed to him had only two words on it: "Ask Eldy."

Zac didn't want to ask Eldy. Eldy was trouble. He wanted to talk to Chelsea. But after several more attempts that week, he finally gave up. Just once, when they met at the water fountain, she passed back to him the fragment of red balloon, along with several others, which he thrust deep into his pocket. Later, all alone in the washroom, he pulled them out and examined them. Overcome by all the dark enigmas in this town and his inability to understand, he threw the colored scraps in the garbage. What good was a bunch of old, broken balloons?

Chapter 15

What's Up?

It rained all the rest of that second week. Sometimes a drizzle, sometimes a downpour. Every morning, first thing, Zac went to his boarded-up window, removed the knot, and peeked out at Porter's Store, where he was now a regular employee. Every morning Sky appeared to greet the new day, always with his umbrella. Sometimes he kept it furled and stood under the awning; other times he opened it and stood in the rain.

On Tuesday, Zac received the promised two blows for failing to steal the umbrella. On Wednesday, his backside still sore, he reported for work after school and met Sky standing in the rain under the open canopy.

"The beauty of an umbrella," said Sky, "is that you've always got a roof over your head. You can be at home wherever you go."

Sharing the umbrella, Zac chanced to look up and was surprised to see …

Nothing.

Overhead, where the canopy should have been, there was only sky. They weren't getting wet, and Sky was definitely holding the umbrella handle, and there was a pleasant pattering sound—but where was the umbrella itself?

"Sky," Zac faltered, "how do you keep dry under this thing?"

"What do you mean?"

"Well, what happened to the—I don't know what you call it—the cloth part …?"

"The canopy?"

"Yeah—it's gone."

"No, it's there. Reach up and touch it."

Fully expecting to plunge his hand into thin air, Zac shot up a fist.

"Hey, take it easy, Zac!"

His fist, striking against something soft and bouncy, nearly knocked the umbrella out of Sky's hand.

"That's quite a right hook you've got! Ever think of going into prizefighting?"

Zac was dumbfounded. Gazing up, he still saw nothing overhead; yet his fist had definitely hit something.

"Try more gently," said Sky. "Just reach up and feel. It's there."

Gingerly now, Zac raised his hand until his fingers brushed against … what? Something satiny, watersmooth, soft as a rose petal. He remembered the feeling from the first time he'd held the umbrella.

"But—" He was still staring up, seeing nothing.

"It's not invisible," said Sky, "any more than the sky is."

Zac's mind boggled. Did that mean … was it really possible …?

"That's right, Zac. The underside of the umbrella takes on the same coloring as the sky, so it looks as if the canopy isn't there."

Zac had a rush of insight. Even indoors, he recalled, the inner surface of the canopy had looked like the sky itself, as if a window were thrown open.

"Just one of this beauty's amazing qualities," said Sky. And with that, moving under the awning, he closed the umbrella, shook the black and silver raindrops from its folds, and held open the door for Zac to go inside. Right behind them a customer entered and engaged Sky's attention, and Zac, though full of questions, had to get busy cleaning shelves.

A customer at Porter's was always an event. Often they came more to chat than to shop, and what they did buy tended to be small odds and ends difficult to find elsewhere: a length of rope or chain, a packet of herbs, an odd-sized nut or washer. It was amazing how much that store contained. Whatever was wanted, Sky managed to find. It almost seemed that if a certain article weren't there when a customer entered, it would be before he left.

Two or three people a day came to have their glasses adjusted or eyes tested. Sky sat them on a stool and had them read an eye chart behind the counter. Before long Zac had memorized the chart's sequence of letters: E - F P - T O Z - L P E D … Sometimes this seemed to him the code to some mystery he couldn't quite decipher. If a customer needed new glasses, Sky brought out a tray of used pairs from which the one that worked best was selected. Often people expressed wonder at how clear the world could look through a pair of secondhand specs. Every day at least one satisfied customer made the old quip, "'I see!' said the blind man as he picked up his hammer and saw." This always got a laugh from Sky, a laugh not so much of humor as of plain pleasure.

The most business, naturally, was from kids buying candy, and from umbrella customers. During this week of nonstop rain, it seemed everyone in the county had an umbrella that needed fixing. Sky took them all, no matter what shape they were in, and returned them in a day or two looking brand-new. As with the eyeglasses, people were often amazed at the transformation.

"Porter, you're a wizard!"

"Not a wizard, Jack," he'd reply. "I just know my business."

He always called people by their first names, though few reciprocated. This made Zac even more squeamish that he, a mere boy, should be on a first-name basis with his boss. He wished he could settle on "Mr. Porter." But having crossed a line into familiarity, it was too awkward to retreat.

The only others who used Sky's name were the old men who sat at the back of the store, keeping warm by the wood-stove, playing checkers or cribbage, chewing the fat. With them it was always "Sky this," "Sky that," as if the whole universe revolved around this one man in an apron. Their other favorite topic was the weather, of which they all appeared to have seen a good deal.

"What's it going to do today, Sky?" one might say. "More of the same?"

"Say, Sky, when will this wet stuff turn to snow?"

"Remember that big blizzard we had fourteen years ago?"

"Same year as the twister."

"Wasn't that the time May Spong found a hailstone big as a honeydew melon and kept it in her freezer?"

At first Zac paid no attention to all this chatter. To him weather was the most boring topic in the world. But the old men's voices made a pleasant hum and he soon warmed to their company, especially as they kept trying to engage him. Always when he arrived for work they greeted him with a chorus of, "Hi, Zac! What's up?"

"Not much," he had replied the first time.

"C'mon, Zac, tell us what's up?"

"I dunno. I just came from school ..."

"No, it's a joke. What's up?"

"A joke?" Zac stared blankly.

"You know—ha ha?" The old men cackled with laughter.

"I don't get it." Zac was usually good at jokes and riddles.

"Well," said one of the old men, "here it is. We say, 'What's up?' and you answer, 'The sky.' Get it? The sky?"

More laughter rippled around the little tables, and this time Zac joined in. Every day after that they asked him, "What's up?" and every day he answered, "The sky," and every day this exchange produced gales of laughter.

Gradually Zac learned the old men's names, which all, oddly enough, had three letters: Sam, Joe, Abe, Dan, Ike, Eli.

Ever since Mr. Pottinger, Zac hadn't paid much heed to old people. But there was something about the old men of Porter's Store that set them apart. They had a gentle, homey quality and they didn't seem to have a care. Unlike the customers who bustled in and out, they had nowhere else to go, nothing else to do. Right where they sat was the only place to be. Cards, chitchat, and climate, far from boring them, seemed unlimited sources of delight. They loved to laugh and they loved to sing. Their musical repertoire ranged from old popular songs ("Singin' in the Rain," "Let a Smile Be Your Umbrella"), to hymns ("Will your anchor hold in the storms of life?"), to childhood ditties:

> *If all the raindrops were lemon drops and*
> *gumdrops,*
> *O what a rain that would be!*
> *I'd stand outside with my mouth open*
> *wide—*
> *That's the weather for me!*

Many of their jokes, too, were about weather: "Hey, Zac, did you hear the Mexican weather report? Chili today and hot tamale."

Zac wished he had a nickel for every time he was up on the ladder, cleaning, when someone called out, "How's the weather up there?" One homespun joke could keep the old men chuckling for several minutes, and the next day they'd laugh again at the same line. Their jokes never wore out.

"The old ones are the best," Ike liked to say. "Like wine and cheese, they improve with age."

It wasn't all jokes with the old men; they could be quite serious, especially when it came to the weather. To them weather was awesome, prodigious, endlessly fascinating, and they loved telling stories of nature's grandest and rarest displays. One man, Eli, had once seen the green flash; Joe had seen a triple rainbow; Dan had seen a hailbow.

"A hailbow?" asked Zac.

"That's right. From the look on your face, you've seen one too?"

Zac nodded, as the day of his mother's funeral came rushing back.

"Very rare and very special," said Dan. "Everything has a meaning."

"What does a hailbow mean?"

Old Dan hesitated, then said, "Means a hard rain's gonna fall. A hard rain, Zac. That's the hail part. But the bow part is this: It will all come out right in the end."

There was a moment of solemnity as they all contemplated this statement, confirming its truth with grave nods. Then Ike said he had a story. He knew a fellow named Rudolph who had the same color hair as Zac. One day Rudolph looked out his window and said, "Looks like rain today." His wife said, "Don't be silly, dear, there's not a cloud in the sky," to which the husband replied, "Rudolph the red knows rain, dear." At this the whole company broke up, the old men slapping their knees and Zac doubled over, and then all together they sang

172

the song. Though it was already mid-December, since coming to Five Corners, this was Zac's first hint of Christmas.

The old men were not always at their tables. In the far back corner was a flight of stairs, and beside it a door. Singly or in pairs the men would drift off, either upstairs or through the door, then reappear twenty minutes or an hour later. Often overhead Zac heard the soft shuffle of footsteps, and sometimes other sounds too—strange cracklings, swishings, gurglings, faint rumblings. He could think of nothing that made sounds quite like that, unless it was some sort of machinery. Recalling the mysterious lights he'd observed on several occasions above the store, he was most curious about the goings-on up above. But he also felt reluctant to ask questions, partly because of the rumors of Porter's being haunted, and partly because the topic seemed somehow off-limits. This was confirmed when finally he did ask, as casually as he could, "What's upstairs? And why do you guys keep going there?"

From the old men came soft explosions—"Oho!" "Aha!" "Well, now!"—and then they fell silent and studied Zac a long time.

Finally Abe ventured, "Sorry, son, but you'll have to ask Sky about that." And they went back to cracking jokes.

Ask Sky? Yes, Zac wanted to ask Sky. He had lots to ask Sky but it wasn't that easy. Sky was obviously fond of the old men and enjoyed joshing with them as he puttered about the store, but he was also different from them. Though much younger, he had an air of authority that set him apart. Zac found it hard not to keep watching him. And the more he secretly studied that homely, beautiful face, the more it seemed that other people almost didn't have faces. Mr. Twitchell's face was frightened; Reverend Cholmondeley's was pitiful and clownish; the Aunties wore masks; Dada's face was a ghostly hole …

The old men had warm, real faces. But in Sky's there shone another quality altogether—some heartwrenching intimacy—which was the very reason Zac did not know how to talk to him. What do you say to someone who always seems to look directly into your heart?

And of course there was the problem of the umbrella. Zac's real job in that store was not cleaning shelves but stalking the umbrella. What turmoil this caused him! Sky Porter was the nicest man he had ever met, but Zac couldn't let himself become attached because his whole reason for being there was to steal from him. And every day he failed meant an added blow from the cane.

Among the old men's jokes and songs were snatches of poetry, including their favorite:

> *The rain it raineth on the just*
> *And also on the unjust fella,*
> *But chiefly on the just, because*
> *The unjust steals the just's umbrella.*

Each time Zac heard this, he wondered whether the old men somehow knew what he was up to. Several times he came close to confessing his predicament to Sky, but then he'd recall the encounter between Sky and Esmeralda when the man had done nothing, nothing at all. However nice the storekeeper was, somehow when it came to the Aunties, his hands were tied.

Once Sky caught Zac staring at the umbrella. As if reading the boy's mind he asked, "What's wrong, Zac? Is there something I can do for you?"

Zac hesitated, then shook his head.

"In this store, you know, you can help yourself to anything you want."

Sky had said this before. Zac assumed he meant candy and snacks.

"Anything?" Zac asked.

"Of course. Make yourself at home. What's mine is yours."

What? Surely Sky wouldn't say this if he knew Zac wanted the umbrella. But then, hadn't he just caught him looking straight at it?

Chapter 16

The Ghost

The old men of Porter's were rarely quiet. Their convivial hum was like the patter of an all-day rain. The only exceptions were those times when the haunting beauty of O's singing carried into the store like a gentle finger of breeze. Then the old men fell silent, entranced, nodding daydreamily. Often O's songs sounded far off, drifting from clear across town, but occasionally her voice seemed so close that she might have been right in the store, or just outside. When this happened, a few of the old men might rise and saunter out the back door, as though to take a breath of air.

Though Zac was unable to learn anything about the second floor, the mystery of the back door was solved, or partly solved, on Thursday when the old men asked him for a hand carrying Christmas decorations from a building out back that they called the umbrella factory. Connected to the store by a breezeway, the place was chock full of umbrellas—clustered in stands, scattered over tables, tied in bundles. Furled umbrellas hung like bats from the rafters, along with open ones like large, exotic butterflies, giving the room a buoyant feel as though one could step up into the air and take flight. As the old men gathered boxes, Zac walked up and down between the long tables examining the clutter of paraphernalia: bolts of fabric, spindles of coarse thread, triangular wooden frames, modified sewing machines with quaint attachments, metal boxes of nubbins and ferrules.

"Hey, Zac," said old Ike. "Three large women went walking under one umbrella, but none of them got wet. Why not?"

"Search me," said Zac.

"It wasn't raining." All the old men guffawed, but Zac was only half listening. There was an odd feeling in this umbrella factory. Obviously a hive of activity, it looked as if whoever worked here had departed just moments before.

"No sign of her today," said Abe.

"Nope," said Eli. "A week of pouring rain, you'd think she'd be here."

"She's got her own ways," said Joe.

"You can say that again," said Dan.

"Who are you talking about?" asked Zac.

"Why, the Lady of the Umbrella Factory," said Abe. "Don't tell me you don't know her. Everyone knows Lady O."

"O?" said Zac. "You mean …?"

"Yup," said Abe. "You've heard her, I imagine?"

"Sure. She's got a nice voice."

"Nice isn't the word for it," said Sam.

"Supernal," said Ike.

"Beatific," offered Joe.

"Why, Lady O," said Abe, "she can sing soft as a snowflake falling on snow."

"Softer," said Sam. "Soft as dew forming on a lily."

"Are you saying she lives here?" asked Zac.

"O doesn't live anywhere," said Eli. "At least, not in any building."

"No roof could hold her," said Joe. "That's why she's so good at making roofs for others."

"You mean umbrellas?"

"She's the one," said Abe. "Makes 'em and fixes 'em."

"O does it all," said Ike. "Refinishes handles, overhauls frames, sews new canopies."

"An umbrella by O," said Dan, "is a thing of beauty forever."

"But I thought …" Zac hesitated. "I thought she was a drunk."

At this the old men erupted in laughter. Zac couldn't help joining in—but what was the joke?

"O a drunk!" Eli squealed. "That's a good one!"

"Drunk on life," said Ike.

"Drunk on herself," said Sam.

"You mean she doesn't drink?" asked Zac.

"Oh, she drinks all right!" chortled Abe. "Like a fish."

"And she works here all day?"

"Hardly," said Eli. "O's never worked a day in her life."

"She works when she feels like it," said Abe. "Never know when she'll drop in."

"But she gets the job done," said Sam.

"You can say that again," said Dan.

"Weaves all the umbrella fabrics herself," said Eli.

"Made Sky's blue umbrella," said Abe. "And what a beauty that is."

The old men fell silent, sighing. And then they all set to work carrying boxes of ornaments along the breezeway into the store, where they spent the rest of that afternoon singing carols and decorating.

That evening Sky asked Zac to stay late to finish decorating the large tree that had been set up in the front window. It was so tall, a good twelve feet, that a ladder was needed for the upper branches. Sky had paperwork to do in his office and he didn't want the old men trying to balance on the ladder, so Zac was left alone with the job.

It was very quiet in the big store at night. The only sounds were the hum of a freezer, the soft flap of flames in the wood-stove, a buzzing light bulb, the mutter of rain. From Sky's office in the back corner, a warm triangle of light fell through the open doorway. One after another Zac drew ornaments out of the boxes and hung them on the fragrant fir boughs. The ornaments were intriguing—clearly very old and handmade from wood, stained glass, brocade. Zac's mind was elsewhere, however, thinking more about Sky and the umbrella, and about the Aunties, whose house he could see through the window as he worked. Each day they put more and more pressure on him, grilling him savagely about every detail concerning the umbrella and (of course) punishing him with the cane.

Holding a large gold star obviously meant for the treetop, Zac had just mounted to the top of the ladder when he heard footsteps overhead. His breath stopped. Who could it be? Sky was in his office. There was no one else in the store, he knew there wasn't; he'd watched all the old men leave by the front door. And these footsteps were not the elderly, shuffling ones he'd grown used to hearing upstairs. This was the firm, purposeful tread of a robust man. But not Sky; Sky's walk was lighter, springier.

The new footsteps, loud in the silent store, approached the front of the building where Zac was. At a spot on the ceiling just above his head, they stopped, and for a few moments all was still. Then, frighteningly loud, came a harsh, spitting crackle like sparks of electricity from a live wire. Zac's whole body tingled and his hair seemed about to catch fire. Shaking with dread, he clung to the ladder as to a cliff in a high wind, but finally lost his balance and fell. Luckily, grabbing a rung, he was able to break his fall and not any bones, and landed in a heap on the floor with the star on top of his head—which is how Sky found him when he came running from the office.

"Zac, you okay?" Seeing the boy's weak nod, Sky smiled. "Looks like you've been decorating yourself instead of the tree." Giving him a hand up, he asked, "What happened? You look like you saw a ghost."

"Yeah … I mean, no … I don't know … I heard footsteps … and some kind of explosion … up above …"

"Explosion? Oh, don't let that bother you. It's just Dad puttering around."

"Your father?"

"Yes. If you like, I can introduce you."

Zac, still shaking from his scare, hesitated. "Sky—I don't know how to say this but … people think this store is haunted."

"I've heard that, yes."

Gathering courage, Zac went on, "But you say it's just your father. I don't get it. People aren't even sure if your father is still alive or not …"

A sharp rap sounded at the front door, and Zac, still spooked, jumped. Turning, he saw the large, livid face of Auntie Pris in the dark glass.

"Why, Priscilla," said Sky, opening to her, "how nice of you—"

"Don't nice me, Porter." She stamped her foot in rage. "What do you mean by keeping the boy this late?"

"He was just helping to decorate the Christmas tree."

"I'll decorate you, Porter, I swear I will. And I'll decorate that boy's behind. You come with me, Boy."

Zac glanced at Sky, the man nodded, and then Pris thrust him out the door and marched him across the street. Esmeralda was waiting for them in the front hall.

"What do you think you're doing, Boy, dragging in here at this hour?"

"I've been working, Auntie. Mr. Porter kept me late—"

"We know that," snapped Pris. "Do you think we couldn't see you in the window, decorating that foolish tree?"

"What about the umbrella?" demanded Esmeralda. "All that time in the store and what have you got to show for it?"

"Please, Auntie, I've been trying to get it … I have a plan—"

"A plan, my eye. I have a plan too, and here it is." She raised her cane.

"Please, Auntie, if I can just—"

"*Bend over!*"

Zac did as he was told, and Esmeralda delivered the four whacks he had coming to him that day, this time all in a row without even letting him say, "Please, Auntie, may I have another?"

"No more fun and games," she declared. "I want that umbrella."

That night Zac couldn't sleep for the pain. Just as disturbing, in a different way, was the fright he'd received in the store. But most painful of all was the fact that Sky, once again, had utterly failed to protect him from the Aunties. With Zac's window still boarded up, his room was totally dark, adding unspeakably to his sense of doom.

Toward dawn he had a kind of waking dream in which the strange, darkly clad boy from the dining room's ancient painting appeared. Stepping out of the ornate golden frame and right into Zac's room, he stood at the foot of the bed and spoke one word: "*Now.*" Though he was only a boy, his voice was that of an old man and it seemed to reverberate deep in Zac's bones.

Troubled, Zac rose and crept to the window and put his eye to the knothole. Soon he saw Sky emerge from the store for his ritual of greeting the new day. The storekeeper looked calm and happy, oblivious to all Zac's pain.

"You coward," murmured Zac. "Why won't you help me?"

As usual Sky held the umbrella, that cursed object that was causing Zac so much distress. And the boy remembered something: When he'd fallen the evening before and Sky had come running, he did not have the umbrella. He must have left it back in the office.

Wheels turned in Zac's head. For some time he wrestled, frightened of his own thoughts, trying to slow them down. But finally, overcome with pain and resentment, he reached a decision. Today, Friday, was the day. Whatever it took, he would get that umbrella. All he had to do was create a distraction, slip into the office and nab it, then disappear out the back door. If that didn't work, he'd simply wait till the end of the day, ask Sky if he could hold the umbrella again, then run like the dickens. He was that desperate. Then it would be up to Sky and the Aunties to sort things out, but Zac's part would be done. All he knew was that he couldn't face another day of anxious scheming or another hiding from Esmeralda. His will was set.

From the moment he reported for work after school, however, things did not go according to plan.

"What's wrong, Zac?" Sky asked right away. When Zac didn't answer, Sky put his hands on the boy's shoulders and looked him in the eye. "I might be able to help."

Those words, and those lucid blue eyes, nearly broke Zac's resolve. Tears sprang and he had to look away.

"Zac, is there something you need to say?"

Zac shook his head.

"Well, then, how about joining me in my office? I'd like to tell you a story."

Chapter 17
Sky's Story

Trembling with fear, relief, confusion, Zac followed the white bow of Sky's shop apron to the rear of the store and through the small door into his office. Set into the side of the staircase, the doorway was so low that Sky had to stoop to enter. Though Zac had never been in this room, he had a sense of déjà vu. His mother's house had had a walk-in closet much like this, tucked under the stairs. When Zac was little, his mother had cleared out this small space for him to use as a clubhouse. There he would play for hours by himself or with friends, swearing all visitors to secrecy with elaborate passwords and codes.

"Have a seat," said Sky. "Looks like you could use a stiff mug of hot chocolate."

He waved Zac to a big leather swivel chair behind a desk—obviously Sky's own chair. As there were no others, after plugging in an electric kettle, Sky pulled over a squat barrel and sat down. He still had the umbrella, Zac noticed, cocked over his arm.

"It's nice to have one room where I can be alone," he said. "I like this one because it reminds me of the room I had upstairs as a boy."

There were no windows, except for a small one at the higher end of the sloped ceiling. Like a porthole on a ship, it was just big enough to admit a glimpse of weather, which today was rainy. When the kettle boiled, Sky rose to make the hot chocolate. Before carrying the two mugs to the desk, he deposited the umbrella in an oddly familiar-looking receptacle in the corner.

Catching Zac's glance, Sky said, "You're right—it's an elephant's foot. They used to be very popular as umbrella stands. In fact there's a lovely old poem that goes—

> *The elephant, a noble beast,*
> *Is met with chiefly in the East,*
> *Also at Southsea, where Aunt Melisande*
> *Keeps its foot as an umbrella stand.*

Zac hardly heard this, so absorbed was he in gazing at the umbrella all by itself in that big gray foot with its square, yellowed toenails.

"Cheers," said Sky, raising his hot chocolate, and the two clinked mugs and sipped together. "Do you realize," Sky continued, "that chocolate is the most delicious food in the whole world, and this very moment we are tasting it?"

At these words Zac's taste buds—indeed his entire attention—awoke as if an alarm clock had rung. Though he'd always loved chocolate, suddenly it seemed spectacularly ambrosial. For a few moments they enjoyed their drinks in silence, warming their hands and watching each other over the tops of the mugs. Everything in Zac began to slow down and relax. His left leg even stopped bouncing.

"Now is there anything you'd like to ask me?"

Sky's question caught Zac off guard, and before he could stop himself, he said, "Why do you always keep that umbrella with you?"

"Ah," said Sky. "Now there's an interesting question. The quality of your life depends upon the questions you ask. A bad question leads down a wrong road, while a good one opens up the universe. But tell me, why do you ask?"

Did Sky have to raise that? "I don't know. It's just odd. I mean, how you always have it, even on sunny days."

"Yes. Well, it's really quite simple. I always want to be prepared for a change in weather. With the weather, one never knows."

Seeing that this answer did not satisfy, Sky continued, "But you're right, I have other reasons. For one it's good advertising for my umbrella business. For another an umbrella's a very comforting thing to hold. I suppose I'd feel almost naked without it. My father always carried one. Like father, like son."

Lowering his eyes, Zac mumbled, "I never knew my father."

"No," replied Sky, "not consciously. But he's there in your genes. There are things you do, and ways you are, for no other reason than that your father did those things and was that way. Even though you never knew him."

"Really?" Zac looked up.

"Sure. Why, there's a good chance you even look like your father. And that's just on the outside."

Though his mother had often said the same, coming from Sky this thought struck Zac differently. After a lengthy reflection he asked, "Is your father still alive?"

"Oh yes, very much so. Those footsteps you heard last night—did they sound like a dead man's?"

"No, I guess not. Then it's not true—about this place being haunted?"

"Depends what you mean by haunted. What frightens one person thrills another. People say this place is haunted because they want nothing to do with Dad. It's a way to keep their distance."

"Why? What does he do upstairs?"

"He's basically retired now, but he still likes to putter around. He built this place. I carry the umbrella partly because it reminds me of him. It also reminds me of a story he often told when I was little, though it didn't sink in till I was about your age. You know how you can hear something all your life without really caring? Then one day the circumstances are just right, and the story fits you like a key in a lock."

Sky fell silent for so long that Zac grew fidgety. "Is that the story you wanted to tell me?"

Jarred back to the present, Sky replied, "Yes, but first let me tell you the circumstances. I was in school then, and my teacher was Miss Esmeralda Henbother."

"Auntie Esmeralda?" exclaimed Zac.

"That's right. She and Priscilla taught almost everyone in this town. Esmeralda was just as stern then as she is today. Your Mr. Twitchell is a cream puff compared to her. She's the one who started that horrid practice with the cane—you know, getting kids to say, 'Please, may I have another?'"

"You know about that?"

"Of course. I got the cane myself a few times."

This news astonished Zac. It was strange to think of adults being kids once and having bad things done to them.

"Auntie Esmeralda had an arm of steel," continued Sky. "She could whip that stick like a hockey player on a slapshot. Everyone was terrified of her. But one day she thought of something that made those beatings even worse. Edgerton Cholmondeley was up there, getting his whacks—"

"Ches's dad?"

"Yes."

"But he's the church minister!"

"Wasn't then. He was just a boy like you. And nobody escaped that cane. Anyway, he'd gotten a couple of whacks when Miss Henbother straightened up and said, 'Children, my arm is tired. Do you know how hard it is trying to knock some sense into you little morons? No, you have no idea what I go through so that you can receive an education. It's about time you got a taste of what it's like on the other end of this stick.' With that, she handed the cane to the boy in the front desk, Bernie Phelps."

"You mean …?" Zac stammered. Bernie Phelps was the mayor of Five Corners—a huge, round-faced man in a bow tie.

"The same. At first Bernie didn't want to take the cane. No child had ever dared touch it. Esmeralda had to force his fingers around it. And when she told him to step right up and take a whack at Edgerton, at first he just stood there. He and Edge were good friends. He couldn't believe what the teacher was telling him to do. But she made it clear that if he didn't take a whack—and a good hard one, too—then he would be next. So finally Bernie hit Edgerton. He had to hit him three times before Esmeralda allowed it was hard enough. And each time Edge had to say, 'Please, Bernie, may I have another?' After that every child in the class had to do the same. It wasn't a large class, just eight students, but the cane went from hand to hand and everyone had to hit Edgerton more than once because nobody wanted to do it."

Sky paused to let the shock of this scene sink in. The students who had beaten the future church minister were, presumably, his present parishioners.

"Eventually the cane passed to me," Sky continued. "But I wouldn't take it. I kept letting it fall to the floor. Miss Henbother practically broke my fingers trying to force me to hold that stick, but I wouldn't. Finally she dragged me to the front and started the whole process again—this time on me. She delivered a couple of good whacks herself and then everyone else had to hit me too. I went home so sore! But at the same time, it wasn't all that bad, because in a way I'd won. I was beaten, but I wasn't. I hadn't given in to hitting any other child, so I had that to hold onto. Until next time."

"Next time?"

"Yes, it happened again. And again. Each time a child was beaten, Esmeralda got everyone in the class to participate.

Except me. I wouldn't. I flat refused. And each time I got dragged to the front and beaten by everyone."

Sky paused again, looking off into space.

"So what happened next?"

"Well, you recall I mentioned a story my dad told me, and how it never really hit home until the circumstances were right? What I've just told you—those were the circumstances. You see, I was wrestling with how long I could go on with these beatings—I was so afraid!—until finally I had to tell my dad. In those days, you know, beating kids in school was commonplace. Corporal punishment, it was called. You didn't run home and cry to your parents. You just took it. But this situation, I realized, was different. This was kids beating other kids. So finally I spilled it all out to Dad. And that's when he reminded me of the story of Jonas Hanway."

"Jonas Hanway?"

"He's the Englishman who single-handedly popularized the umbrella back in the 1700s. This is a true story that hardly anyone knows. Hanway was a traveler, who in visits to places like Italy and Portugal had seen umbrellas used not just as parasols, which was normal, but occasionally in rain or even snow. Hanway thought this was a brilliant idea for England with its wet climate. So around 1750 he brought home an umbrella and began carrying it everywhere. Can you guess what people thought of him?"

"That he was dumb?" suggested Zac.

"Exactly. Though Hanway was a prominent man, people ridiculed him, even former friends. They said he looked silly and girlish; children chased him and teased him; cabdrivers, afraid Hanway would put them out of business, deliberately drove their carriages through puddles to spatter him with mud. This went on for years. But in spite of all persecution, Hanway persisted in carrying an umbrella until finally, just before he died—guess what?"

Zac had no idea.

"The custom caught on. And after that there was no stopping it. Umbrellas became so common that every English gentleman had to have one as part of his wardrobe, just like a hat or tie. For a while umbrellas were even called Hanways. So the world changed, all because of one man's vision and courage. Isn't that amazing?"

Zac agreed. But he wanted to get back to the other story about the cane. "So what happened when you told your dad about the beatings? Did he protect you? Did he stick up for you against Auntie Esmeralda?"

"No, nothing like that. All he did was to tell me this story. But you see, that was enough. It was just what I needed. I thought that if Jonas Hanway could act so bravely for the sake of something as petty as an umbrella, then surely I could do the same for a cause that to me was far more important. My resolve to resist Miss Henbother grew stronger than ever. And after that, strangely enough, things changed."

"Really?"

"Yes. The next time I was hauled up for punishment, she handed the cane as usual to Bernie Phelps. But Bernie wouldn't take it. I don't know why, but something had changed in the very atmosphere of that room. So Bernie just stood there, letting the cane fall to the floor, until finally he got whacked instead of me. But only by the teacher. She didn't hand the cane to any other child and she never tried pulling that trick again. She's very clever, Esmeralda. I think she sensed that the tide had turned and she didn't want to lose her position of strength. After that she always did the beatings herself."

"You didn't try to stop her?"

"I wanted to. But in those days challenging authority was unheard of. And as Dad said to me, 'You can't always stop people from being mean. But you can stop them from making you mean.'"

Throughout Sky's story, outside it streamed rain. Rain drummed against the wooden building and clattered on the window while the man and the boy sat in the tiny office that reminded Zac so much of his clubhouse under the stairs at home. It wasn't just the room that made him feel safe and snug, but the sound of Sky's voice—a soft, compelling voice that, like an umbrella, drew one into a place of shelter.

"You asked me why I carry this umbrella," Sky concluded. "Among other reasons it reminds me of that struggle I went through, and of the radical change one person can make, acting with courage against great odds. The Aunties have their cane, but I have my umbrella."

Chapter 18

World's Smallest Business Establishment

It was late by the time Sky and Zac finished their talk in the office. It was raining harder than ever and Sky, in an unusual gesture, offered to walk Zac across the street, the two of them sharing the umbrella. So absorbed was Zac in Sky's story that it didn't even strike him as odd that they were carrying the umbrella right to the Aunties' front door—the very umbrella that he was supposed to be stealing. Not until Esmeralda answered their knock did the awful irony dawn.

"Good evening, Esmeralda," said Sky. "Zac and I have been having a talk. I just want you to know that I told him the story of the beatings in school."

Esmeralda glared. Without saying a word, she grabbed Zac's arm, yanked him inside, and slammed the door. Pushing him ahead, she propelled him into the parlor where Pris sat on the love seat doing a crossword puzzle. While Zac stood in a corner, Esmeralda leaned down and whispered to her sister.

Please, oh, please, thought Zac, *please let them give up on the cane.* Today, Friday, he knew he had five whacks coming.

Maybe more, since Esmeralda was plainly furious. But did Sky, after all, hold some sway over the Aunties, and would this work to Zac's benefit? Though he quivered with fear, a part of him was still sequestered cozily in Sky's little office under the stairs.

Eventually Esmeralda turned to him and said, "Why didn't you get the umbrella, Boy?"

What could he say? That Sky had so mesmerized him that he'd completely forgotten his mission?

"Speak up!"

"I … couldn't get it … He always has it …"

"He let you hold it once. Have you asked for it again?"

"No, but—"

Esmeralda cut her eyes toward Pris who, like a walrus climbing out of a bathtub, heaved herself from the love seat and stumped toward him. Stopping just inches away, she bared her big teeth in a grisly smile. If her incredibly long black chin bristle had come any closer, it could have scratched Zac's cheek.

"I've been meaning to tell you," she wheezed, "about a little discovery I made. I happened to check the pockets of your suit the other day, hanging in your cupboard. I found this."

She flashed a photograph before Zac's face. It was the picture of his mother in the rose garden, the one memento he had of her. When he reached for it, Pris waved it high over her head like a winning lottery ticket.

"Give me that!" he cried. "It's mine!"

"Not so fast. Of course it's yours. We're just keeping it safe for you. Aren't we, Esmeralda?"

Pris handed the picture to Esmeralda, who tucked it into her purse, a shiny snakeskin pouch.

"That's right," said Esmeralda, patting the purse, "it will be nice and safe right here. Of course, if you really want it back, there is a way."

Zac glared.

"Can you guess the way, Boy?"

"I bet he can," gloated Pris.

When Zac remained silent, Esmeralda continued, "The way to get back your picture is to bring me the umbrella. What could be simpler?" After another fraught silence, she added, "Now bend over."

"What? No!"

"Don't you dare defy me! Bend over."

"No! Give me my picture!"

"I'm warning you, Boy." Esmeralda advanced toward Zac, pointing the cane at him like a rifle. "Will you bend, or do I have to break you?"

What Zac did then shocked himself as much as the Aunties. Erupting in rage, he seized the cane with both hands and yanked it from Esmeralda's grasp. For a moment he just stood there, horrified at his own action. The Aunties, too, seemed struck to stone. Then swiftly Zac backed away, nearly tripping over a footstool. Esmeralda saw her chance and darted toward him but Zac, regaining his balance, raised the cane like a baseball bat.

"Don't you touch me! One more step and I'll smash your head in!" He spat the words out, snarling like a cornered animal. Esmeralda retreated a step, and Zac was surprised to see that she looked afraid of him.

Soothingly she cooed, "Please give the cane to Auntie. There's a good boy. You don't really want that old cane, do you?"

She began inching toward him, forcing him to yell, "Stay away!" But she kept coming. Finally, hardly aware of what he did, he swung the cane with all his might. It swished about a foot from Esmeralda's face and hit a china elephant, smashing it to pieces. Esmeralda recoiled, and behind her Pris made a whimpering sound. Quickly Zac was in position for another blow. Again he swung, this time connecting with a large blue vase. The air went blue with shards, but the silence in the wake of the crash was black.

Something new had entered the room. The broken china made it all so real. Those objects, thought Zac, might have been human heads. He began to shake violently, and seeing this, Esmeralda's eyes glittered with fresh ferocity even as she cooed all the more unctuously. "There, there, now. You don't really want to hurt anyone, do you? Come, give the cane to Auntie and everything will be fine."

In Zac's hands the stick was vibrating so wildly that it seemed animated by more than his fear. It felt weirdly alive. Sick with shock, the boy's arms and whole body drained of strength. With Esmeralda advancing once more, speaking insistently in that hypnotic voice, finally the contest of wills was too much for Zac. With a deep sigh he let the cane slump to his shoulder, and with one easy gesture Esmeralda plucked it away.

For a few moments she seemed to forget Zac altogether as she inspected her precious cane, lovingly caressing it almost as Dada had done. Meanwhile Pris was on her hands and knees, crying over the broken elephant. Zac stood quite still, utterly purged of every emotion, every thought, except for the dim knowledge that in a moment he would be severely beaten, perhaps killed. He barely had energy even to be relieved when Esmeralda said simply, "That's enough out of you today. Get to your room."

The next morning, Saturday, Zac lay in bed for a long time, still numb from last night's ugly scene. He could not believe what he'd done. Now he was in more trouble than ever. His meeting with Sky under the stairs seemed so long ago. What good was Sky's dumb old story now?

When Zac finally got up, he went first to the closet to check on his suit, the suit he'd once scorned but that now he treasured as the sole remnant of his past life, his childhood of goodness and light. He felt in the pocket, but no, the photograph was gone. It was a crushing blow.

What now? Hungry though he was, he couldn't just go down for breakfast with Butler as usual. He had to get out of that house.

Quietly as he could, he stole from the room and crept downstairs. As he reached the front hall he heard voices, and something in their tone made him stop. Muffled but impassioned, they came from the dining room, and Zac soon recognized them as those of Butler and Auntie Esmeralda. Tiptoeing to the closed door, he put his ear to the wood and listened.

"Please, Esmeralda. Not now."

"Come, come. Come to your Auntie."

"Please, I beg you. I've just gotten over a bad spell."

"Poor boy. But it's all better now, isn't it? Doesn't it always get better?"

"I don't know. This time was the worst. I wasn't sure I'd make it."

"Nonsense! I'm only asking you to touch the cane. Just for a moment. That's all."

"No, it's more than that. Much more."

"Butler, haven't I been good to you?"

"Of course, Esmeralda, but—"

"No buts, just take the cane. Here—put your hand right here."

"I can't—"

"Yes, you can. Five seconds and it's done."

"No—"

"How can you deny your dear Auntie? Do you forget who's watching?"

Butler gave a sharp cry.

"Oho—touched a nerve, have we? You know he's watching."

What? Had Zac been discovered? But no …

"Dear Butler, you're only making this hard on yourself. You know the choice you have. It's touch the cane, or the cane touches you. That simple."

"I tell you, Esmeralda, I'm not sure I can survive another spell."

"You think you can survive the cane, then?"

"Please …"

"How long is it, Butler, since I've had to cane you?"

"I don't know."

"Years? You're not going back to that now, are you? Come now, like a good boy. Don't force me."

After a few moments of silence, in a softer voice Esmeralda said, "That's right. That's not so bad, is it?"

Zac had heard enough. So this was the source of Butler's strange illness. Had Zac not experienced it himself? Creeping away, he was soon outside and running down the front walk. He'd made up his mind: He was going to see Sky. Sky would take him into his office again, make another mug of hot chocolate, answer his questions, know just what to say—

"Ho, ho, where are you off to so fast, Boy?"

He'd almost run smack into Auntie Pris.

"Nowhere, Auntie."

"Nowhere? That seems to be your favorite destination."

"Actually I was just going to Porter's. To see about the umbrella."

"Ah, what a good boy. But not just now. Come along, you have an appointment."

"An appointment?"

"Yes, with Barber. You'll like him, he's a dear friend of mine."

Auntie Pris was being too nice. Nothing was mentioned about Zac's outrageous behavior the night before. Instead, was he getting a haircut? Why? He'd had a trim the day before his mother's funeral. So long ago that seemed—though it was only two weeks.

By now Pris had him firmly by the arm and was steering him across the street toward the tiny building with the big sign that read WORLD'S SMALLEST BUSINESS ESTABLISHMENT. About the size of a garden shed, the shop was so small it was the butt of frequent jokes. If there happened to be a few boxes on the back stoop, someone might say, "Look! Barber put an addition on his shop!"

Inside there was just enough room for a counter, one barber chair, a kitchen chair for a customer, and an end table with a stack of magazines. As Pris pushed open the door, a bell tinkled, rousing a very small, very old, very hairy man from his snooze in the barber chair. Moving as quickly as possible, though with painful awkwardness, he scrambled to his feet and stood stiff as a little soldier. Next to Dada, he was the oldest man Zac had ever seen.

"This is Barber," said Pris.

"Hello, Mr. Barber," said Zac.

"Just Barber," corrected Pris.

So the man's name was the same as his profession? Confused, Zac said nothing. Besides looking ancient, Barber really was extraordinarily small, even shorter than Butler, yet like Butler he was no dwarf but a normally proportioned man. What was it, Zac wondered, with all the tiny, old people in this town? Barber's other curious feature was a long gray beard and billows of matted hair that fairly buried him. Apparently he had no use for his own services.

He soon got down to business. Flourishing a sheet of red cloth like a matador, he waved Zac into the chair as Auntie Pris gave instructions.

"You know what to do, Barber. That exploding fluffball has to go."

"No!" cried Zac. His enormous hair was his pride and joy. He made a move to eject himself from the chair, but Pris was there in a flash, pinning him down with one hammy hand. She needn't have used force; her breath alone could have restrained him, along with what she said next.

"Dada's orders, Boy. Do you want Dada mad at you?"

Zac shivered. He had almost managed to forget about Dada.

"I have business uptown," Pris went on, still breathing heavily. "Expect me back in twenty minutes."

"Very well, Auntie," said Barber. "I'll scalp him good, don't worry."

No sooner had Pris left than Barber, perched on a stool, set to work with a very long, pointy set of silver shears. As in a dream Zac watched his precious locks fall about him—another bitter loss.

"Please don't cut it too short," he pleaded.

Barber grunted.

"It's been like this all my life."

"Hold still."

"My mom said I had lots of hair even as a baby."

"You're not a baby now."

After a sullen silence Zac ventured, "Barber, I've seen Mr. Porter come here sometimes. Do you know him well?"

The shears made a clean-sounding *snip-snip* right next to Zac's ear. For a long time the old man said nothing. Was Zac's question, perhaps, off-limits? He decided to try a different tack.

"I heard you call Auntie Pris 'Auntie.' Is she really your auntie?"

Again this query received no response. Zac wondered if Barber had heard him. His hearing had seemed fine a moment ago. Maybe he didn't like being distracted while working?

"Barber," he began again, louder, "why—"

"There's nothing wrong with my hearing," Barber interrupted. "Everything else is wrong—angina, rheumatism, gout—you name it. Eyesight's nearly gone, can't taste anymore. But my hearing, that's just fine. At least I can still hear myself groan, moan, whimper, and sigh. That's some comfort."

Barber had an old man's high, fluty voice—almost, thought Zac, like a woman's. After this surprising outburst he again fell silent. Zac was uncertain how to respond.

"It must be hard growing old," he suggested.

"*Growing* old? If I had a chance to grow, that would be one thing. As it is, I can't tell you what it's like to *grow* old. I haven't the foggiest."

The shears went *snip-snip-snip*. This time the silence extended so long that it began to seem as if nothing had been said at all. Eventually, since Zac could think of nothing else, what was on the tip of his tongue tumbled out.

"Do you mind me asking what's kept you from growing? Is it a disease?"

"Yes. I mean, yes, I do mind. At least, I don't mind you asking, but I do mind me answering. That is, it's not that I mind answering, but Auntie Pris, she minds. In fact she instructed me specifically not to answer any of your questions."

That shut Zac up. What else was there to say? So he was surprised when Barber volunteered more.

"Which doesn't mean I can't ask a question or two of my own, does it? What's your name? Not Boy, I hope."

"Zac. Zac Sparks."

"Ah. I thought so. You're not a Henbother, then?"

"No, I'm a Sparks."

"And your mother—what was her maiden name?"

"Jordan. Elizabeth Jordan."

"No Henbothers in your family?"

"Not that I know of. Just my Aunties."

"Of course. Interesting."

After some reflection Zac said, "They're really my great-aunts, I believe."

"No doubt. Or your great-grasshoppers, perhaps? Or your great-great-rumblebufferballyhoos?"

"Pardon me?"

Again Barber fell silent. Was he daft? No, if Pris had warned him not to answer questions, it must be because he knew too much. Wondering if there might be another way to approach him, Zac said, "Nice place you've got here."

"If you happen to like close quarters," retorted Barber. "Which I don't."

Zac paused to phrase his next sentence carefully. "I suppose if a person was not allowed to leave, even a palace would seem small."

Barber stopped snipping, then resumed. "A shrewd observation."

So, thought Zac—as long as he turned his questions into statements, Barber would respond. Still eager to ask about Sky, Zac said, "Sometimes I see Mr. Porter coming here."

"I can't stop him, can I?"

"I like him. At least, I think I like him. He's a bit hard to figure out."

"He's cracked," said Barber. "Pleasant enough fellow. But quite cracked."

"What do you mean?"

When Barber clammed up, Zac rephrased his question as a statement. "I'm puzzled that you think Mr. Porter is cracked."

"Have you talked to him yourself? That crazy umbrella. And the guy upstairs. And that weird dame who works for him. Completely cracked. And all those wild stories."

"Wild stories?" But Zac's tone held a question and Barber wouldn't answer. So Zac said, "The woman you mentioned: O. She's a mystery."

"Mystery? What's mysterious about a raving drunk? You know what Porter tried to tell me? He said she drinks nothing but water. Ha! I don't believe that for a minute, do you?"

This time it was Zac's turn to make no reply. Eventually he said, "The umbrella—that's another mystery. The Aunties would love to get their hands on it."

"Would they? That's news to me. They don't even believe in umbrellas. Won't have one in the house. Know why? Porter told me. He said the modern umbrella was invented by a man named Samuel Fox, who was walking in the rain one day when he noticed a box of old corsets in a garbage bin."

"Corsets?"

"Girdles. Old-fashioned ladies' underwear reinforced with steel rods."

"Metal underwear?" Zac laughed.

"Yes. That's what gave Fox his bright idea. That same day he traipsed all over town with his new invention, telling everyone what it was made of." Barber chuckled softly. "Porter loves that story, but the Aunties hate it. 'The very idea of parading ladies' underwear in the streets!'"

"I'd like to do that with their underwear," said Zac.

Barber's only comment was to hold his nose, and the two chortled. Then Barber, seeming to catch himself, looked darkly at Zac and said, "You've met Dada, then?"

Once again just the mention of this name unnerved Zac. He wanted to forget Dada. His impulse was to lie, but finally he mumbled a yes.

"I thought so," said Barber. "A person can tell, you know."

"How?"

"*Tch-tch*. Another question. I'll just say this: If you know what's good for you, keep away from Dada." Snipping just over Zac's forehead, Barber paused to look straight into the boy's eyes. "You seem like a smart kid. Find a way. Dada will eat you alive. That's all I can say. Breathe a word of this to the Aunties and I'll cut off more than your hair with these shears."

Barber knew how to stop a conversation. Though Zac had tons more questions, he couldn't think how to ask them. Besides, Barber had switched from shears to an electric clipper, which was loud enough to discourage talk. After a good deal of buzzing, he turned the chair toward the mirror to reveal a severe crew cut.

Zac gasped. With both hands he felt the fine stubble all over his head. The boy he was looking at was *not who he was*. He was about to screech when Priscilla came bustling in.

Leering at him horribly, she sighed, "My, my." Then she demanded of Barber, "Has he been asking you questions?"

"Not at all, Auntie. We've had a pleasant chat but I won't allow questions."

"There's my man."

As Barber unclipped the red sheet and gave it a shake, Pris added, "Your Auntie Esmeralda is waiting in the car, Boy. I'll join you shortly. First I have some business with Barber."

She winked, and Zac noticed the old man wince. He also noticed that Pris had the cane.

Chapter 19

The Voice

As Zac emerged from Barber's shop, the black Cadillac was purring at the curb, Esmeralda at the wheel. He'd been in the Aunties' car only twice: once for his first trip to Five Corners, the second time to go to the Big City. Getting in the car was not good. Through the open window Esmeralda gestured with her thumb toward the backseat, and reluctantly Zac got in.

"Where …?" he began.

"You have to ask?" she snapped. Esmeralda didn't turn but watched him in the rearview mirror.

She was right. Zac knew.

"After your performance last night, Boy, you need some straightening out. And you and I both know just the person to do it."

Like a dark, rain-soaked alley illuminated by lightning, the image of Dada flashed in Zac's mind. He wanted to bolt from the car but his body felt paralyzed. Waiting in silence for Auntie Pris, from time to time he stole glances at Esmeralda in the mirror. Her face was a mask of garish makeup, her long gray hair shone like metal, her small eyes glittered with peculiar energy.

When Pris finally appeared she practically floated out of the shop, her pie-round face and blubbery bare arms flushed with some ecstasy. She even did a little tap dance with the cane before handing it to Esmeralda. She might have been a schoolgirl on her first date. From the moment she got in the car she couldn't stop babbling, and kept it up nearly the whole way to the Big City.

Zac didn't listen. He was busy forming a plan. "Dada will eat you alive," Barber had said, and Zac knew it was true. Already his life was dominated by Dada's demand to steal the blue umbrella. Even if he accomplished that, what would be next? No, he had to find a way out.

Carefully he went over the details of his last meeting with Dada. Obviously the old man had a weird attachment to the cane. He'd made Esmeralda lay it ceremoniously in his lap for him to inspect, sniff, fondle. After that Zac had to place the old man's hand on it and …

But this time it wouldn't go that far. If the old creep tried that again, Zac had a surprise in store. He pictured the cane lying across the paralyzed knees, and Dada summoning him closer. Then, as Zac grasped the cane, he'd just snatch it and run. He'd grabbed it once from Esmeralda; he could do the same again. If necessary he'd bash his way out of that room. After all, if he had to steal something, shouldn't it be that awful old cane? He'd toss it in a dumpster and that would be the end of it.

Beyond this Zac's plan was hazy. The same problem came up whenever he considered running away from Five Corners:

where to go? In the Big City a boy could more easily disappear. People might even help him—perhaps the hospital staff, or the police? Surely someone in this wide world would protect a boy from a crazy old man and his mean old daughters?

As the Cadillac drew nearer to the Big City, the day darkened rapidly. Christmas lights winked on. The gentle drizzle turned to needles of freezing rain, then to white chips of ice that clattered against the car like tiny bullets, taking Zac right back to the day of his mother's funeral. The hail thrummed on the car roof just as it had on the wood of her coffin, except now he was the one inside.

When the air was nearly white with hail, Esmeralda had to seek shelter in a parking garage. In a sudden rage she shouted at Pris to shut up, then got out of the car and paced furiously, banging the cane on the echoing concrete. Pris, obviously hurt, sat still as stone in the car. When the trip finally resumed, not another word was spoken until the three of them, Zac sandwiched between the Aunties like a prisoner between guards, passed through the door with the nameplate that read RUTHERFORD HENBOTHER.

"Ah, my girls! How lovely to see you!" came that voice that sounded like fingernails on a blackboard. As before, the Aunties seemed transformed into tittering teenagers as they rushed forward to attend to Dada—patting his arms, smoothing his furs, asking over and over if he was well and keeping warm and getting plenty to eat.

"Enough," he said finally, and the Aunties withdrew. "You know I can't eat much. Why do you always ask?"

"You need to keep up your strength, Dada," offered Pris.

"My strength, dear, does not come from food. Where does it come from?"

The Aunties exchanged perplexed glances.

"But Dada," said Pris, "the boy is here."

"I see the boy. Do I not have eyes?"

"What can we say?" said Esmeralda.

"That's right, you have nothing to say. Why? Because you have not done my will." The Aunties stared straight ahead, unmoving, while in a voice as low as it was intense Dada said, "Where is it?"

The Aunties looked down. "Dada, I told you on the phone—" began Esmeralda.

"I know what you told me. But I could not believe it until I saw—or rather did not see—with my own eyes. Let me ask you again: Where does my strength come from?"

The window behind Dada was inky with clouds. Inside it felt as if that blackness had entered the room.

"Why so quiet, girls? Full of chatter just a moment ago, pawing over your dear Dada—and now you can't answer a simple question? Then let me answer for you: My strength comes from getting what I want. You have not done what I want. Therefore you are bad girls who must be punished."

"Please, Dada, it's the boy's fault—"

"I'll deal with the boy. Come, Esmeralda, you know what to do."

With obvious trepidation Esmeralda stepped forward and presented the cane to Dada, allowing him to caress it lovingly with cheeks, nose, lips. Esmeralda's thin hands, Zac noticed, trembled, while Pris shifted nervously from foot to foot as if she had to pee.

"You can stop your fussing, girls," he said. "I won't punish you in front of the boy. Come here, Boy."

Zac jumped. He had just been lulled into thinking he might be off the hook. Now, obeying not just Dada's words but something in their tone, he crept forward and stood before the old man. That voice: Always the same hushed monotone, somehow it could convey sternness, wrath, even a shriek.

"Well, well," said Dada. "Barber did a nice job. You look more like me now. See the family resemblance, girls?" Uncertainly the Aunties joined him in a laugh. Then abruptly his tone changed: "Do you see the trouble you've caused your poor Aunties, Boy? How does that make you feel?"

Thinking quickly, Zac answered, "Sad."

"Just sad?"

"Very bad?" he tried.

"Just very bad?"

Zac groped for a word. "Rotten."

"Let me tell you something, Boy. There is no word for what you should be feeling. For a snip of a boy to bring such grief to his elderly Aunties ..."

The head within its cowl of fur moved sorrowfully from side to side.

"Because of you, I must punish them. Is that fair?"

"No, sir," Zac admitted.

"What is fair?"

Hesitating, Zac replied, "Punish me?"

Dada nodded. "But this must be your lucky day, because I will not punish you. Isn't that good of me?"

"Yes, sir."

"Yes, *Dada*."

"Yes, Dada," Zac echoed.

"Do you know why I am called Dada?"

Zac thought hard, searching for the answer that would please. In the car he'd resolved to resist Dada, at least in his own thoughts. But now, standing before him, Zac's resolve was crumbling. He felt himself perched on the lip of a vortex, being sucked down and down.

"Come, Boy. Why am I called Dada?"

"Because you're a loving father?" Zac suggested.

"Don't mock me. I am called Dada because that is my wish. Do you understand?"

"Yes, Dada."

"I have another wish. Do you recall it?"

"The umbrella. You want the blue umbrella."

"What a clever boy. But not clever enough. Why have you not brought it to me?"

Again Zac searched for the answer. "I have no excuse. I'll get it for you next week. I promise."

Zac was surprised by the conviction in his own voice. He seemed to be not merely speaking, but also thinking exactly what Dada wanted.

"There's a good boy. I believe you. And so, rather than punish you, I'll just help you remember. You need help, don't you?"

"Yes, Dada."

"Then come a little closer."

Already Zac was nearly on top of Dada. He knew what was coming. He could feel, could remember in his bones, the cold of the cane, the deathly chill of the old man's fingers. Zac would rather have put his hand in a burning flame than feel that cold again. But Dada's voice drew him like an invisible wire. Leaning closer, eyeing the cane lying across the knees, Zac struggled to focus on his plan. Gingerly he was about to close his fingers around the shaft.

"Now, Boy, you may remove my hat."

"Pardon me?"

"This fur hat, take it off. There's a good boy."

Zac stood paralyzed. This he had not anticipated. The idea of exposing what was underneath that fur—it was unthinkable.

Dada repeated his instruction, but Zac was in another world, numb. He hesitated so long that Esmeralda came forward and lifted the hat from Dada's head. Standing in front of Zac so he couldn't see, she appeared to be tenderly caressing Dada's scalp. When finally she stepped back, Zac nearly fainted.

Like a lamp with the shade removed, the naked bulb of Dada's head was revealed. And the whole horrid face, less like a face than a skull. Shrunken, splotched, bruised-looking, just enough skin stretched across the bone to give a mummified appearance. *Was this person,* thought Zac,—*this thing?— actually dead?* But the pus-covered lips slipped open and the yellowish tongue darted.

"Do not forget, Boy, who it is you serve."

Two caves of eyes, motionless, hypnotic, bored into Zac. Did Dada know? Had he foreseen Zac's planned revolt?

"Now take my hand."

Dazed with dread, Zac could only stare.

Boy!

Not an audible shout, nevertheless it tore through Zac like claws reaching down and ripping out his insides. Automatically his hand darted to Dada's hand and gripped it—too tightly, he sensed, and he muttered a plaintive "Sorry" as he lifted that cold, dead thing and wrapped its fingers around the cane. Instantly a chill shot into his veins like an injection. His hand seemed to be stuck there with Dada's, paralyzed. Gone now was any thought of his careful plan. Gone was any thought at all. There was only Dada, only that stupefying voice. A strange languidness engulfed Zac, a feeling of complete and grateful surrender, almost as if his own mother's arms were reaching out and all he wanted to do was fall into them.

And so he fell. He fell a long way and for a long time.

Presumably he was carried to the bed, as before, while Dada and his daughters resumed their visit. Did the old man fulfill his threat to punish them? Zac had no idea, no memory of this time. The next thing he knew he lay stretched across the cool leather on the backseat of the Cadillac, gazing up at the gables of the Aunties' house in Five Corners. Dimly he recalled being carried upstairs and deposited in bed. And then the night closed over him.

Chapter 20
The Rose

The whole world was melting. That's what it looked like through the window as streams of gray rain ate their way through the dissolving glass. It was Monday morning and Zac Sparks was at his school desk with his head down on his arms, as he'd been told, peeking sideways at the rain, trying to follow one raindrop at a time on its course down the window until it disappeared into the sill.

The other kids were outside for recess, playing in the covered area. Mr. Twitchell would be standing in a corner with crossed arms while the girls skipped rope and the boys shot marbles. Chesterton Cholmondeley, of course, had no interest in marbles. He'd be sitting at the picnic table immersed in some fat book on meteorology. As for Chelsea, she'd be off by herself somewhere, probably frolicking in the rain.

Zac was serving a detention for not paying attention in class. That was fine with him, nor did he mind keeping his head down. In fact that's all he wanted to do—not because of his ugly haircut, though that was bad enough, but because he still felt sick from his meeting with Dada. He'd spent the whole of Sunday in bed, even missing church, and went to school on Monday only because he couldn't stand another minute alone.

Suddenly he was aware of a presence in the classroom. Footsteps slowly approaching, soft footsteps whispering on the linoleum, stopping just behind his desk. Guessing it was Mr. Twitchell, he dared not look up. Then he felt a touch on his back. A finger, just one. It moved down, in a long line, then made a sweeping semicircle. Drawing. Mr. Twitchell was drawing on his back. No, writing. Forming letters. Next came an upside-down V with a line across the middle: an A. Then the first shape again, the long line attached to a semi-circle: D. Then another A, and finally a question mark. The dot of the question mark was made with a little more force than necessary, like a gun poking.

DADA? Someone had written DADA? on Zac's back.

Then the hand touched his shoulder, and two fingers ran like little legs down the length of his arm until they met the back of his hand, and stopped there. Another hand was resting on his, giving it a gentle squeeze. He could see the hand now, and it didn't look like a man's. It was small and white.

Now the person moved from behind Zac to the front of his desk, and without looking up he could tell it was not an adult but a child, wearing shiny yellow rubber boots.

"Leave me alone," Zac whispered. "You'll get me in more trouble."

The hand began stroking his hand.

"Stop it!" he hissed.

The hand withdrew, but then two hands touched him on the head and brushed his bristly crew cut. It felt good. Relaxing, he finally looked up.

"Chelsea! What are you doing here?"

Chelsea's black hair was slick with wetness and her dark eyes shone. Rain dripped from her yellow raincoat, her smiling face gleamed with droplets, and even her eyelashes were studded with tiny wet stars.

"What about the Twit?" Zac whispered.

Like a toddler waving bye-bye, Chelsea glanced at the door and waggled her fingers.

"He went somewhere?"

She nodded. Then again she drew the shape of a question mark, this time on Zac's forehead.

"You know about Dada?" he said.

Slowly, solemnly, she nodded. Then she made an awful face, and again drew a question mark, this one in the air. After making the dot, she left her finger pointing at Zac, and raised her eyebrows.

"Yes, I had a run-in with Dada. How did you guess?"

Chelsea made signs as if she were sick, holding her head, her stomach.

Zac grimaced. "I wish you could talk."

Now it was Chelsea's turn to look down. For a long time she didn't move, and Zac said nothing.

"I'm sorry. I didn't mean …"

She looked up, smiling, and signed OK in the air.

"Chelsea, I'm in so much trouble. I wish I knew what to do."

Smiling radiantly, she bent far forward and took a few small, halting steps like an old, old man.

"Eldy? You think he can help?"

She nodded vigorously.

"But he's like you. He doesn't talk either, does he?"

She nodded even harder.

"I don't know, Chelsea. I wish you were right. But I've got enough problems already with the Aunties, and they made me promise to stay away from Eldy."

Chelsea regarded him sadly. Then, taking both his hands in hers, she gave him a look so piercing, so full of wordless pleading that Zac grew embarrassed and pulled away. He was very glad none of the other kids were there to see Chelsea Cholmondeley holding his hands or stroking his hair.

The bell rang and they heard scuffles outside the door. With a last look Chelsea scooted off to the cloakroom.

"She's a beauty, Bud. There's this big mirror that reflects the sky, and you look into it to read the direction and speed of the clouds. It tells you exactly what's going on even high in the upper atmosphere. Can't wait for this rain to clear to check it out."

Walking home from school with Zac through the gray drizzle, Ches babbled away about his new nephoscope. Zac finally had to tell him to shut up. What did he care about all that weather nonsense?

"What's with you?" said Ches. "You mad about that awful haircut? Looks like you took your finger *out* of a light socket. Ha ha."

Zac didn't respond.

"And why weren't you at church? Didn't the Aunties try to drag you?"

"I was just out of it. Flu or something." Zac was not about to discuss Dada with Ches. Instead he said, "Can I ask you something?"

"You just did."

A while back Zac had made up his mind not to pump Ches for information. It was like trying to milk a giant slug. But right now he needed some answers.

"Ches, what can you tell me about Butler?"

"Little old granny," he said.

"What?"

"He's an old granny. Lived with the Aunties so long he's like one of them."

"Not as big."

"True. Little old baby, then."

"Why is he so small?"

"I just told you: He's a very old baby. Ha ha."

"No, really."

"I've got a question for you, Bud. Why do you ask so many questions?"

"I'm new here, remember? I'm trying to figure out

what's going on in this crazy town. Seems like everybody knows except me."

"Trust me, Bud, enjoy your innocence. Some things are better not to know."

"Like what?"

Ches looked straight ahead and said nothing. Rain dripped off his nose. He was like Barber: You could talk to him as long as you didn't ask questions.

Just then, drifting through the silvery rain, came a sound of singing, far off. Or was it close? With the air so misty it was hard to tell. The music stabbed Zac with sadness, as though a mother were mourning her lost child. He knew right away it was O, but O as he had never heard her before. So plaintive. Standing there in the drizzle, Zac thought of being with Sky in his office under the stairs. But this time he imagined Sky crying.

Ches yanked hard on his arm. "Pick up the pace, Bud. It's just that crazy old drunk."

After that they parted and Zac went straight to Porter's. Earlier that morning he'd wrestled his way to a firm resolve that today was the day he would definitely steal the umbrella. If he didn't, after work the Aunties would beat him black and blue, and he couldn't face that today. He was at the end of his rope.

As he entered the store, the old men sang out, "Hi, Zac! What's up?"

No time for them today. "The sky," he said flatly, and went straight to work sorting bits of hardware. This job placed him in the back corner where he could keep an eye on the open office door. He wondered if Sky was at his desk, as he didn't seem to be in the store. Once he went casually to the door and peeked in just far enough to see the elephant-foot stand. No umbrella there.

The old men were playing cards. Sometimes they played euchre, sometimes cribbage. Their voices murmured like the rain outside. "Fifteen two, fifteen four, a pair is six … Nothing in the crib …"

Time passed with still no sign of Sky. Nervous tension mounted in Zac. He couldn't focus on what he was doing, could barely distinguish between a nut and a bolt.

"Say, Zac, how's the weather over there?" called Joe, as usual evoking laughter from the others. When Zac didn't join in, Joe added, "You look a little peaked, son. You okay?"

"Just flu," he replied. "Any of you guys know where Sky is?"

All the old men put down their cards.

"Maybe," said Sam. "What do you want him for?"

Zac felt their eyes looking right through him.

"I dunno. He's usually around somewhere."

"He's always around if you really want him," reflected Abe. The others muttered agreement.

Sam asked, "Do you really want him, Zac?"

What kind of a question was that? Why couldn't they give straight answers? This was the kind of conversation cracker-barrel locals carried on with a slick stranger to put him in his place. Didn't these fellows know Zac? Hadn't he spent every day with them in the store for over a week, chatting and horsing around?

Descending the ladder, Zac walked deliberately to Sky's office and poked his head in the door. Sky wasn't there. As he turned around, the old men were still boring holes in him. Abruptly he marched past them, heading for the front door. He looked back only to say, "I've had it for today. Tell Sky I'm not feeling well."

Just before the door closed behind him he heard Joe call out, "I hope you find what you're looking for."

Outside the rain had stopped, the sun had just emerged from the low cloud cover, and the whole sky was lit with gold. Like the leading float in a parade, the sun seemed to be marshaling all the day's clouds and pulling them into the west. So beautiful was the scene that Zac had to stand still for a moment to take it in. Everything in sight—streets, trees, fire hydrants, even the Aunties' house—shone with burnished glory from above. Eldy's Balloon and Flower Stand was especially bright, as if doused with a pot of liquid fire.

Then Zac recalled Chelsea's pantomime of Eldy and her confidence that the old man could help him. Drawn to the brilliance that made a ramshackle flower stand look like the end of the rainbow, Zac drifted that way. At first he thought he'd just saunter by and maybe catch a glimpse of what Eldy was up to. But even quite close to the stand he saw no sign of life. Thinking the old man must be busy below the counter, Zac had to step right up to it and peer hard into the brightness till his eyes hurt. And then, though still he saw no one, he heard a voice.

Hello, Zachary.

This plainest of greetings flooded Zac with a strange warmth. Like the first time he'd met Eldy, the words were not audible but seemed to come from within himself, this time flowing across his mind like a banner pulled behind an airplane.

"I don't know why I'm here." Zac didn't say these words out loud, he only thought them. But immediately Eldy responded, again in the flowing interior script.

Oh yes, you do. How are you?

Such a mundane question, yet it made Zac feel that no one before this had ever truly cared about him.

I'm sick, he thought. *And confused.*

Yes, you've been through a lot. Let me give you a flower.

Then Zac saw Eldy, precisely where he was looking, all but lost in the brightness. Bent over as usual, the old man was busy arranging a bouquet of roses—red, pink, yellow, orange. All the colors, Zac thought, of the sunset sky at that very moment.

What color would you like?

Zac hesitated. The last time he'd accepted a gift from Eldy it had fetched him a beating. And why should he want a flower? He didn't even like flowers, except that roses did remind him of his mother.

Red, he thought. *I like red.*

He felt distinctly drawn to a particular red rose, and Eldy's gnarled fingers reached for that very one. His hands moved not like a sighted person's but as if feeling the colors. If hands could smile, these hands, wrinkled and spotted yet glowing as intensely as the sky, smiled. They also trembled, and as they drew the red rose out of its crystal vase, the thorny stem caught and the whole container spilled on the ground.

Dashing behind the counter, Zac knelt down to help Eldy clean up the mess. They were side by side, gathering the scattered flowers and replacing them in the righted vase, when the boy, glancing up, found himself looking into the old man's face. To his surprise it wasn't a face pinched with age or poverty, but rather strikingly handsome and lively. Though certainly old, even ancient, this face was marked less by age than by a sense of wisdom and kindness. Most surprising of all, the eyes—a deep, tender pewter like the first light of morning—rather than having the unfocused look of the blind, seemed to gaze right back at Zac with warmth and humor.

So astonished was the boy that he didn't know what to think or say. All that could possibly be said seemed already expressed in Eldy's eyes. Zac didn't move, didn't reach to pick up any more flowers. He wanted to stay right there, just like that, gazing into that face. But gently Eldy took his arm and lifted him up. It was odd how he did this, remaining bent over himself. But soon Zac was on his feet, looking down again at the brown, bald head fringed with white hair.

Don't be afraid to go back to the Aunties, said the interior voice.

And without lingering, Zac turned to go. After a few steps he realized he was holding the rose.

"Thank you," he called back. It was the only word either of them had spoken out loud.

The sun had set and Zac crossed the street to the Aunties' house beneath a sky clotted with blood-red clouds.

Chapter 21

Trust

The encounter with Eldy left Zac unaccountably buoyant. He practically floated up the front steps and his hand was on the doorknob before he realized he should do something about the rose. Carefully he concealed it in his jacket.

The moment he stepped inside, Auntie Pris confronted him. "Have you got it?"

Thinking she meant the rose, he stared at her openmouthed.

"If you haven't, you know what's coming."

Temporarily residing on another planet, Zac found it odd to feel so happy in the presence of Auntie Pris. She looked far away and almost small.

"Esmeralda! The boy still hasn't got it."

Only when Esmeralda entered, her cane tapping hollowly on the stone floor, did Zac recall the umbrella. He was supposed to steal it, and now he would get a beating. Strangely this knowledge did not distress him. He felt grand and untouchable.

"You have some nerve, Boy, trying my patience like this," croaked Esmeralda. "Bend over."

Zac heard himself reply, "With pleasure, Auntie." And he bent over.

"Don't you dare sass me!"

Auntie Pris grabbed one of his arms and held it behind his back. "We're ready for you this time. Any funny business and I'll break your arm."

Whack!

The first stroke of the cane was like every other time, yet completely different. Physically Zac still felt it—the initial sting followed by deepening pain. At the same time, inside he felt strong, calm, resilient. When he stood up to say, "Please, Auntie, may I have another?" far from cringing with shame, he felt proud.

Whack!

How many times the cane connected with his backside he didn't know. Though it certainly hurt, at the last he stood up straight and looked Esmeralda square in the eye—not with defiance but with power. He saw clearly how this unnerved her.

Deflated, she whispered, "Get to bed. No supper tonight."

The way Zac felt, he could have taken the stairs two at a time. But in an act of deference to his oppressors, he mounted solemnly to his room. Nor did he flop on the bed as usual, but instead paced excitedly. He had such energy! Not only had he survived the caning with ease, but the illness that had dogged him all weekend was gone. He felt free, light, triumphant. If he'd been anywhere else he would have whooped for joy.

Withdrawing Eldy's rose from his jacket, he gazed at it in awe. It was so beautiful, so richly colored. Could this be no ordinary flower? Stashing it under the bed, he hastened to his boarded-up window and removed the knot to peer outside. But Eldy was gone for the day. It was a luminous evening; all was perfectly still. In the curdled cloud cover, a patch had opened where stars gleamed in the loveliest ultramarine sky.

At school the next day he could hardly wait to tell Chelsea about his meeting with Eldy. For once Zac didn't care if the other kids caught him with her. He just wanted to see her face when he told his story. She'd be so proud of him!

However, as the children filed into the classroom that morning, Chelsea wasn't there. Zac was crestfallen. He needed someone to share his excitement. What could have happened to her?

All morning he fretted, much more than was reasonable. He couldn't escape an intuition that something was wrong. Finally at recess he cornered Ches.

"Where's Chelsea?"

"Stayed home," said Ches.

"But she always comes to school. Is she sick?"

"Sort of."

"What do you mean, sort of?"

"She's not sick, exactly. Just real sad."

"Sad? Chelsea? About what? She's always so happy."

When he answered, Ches looked past Zac's shoulder, far off across the school yard. "You haven't heard, Bud?"

"Heard what?"

"About Butler."

"What about him?"

Meeting Zac's gaze, Ches heaved a long sigh and said, "Butler's dead."

"What!"

"Yeah, he kicked the bucket. I thought you knew. It happened in your house, after all."

"In my house? When?"

"Yesterday morning. Doc Murray was there. Then Rev came. And then they took him away. Rev told us last night."

"But what happened?"

Ches gave Zac a long, studying stare. "You tell me, Bud."

As he turned to go, Zac grabbed his arm, but Ches shook him off and stumped away. It was no use pursuing him. If Chesterton Cholmondeley didn't want to talk, there was no forcing him. At least his sister, though silent, was communicative.

After school Zac headed straight for the Aunties' place, not sure what to expect. It was hard to believe Butler was dead. Zac needed evidence, even as horrible thoughts possessed him about what might have happened. Part of him hoped to find Butler, as usual, perched on a stool in the kitchen preparing supper. The other part wondered what to do if he encountered Esmeralda. Ask meekly if it were true? Or hurl himself at her and accuse her of being a wicked witch?

Knowing he wasn't expected at that hour, Zac quietly opened the front door partway. He was about to sneak in when he heard voices issuing from the dining room.

"... the nerve of you, Priscilla, asking for Boy. You know he's mine."

"But Barber's so old."

"That's not my problem. I put up with Butler until the end, didn't I?"

"Please, Esmeralda, can't we share Boy?"

"What a disgusting thought!"

"There's so much life in him!"

"Priscilla, stop it. Boy is mine, Barber's yours. That's what we agreed all along."

"Fine. If you won't share him willingly, I'll use him when you aren't around. See how you like that."

"Shut up this minute!"

"I won't! I've held my tongue too long, Esmeralda. You can't have Boy all to yourself."

Esmeralda, whose voice hardly ever rose above a hoarse whisper, uttered a shriek. "You swine! Have you forgotten who's watching? Bend over!"

"No, you can't!"

"Oh yes, I can!"

"I'm sorry—"

"Too late now."

"But—"

"Your memory is short, Pris dear. Every once in while, it seems, you need a little lesson. Now bend."

Sounds of a scuffle ensued. Then Esmeralda, panting in triumph, hissed, "Would you rather I ram this stick down your throat?"

An interval of silence was followed by a loud *whack.*

Then Pris, in a tiny, plaintive voice, said, "Please, Esmeralda, may I have another?"

"Yes, dear, I think you definitely deserve another."
Whack!

"Perhaps now, Priscilla, you'll remember who's boss …"

Revolted, Zac eased the door shut, crept down the steps, and sprinted across the street to Porter's. Though it was just a short way, by the time he stood inside, he was completely out of breath. He was shaking and covered in cold sweat.

At the back he saw the old men pause in their card playing to regard him curiously. He couldn't face them right now. *Please*, he thought, *please, Sky, be here …*

And there he was—his head popping above the counter, a roll of price tags in one hand and his mouth studded with pins. Removing the pins, he came and stood before Zac, placed his hands on the boy's shoulders, and looked into his eyes. Zac looked back, unblinking. In the space of a few moments, it seemed that everything Zac was feeling somehow passed into Sky—the wild confusion, the pain, the terror. Sky saw in his eyes the unspoken question—*What on earth is going on in this awful town?*—and he heard Zac's silent cry for help. He understood.

"Zac, you look as if a monster's chasing you."

Yes, that was it. Something monstrous had happened to Butler, and next it would happen to Zac. It was happening

231

already. He was in the grip of something he had no idea how to fight. He wondered which was worse: to know that someone had just died—perhaps been murdered?—or to wish that you yourself were dead. In that moment Sky's eyes seemed to reach out and touch Zac like a cool hand on a feverish forehead. Peace, like a warm liquid, flowed through his mind and down through his whole body.

"Think some hot chocolate might help?" Sky suggested.

Zac nodded, and with Sky's arm around his shoulder, they walked toward the back of the store. Passing the tables of old men, Zac saw them gazing with silly smiles, toothless gums showing, their pale old eyes moist, like enraptured moviegoers.

Entering the office, Sky as usual deposited his umbrella in the elephant-foot stand. Zac hadn't been thinking at all about the umbrella, but now he knew he had something to say. Once ensconced in the big leather chair behind the desk, with Sky seated opposite on an upended barrel, Zac could wait no longer. It just popped out.

"The Aunties want your umbrella. That's why they let me work here. They want me to steal it. All this time that's really what I've been trying to do."

"I know." Sky said this as casually as if he'd been told that his umbrella was blue.

"You know?"

"Well, it's pretty obvious from how you've been acting. You look distracted most of the time, shifty. Until today you wouldn't even look me in the eye."

It was true. Now, for the first time, Zac was able to meet Sky's gaze without discomfort. In fact all he wanted right now was to connect with Sky. It's what he'd really wanted all along.

"Every time I come back without the umbrella," Zac said, "the Aunties beat me. Every day I fail, they add one more whack. And it's not just the Aunties, it's Dada. He put them up to it. They're all trying to get their hands on your umbrella."

"And have been for years," said Sky. "I could tell you stories."

"Last week I got so sick of it that I grabbed the cane from Esmeralda and threatened her with it."

"You did? That was brave."

"I don't know. I was so angry. I might have killed her. But I got shaking too much."

"Yes. That cane, Zac, has a power of its own. Best leave it alone."

"But it won't leave me alone. The Aunties are so horrible. I hate them!"

"With good reason. Still, hate makes you a prisoner, not just of them but of yourself."

Mulling this over, Zac said, "But I have to live with them. And it's so weird over there. I mean, Butler just died."

Sky started and leaned forward. "I didn't know."

"And it feels like I'll be next. What can I do?"

Sky appeared lost in thought.

"Please, Sky, can you help me?"

"Ah! Now you're asking for my help. As a matter of fact, yes, I can help. But on one condition."

"What's that?"

"You must trust me. Will you?"

Trust. All of a sudden this seemed to Zac a great deal to ask. Who was this Sky Porter anyway? However, looking steadily into those extraordinary blue eyes, and at that face so warm and present, Zac felt his heart shift. After all, where else could he turn? There was Eldy, but in a strange sort of way Eldy did not seem like a real person. When he talked, his voice sounded inside you, and even his face, most of the time, was hidden. But here was Sky, sitting right there, speaking plainly, his face an open book. Not only was he real—he was the most real person Zachary Sparks knew.

"Yes, I will trust you," said Zac.

"Good. That's always the hard part. With trust, everything is possible."

Chapter 22

Bins, Bags, Barrels, Boxes

Their mugs of hot chocolate drained, Zac thought his talk with Sky might be drawing to a close. But now Sky looked at him with a glint in his eye—a hint of merriment, even mischief. The very air seemed to echo his change of mood, the sun choosing that moment to spill through the room's one tiny window.

"You asked me the other day about my umbrella," said Sky. "About why I always carry it. I gave you a partial answer. I think it's time to answer you fully."

Plucking his umbrella from its stand and making for the door, Sky motioned Zac to follow. To the boy's surprise he headed up the stairs, the ones that formed the ceiling of his tiny office, leading to the very place that had come to hold so much mystery for Zac. It all came rushing back to him— the strange lights he'd seen up there, the talk of haunting, the unknown footsteps and the shock they'd given him. Following Sky's back up the narrow staircase, Zac felt a mixture of excitement and dread. Whatever was up there, would he now learn the secret? Was he about to meet Sky's father?

At the top of the stairs they emerged into one enormous room without a single supporting pillar. It looked like a vast dance hall, the expanse of hardwood floor gleaming as if freshly polished. There were no windows, just three large skylights admitting the golden glow of late afternoon. From the moment Zac entered, he sensed something unusual, as though they'd passed into another world. The atmosphere itself felt different, the light limpid, almost sparklingly clear. It struck him that the entire space was so bright and airy that it did not feel like being inside a building, but like the great outdoors.

How could one room hold so much? The ceiling, crisscrossed with rafters, was high, majestic, cathedral-like—far beyond what seemed necessary or even possible for the hall's proportions. And the walls were lined with the biggest boxes, barrels, bins, bags, and bottles that Zac had ever seen. They were just like the ones downstairs that held candy, flour, buttons, and so on, except these were many times larger. *What could possibly be inside such immense containers?*

Following Sky across the wooden floor, Zac listened to the deep echo of their footsteps, making it seem as though someone else were there too, someone much larger. Upon reaching the nearest container, a glass jar about ten feet tall and as big around as a redwood stump, Zac peered at its contents. Transparent, faintly blueish, the jar appeared to be filled with a clear liquid up to the brim. Sky stood beside him.

"What is it?" said Zac. "Water?"

"Yes. Rain, to be precise."

"You collect rainwater up here?"

"Not exactly. This rain hasn't yet fallen on the earth."

Zac tried to puzzle this out.

"I know, it's not easy to grasp at first," said Sky. "Have a look at some of these other containers."

There were about a dozen of the giant glass rain jars. Beside these, on thick plank shelves, stood rows of smaller, squat jars with screw-on lids. Several of these, like the taller jars, appeared to hold nothing but water.

"More rain?" asked Zac.

"Actually that one you're looking at contains dew."

"Dew?" The word didn't quite register.

"Yes, the moisture you find beaded on grass in the early morning. It's a form of precipitation, so we keep it here with the rain."

"Dew," Zac repeated. "That's a lot of dew. How did you collect so much?"

"Oh, we don't collect it. Again, this is dew that hasn't yet formed."

"Then … where did it come from?"

With his umbrella Sky pointed to the skylights overhead. "It's delivered. Fresh each day."

Zac stared up at the skylights. This was making no sense at all.

Next he turned his attention to some odd-shaped jars on a lower shelf. Like a larger version of the candy jars downstairs, they looked like tilted fishbowls. The contents were not clear but opaque, white and crystalline like salt. Zac looked inquiringly at Sky.

"Frost," he said. "Different kinds, different weights. Of course we also carry frost in loaves. And then there's window frost, which comes in sheets."

Zac stared at the jars, then moved down the row to more fishbowl jars filled with tiny white pellets of various sizes. "I suppose you're going to say this is hail?"

"That's right. I love hail, don't you? One can have a lot of fun with hail."

Noting that the air in the hall was not cold but room temperature, Zac asked, "Why doesn't this stuff melt?"

"Each container has its own self-regulating environment. All the containers are perfectly designed for what they hold, much like your own skin. It's a beautiful system, really."

Beside the jars, piled halfway to the ceiling, were enormous white cardboard boxes. "Here we have snow," said Sky. "All sorts, from large, fluffy flakes to fine granules. Snow is hard to keep; each flake must be perfectly preserved. We don't normally have this much in stock, but Christmas is coming."

For all Zac understood, Sky might as well have been speaking Japanese. "I still don't get it. What do you do with all this stuff?"

"Do? We make weather, of course."

"Make weather? You mean, as a kind of game? You play with hailstones like marbles?"

Sky laughed. "You're right, Zac. It *is* a game, but not in the way you mean. This is the real thing."

Zac made a face of total incomprehension. "This snow here—you say it hasn't yet fallen? When will it fall?"

"Oh, sometime in the next few days or weeks. I can't say exactly. Even I don't know too far in advance. But when I let it go, it will be just the right time."

"When you do what?"

"Release the snow. Let it fall."

"You do that?"

"It's my job. Running the store is not all I do. My real business is up here in the Weatherworks. Weather has to be stored somewhere. And it needs a control center. Think of this as a big bakery where all the ingredients of weather are prepared and mixed. This is where it all happens."

"Happens? But how? How do you do it?"

Sky twirled his blue umbrella like a baton. "Here's the secret. Rain, frost, wind, clouds—they're like paints and this is my brush. You asked me why I always carry the umbrella, and this is your answer. Like flying a big plane, I'm always at the controls."

"You mean you really make weather with that?"

"You bet. Would you like to see?"

Zac's eyes were about as big as the lids on the dew jars. "You're not kidding me?"

"Not at all. I would never lie to you, Zac, or even pull your leg. Unless, of course, your leg was a little too short.…"

Zac laughed uncertainly. "I don't know what to think."

"Don't think. Just watch."

Leading Zac to a large wardrobe of dark, polished wood, Sky opened the double doors to reveal a row of heavy black garment bags on broad hangers. Something about them prompted Zac to ask, "I've seen lights over here, strange lights on top of the roof. People say this place is haunted …?"

"You can judge for yourself. But no, it's not haunted; it's just the work of the weather going on."

"And the lights …?"

"Deliveries. Shipments of weather. They come through the skylights."

"One day last week the lights were beautifully colored, like streamers in the sky—"

"Rainbows. A shipment of rainbows. It's interesting you should ask, because I was just about to release one. Here's where we keep them, in this wardrobe."

Zac gazed in wonder at the line of garment bags that looked as if they held tuxedos for giants. Each one was emblazoned with a brightly colored monogram. "Those are rainbows?"

"You bet. You've noticed all the rain lately? For a rainy season we need rainbows. Not many on hand right now; they don't have a long shelf life. But with the sun just out, we could use one today. What do you say?"

Say? What does one say to a man who suggests taking a rainbow out of a bag and placing it in the sky? Zac's mouth opened, but nothing came out.

Sky had already lifted down a bag and held it draped over his arms. "Here's a beauty. Rain's not over yet, so we don't want anything too splashy. This one's a pale half arch, modest but distinctive." He sounded like a tailor describing a suit. "If you wouldn't mind grabbing the zipper, Zac, just give it a pull."

Zac felt the bag—a rich, creamy leather—then ran a finger over the embossed stitching of the monogram. Finally he took hold of the zipper tab and slowly pulled, wondering what in the world would happen.

Nothing did. The inside of the bag was entirely dark and empty-looking.

"She's in there, don't worry," said Sky. "Rainbows are simply white light separated into component strands. In storage all the colors blend together, so on release they're nice and fresh. Here, you take it."

Zac stretched out his arms as Sky placed the long garment bag across them. It felt almost alive, like a light, sleeping person. *He was holding a rainbow!* Sky, lifting his umbrella over the opening, traced a quick arc shape in the air. Like colored scarves appearing from a top hat, the umbrella's tip seemed to draw something out of the bag and send it flying up through an open skylight. It all happened so quickly that Zac wasn't sure whether he actually saw the rainbow leave or not. But there was no mistaking what happened overhead. Though only a small part of the rainbow was visible through the skylight, it was plainly there—not in the bag anymore but in the sky.

"Wow!"

"Wow is right!" said Sky. "She's a beauty. Still gets me every time." For a minute the boy and the man stood in silence, admiring. Then Sky said, "What'll we do next? What kind of weather do you want?"

"You're asking me?"

"Why not? If you had a bike, you'd let me ride it, wouldn't you?"

"Sure, but …"

"So what will it be?"

Though he appeared to take time to consider, Zac knew exactly what he wanted.

"Say it," said Sky.

"Snow. I love snow. Do you think we could let loose some of that Christmas stuff?"

Sky laughed, a musical riff like a peal of bells. "I thought you might say that. I saw it in your eyes. Okay, let's get started."

In a far corner of the room stood a bank of enormous wooden bins with tall letters chalked on their lids: NW, NNW, S, SSE, and so on. Sky led Zac to the bin marked SW and opened its large, hinged lid. "These are the winds," he said. "If we want snow, first we need a wind to lower the temperature and bring in clouds. This wind's a sou'wester—a dandy one for snow. Will you do the honors?" Sky offered Zac the umbrella.

"Me?"

"You've got hands, haven't you? All you do is stir the wind like a big pot of soup." Sky made a circular motion with the tip of the umbrella. "Here, try it."

Taking the umbrella, Zac was astonished again by its lightness and its exquisite feel of quality. Like a fine motor it practically purred in his hands, or breathed, and was warm to the touch.

"Just point and stir," said Sky.

Aiming the tip of the umbrella into the open SW bin, Zac vigorously stirred. Immediately powerful gusts pummeled the building.

"Whoa, there, Zac! Slow down a little."

As Zac slowed his stirring, the gusts subsided.

"My goodness!" exclaimed Sky. "A few shingles will need replacing today! You've got to be careful with weather, Zac. There are living people out there. It's a good thing you didn't start off with hail."

Zac stared with amazement at the umbrella, and at his own hands. He himself had made the wind blow! All along he'd had a healthy respect for this umbrella, knowing it carried some special secret. Now, suddenly, it was a powerful magic wand.

Guessing his thoughts, Sky said, "It's not magic. At least, no more than the wind itself. It's perfectly natural. Think about what you want to accomplish, make an appropriate motion, and the umbrella follows through."

Next he led Zac to a mountain of white cotton bags resembling huge flour sacks. Piled to the ceiling, they bulged with their odd-shaped contents.

"Can't have snow without clouds," said Sky. "Here you'll find every type that's on that chart downstairs. Stratus, cirrus, nimbus—you name it."

"How do you get clouds into sacks?"

Sky beamed, showing teeth white as cumulus wool. "Easy when you know how. But hard to explain. Some things are not for explaining, they're for doing. But tell me—what sort of clouds do you think we want for snow?"

"You're asking me? I dunno. Nimbostratus?" Zac named the darkest, snowiest-looking clouds he recalled from the chart.

"That would do. Maybe a bit heavy-duty for today, though. How about cumulonimbus? They're a little lighter, and they work well with a southwest wind and a temperature around freezing."

"Okay."

Sky pointed to one of the sacks, a particularly bulky one. "They're just tied with slipknots. Poke the tip of your umbrella …"

My umbrella? thought Zac.

"… into the loop of the knot and pull. It's that easy. As the sack opens, imagine a big bank of snow-bearing cumulonimbus riding in on the wind."

A vivid impression flowed into Zac's mind. Using the tip of the umbrella to open the sack, he saw it deflate, and at the same moment the sunlight that had poured into the room was blotted out. Overhead, sure enough, the skylights filled with ominous-looking dark clouds sliding along like giant sharks.

"Now for some sprinkles," said Sky.

Part of Zac's brain was flipping somersaults, while another part was starting to think it quite natural to see rainbows shoot from garment bags and clouds pop out of flour sacks. He marveled that things in the Weatherworks seemed to happen almost instantaneously, yet he also had the odd feeling that time was somehow stretched in this room, so that really the coming of the wind and clouds took longer than it seemed.

He had a similar feeling about the size of the containers, that they were really even larger than they looked, and he sensed this same illogic applied to the room itself. He knew the dimensions must be equal to those of the store below, yet as he looked down and across the wide expanse of that storeroom, it seemed to go on and on. It was as if walls had been put around all of nature.

Returning to the area where the boxes of snow were kept, they passed the biggest containers Zac had yet seen. They seemed as big as barns, yet they appeared empty. To Zac's question Sky replied, "Fresh air. Different kinds for dusk, noon, plains, mountains. Couldn't do without it."

Sky halted before one of the white snow boxes. At the bottom of each was a small sliding door, reminding Zac of dispensers for powdered detergent in laundromats. "Just lift that hatch with the umbrella tip," said Sky, "and the snow will come down."

Mindful of what had happened when he'd stirred the wind too hard, cautiously Zac pointed the umbrella and lifted the hatch an inch or two. After a moment he said, "Nothing's coming out."

"Not here," said Sky. "Up there."

Looking up, Zac was astonished to see a gauze of downy flakes sifting past the skylights. His heart leapt. Could he possibly be imagining this? No, without doubt the snow was real. Up until then he'd been in a daze, hearing what Sky said but not quite believing it. Now, in the overwhelmingly visible presence of something he loved so much, awareness hit him as if a handful of snow had been tossed in his face. He himself had produced this snow by lifting a little door in a cardboard box. *Wow!*

With fresh awe Zac regarded the umbrella. So light it was, so beautiful, so imbued with power. This was the object that, for the past two weeks, had riveted his attention and provoked an intense struggle between the most important people in his life, a struggle he hadn't begun to understand. Now he understood. No wonder Dada and the Aunties wanted it so much. Who wouldn't? Who wouldn't want to wave a little stick and change the weather?

Eyes wide, Zac gazed around the vast warehouse. Where was he, really? What was this place? What kind of room could hold unimaginable quantities of unfallen snow and dew and frost like grain in silos? He glanced at Sky, who was quietly watching him. Who was this man who had power over the weather? How did he do it? Was the power his, or was it in the umbrella? And how far did that power extend? So many questions!

"Sky," he began, "does all the weather for Five Corners come from this one room?"

"Not just Five Corners. The world. All the weather for the entire world is handled right here in Porter's Store."

"What! How can that be?"

Gently taking back the umbrella, Sky said, "There's only one blue umbrella, and this is it."

"But this snow I made—it's just here, isn't it? It's not snowing everywhere?"

"No, because you intended it to snow here. That's what was in your mind, wasn't it?"

"You mean, if I wanted it to snow in New York or London … or Hawaii …?"

"That's right. The umbrella's range is unlimited."

"But that means … it means you could start another ice age, or flood the whole world!"

Sky gave Zac a look of utmost seriousness. "You're right. But I haven't done that, and I won't. You wouldn't try it either, would you?" Though Zac made no reply, Sky answered for him, "Of course you wouldn't."

Too much information was rushing at Zac; he had to stop and think. Finally he said, "But why here? Why should all the weather for the whole world come from a little place like Five Corners?"

"It has to start somewhere, doesn't it? That's like asking why is your belly button in the middle of your stomach. I suppose it could be on top of your head, but then it would be a head button. And that's how you'd go to sleep at night—just turn off your head button."

Despite his bewilderment Zac giggled.

"So you see, your belly button could be anywhere, but it's not: It's somewhere. Anything could be different from how it is. A giraffe could look like a giant toad with wings, but it doesn't. Things are as they are. Five Corners just happens to be the weather capital of the world."

"And is it just you who makes weather? Or are there others?"

"Just me. Dad used to, but he handed it all over to me. At least the business end of things."

"But why you? Why do you get to have the umbrella, rather than someone else?"

"Like who?"

"I don't know. Anybody. Reverend Cholmondeley, say."

"Oh dear! Would you really want to hand over control of the weather to Reverend Cholmondeley?"

"No, I guess not. But that's just an example. What about someone else? His son Ches loves weather!"

"Does he?"

"Well … he loves studying the weather, and he knows all about it."

"So you'd trust him with the umbrella?"

This didn't take much thought. "Yeah, I see what you mean. But still—I guess I never thought of an actual person doing this job. I thought weather just happened. How come you get to do it?"

"Doesn't someone have to? You can't have the four winds roaming around all by themselves. Weather's like an orchestra—it needs a director."

Zac thrust his hands into his pockets. "But it sounds so complicated. How can you possibly run the world's weather all by yourself?"

"It's simpler than it looks, Zac. All the weather begins in Five Corners and spreads out from here. A wind released here rushes into a low-pressure zone somewhere else, and so on, in a chain reaction. All I have to do is set things in motion.

Occasionally I stir up some new weather over in Portugal or Tasmania, but mostly I just get the ball rolling here and let it roll."

Zac was silent. So much to absorb. Quietly Sky suggested they head back downstairs. On the way Zac thought of another question. "Do you have to be in that upstairs room to make weather?"

"As long as I have the umbrella," replied Sky, "I can make weather anywhere. But I love the Weatherworks. I'm very fond of the containers—all those bins and boxes and bags and barrels …" He smiled. "I like being close to the elements."

"Can anyone work the umbrella?"

"You saw that for yourself, didn't you?"

"Yes, but you were with me."

"Anyone who has the umbrella and knows the secret can make it work."

"That sounds dangerous."

"No more than anything else. If you knew nothing about life, and I told you all about it, you'd say life sounded dangerous. It's dangerous getting out of bed in the morning. There's no escaping danger."

Chapter 23

Buried Alive

By the time Zac left Porter's Store, he was so excited that he did cartwheels in the falling snow—the snow that he had made!—practically leaving footprints on the clouds. Then he stood with his mouth wide open to taste the little cold stars on his tongue—how real they were!—and went dancing along the sidewalk chanting, "Wow! *Wow*! Wowie-wow-*wow*!" He didn't care who saw him. He didn't have a care in the world. The flat-out wonder of what he'd just experienced so filled his soul that, if Dada himself had appeared, Zac might have pinched the old fellow's cheek and wished him a happy day.

In such a state he couldn't go straight to the Aunties. He just couldn't. He was bursting with news and he had to tell someone. Sky hadn't said anything about keeping the Weatherworks a secret. It never occurred to Zac to keep such an amazing revelation to himself.

But who to tell? The obvious person was Ches Cholmondeley. Weather was Ches's passion. He knew everything there was to know about it—except this. He was missing the most important thing of all. How amazed he would be to find out!

Sure enough, a light was on in Ches's room, and Zac saw the square, lumpish form leaning over one of his precious instruments. Not quite ready to go inside, Zac stood in the backyard of the rectory with his face raised to the snow, his eyes shining, his heart soaring. He couldn't get over it. How many people in the world knew what he knew? Who else had given orders to wind and clouds?

Then it hit him: *Why me?* Why should little Zac Sparks, of all people, be initiated into this tremendous secret? Or was he perhaps just kidding himself? Was it possible that everyone in Five Corners *except* Zac already knew about the blue umbrella? Would Ches just grimace and say, "So what else is new, Bud?"

The driveway to the rectory was covered with pea-sized gravel. Scooping up a handful, Zac tossed a few stones lightly at Ches's window. He had to do this several times before Ches finally slid open the balcony door and emerged, looking like a bear rudely roused from winter quarters.

"Down here!" called Zac in a hoarse whisper.

Peering over the rail, Ches spotted him. "What are *you* doing here? Did the Aunties let you out of your cage?"

"*Shh*. I'm not supposed to be here."

"You're telling me. What do you want?"

"Can I come up?"

"I'm pretty busy. Weather stuff ..."

"This *is* about weather. You won't believe what I'm going to tell you."

"You're right, I won't. You think you can tell me anything about weather I don't already know? Thanks, but no thanks."

251

"Come on, Ches, this is important. Please let me come up. Just for a few minutes."

"Well …"

"If you won't listen, then go get Chelsea. I want to tell her, too."

"I don't allow girls in my room. Especially small ones related to me by blood."

"Then I'll go toss stones at her window."

"Hold your fire, Bud. Go to the back door and I'll let you in."

His hair tousled, horn-rimmed glasses askew, and wearing an enormous checkered bathrobe, Ches appeared even older than usual. "This better be good," he muttered as Zac followed him up the back staircase.

"It's good. I promise you."

Once in his room, Ches closed the door. "What about Chelsea?" said Zac. "I want her to hear this."

"I told you—no girls. Get on with it."

Zac moved toward a chair, but Ches remained defiantly standing. "Don't sit. You said you'd keep it short."

Already Zac felt some of his excitement waning. People had their own personal weather systems, and Ches was wrapped in an atmosphere of dense clouds. Still, what Zac was about to tell him was amazing by any standards, and moreover it was specifically geared to his number one passion. Zac could hardly wait to see the Great Meteorologist's defenses crumble.

Just then they heard a light knock.

"Go away!" shouted Ches.

Zac made a motion to open the door.

"Don't," Ches warned. "She has no business in here."

"I need to see her."

"Not in here you don't. Go away, Chelsea."

"Wait, Chelsea. Just stay there by the door. I'll talk loud so you can hear."

Ches turned his back and stared out the window. It was almost as if he sensed the explosive nature of what was about to be divulged, and had already determined to remain unaffected. Zac knew he had to talk fast.

"You know how you told me Porter's Store is haunted? Well, I found out what goes on there. Those strange lights on the roof—I know what they are. Sky—I mean, Mr. Porter—he told me. He took me up there himself and showed me."

Ches did an about-face. "You've been up there? To the second story?" In spite of himself, he seemed impressed.

"You bet. Just wait till I tell you."

Describing the appearance of the upper room with its massive containers, and detailing their contents step by step just as Sky had, Zac sought to reproduce for Ches the gradual unfolding of the mystery. Throughout his speech Ches stood with hands on hips, glowering, with a curious combination of reluctant interest and open belligerence. He was such a poor audience it was hard to keep going; Zac felt like a guttering candle. But the knowledge that Chelsea might be listening behind the door encouraged him. Finally he got to the punch line.

"You see that snow—that snow right out there?" Zac pointed emphatically, but Ches refused to look.

"I have news for you, Bud. That ain't snow."

"Of course it is! Just …" But Zac's words died in his throat. The snow had changed to freezing rain. In the silence it made a tiny clattering sound.

"That there is sleet," announced Ches, immense satisfaction in his voice.

"But it *was* snowing," said Zac.

"Suit yourself."

"Come off it, Ches. You saw the snow. Didn't you?"

Ches remained triumphantly noncommittal.

"You know you did. It *was* snowing," Zac insisted, almost doubting it himself. "Anyway, here's the thing: *I caused it.* I made it snow. Me, Zac Sparks. I know it's incredible, but it wasn't really me, it was the umbrella. Sky had me stand before this big white cardboard box full of snow. I used the umbrella to lift up this little door, and right away it started snowing! And before that I made the wind blow by stirring the umbrella in a bin. At first it blew so hard I had to slow it down. You must have heard it—that big gust a little while ago? Sky said it probably blew off some shingles …"

Again Zac's voice died. What was going on, he wondered, in that big, thick Cholmondeley head? "Don't you believe me?"

"Who is this Sky?" Ches answered. "Who are you talking about?"

"Mr. Porter. Sky. That's his name."

"I've never heard him called that."

"It's what he told me to call him."

"You don't mean the old man? You didn't see some old guy up there?"

"No, it was just Sky—Mr. Porter. The one with the umbrella. But didn't you hear what I said? This man controls all the weather for the whole world! It's all done right here in Five Corners, right across the street."

Ches, his arms now folded tight as a straitjacket, stumped toward Zac until he practically stood on the shorter boy's toes. "Bud, either you're making this up, or you've gone wacko. Which is it?"

"It's the truth, Ches, I promise. I saw it all with my own eyes. I held the umbrella myself and brought clouds; I stirred up the wind and caused snow. I even saw Sky make a rainbow. I hardly believe it myself but it's true."

"Then it's just as I thought: You're crazy. You've flipped your flippin' lid. I warned you not to get mixed up with that place." Ches waggled his finger. "And now you're bewitched or something. There couldn't possibly be a man, a human being, in charge of all the weather. What a load of malarkey! Ha ha. Double ha ha. That's not how weather works, Bud. You want to know what causes snow? I'll tell you …"

As Ches went into one of his long meteorological explanations, it was Zac's turn to tune him out.

"Okay, okay," he said when Ches had finished, "so you don't believe me. But I can prove it. Come with me to Porter's and I'll show you. Sky will show you himself."

"You really have flipped, Bud, if you think I'll ever darken the door of that old spook shack. I'd rather freeze in hell."

Zac had stayed near the door, the better for Chelsea to hear. Now he called out, "You believe me, don't you, Chelsea?" and he reached for the handle and pulled it open. The person on the other side nearly fell through the doorway.

"Mrs. Cholmondeley!" cried Zac. "I had no idea …"

"Yes, dear, I know. I shouldn't eavesdrop, but I couldn't help myself." Mary Cholmondeley wore a faded bathrobe and her face looked even paler—except for her eyes, which shone like a child's. "I don't know …" she murmured. "What you said … it's so wonderful … I couldn't tear myself away …"

"You believe me, then?" asked Zac.

"Is it really true?"

"Yes! Every word of it!"

"I don't know … I want to … Yes, I'd like to believe …"

"Come see for yourself."

"Oh no, I couldn't …"

"Yes, you could. It's right across the street."

"Oh no, dear. You don't understand. Reverend Cholmondeley—"

At that moment they heard the front door open downstairs.

"Oh dear, oh dear," moaned Mary. "He mustn't find you here, Zac. You have to go."

Already Ches had Zac by the arm and was steering him toward the back stairs. "Looks like you've worn out your welcome, Bud."

"Wait!" Zac hissed. "Mrs. Cholmondeley—Mary—please come with me to the store. Tomorrow afternoon. Will you?"

"No, no … You don't understand …"

"I need someone—anyone—to believe me. Please come."

"No …"

Shaking her head, she was clinging to the doorknob as if a mighty gale blew through the hallway. Ches kept pushing Zac toward the stairs.

"Then tell Chelsea. Tell her to meet me at the store tomorrow after school. Please?"

"I don't know …"

Suddenly Zac's feet were on the stairs and he was shoved so hard he nearly fell. He wanted to turn around and belt Ches, but the other boy was both bigger and angrier.

At the bottom of the stairs, Zac stopped. He faced Ches and declared, "Look, whether you like it or not, you're going to believe me. If you won't come see for yourself, I'll show you. I'll bring the umbrella here."

"You bring that blasted thing here and I'll stick it you know where."

"I'll bring it and then you'll see."

Ches slammed the door in Zac's face.

It was darker now, and cold, and the sleet pelted down like a rain of needles. Zac had nowhere to go but back to the Aunties', and he knew very well what awaited him there.

Quietly he eased open the front door and crept in, hoping as usual that by some miracle the Aunties weren't home.

He was halfway up the stairs when Esmeralda's whispery voice stopped him.

"There you are, Zachary. I've been expecting you."

Zachary?

"How was school today, dear?"

Dear? Without answering, Zac turned and stared at her, wondering if this was the same Auntie Esmeralda.

"I suppose you're tired from your work at the store?"

Her voice was so different. Still the same papery rasp, like a voice in a séance. But now the tone was syrupy sweet. She wanted something.

"Come here, my dear, and tell me all about your day."

She was standing in the doorway to the parlor, wearing a long black dress and a fox stole. The fox's eyes seemed to look directly at Zac. Warily he descended the stairs to Esmeralda, who reached out and tousled his hair, at the same time exerting a slight pressure that drew him closer. Stooping, she put her arm around his shoulder.

"Why so quiet, love? Mr. Porter wasn't mean to you, I hope?"

Far from it, thought Zac. At that moment Sky Porter was his only friend in the world.

"No, I suppose not," she went on. "He's really quite a nice man, isn't he?"

There was something else in her tone, something underneath the false sweetness. Zac realized what it was: an uncertainty, a nervousness. What could make Esmeralda Henbother nervous? And why wasn't she asking about the umbrella?

258

"I know why you're so quiet," she drawled. "It's the cane, isn't it? You think you'll get a beating. But I have a surprise for you, a very pleasant surprise." Bringing her face just inches from his, she pronounced the next words with wide-eyed exaggeration. *"No cane.* No cane today, Zachary. Isn't that wonderful?"

Turning up empty palms, she showed that indeed she was not carrying it. Then, straightening, she steered him into the parlor. "No more beatings, Zachary. Aren't you happy about that? I'm sure you're as sick of that old cane as I am. I hate seeing anyone hurt. I've only used it for your own good. But perhaps I've been wrong."

She sat Zac beside her in the pink love seat. After smoothing the creases in her lap, she draped one arm along the back of the love seat, letting her hand rest just behind Zac's head. As she talked, she stroked his hair.

All Zac could think of was Butler. Butler was dead and she had done it. Hadn't she? He wished he'd discussed this with Sky.

"I want to apologize to you, pet," she crooned. "Your mother's death was very upsetting for us all. There have been many adjustments, both for you and for us. Your old Aunties aren't used to having a young man in the house, and I'm afraid we got off on the wrong foot. But it's time for all that to change. Don't you agree?"

Where was all this going? Zac felt such intense loathing that it would almost have been easier to be caned.

"Love, please accept my apologies. I want you to feel welcome here. I'd like us to get to know each other. What do you say? Can we be friends?"

"*No!*" he yelled, erupting off the couch and stabbing a finger at her. "You killed Butler! You *killed* him!"

"What?" Esmeralda looked unsettled. "I did nothing of the sort."

"You did so! I don't know how, but you killed him. And now you're trying to kill *me!*"

"There, there, Boy. Calm down."

As she reached for it, Zac saw the cane lying across the back of the love seat. Beside himself, he lunged with both hands, fit to strangle her. But another pair of arms grabbed his own and forced them behind his back. He was pinned, and Esmeralda jumped to her feet with a look of ferocious outrage.

"Hold him, Pris. If he won't cooperate nicely, there are other ways."

Cane in hand, Esmeralda knelt and drilled him with her gimlet eyes. No, she was not going to cane him; something else was happening, something worse. With a mighty effort Zac jerked his neck forward so that his forehead bashed her on the nose, and at the same time, he released a vicious backward kick with his heel. Behind him Pris grunted deeply. It was enough to buy him a second or two, and he wrestled loose and made a dash for the door, but Esmeralda was right behind and tripped him with the cane. Down he went, bringing her with him, and they struggled blindly on the floor. Once more he squirmed free, and this time made it to the hall, only to see Pris's massive frame barring the front door.

With nowhere else to go, he darted upstairs and sprinted down the hall. Navigating by instinct, he avoided his room but headed for the spare bedroom at the end. Once there he slipped into the closet and quietly shut the door. Groping along the wall, he found the little door, the entrance to the laundry chute he recalled from the night of his confinement. Shoving some coats aside and grabbing the clothes rail like a chinning bar, he managed to swing his feet up and into the chute opening. He didn't know if he would fit, but he had to try. Footsteps sounding like a dozen army boots thundered down the hall.

"You little monster!" screamed Pris. "You can't get away! Every door is locked!"

Every door but one, thought Zac, as he wriggled first his legs, then his whole body down into the chute. He was quite prepared to be trapped there and die of starvation rather than surrender to Esmeralda. To his own surprise he didn't get stuck. Instead he found just enough room to maneuver down until even his head was inside. Spaced every couple of feet, narrow strips of molding enabled him to grip with his fingers and the toes of his sneakers. Arms stretched overhead, he pulled shut the chute door and was swallowed by darkness. And creeping down a few more inches, he waited.

He was certain they'd find him. How stupid he'd been! Surely the sounds of his scuffling in the chute would be audible throughout the house. And he was panting so hard that even this, he imagined, would give him away. After a few minutes Auntie Pris—he knew it was her because her breathing was louder than his own—threw open the closet door and rifled among the coats. But amazingly she overlooked the laundry chute. A person the size of Pris, Zac guessed, would not dream that even a small boy could fit into such a space. For once he was grateful for his littleness.

Moments later Esmeralda's angry voice sounded nearly in his ear, startling him witless. "Priscilla! He must have escaped through the bathroom. I wish you wouldn't always leave windows open." There were some minutes of heated discussion, before Zac clearly heard the Aunties' footsteps clumping down the stairs and the front door banging shut. Then all was silence.

After that he must have waited for over an hour in his metal cocoon, perfectly still and listening like a human stethoscope. The house not only sounded but felt empty, until eventually he wondered if he might attempt a getaway. He couldn't stay there forever, and now might be his only chance. However, when he tried to creep upwards, he couldn't budge an inch. Going down had been a simple matter of slackening his body, but going up meant bending knees and elbows to gain leverage, and the space was too narrow for that. He was, after all, trapped, and this thought threw him into a panic. In the ensuing desperate moments of struggle, he managed only to slip farther down the chute, until finally he knew that he was truly stuck. Entombed, buried alive under the very noses of the Aunties, he saw himself dying there of hunger and thirst, rotting inside his vertical coffin and ending as a skeleton.

In this pit of despair he wished to heaven that he still had the photograph of his mother. If only he could look at her face!

Of course, he couldn't have seen it anyway. But just to know the picture was there, in his pocket, to touch it …

It was some minutes before an obvious thought struck him. Why not just keep going down? At first this brought no comfort. The idea of descending deeper and deeper through total darkness to an unknown destination filled him with dread. For the first time in his life, he felt terrified of insects, spiders, rats. Or what if some greater monster lurked below? Irrationally, in this predicament Zac felt more frightened than at any other time since coming to Five Corners.

Still, what choice did he have? He had to go down—or die. Mustering all his courage, and sucking in his breath to make himself small as possible, he began a slow, wriggling descent, crabbing from one narrow ridge of molding to the next, all the while his heart pounding in the veins of his temples. How long this went on he didn't know; it seemed hours. The chute felt bottomless and the darkness, if possible, deepened and deepened until it seemed to squeeze him.

At last he reached a place where his toes could not locate another ridge. Stretching one leg down as far as possible, and kicking this way and that, he felt his foot dangling free of the chute. He had reached the other end. Now what? He could have relaxed his whole body and simply dropped. But how far would he fall, and what was down there? So he stayed that way with one leg hanging, trying not to think of monsters, trying not to think of a fall that might go on forever. And finally, bracing himself for the best outcome he could imagine—a rough landing on concrete—he let go.

As it turned out, his fall could hardly have been better cushioned if a bed of feathers had been waiting. For he landed, of course, in a pile of clothes—rank, smelly laundry, but at least it was soft. Nearly laughing out loud with hysterical relief, Zac thought: *Yes, there* was *a monster at the end of the chute—the Aunties' dirty underwear! Yuchhhh!* Picking himself up, he scrambled away as quickly as from a heap of manure.

Peering around, he saw he was in the cellar. Bare concrete walls, unfinished rafters, a great gangling furnace. Dust and cobwebs. A rickety staircase at the far end. Under the stairs one light burning in a small window.

A light? Yes. It was in fact the only source of illumination. Without it he wouldn't have seen a thing; but it also meant that he could be seen. Quickly hiding behind a pillar, he watched and waited. There appeared to be no movement, no sound, nothing.

Cautiously he made his way toward the light, stopping at another pillar about ten feet off. From here he had a better view of the window beneath the stairs. Beside the window was a door, unusually small, just right for someone Zac's size. It reminded him of his clubhouse under the stairs in his mother's house. Through the window he could see the source of the light—a candle-shaped lamp on a round bedside table. He could also see part of the bedstead, and a framed picture on the wall, a photograph of a boy. The boy was tiny, about six years old, and he stood beside a swing set on a playground. He looked vaguely familiar.

The sensible part of Zac's brain yelled at him to run up those stairs and get out of that house as fast as he could. But curiosity restrained him. Who could possibly have a clubhouse under the stairs in, of all places, the Aunties' cellar? Creeping closer to the window, he was able to gain a wider view of the room within. More pictures, a bookshelf, a bed with a green blanket. Though he couldn't see the whole room, he guessed no one was within. Approaching the door, he put his ear to it and listened. Nothing.

As carefully as if defusing a bomb, he eased open the door a crack. Then two cracks. Finally he stuck his head in.

The first thing that greeted him—overpoweringly—was a heavy, acrid odor. Urine? And next he realized, to his alarm, that the room was not, after all, empty.

Someone lay in the bed. A small person. And still. So small and still that the slight mound beneath the blanket had escaped Zac's notice. Catching his breath, he nearly bolted. But the person, whoever it was, did not cry out, did not move, showed no sign of being disturbed. Asleep?

Again curiosity got the better of Zac, and tiptoeing to the bedside, he peered down at a perfectly bald, ovoid head on the pillow, with a longish, fantastically wrinkled face.

Chapter 24

Pethybridge

"Butler!" breathed Zac.

He looked shockingly older than when Zac had last seen him. But alive! His face was ghostlike, pale as paper and sunken, all his features barely clinging to the bone. Only the faintest up-and-down motion of the blanket showed any sign of life.

Obviously he was asleep. Or in a coma? Had he, perhaps, been taken for dead and later revived? Why wasn't he in the hospital? Did people know he was here? Butler's woefully small form beneath the blanket struck Zac with pity. He seemed an old, old, little child. His room, too, was like a child's room—small, oddly shaped, homely. And stinking of urine.

More troubled than ever about the sordid scene he'd overheard between Butler and Esmeralda, Zac now longed to know everything he could about this man. Did he dare try to rouse him?

"Butler, Butler," he called gently. The withered eyelids fluttered but otherwise there was no response. Lightly Zac stroked the wrinkled brow. "Butler!" he called louder.

Suddenly two eyes wild with terror stared back. "Don't … please don't … no more …"

"It's just me—Zac. I won't hurt you."

"Boy?"

"Yes."

"Are you alone?"

"Yes. I thought you were dead!"

Butler heaved a profound sigh and turned his face to the wall. "I wish I was. I might as well be. I'm no good to anyone anymore."

"Why are you here? Why aren't you in the hospital?"

"Hospital? Do you think they care? No one does. Not one person in this town cares that I'm dying." Butler's voice, like the rest of him, was piteously drained of strength and color.

"I care," said Zac.

For some time Butler lay completely still. When he answered, his voice was even fainter than before. "Why would you? I haven't done you any favors."

Zac thought for a moment. "Remember that plate of sandwiches at the party? You never told on me."

For the first time Butler betrayed a hint of a smile. "I was proud of you."

"Butler," said Zac, "the Aunties are mean, but you aren't. I like you."

Like clouds scudding across the moon, a wave of emotion passed over Butler's wan face.

"Friends?" offered Zac.

Butler's eyes filled with gratitude. "All right. Friends. Thank you, Boy."

"Good. And now let's do something about these sheets."

"But …"

"Just relax." Having spotted a shelf with some fresh linen, Zac set about changing the bed with Butler still in it. Thankful to discover a plastic sheet underneath, he made no comment but wiped it as best he could with a cloth and deposited the soiled sheets in the laundry pile.

As he worked, he said, "By the way, don't call me Boy anymore. My name's Zac. What's yours? Not Butler, I bet."

At this Butler burst into tears. "Oh dear, oh dear," he blubbered.

"What's wrong?"

"I hate it, I hate it!"

"Hate what?"

"My name. I can't even say it." Butler's weeping, pitiful though it was, at least showed signs of life.

"It can't be that bad," said Zac. "Try me."

"Well … you won't laugh?"

"Promise."

After some deliberation, Butler motioned Zac to draw closer. At first he said the name so softly that Zac had to ask him to repeat it. The name itself sounded like a whisper: "Pethybridge."

"Pethybridge?" echoed Zac, wrinkling his nose. He nearly smiled but quickly gained control. "What's wrong with that? It's a fine name, full of character."

"You really think so?"

"Sure. But what about your first name?"

The poor little man again started crying. "I have none! Only Pethybridge."

"You must have another name."

"Noooooo," he moaned. "That's what's so terrible. My parents never even named me. They didn't care." And he began to wail like a siren.

"*Shhh*," hushed Zac. "The Aunties might hear."

Abruptly Pethybridge stopped crying. "Where are they?"

"I don't know. Out, I think. But finish what you were saying—about your parents."

Quietly now Pethybridge continued, "They deserted me at birth. Both of them. My grandmother took me in but she was a crony of the Aunties, and just as weird. She called me Pethybridge after her pet bird that had died."

Zac restrained a giggle.

"All the kids laughed at me. I was one big joke. When my grandmother died and I came to live here, I didn't mind at all being called Butler. I was happy for the job, too. For once I felt important." Again Pethybridge looked agitated. "The Aunties—are you sure they're out?"

"I think so. They don't know where I am. I escaped."

"Escaped?"

"Yes. I'm not going back."

"No, you mustn't. But they'll hunt you down. They'll find you."

"No. I won't let them."

"They will. They need you. Esmeralda especially."

"Need? Why?"

269

"You don't know?"

"Not really. At least, I have a hunch ..."

"Believe me, it's more terrible than you realize. Tell me your hunch."

"Well ... I overheard something ... between you and Esmeralda."

"Yes?"

"It's the cane. It makes you sick."

Pethybridge rolled his eyes. "I wish that's all it was."

"What do you mean?"

"Look at me—I'm dying. I won't last long. Don't you know why?"

Zac said nothing. At some level, perhaps, he did suspect the truth, but hadn't dared to let on to himself.

"They suck the life out of you," said Pethybridge. "Literally. A week, a month, sometimes six months at a time. I don't know what happens when I'm unconscious. But I wake up older. Not just sick, but older."

"What?" said Zac, even as he thought *no, no, no.* What he was hearing was too horrible. He wanted to run, get out of there.

"Little by little," Pethybridge continued, "Esmeralda has stolen all my life away and sucked it into herself. She doesn't age, but I do. Surely you've noticed her energy? It's all mine, while I've wasted away until now I'm nearly gone. Such a short life!" He paused, and two tears slid down the creases of his cheeks.

Though obviously it cost Pethybridge a great effort to talk, an urgency drove him. And as much as Zac didn't want to believe it, the pieces of a horrid puzzle were fitting together. After a long silence he asked the question that most troubled him.

"Pethybridge ... how old are you?"

The little man pointed to the photograph on the wall. "You see there? That's me, five years ago, when I was six. So in real time I'm eleven. And now I'm dying of old age."

That was when it hit Zac: the truth, the whole, horrendous truth. Trembling, shocked, he stared at the photograph of the boy on the playground, then back at the shrunken, wasted figure in the bed. He could hardly believe the contrast, yet he had to. And the same fate, he realized, was poised to overtake him.

Vividly his mind filled with the memory of his two encounters with Dada, and how sick he'd been after each one. Had Zac already given away some of his life? His precious youth? How much? How much was already gone?

"So you've met ... Dada?" he asked.

"That's how it starts," said Pethybridge. "Dada's a magician. With the cane he makes some sort of opening into your soul. After that the Aunties are free to drink their fill. Of course Dada himself also needs youth to survive. But ... there are children in that hospital."

Zac's mind churned trying to follow the convolutions of this horror. "Is he locked up there?"

"Oh yes. He was caught doing something bad—I don't know what. He should have gone to jail but he was judged insane."

Zac almost whispered his next question. "How many are there? Kids who've lost their youth?"

"Here in Five Corners, just me and Barber now."

"Barber!"

"Yes. There were others before us."

"And they're …?"

"Dead, of course."

A dreadful silence filled the room. Finally Zac said, "So Barber is one?"

"He belongs to Pris. And I'm Esmeralda's. We're their personal fountains of youth. They're too jealous of each other to drink from the same fountain."

"How old is Barber?"

"In natural time? Same as me, I think. He still has some life in him, though not much. Now that you've disappeared, and I'm almost gone, they'll fight over him. Without regular drafts of youth, they're finished. If their true ages ever caught up with them …"

"How old are they?"

"Old as the hills."

"How old?" Zac leaned over the bed.

"You know all those china ornaments upstairs? The elephants and vases and so on?"

Zac blinked. "They always give each other one on their birthdays."

"Exactly. Ever bothered to count them?"

Zac pictured the shelves, sills, whatnots, end tables all crowded with knickknacks. "There must be … hundreds?"

"By my count," said Pethybridge, "155 elephants and 152 plates, vases, still lifes. Of course, you broke three elephants and a vase. And probably others have broken."

Zac's mind slowed. Could the Aunties really be that old? Could anyone live so long? Could it even be called living—feeding off others?

"And Dada?" he whispered.

Pethybridge gave him a sizing-up sort of look. "You've seen that oil painting in the dining room?"

"The really old one of a boy in black, who looks like some ancestor?"

"I have news for you: That's no ancestor."

"It's …?"

"Dada as a boy. It dates, I'd guess, from the 1700s."

Zac's flesh crawled. No wonder this picture had had such an eerie effect on him.

"Dada's bewitched it," Pethybridge confirmed, "so it's like he's really in the room. He's actually keeping watch here."

Shuddering, Zac asked, "Why didn't you tell me all this before? Why didn't you warn me?"

Pethybridge sighed deeply. "I … don't know.… Dada is so powerful … and the Aunties … Besides, what if I just had some strange disease? I wasn't sure … Now, of course, I wish … But at death's door everything looks different."

"Do the Aunties know you're still alive?"

"Oh yes. Esmeralda didn't want to take all of me until she was sure of a replacement. Which is you. She's desperate, I tell you. She needs you more than food."

Zac dug his fingers into his forehead, trying to absorb everything—or block it out. Throughout this conversation all the grief and terror of the past few weeks had been swelling inside him like rain clouds. He wanted to cry, to let it out, but he couldn't. He'd hardly cried at all since his mother's death. It just wouldn't come.

"What's wrong with this town?" he exploded. "Why don't people stop all this stuff?"

Pethybridge shrugged. "Dada's got us all under a spell."

"We have to do something. What about Barber? We need to warn him."

"No use. Barber's as stubborn as I was. And proud."

"Proud! Of what?"

Sinking lower in the bed, Pethybridge said, "Try to understand. We're both orphans. No one ever cared about us. The Aunties … at least they wanted us."

Zac stared again at the photograph. "But how is it possible? How can anyone suck away your youth?"

"I told you—it's the cane. You don't know about the cane?"

"I know what it feels like on my backside."

"That's nothing compared to its true power. It used to belong to old Mr. Porter."

Jolted, Zac leaned forward. "You mean …?"

"That's right—the man upstairs. The ghost of Porter's Store. Oh, that place is haunted, all right. No question about it."

"But—"

"I don't really understand it. But you know how young Mr. Porter always carries that umbrella?"

"Sure."

"Well, his father did too. Not the same umbrella, a different one. And the story goes that he tried to kill Dada with it."

"What!"

"I don't know all the details. It was a long time ago, when Dada used to live here in this house. He and old Porter never got along. They got into a fight and Dada ended up paralyzed. He and the Aunties have blamed the Porters ever since. But Dada also got away with the umbrella handle."

"You mean ... the cane?"

"Yes."

Having seen both cane and umbrella up close, Zac realized they were much alike. The cane was darker, but both had an enchanting grain, so vividly patterned it seemed to be moving.

"But how?" he began. "I mean, Mr. Porter's umbrella doesn't do ... bad things."

Pethybridge closed his eyes. "Are you sure?"

The strain of so much talk finally overcame him. He began to cough and couldn't stop. Zac tried giving him water, plumping his pillows, raising his head, but the coughing went on and on. It was hard to know how a small, frail body could stand such violent spasms. When at last the attack subsided, Pethybridge lay so still that Zac was afraid he'd died. But no, there was still a faint pulse.

For a while Zac simply watched him, trying to sort through the incredible tale. Then, rising, he went to the small, curtained window on the far wall and hazarded a peek outside. It was dark. Dimly he made out the shapes of familiar buildings—Porter's Store, St. Heldred's, the World's Smallest Business Establishment. Few lights shone, and Zac realized how late it must be and how tired he was. Finding a blanket and cushion, he spread them on the floor in the narrow space between the bed and the wall. Even if someone entered the room, he would not be immediately visible, and he could always slip under the bed to hide. The moment he lay down he fell into a deep sleep.

Upon awaking, he found himself thinking about roses. Had he dreamed of them? It dawned on him that, when he'd been so sick after his last encounter with Dada, a single rose from Eldy had wonderfully restored him. He'd felt so strong and happy!

Hmm.

Was it possible that the rose had reversed the effects of Dada's spell? Taking a leap of faith, he thought: *Might the same cure work for Pethybridge?*

If only Zac had held onto Eldy's rose! Unfortunately it was still up in his room, under the bed. Too dangerous to go there now. But there were lots more where that one came from. Excitedly Zac went to the window and peered across the intersection. He must have slept a long time, for already the sun shone brightly on Eldy's humble stand. But Eldy himself was nowhere in sight. His shutters were closed and no balloons or flowers were on display. Where could he be? He was always there from crack of dawn till dusk.

All afternoon Zac watched and waited while the frail form of Pethybridge slept soundly. Still full of questions, Zac considered waking him up. But even in sleep Pethybridge looked utterly spent, and Zac let him be.

With hunger gnawing at him, Zac found a packet of granola bars and demolished them. But as the sun sank toward the west, he knew he couldn't wait much longer. Pethybridge was dying and a rose might save his life. In Eldy's absence Zac wondered about Sky. Surely he could help? But Pethybridge had hinted that Sky and his umbrella might not be entirely safe. And what if the Aunties caught Zac at Porter's and the storekeeper, as before, would not protect him?

Finally Zac made up his mind. With dusk to cover him, it was now or never. Holding Pethybridge's hand, he whispered, "Don't worry, everything will be all right. I'm going to get help." And with that he left the room and stood listening at the bottom of the cellar stairs. Earlier, briefly, he'd heard footsteps above, along with the telltale *tap-tap* of the cane. But nothing now. Gliding like a shadow up the stairs, he slid out the back door and, hugging the outside walls and keeping below window level, he made his way to the far side of the garage where he was well hidden. The black Cadillac was gone. With no one else about, he was able to make an easy dash across the street into an alley beside Porter's Store.

There, by a stand of garbage cans, someone grabbed the collar of his jacket. Adrenaline spurted. After almost a day of anxious waiting, Zac's nerves were at fever pitch and he was ready to smash, kick, bite, kill. His first punches landed in air, then he stumbled backward and fell. Struggling to rise, he found himself staring up into the dark, flashing eyes of his assailant.

Chapter 25

Rumblings

"Chelsea!" Even in the dark of the alley the little girl's broad smile shone. "I thought you were the Aunties! What are you doing here?"

Chelsea made some signs, gesturing toward the second story of Porter's.

"Oh, I remember. I asked your mother to have you meet me here after school"—was that just yesterday?—"and you came!"

Chelsea nodded.

"I'm sorry, I completely forgot. So much has happened. You won't believe what I've found out. But listen, we can't talk now, we have to find Eldy. Do you know where he is?"

Chelsea made a series of elaborate signs, moving so quickly that Zac couldn't follow.

"Hey, go easy. Run that by me again."

More slowly, Chelsea made gestures that Zac still couldn't understand.

"Listen, Chelsea. This is really, really important. Pethybridge—I mean Butler—is dying."

Chelsea's eyebrows shot up.

"That's right—he's alive. I just saw him myself. But he'll be dead soon if we don't do something. And Eldy's the only one who can help. You've got to tell me where he is."

Chelsea began again her dance of incomprehensible motions.

"No, stop. There's no time. Don't you see? A life is at stake. Just this once, can't you open your mouth and tell me? I'm your friend. Please?"

Chelsea hung her head. She looked so completely dejected that Zac knew he must be asking the impossible.

"All right, I understand. I mean, I don't, but it's okay. Look—if you can't tell me where Eldy is, can you take me to him? Can you show me?"

Chelsea turned up empty palms.

"What? You don't know where he is either?"

She shook her head.

"Why didn't you just say so?"

Zac scowled and looked away, but tugging his sleeve, Chelsea pointed to Porter's Store.

"You're right. We need to talk to Sky. Let's go." Seeing Chelsea's puzzlement, Zac added, "Mr. Porter, I mean. His name is Sky."

Making sure the coast was clear, they left the shelter of the alley and approached the front door. Finding it open, they slipped inside. The interior was quiet and empty looking. Though the old men had gone home, their voices seemed still to hang in the air. Just one light burned at the back.

"Sky must be in his office," whispered Zac.

They made their way to the back, to the doorway under the staircase, and upon spotting the blue umbrella in its familiar elephant-foot stand, Zac felt a surge of joy. He poked his head in the door, and sure enough, there was Sky Porter, seated at his desk. He almost seemed to be waiting for them.

"Hello, Zac. I missed you this afternoon."

"Sorry, Sky. I couldn't come. I got into trouble with the Aunties. But I've brought someone to meet you. A friend. Is it okay?"

"Of course."

Zac motioned to Chelsea to come in. Timidly she peeked around the corner, then entered on tiptoey steps to stand before Sky with hands clasped shyly.

"Hello, Chelsea," said Sky. "I wondered when I might have the pleasure of meeting you."

Chelsea made no response.

"She doesn't talk," explained Zac. "I don't know why, but she hasn't said anything in years."

Sky made a quick motion with his right hand and Chelsea smiled. Then he gestured with both hands and she laughed out loud. Before this Zac had often seen her face wreathed in giggles, but always soundlessly. Her laugh in Sky's office was the first real noise he'd heard from her.

Sky made more gestures and Chelsea signed back. They both laughed. Then the gestures flew back and forth in a long, complex, entirely silent conversation. Having no clue what they were saying, Zac began to feel left out. He was impatient to get on with rescuing Pethybridge. He was about to interrupt when Sky rose and withdrew the umbrella from its stand. He handed it to Chelsea, who cradled it lovingly in two arms as if it were a baby.

Motioning the children to follow, Sky led the way out of his office and up the staircase into the Weatherworks. Upon seeing the place again, with its enormous and unlikely containers of wind and dew, rainbows and frost, Zac felt caught up once more in all the exhilaration of the day before. As for his problems, so urgent just moments before—Pethybridge's desperate plight, the villainy of Dada and the Aunties, the threat to Zac's own life—all seemed to fade away before the sheer awe of being in a warehouse where somehow the whole world's weather was stored. If possible, it was even more thrilling to see this place now through Chelsea's eyes.

Just as Sky had done with Zac, he took Chelsea on a short tour, introducing her to the jars of rain and hail, the boxes of snow, the sacks of clouds. He also showed her things he hadn't shown Zac: breezes in brown paper bags, sheets of window frost, and what appeared to be balls of glowing light in stoppered flasks.

"Sun dogs," explained Sky. "We carry them in white and rainbow-colored, and in different shapes: circles, crosses, swords. And over here"—he indicated a row of giant test tubes on a wooden rack—"are halos for the sun and moon. Coiled, of course; we couldn't possibly store them in the round."

Struck by a thought, Zac asked, "What about the sky itself? It's so big, but you've got to have it in different colors and so on, don't you?"

"Ah, now there's an interesting question. Yes, we have sky—lots of it. But not in any of these containers." Pointing to the umbrella, Sky said, "Open it up, Chelsea."

With solemn reverence Chelsea undid the umbrella's strap and slid the golden ring slowly up the shaft. As the canopy opened, it made a rustling sound like a flock of birds. The inner surface, the children noticed, was not the same blue color as the exterior. Instead it was a luminous ultramarine splotched with moving patches of inky black.

"Hold it up," said Sky.

Raising one arm as high as she could, Chelsea held the umbrella aloft toward a skylight, where the umbrella canopy and the sky itself could be seen side by side. Though Zac knew what would happen, still it amazed him. "Exactly the same!" he whispered.

The inky shapes on the umbrella's canopy, it turned out, were the same dark clouds that even now were scudding across the sky. It was just as if a new, round, scallop-edged window had been opened in the roof.

"So the umbrella is the sky's container!" exclaimed Zac.

Before their eyes the first star of evening appeared in the canopy, so vivid they might have reached up and plucked it like a white grape from a vine. Chelsea was so delighted she began to dance, skipping and laughing, twirling the sky above her like a parasol. Wherever she moved, the sky-window moved with her. Unable to resist, Zac joined in and together they transformed that warehouse into a celestial ballroom. As though mere earth had vanished, the sky now seemed not just overhead but everywhere. More stars came out and whirled around them thick as snowflakes. So strangely caught up was Zac that he did something he hadn't done in a long time: He sang out loud! It was a made-up song all about Chelsea and Sky and himself, and the old men of Porter's Store were in it too, and even Eldy and O …

How long this went on Zac had no idea, but in the end the two children found themselves stretched on their backs gazing up into the starry dome of the umbrella, now completely clear of clouds—as if they'd danced and sung them away. *What just happened?* Zac wondered. What would the kids at school think if they saw Chelsea and him prancing around Porter's Store with an umbrella!

"Look at that," said Sky. "I wasn't expecting it to clear up so soon."

Zac was startled. "You mean you don't know what's going to happen?"

"When an artist begins a painting, does he know how all the details will look?"

Mulling this over, Zac had an idea. "Sky, do you think Chelsea could have a turn at making weather? Like I did yesterday?"

"I don't see why not."

"Hey, Chelsea, you can make it snow just like I did! But first you need a wind …" Closing and furling the umbrella, Chelsea followed Zac to the big wind bins while he excitedly explained the whole process of producing snow. She watched and listened, interested, but without appearing to share his enthusiasm.

"What's wrong? Don't you want to try it?"

"Maybe she'd like to do something else," suggested Sky. "Each day's weather is as unique as a snowflake. What'll it be today, Chelsea?"

Her dark eyes shining, Chelsea peered carefully all around the enormous room. Not seeming to find what she was after, she raised both hands over her head and brought them together in a single loud clap.

"Ah," said Sky. "You've asked for something very difficult. At least, difficult for you." Zac noticed that Sky was now addressing her in words. "The thing you want is contained in those steel drums along the far wall."

When they'd gathered beside the drums, Sky continued, "What's hard about this is that these containers have no lids or levers, no spouts or spigots. There's only one way to access their contents. Do you know what that is?"

Chelsea shook her head. Sky, dropping down on one knee, took her hands and moved them along the curved wood of the umbrella handle. "Feel how smooth it is? Shift your grip until it's perfectly comfortable, until the umbrella feels like a part of your arm. Okay?"

Chelsea nodded.

"Now point the umbrella at one of the drums and imagine the thing you want to happen. Ready?"

Again Chelsea nodded. Standing there with the umbrella held out like a sword, she looked as fiercely determined as a warrior.

"Now, Chelsea, there's something else you must do. You must say the name of the thing. You must speak the word aloud. Can you do that?"

At this, like a drooping flag, the umbrella slowly lowered to the floor and Chelsea hung her head.

"Yes, I understand," said Sky. "Well, then, I suppose you must try something else. Because there's really no other way."

For some time Chelsea remained with her head bowed, staring down at the slack umbrella. Then, slowly, she looked up and once more raised the umbrella until it was leveled at the drum. Zac felt something come into the room, an almost visible tingling, as if every molecule of air were a tiny angel on tiptoe. Gazing intently at Chelsea, he saw the black hair, the dark eyes, the small, bright visage, normally so cheerful, trembling now with somber emotion. He recalled a saying of Sky's: "With trust, everything is possible." Then Chelsea's jaw dropped slightly and her lower lip moved, as if purposefully forming … as if trying to utter … a word.

"No," said Sky, "it's not enough to say the word under your breath. You must speak it out loud, loud enough for the air to hear."

At once Chelsea jabbed the umbrella forward like a fencing foil and—she spoke! She actually said a word! It was just one word, and despite the force of her gesture, the sound was soft. But beyond any doubt she spoke aloud—and oh how sweet and majestic was her voice! Chelsea Cholmondeley spoke! And the word she said was—

"*Thunder!*"

Far off in the distance, like a long freight train grinding to a halt in a remote canyon, thunder rumbled. The sound was so clear and sudden that Zac's skin crawled and the hair on his neck stood up. When the reverberations died out, little Chelsea stood there with a grin on her face wide enough to drive the Aunties' Cadillac through. Then Sky took one of her hands, and Zac took the other, and the three of them danced in a joyous circle, leaning far, far back until they were nearly flying. Oh what a giddy, merry celebration they made of Chelsea's thunderous victory!

"Can I try it too, Sky?" cried Zac. "Can I make thunder? Please?"

"I think not, Zac. We're not cooking up a storm today. Chelsea's thunder was just for her."

"What did it feel like, Chelsea? What's it like to talk for the first time in—how long?"

They had stopped dancing but still held hands in a circle. Chelsea opened her mouth but nothing came out. Frowning, she broke the circle and dropped her hands.

"Come on, you can't stop now," Zac coaxed. "Talking's like eating potato chips—one word leads to another and another …"

Chelsea gazed helplessly at Zac.

"Besides, you have to tell Ches all about the Weatherworks. He won't believe me but he'll believe you. Especially when he hears you talking."

Chelsea began to shake her head.

"What do you mean? You *are* going to tell him, aren't you?"

She shook her head harder.

"But that's not fair! You have to be my witness."

"Maybe she needs time," said Sky. "Maybe one word is enough for today."

"But … what about Ches? I told him all about the Weatherworks but he refuses to come see for himself."

"That may be just the way he is. People believe what they want to, and beliefs don't easily change. Even in the face of truth."

"But he's crazy about weather. Of all the people I know, he's the one who would totally fall in love with this place."

"Maybe, maybe not. If he's worked hard to acquire his knowledge, that may be all he can see."

"But if Chelsea could tell him …"

Chelsea shot a look that made it perfectly clear this was not going to happen. For some time no one spoke. It had grown quite dark in the upper room and Sky, who now had the umbrella, pointed it toward the stairs and said softly, "Time for me to be closing."

As the children followed him down to the store, Zac was struck by a thought. "Sky, you said the umbrella will work anywhere, is that right?"

"Sure."

"And anyone can do it?"

"Yes, anyone who knows the secret."

"Well, I know this is asking a lot—but do you think maybe I could *borrow* the umbrella? I mean, just for a few minutes? I only want to run across the street and show Ches how it works. I'll keep it small—not thunder or a storm or anything—maybe just a little wind? Oh, please, Sky. It would mean so much to me to have Ches on my side …"

Zac could hardly believe his own nerve. What made him think he could take charge of all the world's weather, even for five minutes?

"I'll bring it right back. I promise. Please?"

The umbrella hooked on his arm, Sky formed a cage with his fingers and regarded Zac through it with faint amusement.

"Well, I don't see why not," he said.

"Really? You're not kidding?"

"I don't kid, Zac. Especially not kids. Here you go; she's all yours."

Without a hint of ceremony Sky offered the umbrella to Zac. His gesture was so abrupt that for a moment Zac wasn't sure whether to accept or not. Was this really what he wanted?

When he did take the umbrella, it felt surprisingly different—not light as before, but heavy, as if it held the growing darkness of the night.

"I think you know the responsibility you carry," said Sky. "But I've asked you to trust me, and I want you to know I trust you as well."

These words too had a curious weight as they came to rest in Zac's soul. More than anything else Sky had ever said, they would ring in his ears.

Chapter 26

Who Done It

Zac and Chelsea stood just inside the door of Porter's Store, studying the lay of the land. Across the five corners Ches was visible at his desk, poring over a book, no doubt absorbed in meteorological studies. At the Aunties' house there was no sign of activity.

The Aunties' house! Suddenly Zac remembered Pethybridge, languishing in his tiny basement room. He'd meant to ask Sky about him, but so enthralling was the Weatherworks, he'd completely forgotten. And now, with the umbrella in his hand, this new mission seemed equally important and it wouldn't take long. Even if Pethybridge could be helped, the problem of Dada and the Aunties remained, and for that Zac needed all the support he could get. With Ches on his side, perhaps they could win over other kids and launch a protest.

"Are you ready, Chelsea? This has to be quick. I haven't told you yet, but I've officially run away from the Aunties. I can't let them catch me, especially with the umbrella."

Chelsea nodded solemnly. Even without talking, she was a wonderful companion.

"Let's go," he said.

A minute later, the umbrella tucked under his jacket, Zac and Chelsea were tiptoeing up the back stairs of the rectory. As they reached the upper hallway, a faded nightgown came drifting along it.

"Mom!" said Chelsea.

Startled, Chelsea's mother looked straight at her, a flicker of life in the tired old face.

"Chelsea, you just …"

"Yes …"

Chelsea herself looked completely astonished at the words that flew out of her mouth like doves from a magician's hat.

"Oh, Mom … that awful man … I just couldn't …" Breaking into sobs, she fell into her mother's arms.

Mary enfolded her and stroked her shiny black hair. "Dear Chelsea, I know. My dear, dear daughter. It's all right now, it's all right …"

Even when Chelsea's tears subsided, the two hugged for a long time, then retreated to Mary's room where they sat on the edge of the bed and continued to talk in low tones. Zac lingered uncertainly outside the door until Chelsea called to him.

"Come and show Mom the umbrella. I've told her all about it."

"It's fine, dear, I don't need to see it."

"But it's right here and it's amazing! Without the umbrella I wouldn't be talking." Remarkably Chelsea spoke fluidly, though still with a sense of self-conscious awe. Her voice was a bright, musical burble that matched her sparkling eyes.

Zac, entering the room, unzipped his jacket and held out the umbrella to Mary, inviting her to take it.

"Oh my," she said. "I really don't think I should."

"Why not, Mom? It won't bite."

"Well, perhaps just a touch." Reaching out to run her fingers along the curved wood of the umbrella's handle, Mary exclaimed, "So smooth! Like ... nothing I've ever felt before."

"That's exactly where my hand was when I said my first word."

"So it's true? You really spoke to the thunder?"

"I did! You heard it, didn't you?"

"Oh, yes. And I sensed something unusual in that thunder."

"Really?"

"When it happened, I was lying right here in bed, and it made me sit straight up. Then when I heard your footsteps on the back stairs, I knew you would talk to me."

"How?"

"I dreamed it. I've had the same dream for years and last night it came more vividly than ever. I have the most beautiful dreams, you know. But my waking life, I'm afraid, is sadly lacking. I wish I'd been a better mother to you, Chelsea."

"Oh, Mom."

While Zac sat in a chair in the corner, Chelsea and her mother shared regrets, memories, and hopes as bright as the stars that shone through the small window. Eventually Mary said, "Perhaps that's enough for now, dear. We don't want to overdo it."

"But I have so much to tell you!"

"And I want to hear it all. But now I must rest."

They left her then, stretched out on the bed with an afghan tucked round her, looking happy but exhausted. Out in the hall Zac whispered, "Why is she so weak?"

"Years of sadness," said Chelsea. "That's what Eldy told me."

Sadness. Eldy. Zac's mind filled with a picture of poor Pethybridge lying in his damp bed.

"Chelsea, we really need to find Eldy. Are you sure you don't know where he is?"

"I was trying to tell you that every winter he closes up his stand. Today's the first day of winter, so he's gone. Where, I don't know." She looked dismayed. "Last winter was so hard for me, not seeing Eldy. That's why he gave me all these."

They had just entered Chelsea's room, which was full of balloons: piled on the window seat, overflowing from the closet, wedged in the bookshelves, tied in clusters to the bedposts. Zac had to laugh, and Chelsea joined him, making a lovely ripple like a stream in a sun-dappled wood. Shooing aside some balloons, she motioned him to sit beside her on the window seat, which gave a beautiful view through tree branches of Wind Mountain.

"You know what's really funny?" she said. "My mom's room is full of balloons too, only she doesn't know it. I mean, she knows they're there, but she has no idea what they do."

"They do something?"

"Of course. You don't know?"

Zac thought back to his experience with Eldy's balloons—chasing them up the mountain and then returning them. Eldy had given him one but then Auntie Pris had popped it.

"I'm not sure," said Zac.

"Dreams," said Chelsea. "They give wonderful dreams. Didn't you notice?"

Come to think of it, the night Zac had slept with the empty shell of the balloon in his pocket, he'd had beautiful dreams of his mother. And one about his box of toy soldiers …

"Full of air," Chelsea continued, "they give the sweetest daydreams. Empty, they give night dreams. My mother's not supposed to have them in her room; Dad won't allow it. But he doesn't know about that blue vase on her bedside table. I put my old balloons in there. Mom knows I do it, but she doesn't know why."

"You haven't told her?"

"We never discuss Eldy. Because Dad hates him. He forbids me to see him but I do it anyway."

"How do you get away with it?"

"He doesn't exactly pay attention. Besides"—Chelsea shrugged—"no one can stop me. Some things are just too important."

It was astonishing to hear this from a nine-year-old girl. Zac asked her how she got so brave.

"Eldy. If I stopped seeing him, I'd be as unhappy as everyone else in this family. In this town. But Eldy helps me with all my problems. I can ask him anything."

"But he doesn't say anything—he's dumb."

Chelsea threw back her head and laughed. "He's nowhere near as dumb as you, Zac Sparks! Of course he's not dumb."

"You mean he does talk?"

"You haven't figured that out?"

Zac had—and he hadn't. He needed Chelsea to confirm his own intuition. "Eldy doesn't talk out loud," he insisted.

"No. But you've still heard him, haven't you?"

Zac couldn't deny it. In some ways Eldy's interior voice was clearer than any spoken words.

"What's he said to you?" Chelsea asked.

Zac made a sudden connection. "He told me a sword would pierce my balloon, and then Pris burst it with her hatpin. He also told me no sword could destroy it, but I destroyed it myself by throwing it in the garbage."

"What! How could you?"

"I didn't know." Zac grew thoughtful. "Listen, Chelsea, have you got any roses?"

"Roses? No, why?"

"Don't you know about the roses? I mean, I'm not sure about this; it's only a guess. But the last time I saw Eldy, I was really sick. He gave me a rose and right away I felt better."

"Really? That's amazing! I remember seeing you at school when you looked so sick. I had a feeling it was …"

"Yeah …" Cautiously Zac asked, "Have you … met Dada?"

Staring out the window at the bare tree branches, Chelsea said, "I only wish I hadn't." She was silent so long that Zac grew concerned she might not speak again.

"Chelsea?"

Hopping down from the window seat, she strode to the other side of the room. With her back still turned, she said in a voice barely audible, "Dada is the reason I stopped talking."

Zac waited for more, but she remained silent, staring at the wall. Zac went to stand beside her. "Can you tell me about it?"

She shook her head. Zac was struggling too. The topic of Dada evoked such distress in him that he had no wish to pursue it. But they had to.

"Okay," he said, "I'll go first." And he proceeded to tell Chelsea everything that had happened between him and Dada: the strange power of the old man's voice; how he'd persuaded Zac to try to steal the umbrella; the horror of his appearance beneath the fur hood; and how he'd forced Zac to touch the cane, not just once but twice, and the sickness that followed.

"I know now, Chelsea, that what he and the Aunties do is steal life from kids. Just talking about it scares me. I don't want to get old and sick and ..."

Finally she turned around, her eyes wide and glistening. "Oh, Zac, I'm so sorry. I thought he must have got to you, but I wasn't sure."

"And you?"

"He tried, but I wouldn't. I just wouldn't do it. I set my mind against him and he couldn't break through. Twice the Aunties took me. And then Dad came—"

"Your *father*?"

"Yes. They all tried to make me. They beat me but I wouldn't give in. That's when I stopped talking. I didn't mean to, it just happened. I was only five and so frightened. After that Dad wouldn't talk to me either. When I kept visiting Eldy, Dad basically disowned me. But it was Eldy who gave me the strength to resist Dada."

"And what about Sky? Did you ask him for help?"

"I couldn't. I was scared of him. Ches convinced me Porter's was haunted. And I had a bad experience there when I was little ..."

Recalling the fright he'd received while decorating the Christmas tree, Zac said, "Yeah, I understand."

"And people said Dada used to go there a lot. I got the wrong idea, I guess."

"Does Ches know about Dada?"

"Sure he does. Dad took him there too."

"And he also refused?"

"No. He gave in."

"You mean he ...?"

"Yes."

Zac was confused. Why wasn't Ches an old man like Pethybridge, then?

"My brother only lost a few years," continued Chelsea. "He was Esmeralda's boy, but just for a while. For some reason it stopped, maybe when Butler came along. There was some deal, I think. Ches knows but he's not talking."

"He doesn't talk about much, does he?"

"Only the weather."

Zac sat on the edge of Chelsea's bed, and she sat beside him. Suddenly he felt tired. If this hadn't been a girl's room, he would have lain down. All this talk of Dada was depressing. Putting his hand on Chelsea's shoulder, he said, "I'm proud of you for not giving in."

Just then a shadow fell over the doorway, followed by the bulky frame of Chesterton Cholmondeley.

"Well, well," he said. "Looks mighty cozy in here. Got yourself a new boyfriend, Sis?"

Chelsea glared but said nothing. Zac stood up.

"Don't you know you've worn out your welcome here, Bud?"

"Ches, listen. The reason I came today was to see you. It's really important. Look what I brought."

Zac held up the umbrella.

"Very nice," he sneered. "A bumbershoot. You think I haven't seen one before?"

"It's not just any umbrella. It's the blue umbrella from Porter's, the one I told you about that makes all the weather."

"You brought that creepy thing here? Take it away."

"But Ches, I can prove it to you. I'll make some weather right now!"

"Look, Bud, I don't believe it, see, and I won't. Not ever."

"Then how do you explain …?"

"Don't need to," snapped Ches. "That Porter is bad news. He's got you under a spell or something."

"Then I suppose it's a spell that Chelsea is talking now!" Zac turned to her triumphantly. "You tell him, Chelsea. Go on."

Refusing to meet Zac's eye, Chelsea stared straight ahead, her face frozen, her whole body rigid.

"If this is your idea of a joke," said Ches, "it ain't funny. Besides, even if it's true about the umbrella, I think there's one little thing you're forgetting."

"What's that?"

"Didn't you tell me your mother was killed by lightning?"

"Yeah …"

"Well, lightning's *weather*, isn't it? If Porter controls all the weather, that means he also dishes out lightning, right?"

Now it was Zac's turn to fall silent, to stare straight ahead, to feel suddenly frozen inside.

"I mean," Ches continued, "he's just like old Zeus, right? Hurling thunderbolts?"

As Ches paused for effect, the silence in the room was much louder than any thunder.

"I hate to break this to you, Bud. But if Porter is who you say he is, then he's a murderer. He killed your mother."

Chapter 27

Betrayal

Zac stared at the blue umbrella in his hands. Sky Porter, a murderer? His mother's killer? How could that be? At the same time, how could it not be? If Sky controlled all the weather, then it followed he must also be in charge of lightning. How could Zac have overlooked this perfectly obvious fact?

He hadn't noticed any containers for lightning in the Weatherworks. But then, he hadn't looked. The thought of lightning had never occurred to him. And yet hadn't he just witnessed Chelsea producing thunder? Where there was thunder, there was lightning.

"No, no," he moaned. "It can't be."

"Must be," insisted Ches. "Porter bumped off your old lady. And he did it with that umbrella."

Zac had once seen a picture of an umbrella with a tiny gun concealed in the shaft. A respectable gentleman could have walked down a busy street, nonchalantly pointed his umbrella at someone, and *bang*! Sky Porter's umbrella, Zac realized, was just like that: a deadly weapon in disguise. Moreover, if Sky had caused one death, he'd caused a million. How many other people had been killed by lightning?

And what about floods, tornadoes, hurricanes? That was all weather too.

Zac's whole body was shaking violently. He was holding this thing, this wicked instrument of death, in his own hands. He felt like throwing it out the window. Or in the garbage. Or going and smashing Sky Porter's skull with it. That big story he'd told about his bravery in school, standing up to Auntie Esmeralda with her cane ... why, a few whacks with a cane was nothing compared to zapping people with lightning bolts!

Zac was betrayed. Deceived, taken in, suckered. It was Mr. Pottinger all over again: the friendly, fascinating neighbor who kept promising great things that never came to pass. All lies. Didn't Zac know better than to trust any adult, especially a man? The only adult who'd ever been worthy of trust was his mother. Now she was dead—and who had done it? A man! A man who seemed so nice, so wonderful. But underneath ... a murderer.

Blind with hurt and rage, Zac jumped to his feet, elbowed past Ches in the doorway, and bolted from the room. Behind him he heard Ches say, "Sit tight, Sis, you aren't going anywhere." Then he called after Zac, "So long, Bud. At least you've got cover if it rains. Ha ha."

Outside it was fully dark. At the moment Zac emerged, as if to rub salt in his wound, thunder rumbled in the distance. He paused to search the horizon. The sky was clear and star-studded, except in the west toward the Big City, where sheet lightning glimmered among inky clouds. What was Porter up to now? Would more people die tonight? How much could he do without the umbrella?

A wind stirred and it was cold. Zac zipped up his jacket, tucking the umbrella inside. Huddled behind a hedge, he peered into the night and felt as if all good had fled from the world. Across the street the Aunties' house blazed with light. For some reason his eye was drawn to the one dark corner, the windowless dining room. He recalled the oil painting that hung there, the one of a smirking boy in old-fashioned clothes. Dada. Though he'd seen that portrait just once, he saw it again now as vividly as if it hung not inside the house but outside, facing him. Its eyes locked into his and, as before, Zac had the strange impression that the boy in black spoke to him.

Suddenly he knew what he had to do. At one level he knew it was not a good idea, but it was so compelling that it carried him along. Making sure no one was about, he darted across the street to the dark corner of the Aunties' house, then crept along the wall toward the lighted parlor window. There, silhouetted in the wingback chair, was the lanky, black-suited form of Reverend Cholmondeley. Zac imagined the Aunties opposite him, seated primly on the love seat in all their glittering vileness.

He nearly turned back. But no, he had to do this. He needed to do something bad. To get back. Besides, the Aunties had something he wanted, and he intended to get it. Nothing else mattered anymore.

Should he ring the doorbell? Waltz in boldly and announce himself? Or sneak in? For no other reason than just to please himself, he opted for sneaking. He could do anything he wanted now. No one had a hold on him anymore. He was free from them all.

After stashing the umbrella in the bushes, silent as a cat he stole onto the Aunties' porch, slipped through the front door, and stood in the brightly lit hallway. Voices drifted to him from the parlor.

"… haven't seen him anywhere, I assure you," Reverend Cholmondeley was saying. "I wonder if Porter has him?"

"Curse that man! He ruins everything."

"Calm yourself, Pris. Even if the boy is with Porter now, he's bound to come looking for Chesterton."

"Chesterton! That son of yours was supposed to keep an eye on him."

"And he has, Pris, he has. He's done a good job of befriending the boy. I promise you, that scalawag won't go far."

"He'd better not, Edgerton, or your son will be next." This came from Esmeralda, her voice sounding eerier than ever. "You know what I need, and Barber can't last forever."

"You're not using Barber!" snapped Pris. "There's no reason Chesterton can't supply you."

"Now, Priscilla," said the Reverend.

"Pris, I'm sick! I will use whomever I please."

"Ladies, ladies, everything will work out, I'm sure. It's just a matter of waiting for the mouse to emerge from his hole."

And then Zac Sparks stepped into the parlor. Three pairs of eyes drove into him like nails.

"Seize him!" cried Pris.

Reverend Cholmondeley leapt from his chair and in three strides was across the room. Face to face with Zac, however, he seemed uncertain what to do. Meanwhile Pris stumped heavily over and pinned Zac's arms behind his back. Zac let it happen; it didn't matter to him. Only one thing mattered.

Esmeralda remained reclining on the couch, covered with a blanket. Staring straight at her, Zac said, "I'm sorry I ran away, Auntie. I was only trying to do what you asked me to. And now I've done it."

Slowly, with obvious effort, Esmeralda rose to a sitting position. "What's that? What are you saying?"

"I have what you want, Auntie."

Pris gave his arm a hard twist. "Don't fool with us, Boy, if you know what's good for you."

"I'm not fooling! I promise you. Let me go and I'll show you."

Esmeralda, sinking back down, said weakly, "Bring him here, Pris."

Zac let himself be manhandled across the room until he stood just inches from Esmeralda. He was shocked at her appearance. She looked about a hundred years older.

"All right," she whispered, "what's your game?"

Zac couldn't help staring. She barely looked human. Finally he said, "It's no game, Auntie. I've done what you asked. All I want is one thing in return."

Again Pris wrenched his arm, snarling, "You dare to bargain with us?"

"Just a small thing!" he cried.

"A small thing?" said Esmeralda. "I, too, have a small thing I want from you." Her eyes bored into him hungrily.

Her words didn't quite register. Zac had only one thing on his mind.

"I have the umbrella," he said quietly. "Do you want it, or don't you?"

The three adults gasped. Esmeralda half rose from her couch and seized the collar of Zac's jacket.

"The umbrella!" she wheezed. "You have it?"

"You'd better not be lying!" barked Pris.

"I'm not lying. I can give it to you right now. All I want is the picture of my mother. The one you stole."

"The umbrella?" Esmeralda repeated. "Porter's umbrella? The blue one?"

"Yes, yes, I have it. It's hidden outside. But I want the picture. Is it a deal?"

Esmeralda's eyes blazed. "Give me the umbrella right now and you'll have your picture."

"No," insisted Zac. "The picture first, then the umbrella."

Esmeralda, emitting a long, rattling sigh, reached beneath the blanket and drew out her snakeskin purse. Snapping it open, she produced the small photograph, which she held aloft before Zac's eyes. Then abruptly she crumpled it into a tight ball and thrust the wad of paper into his jacket pocket.

"Don't let go of him, Pris. And you, Edgerton, go with them. Be back in two minutes, Boy, or more than that photograph will be crushed."

Infuriated, Zac wanted to kick her in the face. But he did have the picture now, and just having it in his pocket soothed him. Dully he let Pris frog-march him to the front door, Reverend Cholmondeley at their heels, and he led them straight to the bush where he'd concealed the umbrella. He was almost surprised to see it still there. Pris snatched it up and a minute later they were back in the parlor.

"Can it be true? Is this really Porter's umbrella?" Esmeralda, cradling it in both arms and gazing raptly, ran one clawlike hand along the curved handle. Then, comparing it with her cane lying on the back of the couch, she whispered, "This is it, Pris."

The heads of the three adults bent together. No one held Zac anymore; he could have escaped. But he didn't. He was in a kind of trance, stupefied. What had he done? Already, somewhere far out on the horizon of his heart, a dull horror was lifting its head. The black boy in the oil painting would be not just smirking now, but laughing.

"I have to hand it to you, Boy," said Esmeralda. "You've exceeded my expectations. How did you get it?"

"I convinced Mr. Porter to loan it to me," said Zac, "just for a little while. And then I brought it straight to you."

Everyone was plainly amazed.

"Congratulations!" enthused Pris with something akin to genuine heartiness. "We thought Porter had you wrapped around his little finger."

"Porter's no friend of mine," Zac heard himself say.

"Remarkable," said Reverend Cholmondeley, stroking the umbrella's canopy. "Simply remarkable."

"Open it up, Edgerton," said Esmeralda. "I want to see for myself."

Taking the umbrella, Reverend Cholmondeley handled it as carefully as a stick of dynamite. After undoing the strap and letting the furls of the canopy fall loose, he paused, as though anything at all might emerge from within. Already the interior was partially visible. It was quite black, so much so that darkness seemed to leak into the room from the trembling folds of cloth. With the sliding of the golden ring up the shaft came the familiar rustling sound, then a surprising rush of cold wind as though some large, winged creature had flown through the room, bringing the night with it. In quivering hands the Reverend carried the open umbrella to the parlor window where he held it up beside the dark glass. Everyone saw how the underside of the canopy perfectly matched the outer sky. Reverend Cholmondeley was so startled he dropped the umbrella.

"Enough!" croaked Esmeralda. "Close it up."

Clearly the weird sense of the night being brought inside had an unnerving effect on everyone in the room. So when Esmeralda said, "Come here, Boy," Zac went and stood beside the couch without thinking. Esmeralda didn't worry him; he was beyond her. His hand was around the little ball of paper in his pocket, smoothing it. Everything would be all right now.

"You've done well," she said, "though I can't help but question your motives."

"It's only an umbrella," Zac lied. He saw no point in letting on that he knew anything.

"Never mind that. But in return for your help, I'd like to give you something."

Surprisingly she held out the cane to him.

"Take it. Please. My gift."

Puzzled, Zac put his hand on the cane. Immediately he felt Esmeralda's fingers close around his. Her grip was like a bite, the long nails puncturing his skin. He could not tear his hand away, and he felt his other arm pinned behind him.

How stupid he'd been! So consumed was he with getting back at Sky and retrieving his mother's photograph, he'd completely overlooked what more this might cost him. Now, trapped, he surrendered. He could not take another betrayal. Why care about anything anymore? The very ground beneath him crumbled and he felt himself sliding down, down, down.

"There's a good boy," sighed Esmeralda.

He was tired, so tired. His stomach turned over, his head swam, he lurched forward onto the couch, and deep inside him something wavered and went out like a candle flame. Finally Esmeralda roughly shoved him aside and, now revived, erupted to her feet.

"Give me that umbrella, Edgerton. Oh, I feel like a girl again! I could dance!"

"Why, I've never seen you dance in my life," said the Reverend.

"Put on some music, Pris. Let's celebrate!"

"Esmeralda, control yourself. Be careful with that umbrella. We have to call Dada."

"Forget Dada. I'm going to dance with the umbrella …"

Dimly Zac was aware of Esmeralda's ecstatic babbling. And then he was gone.

He awoke to the buzz of voices. Loud voices. At first he didn't know what they were saying. Didn't care. *Please*, he thought, *just let me sleep*. But the voices kept rising. An argument. Two women. One with a husky growl like a bear's—he could feel it right through the floor—the other whispery but forceful, penetrating as the hiss of a snake.

He opened his eyes. He was in his room at the Aunties' house. It was dark. Window boarded up. Not pitch dark; dimly he could make out objects drained of color. A crack of gray light leaked from under the door.

As if bursting from underwater, he awoke to full consciousness. His ears popped open and now the voices were so clear that, though he knew they were downstairs, they sounded present in his room.

"No, Esmeralda, if you use it, Dada will be livid."

"He's always livid. Besides, Pris, he wants it warm too. You know he does."

"Warm! You mean to raise the temperature?"

"Of course."

"No, you don't. If anything, we'll make it cold."

"Cold? I've been cold all my life. I'm sick of living in these furs."

"Don't you think I'm sick of sweating?"

"It's your own fault for being such a fat pig."

"Esmeralda!"

"It's true, Pris. Why don't you lose some weight?"

"I'm not fat, I'm just big. If anyone should lose weight it's you—from your fat head."

"We'll see who's fat when I turn up the temperature."

There were sounds of a scuffle.

"Take your hands off this umbrella!"

"No—you can't use it."

"I *will* use it. I'll make it hot, nice and hot."

"Then I'll make it cold."

"Hot!"

"Cold!"

"Hot!"

"Cold!"

Zac pictured the Aunties tugging the umbrella back and forth. A heavy thud told him they'd fallen to the floor. Furniture scraped, china shattered. There were grunts, squeals, screams …

A tremendous concussion shook the house, like two locomotives crashing in midair. At once Zac's room was engulfed in thick white smoke and the walls seemed to rush toward him.

Frightened, bewildered, he felt in his pocket, but the photograph, of course, was gone. Overcome, he closed his eyes and fell a long way back into sleep.

Chapter 28

Christmas Adam

He awoke to silence. And whiteness. A cottony haze that felt like being inside a cloud. He rubbed his eyes but could see nothing. He seemed to have lost his sight.

Then, suddenly, he could see. Not much, but a little. Just as suddenly the filmy whiteness returned; then parted like veils; then closed again. For a long time he lay still, drifting in and out of the gray gloom, trying not to think. Trying very hard not to enter the painful realm of consciousness. But one thought, one terrible memory, he could not avoid: his last encounter with Esmeralda.

He, Zac Sparks, of his own accord had given that evil witch some of his youth. How much, he didn't know. How much older was he today? How much closer to the grave?

On the heels of this terrible thought came another: the blue umbrella. Had he really surrendered it to the Aunties? Yes, and a part of him was still—in a bitter sort of way—glad. Why should he care who had it? After all, on the one hand were the Aunties who took their time murdering people; on the other hand was Sky Porter who did it swiftly. Some choice.

310

But this brought him to a third terrible thought: Pethybridge. Two floors below, on a cot in a small room, lay a man—no, a boy—who was dying from a disease that Zac also had. How could Zac have deserted him? Smitten with guilt, he saw how selfish he'd been. Of course, the discovery that Sky Porter was a killer had come as a shock. But Sky was also the only person who might know where Eldy was, which was why Zac had gone to see him in the first place—to get a rose to cure Pethybridge.

A rose! Jolted alert, Zac sat up in bed. Though his head swam and the cobwebby haze still clung to his eyes, he managed to put his feet on the floor. Kneeling down, he peered under the bed but saw nothing. Lying flat, he reached as far as he could and felt all around. But no—there was nothing except the chamber pot. His rose was not where he had left it.

Distraught, he sat on the floor and tried to steady his whirling thoughts. Whatever else he'd done wrong, neglecting Pethybridge was the worst and he had to set that right. He had to get a rose for his friend. But what if Pethybridge was already dead? What if he perished, finally, not just from the cane's dark magic but from Zac's neglect?

Stumbling to the window and removing the knot, Zac pressed his eye to the hole. Even outside he couldn't see a thing. It was obviously daytime, but the light was grayish, woolly, opaque. Groping, swept with nausea, somehow he made his way to the door and out into the hall. Periodically the air cleared enough to reveal drifting rags of mist like little clouds. He paused, debating which way to go to check on Pethybridge.

His best hope, he decided, was to escape out the front door, counting on the poor visibility for camouflage. Once outside, he could creep around back to Pethybridge's window.

He felt his way along the banister to the bottom of the staircase, where he stopped to listen. Silence. Everything seemed dead. As he pressed on across the front hall, it seemed such a long way; any moment hands might reach out to grab him. At one point his foot brushed a large china vase on the floor. It shifted, rocked on its base, but didn't topple. In the eerie mist its hollow clatter sounded hugely magnified. But finally the echoes died and all was still.

Slipping out the front door, Zac was met by a wall of white. Dense, moist, palpable. Inside he'd been able to make out ghostly shapes, but now he couldn't even see his hand in front of his face. The air felt heavy as wet wool and it smelled like freshly dug earth.

Fog. Must be fog—impossibly thick, so white it was dark. Zac was blind. How strange: able to see, yet seeing nothing. As if the whole world were a blindfold.

Inching across the porch, feeling ill, dizzy, he searched with his toe for the edge of the steps. Though he felt solid wood, nothing else was solid. In no time he was completely disoriented. Though he'd just left the house, already he had no idea where it was. Front, back, left, and right had disappeared. Even up and down seemed uncertain, as if the bandaging whiteness affected not just his eyes but also his mind.

Taking baby steps, sweeping his hands before him, he sought a post, a wall, anything. How could a mere porch be so vast? Finally he stood still, trying desperately to get his bearings. Nothing. Nothing but blank, vacant whiteness.

He was lost. Standing outside a familiar house in a place he had come to know well, Zac Sparks was utterly lost. And so sick. If only he could lie down again …

Then he heard a sound. At first he took it for a bird singing, far off. One note, two notes, repeated. High, lyrical, the music pierced the fog. Gradually other notes were added and the melody grew more and more elaborate. Couldn't possibly be a bird; must be a person. Not a radio, either, but a living person. Someone was singing.

Zac knew that voice. He'd heard it before.

O?

Yes, it was O, the town drunk, singing her heart out. Nearer now, so near. And oh how beautiful! Pure, bell-like, perfect in tone and clarity—more lovely than a meadowlark, more incredible than an angel. It was a kind of Celtic melody, intricately woven in an endless pattern of interlacing whorls. Zac was enraptured. As the dense fog smothered his mind, so O's song lightened his heart. Though the music was wordless, there seemed to be a message: "Come … Come to me …"

So close was the voice now that he could almost pinpoint its location. Just across the street? Somewhere behind Porter's Store? As much as Zac disliked the thought of going anywhere near that place, he did want to follow this voice. He needed to. The song was for him.

As if taking hold of a thin, silken rope tossed to him through the white night, he set out to follow. He still couldn't see, but he had a sense of direction, of bearings. Finding the edge of the steps, he descended confidently, not even steadying himself on the railing. He sensed when his feet would touch the gravel path, knew exactly the number of paces to reach the cement sidewalk. He walked not tentatively but easily, normally, forgetting all about his queasy dizziness and the fog. He moved as if all around him were plain as day, and with each step O's song grew clearer and lovelier.

He crossed the street. He entered the alley beside the store. He followed the lane to its end, then headed toward the smaller building behind the store. All this without being able to see a thing—yet he knew exactly where he was. Arriving at the rear door of the umbrella factory, he put his hand on the latch. Though he'd never entered this way, he knew he had to. The song was just behind this door.

Lifting the latch, he peered inside. Suddenly he could see. There were the long tables with the big rolls of fabric for making umbrella covers. There were the smaller tables with sewing machines, and the rows of green-shaded lightbulbs hanging from the ceiling. And there were the completed umbrellas, some furled in stands, some tied in bundles, others open and suspended in air. It was all just as Zac had seen it before with the old men, except now the room was partially obscured by shifting veils of mist. Visibility, for some reason, was better indoors, whereas outside the fog bulked against the windows like the fur of some great albino animal.

Zac's eyes combed the room. Though O's song was clearer now than ever, he saw no sign of anyone. Having never met O, he had no idea what to expect. But he was not afraid; instead he felt a luminous peace. The song seemed to be coming from one of the sewing machines in the far corner. Though the machine was visible, the chair behind it was hidden by a curtain of mist.

Making his way between the long tables, he moved closer. The sewing machine was operating, thrumming like the rapid beating of small wings. Above this floated the song, piercingly lovely, like aural threads of gold and silver stitching molecules of air into an exquisite design.

About three steps from the small table, he stopped. The veil of mist was moving, parting. And there, seated at the machine, appeared the form of a woman, her face, inclined slightly as she pored over her work, obscured by a cascade of shimmering hair. She was young and beautiful. Could this possibly be the old hag whom everyone knew as the town drunk? Could a hag sing so beautifully and have such lovely hair? Somehow that hair—radiant, chocolate brown—brought a lump to Zac's throat. And that white dress with the lace collar and poofy sleeves—where had he seen that before? And the way those fingers moved, and that certain manner of tilting the head, and …

Zac started to cry.

The woman, still singing, looked up. She smiled at him, her whole face bathed, not just in the overhanging light, but in its own inner glow.

"Mom!" he cried.

There was no doubt about it: The woman at the sewing machine, singing as only O could sing, was Zac's mother. He wanted to rush to her and bury his face in her hair, his whole self in her arms. But his feet stayed put. Somehow he knew not to come any closer, even as her song reached out to him wordlessly in welcome, enfolding him like a hug, bathing him in kisses, showering him in tender love. Without so much as touching fingers, he felt no distance at all between them. The terrible gap of the past few weeks, the awful chasm of the grave, closed and Zac was with his mother again, closer than ever before.

She stopped singing, and now the silence that rested between them, like a dove alighting, was even more beautiful than her song. Zac's soul swelled with the music of pure love, and with it love's perfect understanding. His mind, meanwhile, understood nothing. His thoughts protested, *How can this be?—she's dead!*

Then, wonder of wonders, she spoke. "Hello, Zachary. How marvelous to see you again!"

Zac was speechless.

"Do you know what today is?"

He shook his head.

Leaning closer, she whispered as excitedly as a little girl, "It's Christmas Adam!"

Christmas Adam. If Zac had any shred of doubt that this really was his mother, it fled now. Only his own mother could know about Christmas Adam. She and Zac had invented it themselves. On December 23, when he was six, he'd asked her seriously, "If tomorrow is Christmas Eve, does that make today Christmas Adam?" She'd laughed long and musically, then explained that Adam and Eve did not really figure in Christmas.

316

Still, it struck her as a fine idea and why shouldn't they celebrate? And so was launched their first Christmas Adam party, complete with singing carols, reading stories, baking cookies, doing crafts. And always after that, come December 23 they said, "Today is Christmas Adam, tomorrow's Christmas Eve, and the next day we raise Cain!"

Zac's eyes brimmed with tears as the memories flooded.

"Do you remember those special cookies I used to make?" said his mother. "Peanut butter chocolate chip with cornflakes on top?"

Did he ever! They were the best cookies in the world. He could practically taste them right now. It was something else that only Zac's own, real mother could possibly know.

"You were always doing special things for me. You loved me so much!"

"I love you still, Zachary. Love never ends."

In the silence she resumed her sewing. The machine hummed, then stopped.

"Do you remember," she said, "when you picked all the roses in my garden—every last one—and brought me a bouquet?"

Zac felt a twinge of embarrassment. But his mother was laughing.

"Oh, Zachary, how lovable you are! Always so full of life."

His mother's words both melted and stung him.

"Mom, you don't know … I mean, right now I'm so messed up …"

"Yes. That's why I want you to do something for me."

"For you? Anything."

"I want you to have a merry Christmas."

Merry Christmas? With all that was happening, Zac hadn't had time even to think about Christmas, let alone be merry about it. Again he filled up with tears.

"Oh, Mom, I've been so bad."

"Have you? Then just be good again."

"You don't understand. I've done some things … terrible things …"

"Well, now do something wonderful. Something to change it all."

Her tone was so hopeful!

"But how? What do you mean?"

"Christmas is for giving. That's how to make it merry. You know what you can give, don't you?"

Yes, he knew.

"You have some Christmas shopping to do. What you're looking for—you'll find it upstairs."

With these words the woman at the sewing machine vanished behind a veil of mist.

"Don't leave me!" he cried. "I'm so alone—"

"You're not alone, Zachary," came her voice. "No one is ever alone."

She was gone. Zac waited for the mist to clear, but it did not. He waited quite a while, fervently willing, praying. Nothing.

At last he knew he must go.

Chapter 29

The Man Upstairs

Zac left the umbrella factory, not by the rear door where he'd entered, but along the breezeway that connected to Porter's Store. Here the fog, once again, was dense as a witch's brew and he had to feel his way along by the railing. Twice he halted, not just disoriented but dismayed. His mother had directed him upstairs, and he knew she meant the Weatherworks. He didn't want to go there—what if he ran into Sky?—but he knew he must. With the image of his mother still before him, he pressed on.

Inside the store the fog again thinned to drifting scarves of mist. He paused to listen for familiar sounds—the ring of the cash register, the old men at their card games, Sky's voice. But no—all was quiet. Good. It dawned on Zac that if today really was December 23, he must have slept away two full nights and a day. Just thinking this brought back his sick, weak feeling and he had to collapse on one of the old men's chairs. Peering around, his eyes fell on the Christmas tree, glowing quietly in the front window. But this only reminded him of the shock he'd experienced while perched on a ladder inches below the upper floorboards. Hearing those footsteps again in his mind, he shivered. Whoever—or whatever—lived upstairs, he had no desire to meet it.

From where he sat, a few feet from Sky's office, he could almost see inside, and this spooked him too. What *would* he say to the man whose most precious possession he had stolen? Straining his ears, he listened. Silence. Yet it was the sort of silence that seemed to shimmer with presence. Though the building looked empty, it didn't feel so.

Finally Zac had to force himself to stand up. Filled with trepidation, he mounted the staircase. Each step made a noise of its own—a creak, a groan, a nearly human sigh. He struggled to go on. As his eyes reached the level of the upper floor, he stopped. Still nothing.

Finally he was standing in the vast storeroom of the Weatherworks. It was dim, nearly dark. With fog clogging the three skylights, just enough light leaked through to make ghostly shapes of the large barrels, the jars, the boxes and sacks and bins that held the weather. It was impossible even to tell the time of day. It might have been the dawn of creation, or twilight at the end of the world.

What to do? His mother had spoken of Christmas shopping; she said he would find what he was looking for up here. But where? Hugging a wall beside the stores of weather, he crept through the grayish gloom. Rain, hail, dew, clouds— the familiar commodities seemed so strange, like the mystic potions of alchemy. Almost alive, they sat brooding, each with its own primitive personality. As Zac knew only too well, there *was* a personality behind them, a real person whom fearfully he

320

expected to meet at any moment. Stealing along, he felt like a thief—and then remembered he was one.

He saw a light. In a corner at the far end of the building, a single light burned. Drawing closer, he saw a naked bulb in a conical green shade, like the ones in the umbrella factory. This one hung inside a glassed-in office he had not noticed before. The glass was pebbled, milky, except for one clear panel in the door. On the small pane of clear glass was a line of gold lettering. Zac had to come very close to decipher it. In old-fashioned script it read:

$$\mathscr{E}.\ \mathscr{P}orter,\ \mathscr{P}rop.$$

Puzzling over this inscription, suddenly he became aware of a presence behind him. Whipping around, he gasped to see a tall, hovering figure. At the same time, he recognized something he'd seen before—a bulky, woolen sweater, dark blue. And he found himself looking up into a face that also seemed familiar—weathered, dark-complexioned, aged yet handsome.

"Welcome, Zachary. I've looked forward to meeting you again face-to-face."

That voice, too, rang a bell. Uncertainly Zac stared at the tall man. He wanted to ask, "Have we met before?" but the words stuck in his throat.

"Yes," answered the man as if he'd heard. "But the last time was outside. Though one can hardly call the Weatherworks inside."

What was he talking about? Who was this person?

"Are you the ... g-ghost?" Zac stammered.

Throwing wide his arms, the man laughed. "Do I look like a ghost?" Indeed he did not. He fairly burst with robustness. "Perhaps I should introduce myself." Sweeping one arm across his stomach, the other behind his back, he bowed low and held that pose for several seconds, so that Zac found himself staring at a bald pate fringed with white hair and dotted with dark brown age spots—as many, it seemed, as the stars in the sky.

Then Zac knew him.

"Eldy!"

"Yes, Eldy Porter, at your service." Straightening up, he was a good six feet tall.

"But ... why aren't you all bent over?"

"Goodness, I can't hold that position forever, can I? Would you like to bend over all the time?"

"Uh, no. But I thought that's just how you were."

"That is how I am at the balloon and flower stand. But here I like to stretch a little."

"But why ...?"

"Why the disguise? It's not, really. A disguise hides true identity. But I don my other appearance to reveal myself. For years I went around openly but was never accepted. Alas, people were afraid of me. I love people; I love being with them. So now I'm just a little old man who sells balloons and flowers." Eldy's smile was as warm as sunshine.

"You called yourself Eldy Porter," said Zac. "Does that mean you're Sky's father?"

"The same," said Eldy.

"But … you don't look anything like Sky!"

It was true. Sky's face was decidedly homely, whereas this man, despite his age, glowed with good looks.

Eldy chuckled. "Poor Sky—he takes after his mother. For that very reason I hoped he'd be more approachable, less threatening to people. But sadly they're as leery of his power as they were of mine."

"You mean … over the weather?"

"That's it. When people find out about the blue umbrella, they tend to back off."

Awkwardly Zac looked away. Did Eldy know what he'd done?

"My goodness, Zachary, I'm forgetting my manners. Would you like some hot chocolate?" Extending a hand, Eldy Porter invited Zac into his office. It was small, square, sparsely furnished, dominated by a large drafting table covered with blueprints. On the wall hung a cloud chart.

Using almost the same mannerisms as Sky, Eldy opened two pouches of hot chocolate, emptied them into mugs, and set the kettle to boil. Also like Sky, he directed Zac to the upholstered swivel chair at the drafting table, while he pulled up a wooden stool.

"This is where I hole up for the winter," he said. "I'm here every night, too. Sky does all the weather now; I just handle deliveries, mainly after dark. It's a good arrangement, lets me keep my hand in."

"Deliveries?" said Zac.

"Through the skylights."

As Eldy gestured overhead, Zac flashed back to his first night in Five Corners, to the bright lights he'd seen over the store. When he described this, Eldy said, "Yes, come to think of it, that night we got in a shipment of lightning."

"Lightning!" Zac stiffened. So it was true. Sky and his father really did deal in lightning bolts. One stored them, the other released them. What was Zac doing, talking to such a man? Before, the mystery of the flashing lights had fascinated him. Now he was repulsed.

The old man was studying him. Reading his thoughts? If so, Eldy didn't let on.

"We keep lightning in porcelain urns," he said casually, "something like those large vases in the Henbother house. But of course on a grander scale." He grinned. "Porcelain's a fine insulator, so the lightning's quite safe—though it's a job getting the bigger bolts into the urns. Bit like rasslin' broncos."

Zac was horrified. How could someone talk so lightly about the weapon that had killed his mother? At the same time, he was intrigued. "One night last week I was decorating the Christmas tree downstairs, and I heard ... or felt ... like a loud crackling ..."

"Yup," said Eldy, "that was me, manhandling bolts. There's a whole lot of popping and sparking goes on with those brutes."

Zac's mind raced. Despite the subject something about Eldy's voice, his whole presence, was reassuring. Gentle, calm, friendly. Confused, Zac studied the blueprints on the drafting table: creamy, midnight-blue sheaves etched with white lines that glowed softly like starlight.

"Lovely, aren't they?" said Eldy. "Weather doesn't just happen; it has to be planned. That's mainly what I do up here. I love these long winter nights, poring over plans for the new year. And deliveries are so much easier now. In the old days, every morning I'd hitch up the horses and drive up Wind Mountain to the mine, load the day's weather, and haul it back to the store. Used to be a ramp outside so I could bring the carriage right up top to the big double doors."

Surprised, Zac looked up. "You got weather from a mine?"

"Where'd you think it came from?"

Zac waved vaguely. "Out there, I guess. Up above."

"Yes, weather does come from above, but also from below. There's weather at the earth's core."

At Zac's perplexed look, Eldy continued, "Consider a beautiful sunset. What do you think makes all those colors?"

"Sunlight?"

"Right. But also dust. It's the two together. Or take rain: Though it falls from the sky, it originates in bodies of water fed partly by underground springs. So you see, earthly ingredients are necessary. Weather is really the interaction between four elements—earth, air, water, fire."

"Fire?"

"Sure. Fire comes down from the sun, but also up from below in volcanoes. Volcanoes have a huge impact on weather."

This was all very interesting, but Zac was stuck on the lightning problem. And he was still struggling with the mystery of this wizard of weather being the same person who sold balloons and flowers from a stand.

"Sky built a tunnel," Eldy went on, "from the mine to the store, making use of the natural cave system under the mountain. We thought if the really big weather, at least, could be conveyed more discreetly, people might be more accepting. But it hasn't worked out that way. Sky is still shunned, as I was."

Zac squirmed. Hadn't he, too, turned against Sky, alienated by his power?

Hearing a noise, they looked toward the door. Someone was there, just outside, someone whose head barely came up to the bottom of the window. Eldy rose to open the door.

"Well, look who's here."

"Eldy!" cried a small voice.

Eldy stood aside as a black-haired girl entered the office.

"What are you doing here!" exclaimed Zac and Chelsea at once.

She answered first. "I followed O's song and met Eldy down in the umbrella factory."

"What!"

"I was so surprised to see him standing upright. And we both talked *out loud*!" Then to Eldy she said, "But how can you be up here, too?"

"He's been here all along," said Zac. "But what about my mother? Did you see her down there?"

"Your mother? I don't even know your mother. You said she died."

"Yes, but …"

"Perhaps I can explain," Eldy interjected. "You both followed the sound of O's voice through the fog, and you both met someone different. That's because when O appears, she takes the form of the person you love most. For Zachary, that's his mother. For Chelsea, I'm honored to say, it's me."

Readily accepting his explanation, Chelsea said, "I do love you best of anyone, Eldy. No one's ever been as good to me as you have."

Zac was more skeptical. "You mean that wasn't really my mother?"

"Of course it was. She told you things only your mother could know, didn't she? O doesn't lie; she's not an impostor."

"Is O … real?"

"She's real, all right. She's just completely self-effacing. She shines through everyone who loves, so they're seen and known as they truly are. Even people who are no longer here."

Zac pressed his hands to his head. "But Eldy, how could you—or O—be in two places at once, both downstairs with Chelsea and up here with me?"

Eldy scratched his bald pate. "Well, let's just say love is a mystery. It has no limits."

Chelsea was beaming. "Eldy, will I always be able to find you in winter now?"

"Any time you wish. Just listen to O."

Eldy peered out at the fog that now, even in the Weatherworks, had grown denser. "If it's like this on Christmas Eve," he reflected, "Rudolph will have his work cut out for him."

"Rudolph?"

"The red-nosed reindeer. But it's no joke. A fog like this can kill."

"Really?"

"Oh, yes. Traffic accidents, drownings, respiratory problems. Ike and Joe and Abe—they all have lung conditions."

A terrible feeling crept over Zac. He didn't want to say anything but his question spilled out anyway: "Are people dying in this fog?"

"Too soon to say," replied Eldy. "But frankly, I'm concerned. It's so heavy and it's come up so quickly. You don't happen to know anything about it, do you?"

The look Eldy gave Zac was impossible to interpret. Why would he think Zac knew something about the fog? Until that moment, Zac himself had not deduced its cause. But recalling the Aunties' fight over the umbrella—one wanting it hot, the other cold—suddenly he understood. Their two opposing wishes must have created extreme hot and cold fronts that, colliding, had produced a remarkably thick fog.

Zac's left leg started jiggling. He felt defensive, afraid. Realizing Sky was responsible for his mother's death had made him angry. Now it appeared that many more people might die from the fog, and who was responsible for that? Zac Sparks. And how much more harm might the Aunties do with the umbrella he had given them?

As much as Zac wanted to change the subject, he answered Eldy's question. "Yes, I do know something about this fog. It's all because of me. Sky let me borrow the umbrella, just for a little while, so I could show it to Ches. I meant to return it right away but … something came over me and … I gave the umbrella to the Aunties."

"You *what*? Zachary Sparks—how could you do such a thing?" Chelsea was yelling. Now that she was talking, it was clear she had a good set of lungs. As for Eldy, he didn't bat an eye.

"I don't care," Zac blustered, "I'm mad at Sky! He killed my mother. He murdered her with a lightning bolt! It's no wonder people don't like him." Immediately he wanted to take back these words, but it was too late.

"Are you sure it was Sky?" asked Eldy gently.

"He makes the weather, doesn't he? He's the one who throws lightning bolts."

Rising, Eldy came around the drafting table and took the boy's two hands in his. "Listen to me, Zachary. My son is not a murderer. What Sky and I do here in the Weatherworks isn't the only factor that affects the weather. People have a vast impact, mostly through pollution—smog and so on. The blue umbrella doesn't do any of that. But among all the bad influences, the worst is the cane."

"The cane! You mean it affects the weather too?"

"Oh yes, that cane plays havoc."

Recalling what Pethybridge had told him, Zac asked, "Is the cane really the blue umbrella's old handle?"

"It is," said Eldy. "That cane is rightfully mine."

"I bet you never used it to beat children!" said Chelsea.

"Oh no, it was never meant to be used on people at all."

Before Zac could stop himself he blurted, "But you tried to kill Dada with it!"

Frowning, Eldy resumed his seat on the stool. "I don't know what you've heard, but let me tell you what really happened. Rutherford Henbother lived across the street. I watched Esmeralda and Priscilla grow up. Rutherford also watched me. He was curious about my umbrella and how every morning I drove a wagon up Wind Mountain. In those days everyone knew I controlled the weather; it was common knowledge. But not many knew how, nor did they care. One morning, however, Rutherford followed me up the mountain. The weather that day began calmly, but with the umbrella I released some dramatic effects. Guessing its purpose, Rutherford coveted the umbrella for himself. And so he attacked me."

"You mean you weren't out to get him?"

"I'm not out to get anybody. Rutherford attacked me from behind. As we wrestled, both tugging at the umbrella, he stumbled off the edge of the mountain. I tried to hang onto him—he had the curved end of the handle, I had the other—but the canopy came off in my hands." Eldy sighed. "Rutherford fell thirty feet onto a rock ledge. It broke his fall but also his neck. He was left paralyzed."

"And that's how he got the cane?"

"Yes. As for the umbrella, O made a new handle for the old canopy."

"But Dada also has power over weather?"

"He does a lot of damage, yes, but in an unpredictable way that frustrates him. He doesn't really know weather's secrets. And another thing: The way he uses the cane also affects *soul* weather—in a word, people—which in turn changes weather. Every time that stick is raised in anger, the whole world feels the blow."

Zac recalled the time when he himself had raised the cane angrily, and how he'd felt a weird energy course through it. "It sounds even more powerful than the blue umbrella," he muttered.

"Not at all. Without the canopy the cane's power is much less. And the umbrella could also be used on people, but it isn't."

"What do you mean?"

Eldy hesitated. Finally, folding his arms and looking steadily at Zac, he said, "There's something you don't know about the umbrella. Its power is not just over weather. The truth is, it can do anything."

"Anything?"

"That's right."

Zac was stunned. Like his introduction to the Weatherworks, this was an amazing revelation. But it also felt ominous.

"Eldy," said Chelsea, "could the umbrella make my father talk to me?"

"Yes. But also—no. You see, from the beginning it was decided that, though the umbrella can do anything, it would be used only for creating weather."

"Why?"

"Great power must be greatly limited. Otherwise it robs people of freedom. It's no good making your father talk to you; he has to want to. Right?"

Slowly Chelsea nodded.

"It's the difference," Eldy continued, "between magic and miracle. Miracles, astounding as they seem, are rooted in nature, whereas magic is a violation of nature. Rutherford uses the cane for magic."

"Like sucking life out of kids?" asked Chelsea.

"Exactly. The cane can be very strong when combined with a strong will. Rutherford uses it to acquire the thing he wants most: to live forever."

Zac ran his hand over his hair, still surprised at how short and prickly it was. Lost in his own thoughts, he said abruptly, "Are you telling me it was Dada? He killed my mother with that lightning bolt?"

"Not quite, Zachary. When it comes to weather, Rutherford doesn't know what he's doing. He's what you might call a rogue interferer."

Zac rocked back and forth, trying to comprehend. "So does Sky control the weather—or not?"

"Oh, he's in control, all right. But even a king has subjects who refuse to obey the law. So there's room for disorder, tragedy, destruction."

"But why? Why have lightning at all? Why don't you just get rid of it?"

"Lightning has many beneficial effects. It replenishes the ozone layer, injects nitrogen into the soil, causes forest fires …"

"Forest fires! What good are they?"

"Fires are necessary to stimulate new growth. It's nature's way."

"Nature's? Or yours?"

Zac shot Eldy a defiant look. For a few moments they locked gazes, until finally Zac had to drop his eyes. When he looked up, Eldy's back was turned. He was peering through the office window into the clouded vastness of the Weatherworks. Without turning around, he said, "Zachary, your mother's death was a complex event. You'll have to decide for yourself who killed her—or whether, indeed, it was murder at all. You can choose to trust Sky and me, or not. It's up to you."

Chapter 30
Big Stuff

A black mood had settled over Zac. Eldy and Chelsea kept chatting away but he wasn't listening. How could he trust when he still had so many doubts and questions? If the blue umbrella was really all-powerful, then even if Sky didn't actually throw the bolt that had killed Zac's mother, couldn't he have prevented it? Why did everything have to be so complicated?

At the same time, Zac felt increasingly agitated over the role he himself had played in causing a potentially killer fog, and perhaps even worse disasters to come. Somehow he had to undo his wrong. He had to fix it.

"Eldy," he said, "I have to go. I have to get that umbrella back. People could be dying and it's all my fault."

"Esmeralda and Priscilla caused this fog," said Eldy, "not you."

Zac drummed his fingers on the drafting table, his leg jiggling wildly.

"Wallowing in guilt won't help," said Eldy. "Yes, it was very wrong to give away the umbrella. And yes, we must find a way to retrieve it. But that may not be easy. Meanwhile, instead of dwelling on the bad you've done, is there perhaps some good you might do? Is there someone you could help?"

In Zac's darkness a light went on. He remembered his mother's words and why he had come here: *You're looking for something. You'll find it upstairs.*

"Pethybridge," he said. "He's dying and he needs a rose. Eldy, can you give me a rose for Pethybridge?"

"I thought you'd never ask."

As the children followed Eldy out of his office and back through the Weatherworks, Zac told Chelsea his adventure of escaping down the laundry chute and finding Butler/Pethybridge in the Aunties' cellar.

"Oh dear," she kept saying. "That boy has suffered so much."

"You know …?"

"That he's really just a boy? Of course. I can almost remember him before he lost his hair and got so wrinkled." Chelsea made a prune face that made Zac laugh.

By now they had reached a cupboard at the back of the store where Eldy kept paraphernalia from his stand. Rummaging within, he said, "Here we are. I just happen to have three fresh roses left. You might as well take the lot."

Zac could think of no reason to accept three roses, but Eldy insisted. The moment his hands touched them, he felt a surge of energy. "Whoa!" he cried, bouncing up and down. "Wait till Pethybridge gets a whiff of this!"

Meanwhile Eldy, finding a lily plant, cut off one large

bloom and handed it to Chelsea, saying, "You'll need something to light your way."

Understanding it was time to take their leave of Eldy, the children had no idea what his last words meant until they got outside, where the lily emitted a soft white glow in the thick fog. It was just enough light to let them take their next step. In this manner, one step at a time, they found their way to the Aunties' backyard and then to the cellar window of Pethybridge's room.

Zac's heart raced. Was Pethybridge even here? Was he still alive? What if they'd come too late? Fortunately the window opened easily; Zac scrambled inside and gave Chelsea a hand.

A cloud of fog obscured the bed. Even standing right beside it, Zac felt Pethybridge before he saw him. A hand, an arm, a shoulder. As Chelsea drew near and shone the lily, in the soft bubble of light a still, white face appeared, looking like a dried flower.

Zac leaned close and whispered, "Pethybridge, it's me, Zac. I'm sorry I took so long. I brought you something. A Christmas present."

Pethybridge showed no sign of awareness.

"Just give it to him," whispered Chelsea. "Put it in his hand, or let him smell it."

Carefully Zac took the thin, old fingers, so fragile they seemed ready to break off, and closed them over the gold foil around the stem of the rose. Then, bending the elbow, he lifted the flower right up to Pethybridge's nose.

The effect was immediate. As though the aroma became visible, color rushed into Pethybridge's cheeks and then suffused his whole face. Though his eyes remained shut, he looked more peaceful, even happy, as if some great strain had passed away.

And this was just the beginning. What happened over the next few minutes was as dramatic as watching a speeded-up film. All over Pethybridge's face the fantastic road map of wrinkles tightened and smoothed. The red bumps on his nose shrank, the pouches under his eyes vanished, his skin lost its splotched and wattled look and turned clear and creamy. His lightbulb of a head diminished in size and, most amazing of all, began to sprout hair—a pale blond cascade that grew and grew until it brushed his shoulders.

Before their eyes the figure in the bed was utterly transformed from a dying old man to a young boy! When the boy's eyes—large and bright green—finally flickered open, they could not have been more astonished if he had just been born into a new world. His hands flew to his face.

"What's this? Young again? How …?" Grabbing fistfuls of gleaming hair, he brought it to his lips and kissed it passionately. Then he threw off the blanket and sat bolt upright. Zac and Chelsea reacted as if a corpse had just sprung from its coffin.

"What's wrong?" he cried. "You don't think I'm going to stay in this smelly old bed, do you?"

The transformation of Pethybridge was truly shocking. Zac had hoped the rose, as it had done for him, might provide a fresh infusion of health and energy. But he had never dreamed that an old man could actually be turned back into a boy.

"Wow!" was all Zac could say. "Wowie-wow-*wow*!"

"Welcome back, Pethybridge," said Chelsea, extending a hand.

Pethybridge did a double take. "What? You talk? Well, it's a day for marvels. You're talking and I'm eleven. Hurray! I've never been eleven before. At least, not for long. About two weeks, I think. I waved at eleven as I raced by. But now I'm back. Eleven, eleven! I should have a birthday party. And what about ten, nine, eight, and seven? I missed them all. I should have five birthday parties at once!" Pethybridge was giddy with joy. "I feel so … tingly. I should turn cartwheels! Not that I ever turned a cartwheel in my life—but I bet I could right now. I would, too, if it wasn't for this … what is it? Fog?"

It was hard to follow his babbling. Even his voice was changed, high and skittish as though he'd breathed helium. And he certainly was an odd-looking kid. Gangly and long-faced, everything about him was long: arms, legs, fingers, hair, even his nose. In the globe of light from the lily, he perched on the bed hugging his absurdly bony knees, green eyes wide and staring, ears antennalike. It wasn't only on account of his name, Zac guessed, that he'd been laughed at as a child.

"No, I won't do a cartwheel," he prattled. "But I must do something. I'm so happy I could dance! Yes, I'll dance! But no, on second thought, the one time I danced, I tripped myself and three other people. Oh, what to do? It's not every day a person sheds seventy years! Let me think. What would an excited, delighted boy of eleven do?"

Zac and Chelsea couldn't help laughing. Though the old man was definitely gone, young Pethybridge was even more preposterous.

"Go ahead and laugh. You won't dampen my spirits. I feel so … ebullient. Yes, that's it—*ebullient*!" Several times he said the word, each time a little louder, until his eyes, already huge, grew about three sizes and he exploded, "Eureka! I know what I'll do!"

Puffing out his chest like a rooster, he balled his absurdly long fingers into a semblance of fists and beat them on his chest while emitting an earsplitting Tarzan yell.

At first Zac was too shocked to react. Then he seized the boy's arms and shook him. "No, Pethybridge! Stop it!"

"Let me go! Can't I express a little ebullience?"

"Pethybridge—the Aunties! We have to be quiet."

"Aunties-panties! Don't even call them Aunties—unless you mean they're anti-everything: antilife, antigoodness, antijoy. But they're nobody's aunties, that's for sure. Not mine, not yours, not anybody's."

"I think they're my great-aunts," corrected Zac.

"Rubbish. If they're your great-aunts, then I'm your great-grandfather and you're a great big baboon."

"What? You mean …?"

"Of course I mean. They stole you, Zac Sparks, just like they stole me and Barber. They're nothing but kidnappers."

Zac was flabbergasted. This thought had never occurred to him. Something erupted inside him: anger? dread? joy? At the same time, weirdly, he felt more abandoned than ever before.

Blood relatives, even bad ones, were at least family. But now he truly was all alone in the world, an orphan.

"Anyway," continued Pethybridge, "don't worry about the so-called Aunties. They left just before you came. With Dada."

"*Dada?*" said Zac and Chelsea together. "He's here?"

"Was. Right in this house. I heard him talking to the Aunties." Pethybridge shuddered. "That horrible voice! It creeps right under your skin—"

"But how did he get here?" said Chelsea. "He's supposed to be locked up."

"Your father brought him in a wheelchair van."

"My father? Why?"

"Christmas. He's out on a Christmas pass. But really it's something to do with the umbrella, that blue umbrella Mr. Porter carts around. Or used to. Dada and the Aunties have it now. They kept raving about it. I thought they disapproved of umbrellas. Normally they won't even have one in the house. But now …"

"This one is different," said Zac. "It controls the weather. Wind, sunshine, rain, even this fog—it's all done with the blue umbrella."

Understandably perplexed, Pethybridge sat perfectly still as Zac and Chelsea told him the whole story of Sky, Eldy, the Weatherworks, and the umbrella's amazing power. When he looked skeptical, Zac said, "But see what Eldy's rose did for you! Just one touch and you're right as rain. What we're telling you about the umbrella is no stranger than that."

Pethybridge had to agree. When Zac got to the part about how the Aunties came to possess the umbrella, he couldn't tell it. Chelsea had to speak for him, as Pethybridge regarded him with increasing horror.

"But how could you do that?" he cried. "Don't you hate the Aunties?"

Then Zac explained how his mother had died by lightning and how he figured only one person could have done it.

Pethybridge stared out the window, processing. At last he said, "Well, he's a strange man, Porter. No doubt about that. Still, it's hard to believe he would kill your mother. Are you sure?"

Zac felt intensely frustrated. Why wouldn't anyone believe him? He was the one who had lost his mother. No one else seemed to take her violent death seriously.

Chelsea, changing the subject, said, "Pethybridge, do you know where Dada and the Aunties have gone?"

"To your house. I don't know why."

Chelsea looked worried.

"After that, Dada was bent on going up to the mine."

"On Wind Mountain?" asked Zac.

"Yes. The Aunties tried to talk him out of it but he shut them up. He kept raving about *big stuff*, that's what he called it, stored at the mine: tornadoes, hurricanes, earthquakes. I thought he was off his rocker, but now I wonder: Is he planning to unleash some of that big stuff with the umbrella?" Zac and Chelsea exchanged grim glances. "He said the umbrella is the key to global domination."

Zac dropped his head into his hands.

"So it's true? About big stuff being kept at the mine?"

"I don't know," moaned Zac. "Sky never mentioned it. Eldy talked about the mine but he never said anything about earthquakes or hurricanes." But he had, Zac realized, mentioned volcanoes—and now Zac recalled his time on Wind Mountain, while chasing Eldy's balloons, and what he'd heard as he leaned over the mine shaft: deep rumblings and roarings like prehistoric monsters dueling underground.

Zac looked up. "It's hard to imagine stuff like tornadoes being kept in jars at the store. Big stuff would need a really big container—like a mountain."

For a minute the children fell silent as they contemplated Dada at large with the blue umbrella on Wind Mountain.

"He really is crazy," said Chelsea.

"Not just crazy, but highly intelligent," added Pethybridge. "A bad combination."

"He's also something much worse," Zac reflected. "He's evil."

Saying this word, he felt a jolt, like something kicking his insides. His next words spewed out: "I have to stop him! I have to go up there and get that umbrella!"

Chapter 31

A Fair Exchange

"Up the mountain?" said Pethybridge. "But no one's allowed up there."

"Someone should tell that to Dada," said Zac.

"You're not going alone," said Chelsea. "I'll come too. What about you, Pethybridge?"

"Me? Against Dada? I'd have to be crazier than he is."

"I suppose you'd rather get blown away by a hurricane?" Chelsea pointed her chin at him.

"Perhaps I would. Yes, now that you mention it, I think a nice hurricane would be much preferable to facing Dada."

"Don't try to talk him into it," Zac said. "This isn't for the faint of heart."

"Faint of heart!" bleated Pethybridge. "I'll have you know, Zac Sparks, it's taken more than faintness to live with those two witches all these years."

"I'm sorry, Pethybridge. I just don't want you feeling obligated to go up the mountain. You're welcome to stay here."

"Stay here? All by myself?"

After a good deal more hemming and hawing, Pethybridge agreed to accompany the others. First, however, he raised another matter. "What about Barber? He needs a rose too."

Eager to be off, Zac argued that Barber could be rescued later. But Pethybridge was adamant and Chelsea sided with him.

"It won't take long," she said. "And why else would Eldy give us extra roses? He must have had Barber in mind."

Pethybridge's rose, Zac noticed, lay completely shriveled on his pillow. Studying the remaining two, their intricate petals quivering with life, reluctantly Zac gave in. With Chelsea's lily lighting their way, the children set off for the World's Smallest Business Establishment. They were practically on its doorstep before the tiny shop loomed out of the fog. When, in answer to Zac's knock, the little walking haystack of Barber appeared, he seemed to have stepped from long ago out of the mists of time.

"Barber, can we see you?"

"Feast your eyes."

"I mean, can we come in?"

"Where did you learn your grammar, Boy? Not can—may."

"All right, then, may we come in?"

"No questions, remember?"

"Barber, you're wasting time. We're here on very important business. I've brought Chelsea and ... ah ... another friend."

"Chelsea Cholmondeley? Certainly not. I'm a barber, not a hairdresser." Then, peering at Pethybridge, he asked, "And who's this girl?"

"He's not a girl, he's—"

"Ah, I see. Here for a haircut. Well, that's another matter. Come right in."

As the three children crowded into the tiny room, it began to feel like one of those circus stunts cramming clowns into a car. Barber, flourishing his red sheet, stood beside the chair.

"Step right this way, young sir. I'll have those golden locks off in a minute."

"Barber, ah, we're not actually here for a haircut."

"I know *you* aren't, Boy. But this young lad hasn't had a trim in … years? What's your name, son? You look vaguely familiar."

Pethybridge stuck out his hand. "Hello, Barber. I'm Butler."

"Butler! Why, of course. Such a strong resemblance. I never guessed the old boy had family. Quite amazing."

"I'm not related to Butler. I'm him. I'm Butler."

"Yes, and I'm the King of Balderdash. Now sit right down and let me have a go at that mop."

"Barber, it's true," said Zac. "This really is Butler, except his real name is Pethybridge. Why don't you have a seat in that chair yourself and we'll tell you what's going on."

As the three children eased the old fellow into his chair, he looked a mixture of resistant, bewildered, and helpless, as if a part of him already sensed the truth. There was no containing the children's excitement as they spilled out the whole story, interrupting one another in their haste to tell all the details. When they came to the part about the rose, and to Butler/Pethybridge's remarkable transformation, Barber's eyes grew wide with wonder. Speaking to himself, he murmured, "So it's true. Porter kept warning me, but I thought he was cracked."

Barber explained that occasionally—when the Aunties were away—Mr. Porter would stop by his shop for a chat. They'd discussed many things, from local news and weather (naturally) to what Porter discreetly referred to as Barber's "condition." Barber didn't want to admit he had a condition, but Porter kept bringing it up.

"How was I to know? I'd never grown old before. Maybe this was just how it happens."

In the midnight of his soul, he knew something was terribly wrong. Still, he'd politely scoffed at Porter's admonishments to procure one of Eldy's roses to reverse the aging. He found Porter a pleasant enough fellow, but one had to take everything he said with a grain of salt. Like most folks in town, Barber believed Porter's Store was haunted and that young Porter, like his father, was batty.

"In a way I wanted to believe him," he said. "But it was too scary. I had to laugh it off."

"It's no joke," said Pethybridge, "living with the shame, the secrets, the lies."

Barber stared hard at him. "I can't get over it. You really are Butler?"

"Pethybridge," he corrected.

"Well, I'll be a monkey's uncle."

"If you ask me," said Pethybridge, "you look more like an Auntie's monkey." And they all laughed.

"But we can change that with this rose," said Zac. "You'll be young again. We'll give you a haircut you won't forget."

"No you don't!" yelped Barber. To everyone's surprise he shrank away as if he'd been offered poison. "I'm used to being old. I *like* it. Have you thought of that? Being grown-up has its advantages."

"Like dying?" suggested Pethybridge. "There aren't many grown-up advantages on your deathbed. I found that out for myself."

"Everyone has to die," said Barber. "I'm ready."

"You haven't even lived!" protested Chelsea. "How old were you when the Aunties got you? Three? Your whole life has flown by while you're cooped up in this crummy little shop. It's like a coffin in here!"

"Don't go insulting my business, missy. I'm proud of this place."

"It's not even yours," said Pethybridge. "Pris owns it. She owns you, too. And Dada owns her. Dada, not Porter, is the crazy one. And you've sold your soul to him."

Barber fell silent, chewing his lips, chin jerking nervously.

"How about an experiment?" suggested Zac. "You don't have to touch the rose. Just smell it. I'll bring it up to your nose and you take one whiff. If you don't like it, I'll take it away."

Barber's broad, veined nose twitched dubiously.

"Just one sniff," coaxed Chelsea.

Almost imperceptibly Barber nodded.

What happened next was not just quick but instantaneous. When Zac gently wafted the rose under his nostrils, there was a loud *pop!* like a blown-up paper bag bursting and Barber's whole body seemed to implode.

Then they heard another sound, smaller but somehow menacing: the tinkling of the door bell.

They all turned to see a form emerging from the fog. An improbably large form that bulked into the small room like a whale breaching in a pond. A form almost the same color as the fog, then suddenly distinct in a bright pink muumuu and a bobbly flowerpot hat.

Auntie Pris!

As always in a doorway, Pris had to turn sideways to get through. So preoccupied was she with managing this maneuver that at first she wasn't aware of the small crowd of alarmed witnesses. Finally turning to face them, she stopped cold. The moment could not have been more fraught. Pris's gaze fastened hard on Pethybridge, her tiny eyes twitching with bewildered recognition, straining to grasp the impossible. Then, as she turned to the figure in the barber chair, she screamed, "*What have you done to him?*"

Her hands flew to her head as if she'd just been stricken with an ax. "What's happening? Oh, what have you done!" In a strange dance she began bowing her head, then her whole upper body, back and forth like a wavering flame, at the same time stamping her feet like a child throwing a tantrum. "Stop it! Stop it!" she bellowed. The whole building shook with her heavy stomps.

The children, terrified, couldn't take their eyes from her. She looked like a huge pink grizzly, mad with rage, about to attack them all. But abruptly the stamping stopped, and the screaming, and she sank to her knees. Then Zac noticed her hands, still covering her face: They were brown, twisted, and rough like gnarled tree roots, and behind them her head was like a rotted stump. Her fingers weren't just covering her face now but digging into it, sinking in, head and hands becoming one knotted burl. Then the whole, great, blubbery bulk of her began to shrivel, sagging to the floor and collapsing into itself like a deflated dirigible. From somewhere inside this diminishing shape came an unearthly moan, the most ghastly, piteous sound Zac had ever heard, as if the woman's lips were sewn shut, her throat sealed off, yet still the ghost of a voice escaped.

"Lost ... lost ... lost ..." said the horrified whisper until finally it faded away to nothing ... as did she.

Incredibly, she was gone. The preposterous immensity that had been Priscilla Henbother was no more. It seemed not just one but ten people had left the room. All that remained were a few bones topped by a pot of plastic flowers—her sad little hat—as though the deceased had anticipated her own funeral.

Appalled, Zac turned away to see a sight equally startling but entirely different in nature. There, on the barber chair, sat an odd-looking creature who appeared to be a young boy but whose chin was covered by a long gray beard. Between that and a mountainous mop of tangled, ashen hair, the boy's face was all but hidden. Even so, the slightness of his body and the dewy largeness of his eyes left little doubt that this was a child—one so startled and fresh-looking that he might have just popped out of a box.

As the others stared, he burst into tears. "Now look what you've done! I told you! Why couldn't you just leave

349

me alone?" Sobbing in frustrated rage, he seized his beard, tore it from his chin, and dashed it to the floor. It was fake! Then, grabbing his haystack of hair in both hands, he lifted it straight off his head and hurled it across the room. A wig! Underneath was a fuzz of golden brown atop a small, oval, baby-smooth face. Hopping down from the chair and catching sight of himself in the big mirror, he gasped and hid behind his hands.

"What on earth …?" said Pethybridge.

Chelsea tried to touch him but he waved her away.

"Are you …?" Zac began.

"Barber?" said the boy angrily. "Not anymore. Now, thanks to you, I'm … Iris."

"Iris!" exclaimed the others.

"That's what Mr. Porter called me. 'Lovely as the flower,' he kept saying. Ha! I wish."

"But," said Pethybridge, "isn't Iris a girl's name?"

"What do you think I am—a leprechaun?"

As they all leaned in for a closer look, Zac recalled the high, feminine-sounding voice of the old Barber.

"But the beard …?" he asked.

"You saw me rip it off, didn't you?"

"Yes, but why …?"

"Why dress as a man? Pris made me. She wanted a boy, like Esmeralda had, but all she could get was me."

"Oh, sick!" said Pethybridge.

"Pris said I looked like a boy anyway—and I do! I hate myself!" As Iris succumbed to a fresh wave of tears, no one said anything. For the simple truth was that she did look like a tomboy.

"Maybe when your hair grows back …?" suggested Pethybridge.

"No!" she yelled, stamping her foot. "My hair is ugly, *ugly*! And so am I! That's why I didn't want your stupid old rose."

Zac wanted to say, "But you're not nearly as ugly as Barber"—but whatever words he thought of sounded not quite right. There was just no denying it: Iris did not look much like a flower. Especially when she was so mad.

"Iris," said Chelsea, "you said Auntie Pris wanted a boy. But I bet there was more to it. Maybe your disguise was a way of hiding you. I mean, from your real family."

From the look on Iris's face, this obvious thought had not occurred to her.

"Do you know who they are? Where you came from?"

Iris shook her head. "I don't even know my real name."

Distracted from this thought by the pile of rags by the door, Iris cautiously approached and whispered, "Is that you, Priscilla? Good-bye, old hag. Can't say I'll miss you." Looking back at the others, she made as if dusting off her hands. "Well, I guess she got what was coming."

"I don't get it," said Pethybridge. "She just withered away, kind of melted, like the Wicked Witch of the West."

"She *was* a wicked witch," said Iris, "and now she's dead. She really died a long time ago—or should have. But

351

she kept herself alive by feeding off me, as I grew older and older. Eldy's rose reversed all that. The years Pris stole from me caught up with her. She died of accelerated old age."

"You sound as if you knew exactly what would happen," said Zac.

"I did," replied Iris. "Porter told me everything. I just didn't believe him." To Pethybridge, who was staring down at Pris's remains with an expression of grim perplexity, she added, "Don't feel sorry for her."

"I'm not sorry. It's something else. I'm not sure what." In agitation Pethybridge began pacing about the tiny room, until abruptly he stopped and pointed his finger at Iris. "If this happened to Pris when you regained your youth, then when I regained mine, the same must have happened to Esmeralda!"

One could have heard a lock of hair fall in that room. And then all together they exclaimed, "That's right! Esmeralda's dead too! The Aunties are dead and gone!"

Chapter 32

Flower, Photo, Fur, Fire

Spontaneously the children joined hands and danced around the barber's chair, chanting, "Dead and gone! Dead and gone! The mean old Aunties are dead and gone!" Punctuating the chant with whoops and hurrahs, they kept it up until Chelsea stopped, broke the circle, and stood there with her head down.

"What's wrong?" asked Zac.

"It's just … well, the Aunties were human. People like you and me."

"They sure didn't act like it," said Iris.

"How could they? All they knew came from Dada. It's no wonder they turned out like him."

For some time no one spoke. Then Zac added, "And Dada's still alive."

At that instant a burst of light flooded the room, as though someone had just taken their photograph. They felt it in the air and on their faces and hair, a tingling of static electricity. A moment later came a tremendous, lingering crash that seemed to roll down from the mountain like a giant snowball.

"Thunder!" said Chelsea.

"Dada," said Zac. "He's got the umbrella."

The other children crowded to the door to look out, but Zac didn't move. Within moments came another flash of lightning. In the fog no jagged fork was visible, but the whole misty atmosphere lit up with a crackling, bluish light. When the thunder came, it was even louder than the first time. As the rumbling died away, Chelsea made a move to step outside.

"Stop!" cried Zac. "We can't go out there."

"I thought we were going up the mountain," she said. "Remember? To get back the umbrella."

"No. Not now. Not when there's lightning. I can't."

"What's this about an umbrella?" asked Iris.

"But we *have* to," insisted Chelsea. "We have to go after Dada and stop him."

"Dada's here?" cried Iris.

"You bet he's here," said Pethybridge. "And he's about to take over the world."

Briefly they explained to Iris all about the blue umbrella and Dada's plan to release catastrophic weather from the mine on Wind Mountain.

"Porter was always talking weird," reflected Iris, "but he never said a word about his umbrella. I wouldn't have believed him anyway. But now … I might believe anything."

"Will you come with us?" asked Chelsea.

"After Dada? Tell you the truth, I'd rather jump into a pot of boiling oil. But yeah, I'll come."

"Then let's go. Zac, you ready?"

"No, Chelsea. I told you, I can't. Dada's out to get me. I can feel it. That's what the lightning's about."

Zac had hardly finished speaking when the room lit up again. He shut his eyes tight but the flash still scalded the lining of his lids. When the thunder came, it rattled the bottles of hair tonic on the glass counter until one fell off and broke. Zac cried out.

Chelsea took hold of his shoulders. "C'mon, Zac. We have to do this."

"No. I won't. You can't make me …"

He was on the verge of tears. Then, in the peculiarly deep stillness that follows thunder, they heard a sound. Mournful, human, at first it seemed like a baby crying. Not just crying, but wailing.

"Some little kid frightened by the storm," said Pethybridge.

But as they crowded to the doorstep to listen, they realized this was no infant but an adult. A woman. Somewhere nearby, a grown woman was bawling like a baby, sobbing as if she'd lost her child.

"I know that voice!" exclaimed Chelsea, and she ran into the street. All they could see of her was the glow from the lily, bobbing up and down as she ran. "Come on!" she called back. "It's my mother!"

Racing ahead of the others, Zac caught up with Chelsea on the front porch of the rectory. From here the sound of the heart-wrenching sobs was much louder, clearly coming from inside the house. Chelsea's hand was on the doorknob, ready to enter, but as Zac passed the front window something caught his eye.

"Chelsea, stop!" he hissed. Grabbing her elbow and spinning her around, he forced her to a crouch below the window. "Look!"

Just inches away in the living room was the back of a person. A very tall, slim woman dressed in a silvery fur coat.

"Esmeralda!" breathed Chelsea. "But how ... how can she still be alive?"

By now the others had caught up and Zac pulled them down out of sight. Pethybridge, seeing the ghostly form in the window, gasped.

"She's supposed to be dead!" he whimpered. "I thought it was all over. Oh, I can't bear this—"

"Shh!" Zac urged.

"I have to go in there," whispered Chelsea. "Something terrible has happened."

Zac gripped her arm. "Wait. Let me think."

While the four children watched from just below the window, Esmeralda moved away.

"If that witch has done anything to Mom ..." hissed Chelsea.

Zac thought hard. Finally he told Pethybridge and Iris, "You wait here. Chelsea and I are going in." Then to Chelsea: "You go straight to your mother. Leave Esmeralda to me."

They took a deep breath, stood up, and opened the door. Esmeralda was just a few feet away, warming herself by the fireplace. Startled, she turned. On the far side of the room, kneeling beside a leather couch, was Mary Cholmondeley, her frail form racked by sobs. Chelsea ran and threw her arms around her, but Mary was so distressed she barely noticed. On the couch before her lay a third person—the small, shriveled form of an old, old man.

Esmeralda, recovering quickly from the surprise entrance, gushed, "Zachary, how lovely to see you! Auntie Pris and I have been so worried."

"I'm sorry, Auntie," said Zac. "I really am. I've been trying to find you."

"I'm sure you have. And now here we are, together again. And you've brought dear little Chelsea, too. How nice! I can't tell you how fond I am of children. Just being near them makes me feel … young again."

Zac's thoughts whirled. Was Esmeralda taunting him, testing him … or what? He noticed she didn't have the cane. Had Dada taken it with him up the mountain?

"Zachary, I know it's hard for you to understand, but everything Priscilla and I have done has been for your own good. We so want you to feel at home with us."

"I know, Auntie. You've been very kind. I've just had a hard time adjusting. I feel better about things now …" Though he spoke as evenly as he could, his whole body trembled.

Meanwhile, out of the corner of his eye, he was taking in the scene by the couch. Chelsea, who'd been hugging her mother, now released her and began caressing the head of the prostrate figure. Who was he, that old, old man?

Suddenly Zac knew.

"Oh, Ches, what has she done to you?" cried Chelsea. "Speak to me, Ches." She patted his cheeks, rubbed his hands.

357

"It's no use!" sobbed Mrs. Cholmondeley. "He's dead! Oh, my son. She killed him!"

Chelsea, standing up, glared at Esmeralda and shrieked, "You murdered my brother!"

"My goodness, little girl," cooed Esmeralda, "what a surprise! After all these years you seem to have found your voice. What a shame you have nothing nicer to say."

"You witch!" shot back Chelsea.

In a flash Zac guessed what had happened. Esmeralda, at death's door, had seized on Ches to revive herself. She must have sucked away his entire remaining life—over half a century!—every precious drop of which she needed to stay alive.

Carefully slipping one hand behind his back (the hand that still held the third of Eldy's roses), Zac began inching his way toward the body of his friend. But Esmeralda was too quick for him. With two long strides she planted herself between Zac and the couch.

"Not so fast. I know all about your little tricks with flowers. Give me that rose."

Too much was happening at once. Zac had to do something—fast—but he was still reeling from the shock of Ches's death. *It's all my fault! He died because of me. I rescued Pethybridge and Iris but I can't help Ches. It's too late …*

"Now!" said Esmeralda. "Hand over that rose."

Zac stalled. Was it really too late? Or might Eldy's rose revive even a corpse? He made a move toward the couch.

"Wait, Boy. I have something you've been wanting."

Esmeralda's leopard-skin purse dangled from one arm. Snapping it open, she drew out a small, yellowed square of paper. Zac's heart stopped. She held the most important thing in the world to him.

"Remember this?"

She held up the photograph and Zac's eyes locked onto the face of his mother.

"I've enjoyed carrying this little memento," crooned Esmeralda. "But I know it's worth much more to you than to me. And you may have it. All you have to do is *give me that rose*."

Zac's feelings churned.

"Hurry up! You want the picture, don't you? If not, here's a nice, hot fire and I'll just throw your mother into it."

"No!"

"Then give me the rose. There's a good boy."

Zac brought out the rose from behind his back. He inched it toward her, then suddenly drew it back. "No! It's no deal."

With a flick of her wrist Esmeralda tossed the photo like a playing card into the fireplace. Instantly flames licked it and the edges curled and blackened. Zac yearned to run and save it—to save *her*. But he had to guard the rose.

In that split second of indecision, Esmeralda once again outmaneuvered him. She grabbed Chelsea from behind and pinned the girl's neck with one bony arm, nearly choking her.

"No!" screamed Mary. "Not my baby!"

"Keep away, both of you, or I'll break her neck! Boy, I've

had enough of your fooling. I killed her brother and I'll kill her, too. Now give me that rose this instant."

What could Zac do? He handed the rose to Esmeralda, who crushed the flower in one hand and flung its petals into the fire. Chelsea, released, flew to her mother's embrace and the two of them huddled beside the still body on the couch.

"Well," said Esmeralda, "I think we've established who's in charge here. Now, Zachary, I'd like very much for you and me to be friends. Wouldn't you like that too?"

Helplessly Zac stared into the fire. His photograph was gone. The rose was already reduced to charred, papery flakes. Watching it was like watching the body of Ches himself burn up.

"Come, let's make up. You want to be on the winning side, don't you? Here's my hand—let's shake on it."

As Esmeralda extended her withered claw, Zac noticed a movement through the window.

"You're right, Auntie. I can't keep fighting you."

"That's a good boy. Just come to me and everything will be all right."

"Yes, Auntie, I do want us to be friends. It's really what I've wanted all along."

"Zac Sparks!" yelled Chelsea. "How could you!"

"It's no good, Chelsea. I have to do this."

Head hanging, Zac slouched toward Esmeralda. As he drew near, she touched him under the chin and lifted it until he looked up directly into her eyes.

"What a good boy," she said softly. "We'll have such beautiful times together."

As hard as he could, Zac kicked her in the kneecap. Thrown off balance, hobbling on one leg, she crumpled almost on top of him, and with one mighty heave he pushed her into the fireplace.

Chapter 33

News from Beyond

For a moment Esmeralda simply sat in the fire, flames licking at her fur coat. Her face had the oddest look, one that might have been mistaken for passionate pleasure. She had, after all, been cold all her life.

Then she screamed—an intense, full-throated shriek that ran the gamut of pitches like a coloratura soprano's dying aria. Struggling to rise from the fire, she did a fair imitation of her sister Priscilla heaving herself off a couch. Finally managing it, she stood dancing on the hearth in a shower of sparks, slapping her rear end with both hands and whooping like a savage.

Zac seized the opportunity to dash to the couch and kneel beside the body of his friend. He could not quite believe Ches was really dead. He checked his pulse—but no, nothing. Ches was barely recognizable, his features sunken, his flesh the color of ditch water. He looked ready to be shoveled into the ground. Zac was swept with emotion. True, Ches had been no real friend to him, yet entwined with his meanness was an eccentricity, a fierce individuality that from the start Zac had admired.

Mary Cholmondeley still wept softly as Chelsea clung to her. On the floor beside them Zac noticed the lily that Chelsea had carried to light their way through the fog. Sorrowfully he picked it up and placed it on Ches's chest.

"Good-bye, my friend."

As in a dream, he looked up to see the enraged and smoking Esmeralda advancing on him with an iron poker brandished aloft.

"You'll pay for this," she snarled.

Zac did not react. He felt so sad, so tired. Hadn't he done enough fighting, struggling, running away? And it didn't seem quite real, the notion of an old lady in a fur coat bludgeoning him with a poker. Or perhaps, in that moment, he wouldn't have minded dying.

Just then the door flew open to admit Iris and Pethybridge, one with a rake and the other a shovel.

"Drop that poker, Esmeralda!" cried Pethybridge. "Or I'll cave your head in. I swear I will."

It was hard to tell which shook more violently—Pethybridge himself, his voice, or the shovel he held aloft with both hands. Beside him Iris gripped her rake like a baseball bat.

Esmeralda whirled around, froze, and for several seconds said nothing. When she did speak, she nearly choked on the name of the person standing before her.

"Butler! Is it really you ...? You ungrateful imp! After all I've done for you!" Then her attention turned to Iris, and a visible shiver of recognition ran through her. "You ... what have you done ... with my sister?"

Iris, who appeared more in control than Pethybridge, answered evenly, "Priscilla, you'll be sorry to hear, was called away to a sudden dinner engagement. This very moment she's being eaten by worms."

As if hit by a spray of bullets, Esmeralda dropped the poker, clutched her stomach, and fell to the floor groaning and whimpering, writhing back and forth like a snake. What was happening? In less than a minute the twitching convulsions stopped and she had curled into a crumpled ball of silver hair and fur. One final spasm flipped her onto her back where she lay completely still, gazing wide-eyed at the ceiling even as her head withered up like a dried apple and collapsed into white bone. Soon nothing was left of her face but a paste of makeup—patches of rouge, pools of eye shadow, a crooked smear of lipstick—glued like a gaudy mask onto a skull.

Zac, tearing his eyes away, was surprised at the looks on the faces of Iris and Pethybridge. Instead of the somber, horrified expressions of those who have just witnessed a gruesome death, what he saw was astonished joy. He realized they were looking, not down at Esmeralda, but somewhere over his shoulder. Before he could turn, a familiar voice behind him said, "I don't know what you're so fascinated with, Bud. The real attraction's over here."

Zac spun around, and there stood Chesterton Cholmondeley—holding the lily! Dead no more, not even old, he was a boy again, a boy even younger than when Zac had first met him. Like a kid who'd just gotten off a wild carnival ride, he looked both shaken-up and exultant. Bouncing on the balls of his feet and flapping his arms, he crowed, "Whoopee! I'm so light I could fly!"

Chelsea and her mother, still kneeling beside the couch, gawked, too overjoyed to speak. Finally they leapt up and embraced him.

"Hey, watch my lily, will you?" Though pretending aloofness from his family's crushing attentions, Ches was, for the first time Zac could remember, smiling.

"We thought you were dead!" Zac blurted.

"Well, I'm alive now, aren't I?"

"But how?"

Ches knuckled his eyes. "All I know is I was in a really dark place, and then this lily comes along and lights it up like a thousand suns, and I follow its light through a long tunnel, and now I'm here."

"Ches," said Mary Cholmondeley, her eyes brimming tears, "Ches. Let me look at you."

Slender now and slightly shorter, Ches had lost his look of lumbering chunkiness. With fine, chiseled features and a shock of black hair, he was actually quite handsome.

"Gaze your fill, Mom. I'm not planning on crawling back into the grave again. Not now that Miss Skullface here has kindly swapped places with me."

Then Ches filled them in on what had happened, confirming that Esmeralda had sucked away every minute of his life. "The last thing I remember is Mom wailing and Esmeralda cackling like a maniac." He admitted that Dada, years before, had stolen some of his youth and a lot of his spunk. "The old devil tried to get me to swipe Porter's umbrella. I said I would if he backed off, so that bought me some time. But when I started studying meteorology, he finally left me alone. He said my knowledge might come in handy for some big plan he was cooking up."

"With the umbrella," explained Zac. "I tried to tell you it controls the weather, but you wouldn't listen."

"Controls weather? A lousy umbrella? I doubt it," scoffed Ches.

"You still won't believe!"

"Why should I believe what isn't rational? I believe in science, not magic. Rain falls because water evaporates, rises, forms clouds, and so on. It's nothing to do with some old umbrella."

Though restored to youth, Ches's pedantry remained intact, his dark eyes flashing with the passion for logic. Meanwhile his mother gazed at her son adoringly. He could have said anything and she would have been happy.

But not Chelsea. So far she had kept silent, but now she planted herself in front of her brother, rose on tiptoes, stabbed a finger into his chest, and yelled, "You're impossible! You've just come back from the dead and you still won't believe in anything except dumb old science."

She had his attention. He stared hard at her, speechless.

"If you think science is the reason you're standing here right now," she ranted, "you're the dumbest person I know. I'm ashamed to call you my brother." Crossing her arms, she turned her back on him.

Ches's expression had gone from lofty arrogance to profound perplexity. Finally he cleared his throat and asked, very quietly, "What did you say?"

"You heard me," retorted Chelsea. "There's nothing wrong with your ears. It's your head that's the problem."

Ches looked as if his head had just received a blow depriving it of all intelligence. Groping for words, he murmured, "But … you just … spoke!"

Her face flushing, Chelsea whirled around to confront him. "Of course I spoke, you moron. It's about time, don't you think?"

"But … how …?" For the first time in five years, Ches was hearing his sister's voice. It was also the first time he had found himself at a loss for words.

"If you want to know why I'm talking," said Chelsea, "it's because I have something to say. And it's this: Everything Zac told you about Mr. Porter and the umbrella is true." She went on to describe how Sky had let her use the umbrella to make thunder, and how the experience had restored her power of speech. "At least, I speak to people who listen. But with you—what's the use?"

Then Ches surprised her by saying, "I'm listening." Indeed his normally stolid features had arranged themselves into a soft, searching look.

"You may be listening but you're not hearing," said Chelsea. "You won't believe."

Ches licked his lips. "I might. I might believe *you*."

Now Chelsea was the one to look skeptical. "What?"

"I mean, give me some time. If it's enough to make you talk, maybe there's something to it."

Chelsea threw her arms around her brother. Their mother

beamed. Deciding the hug had gone on long enough, Ches appeared to notice Iris and Pethybridge for the first time.

"So who's this?" To their account of the amazing powers of Eldy's roses, Ches responded, "No kidding! All this time Barber's been a girl? And *Pethybridge*—what kind of a name is that?" Finally he turned to Zac. "And who's this freak here?"

"I'm Zac! Don't you know me?"

"Just kidding, Bud."

Introductions over, Ches rubbed his hands together and declared, "Hey, it feels great to be alive. We should have a party."

"It's not party time yet," said Chelsea. "Not with Dada on the loose. We have to hunt him down and get back the umbrella."

At the mention of Dada, lightning flickered outside.

"That's him now," said Chelsea, "up on Wind Mountain." Even as she spoke, a tremendous crack of thunder rattled the house.

Everyone was silent, until Ches said, "Well, what are we waiting for?"

Zac, flopping on the couch where Ches had lain, covered his face with his arms.

"What's with you, Bud? Afraid of a little fireworks?"

"Leave me alone," said Zac.

"He's afraid of Dada," said Chelsea. "He thinks Dada's after him."

"So what else is new?" said Ches. "He's after all of us, isn't he? If we don't get him, he'll get us." Ches was prying Zac's arms away from his eyes. "C'mon, Bud. That couch is for the dead, remember? You've got work to do. If that umbrella is really what you say, we've got to get it back. Otherwise the whole sky's gonna come down on our heads. Right?"

Zac was listening. Ches's voice had a bluff robustness that was hard to resist. Opening his eyes, Zac sat up and asked, "Ches, were you really dead?"

Ches shrugged, turning out his palms as if testing for rain.

"But what was it like?" pursued Zac.

Mulling this over, at last Ches answered, "Like I say, it was dark."

Zac was crestfallen. "That's all?"

"Well, not exactly … I don't know how to describe it.… I saw, like, all these colors … like rainbows … beautiful.… Tell you the truth, I didn't want to come back. But that lily was so bright I had to follow. Some things you do whether you like it or not."

Vague as this was, Zac found what Ches said—or rather, how he said it—strangely comforting. Along with Zac's encounter in the umbrella factory, it seemed further corroboration that his mother might be safe, even happy—indeed, that everything might turn out all right in the end. So on the strength of that certain tone in Ches's voice, Zac got to his feet and prepared to head up Wind Mountain to face Dada.

Chapter 34

Wind Mountain

"No!" cried Mary Cholmondeley. "No children of mine are going chasing after Dada."

"But Mom," observed Ches, "aren't you forgetting something? I'm not just a kid anymore—ten minutes ago I was older than you are, right? Ha ha."

"It's no joke, Chesterton. That man will stop at nothing. And the fog … it's too dangerous … the police are telling everyone to stay indoors."

"Mom," said Chelsea, "this family—this whole town—has been stuck in fog for too long. It's time to do something. Why don't you come with us?"

"Oh, no, I couldn't." Wringing her hands, Mary sank down on the couch.

"Then at least let us go," urged Chelsea. "Maybe this is a job for kids."

Finally she waved them off, and the five of them set out—Ches, Chelsea, Zac, Iris, and Pethybridge—an unlikely little band of the young and the formerly old and dead. Iris and Pethybridge wanted to bring their rake and shovel but

Zac said, "What good are weapons? Would you clobber a paralyzed old man in a wheelchair?"

"If he's paralyzed," asked Iris, "how can he use the umbrella?"

"Maybe he's got someone with him," suggested Chelsea.

"Maybe the whole town's up there," said Ches. "I wouldn't put it past them."

Indeed as they made their way across the main intersection of Five Corners, not a soul was in sight. The fog was lighter now and it was possible to see some distance along the streets. No car moved, not a curtain fluttered at a window. Eldy's stand, as before, was deserted. All that stirred were some thicker fog patches drifting through the streets like townspeople turned to ghosts. Even Porter's Store appeared empty and dark, but for the tall Christmas tree aglow in the front window. Here Zac paused, uncertain how to proceed. He would have welcomed Eldy's help, but he still wasn't ready to face Sky.

Chelsea tried the door but found it locked. Repeated knocks brought no answer.

"Should we try around back?" suggested Pethybridge.

"No," said Zac. "We have to press on."

"But it's Sky's umbrella," said Chelsea. "He'll know what to do."

"No, Chelsea. I got us into this mess and I've got to get us out."

"What do you mean?" asked Ches. "It's not your fault Dada's on the rampage."

When Zac answered with silence, Chelsea said, "Zac's the one who gave the umbrella to the Aunties."

"*What*? First you tell me how great the umbrella is, then you surrender it to the enemy? I don't get it."

Zac fixed Ches with a hard stare. "You made me. Telling me Sky killed my mother."

"Oh, so it's my fault?"

"Maybe not all. But if you hadn't been so mean and stubborn—"

"You didn't have to believe him," said Chelsea. "Thinking Sky had anything to do with your mother's death is just dumb."

"Is it? Even if he didn't hurl the lightning bolt himself, he didn't stop it, did he?"

"I don't believe you, Zac Sparks! Who's being stubborn now?"

"I'm just saying I'm not sure."

"Then why not ask Sky about it yourself?"

"Yeah, I just bet Sky will admit he murdered my mom. Maybe he'll even apologize. 'There, there, little Zac, it's too bad but that lightning bolt just slipped out of my fingers …'"

In mingled grief and rage Zac kicked the door.

"Help me out here," said Ches. "I told you all along not to trust Porter. But oh no, you insist he's such a great guy. And now you make out like he's just as bad as Dada. Which is it? Is Porter a good guy or a bad guy?"

Despite his anger a series of scenes swam before Zac: his first sight of Sky with that uncomely, unforgettable face; his first day in the store when Sky so gloriously strewed nails all around; Zac's awesome introduction to the Weatherworks; the time with Chelsea when Sky coaxed out her first word … Yes, like him or not, Zac had to admit that Sky was not bad. Still, some puzzle pieces would not fit, and Zac had had enough of people telling him how to think and what to do.

"Chelsea," he said, "you've lived in Five Corners all your life. But you never bothered to cross the street to meet Sky until I introduced you. How come?"

Chelsea dropped her eyes. "I told you. I was scared. And confused."

"Well, maybe I'm confused too." Zac picked up a handful of gravel and threw it towards the mountain. "Look, even if Sky's a good guy, what's to say he'll help us against Dada? He never lifted a finger for me against the Aunties. Anyway, I can't face him without the umbrella. I stole it and I have to get it back."

At that a great tree of light appeared, a colossal lightning fork that split the sky over Wind Mountain. Even through mist the bolt was dazzling and utterly clear and right behind it came a peal of thunder so mighty it shook the ground.

Faint with fear, Zac fell to his knees and the others gathered round him.

"Ches," he breathed, "please … I have to do this.… Help me."

Hoisting Zac to his feet, Ches started him walking and announced gruffly, "Okay, gang, let's get on with it."

And so they headed up the mountain, passing through

drifting fog patches that seemed like smoking fires touched off by the lightning. In this nightmarish landscape Zac recalled his dream the night he'd slept with Eldy's balloon. A strange man had brought him his box of soldiers, the ones he'd had to leave behind when the Aunties took him away. Who, he wondered again, was that man? And where were Zac's soldiers now?

Looking around at Ches, Chelsea, Iris, and Pethybridge, he realized: Here was his army—not toy soldiers but real ones. For the first time since coming to Five Corners, he wasn't alone. He was surrounded by friends. They were a small army of friends advancing against one insane old man who had no right even to be alive. How many young lives, Zac wondered, had Dada cannibalized to prolong his own obscene existence?

Not far past Porter's, as the ground began to rise, so did the temperature. Before long it was not just warm, but hot. They'd been aware of this for some time before Pethybridge said, "Whew! I wish someone would turn down the thermostat."

"Dada's always cold," said Zac. "He's using the umbrella to raise the temperature." They were surrounded, Zac realized, by an entirely private weather system. The heat, the ghostly tatters of mist, the spasmodic lightning, the gathering storm—all this was just a foretaste of what was bound to occur with the blue umbrella in the hands of someone who cared only for himself. What would happen when they encountered him? Could such a villain really be stopped? Who could tell what tricks or spells he might perform? And that voice of his! If a skeleton could talk, its voice would be warm and friendly compared to Dada's.

Would even a real army, let alone an army of kids, stand any chance against Dada?

Like a bomb going off, a tremendous ball of light exploded right over their heads. With it came an awful splintering sound, as though somewhere off in the mist a tree (or a house?) had been hit. Zac's army halted. For some time no one spoke or moved. They barely breathed. Occurring at almost the same instant, the thunder and lightning had an eerily supernatural power. Even Ches looked ready to turn back.

"Pethybridge," said Zac, "you know that Tarzan yell you did back at the Aunties' place?"

"Yeah."

"Can you do it again?"

"Now? Here?"

"Why not?"

"Well, for one thing I don't feel like it. For another thing I'd look silly. And for another thing—"

"Pethybridge, it could be important."

"Really? Well, okay, I'll give it a try."

Looking scrawny and frail as a chicken, Pethybridge puffed out his chest, beat his small fists upon it, and gave a few halfhearted whoops.

"That was puny," said Zac. "I want a *yell*!"

This time, as Pethybridge struck his pose and opened his mouth, the sound he produced was so bloodcurdling it nearly knocked everyone down. Inspired, Zac copied him, pounding on his chest and yelling with utter savagery. How thrilling it was! Ches followed suit, and finally even the girls joined in.

The sound they created might not have been as loud as thunder, but inside their own bodies it felt louder, like a great war drum, and it echoed impressively off the mountainside.

Reinvigorated, they set off again at a brisk pace and soon reached the end of the trodden path and the big billboard that blared, in tall yellow letters on a striped background, KEEP OUT! When Pethybridge hesitated, Zac said, "C'mon, I've been up here before."

"You have? And you didn't get caught?"

"Pethybridge, I've been caught ever since I came to Five Corners. This place is one big prison. Now I'm breaking out."

From this point on, here and there in the soft dirt appeared a pair of thin tire tracks. Though they all saw this, no one commented until finally Iris said, "Imagine coming up here in a wheelchair. I wonder who pushed him?"

The only answer was a clap of thunder. Electrical activity was increasing, but otherwise the air was deathly still. When at last they emerged from the fog, the twin spires of the mountain peak seemed to jump out. The stark superstructure of the mine with its age-blackened timbers loomed like a scaffold. Though it was late afternoon and the light was fading, Zac found the sudden clarity disturbing. At least the mist, though eerie and disorienting, had also provided protection. Now, standing on the path in plain view, he felt exposed. Dada, and whoever was with him, could be looking at them right now. It was hard to imagine a more perilous situation: out in the open, on a mountaintop, with a maniac hurling thunderbolts.

Searching the slopes above, Zac saw no sign of movement. In the absence of wind, no song came from the twin peaks. The skyful of low black clouds churned slowly like a steaming cauldron. Out of this roil came skittish pulses of lightning and a nearly continuous growl of thunder.

"Weird weather for Christmas," commented Iris.

"So hot," said Pethybridge, "and the sun's not even out."

"Dada doesn't like sun," said Chelsea.

They spoke in whispers, hushed by foreboding.

"He's impossible to please," said Ches. "Even now, with the weather exactly the way he wants it, I bet he's miserable."

Just then, like sparks arcing across electrodes, a thick blue-white fork of lightning jumped between the mountain peaks. And in the dazzling flash they all saw the wheelchair. Parked beside the mine, wheels glinting silver, it was empty. Why? Dada's fur robe lay folded over the seat. Had they arrived too late? Had he already descended, with the umbrella, deep into the mountain? Was he under their feet at that moment, preparing a volcano or an earthquake?

Though Zac's thoughts raced with lurid possibilities, he urged the others on. "Let's go. If Dada's out of his chair, he'll be weaker."

Warily they picked their way toward the spot where the chair had appeared. Now darkness rushed upon them—not of night, but of something preternatural, a mix of the black, boiling clouds and of their own whirling thoughts. A pungent, sickroom odor told them Dada must be near, somewhere. Were they hunting him or was he hunting them?

Eventually they reached the barrier of rough boards around the mine shaft. Gawking up at the silhouetted scaffolding with its rusted housing and dangling ropes, it was easy to believe such a structure was meant for human execution. Adding to the macabre aura, out of the mine's depths came the ominous sounds Zac recalled so vividly from his last visit—rumblings, crashes, booming waters, a roar of winds—like dragons gnashing to be released from underground cages. With thunderings above and thunderings below, the mountain itself seemed alive.

Suddenly one tremendous sword of lightning leapt almost directly at Zac. Shuddering, he nearly passed out from shock. Nothing in the world frightened him so much as lightning. But in that fulminating flash, something even more frightening was revealed, stark as a nightmare.

There, just yards away, enthroned in the crevice of a massive rock, was Dada.

Chapter 35

War of Words

Bareheaded, hideously decrepit, pale as mushrooms, he seemed barely human. He was clad only in a thin black robe and the cane was propped at his elbow like a scepter. The two soaring peaks of Wind Mountain, though some distance beyond him, appeared to sprout like gargantuan wings from his stone throne.

More than ever Zac knew he had not the slightest idea who this creature was or what he might do. Was he a man, even, or something else: a shade? a force? a devil? Older than sin, colder than bone, he looked like something long dead, dug up from the grave. But plainly he was alive, for his stringy neck turned slightly, his hollow eyes flashed, his fleshless lips parted, and he spoke.

"Welcome, children! I've been expecting you."

There was no wind; the air was utterly still. Yet Dada's voice had the effect of a thin, moaning wind curling desolately among the rocks. He appeared to be speaking into the crook of the cane, held just under his chin like a microphone.

"Is it warm enough for you? Ah, lovely heat! Just a taste of what the blue umbrella can do. Here's another taste." And with a laugh that left not a shred of doubt that he was out of his mind, he wailed, "Do it again! Do it again for our little friends!"

Then a different voice, louder, shouted the one word, "Lightning!" and instantly a fiery fork rent the clouds, followed by a boom of thunder.

"Hear that?" crowed Dada. "It's the sound of the Devil hauling coal."

In the illuminating flash Zac noticed a tall, dark figure standing beside Dada, holding aloft the distinctive shape of a furled umbrella.

"Rev!" exclaimed Ches. "What are you doing here? And what's wrong with you …?"

Reverend Cholmondeley, gaunt as a shadow in his black morning coat, glassy-eyed and scruffy-whiskered, presented a figure almost as eerie as Dada himself. From whatever remote wasteland his soul had withdrawn to, he now turned his attention to his son.

"Chesterton, you have no business here. Go home and take the others with you."

"No, Edgerton, let them stay," ordered Dada. "Children are just what we want. How can you be a minister of the church and not love children? Come, my little ones, come see our pretty fireworks. Do it again, Edgerton. Do it again!"

Once more Reverend Cholmondeley stabbed the umbrella into the sky and loudly croaked, "Lightning!" This time the jagged bolt struck the summit and dislodged a boulder that came rumbling down so close to the children that they had to scramble out of the way. Dada's peal of laughter, though no louder than rustling grass, was somehow as penetrating as the thunder itself.

"My lovely umbrella! Guns, planes, bombs—all nothing compared to this. It's the ultimate weapon and now it's mine. All mine! Let everyone bow to the all-powerful Dada!"

So hypnotically persuasive was his voice that then and there the children might have succumbed to him—were it not for what happened next. To Zac's astonishment, Pethybridge stepped forward and, shaking his fist at the figure on the stone throne, shouted, "You're nothing but a big bully!"

This challenge, though fantastically brave, seemed to fall into a bottomless chasm. Dada lost no time in answering.

"And you, my little runt, are nothing but a filthy bed wetter who wears diapers at night and sleeps on plastic sheets! I bet you're peeing your pants right now."

The effect of these words on Pethybridge was staggering. Doubling over as though he'd been kicked in the groin, he collapsed.

"Oh yes, I know you, little Pethybridge." Dada spat out the name. "Too bad you're young again; as a little old man you were so cute. Especially as you lay in agony on your deathbed. And now, poor boy, you die anyway."

The others rushed to Pethybridge, who was curled tightly on the ground. They spoke to him, stroked his brow, hugged him, but it was no use. He was stiff and unresponsive as stone.

"What have you done to him?" cried Zac.

"Me? I've done nothing, my boy. Can I help it if he pees his pants? Maybe all that pee has rusted him."

Dada's chuckle was like dry leaves scuttling along a gutter. Before anyone could respond, the terrible voice began speaking to Iris: "Let's see now, who is this little miss? Or are you really a mister? Hard to tell from that ugly mug of yours."

In a moment of insight, Zac called out, "Plug your ears! His power is in his voice!" But though they all covered their ears, Dada's poisonous words pierced through, intimate and seductive as thought.

"You liked being a man, didn't you, Barber? Why? Because there's nothing feminine about you. *Iris*—ha! You're no flower, you're a weed. No wonder your parents rejected you."

He spoke so casually, like a snake sliding over a rock, but the effect on Iris was devastating. Like a plant singed by intense heat, she wilted to the ground. Again the others ran to help her, cradling her head and patting her cheeks, but they could rouse no response.

"It's no use," said Dada. "She got what was coming to her for killing my daughter Priscilla."

"Rev, stop him!" cried Ches. "He wants to use the umbrella to cause storms and disasters that will kill millions of people. Don't you care?"

Reverend Cholmondeley, in a burst of animation, piped up, "You're wrong, Chesterton. Dada doesn't want to *cause* storms but to *prevent* them." Warming to his topic, he lifted his voice and arms as though speaking from a pulpit. "Why, hurricanes, floods, earthquakes already abound. How many precious lives

382

are lost every day? Dada, by controlling the weather, will *stop* all that. He wants to bring order into the chaos. Let me tell you about his plan—"

"Enough, Edgerton," said Dada. "We don't want to bore the children."

"Rev," pleaded Ches, "you can't really believe all that stuff. It's lies! You should be ashamed—"

"Give up, Chesterton," interrupted Dada. "Your father listens only to me. Isn't that right, Edgerton?"

Reverend Cholmondeley, all animation draining away, his face a mask of lostness, nodded gravely.

"Chelsea, you talk to him," urged Ches. "He hasn't heard your voice yet."

Chelsea struggled to speak, but no sound came out. Finally she was able to say, "Dad, I love you."

"Chelsea? You spoke …?" As though awakening from a trance, the Reverend sounded tender, mystified.

"Love?" scoffed Dada, again with that dry, dreadful, deadening laugh. "What do you know about love, you brat? Your own father doesn't love you. Isn't that so, Edgerton?"

Reverend Cholmondeley hesitated.

"Go on. Tell your daughter you hate her."

After a tense silence, with resigned obedience the Reverend muttered, "I … hate … you." They were the first words he had said to his daughter in five years.

Chelsea looked stricken. Like a pricked balloon her whole frame deflated. Her hands fell to her sides, her chin dropped to her chest, her knees sagged. Ches grabbed her shoulders and pleaded with her, but she gave no response. Though still standing, she seemed not even to be there.

"She's mine now, Chesterton," intoned Dada, "just like your father. Your whole family is mine and you're powerless to help. You're nothing but a big wimp."

Swelling with anger, Ches charged at Dada, hands poised to throttle the scrawny neck.

"Edgerton, stop him! Open the earth!"

Reverend Cholmondeley, his face set, pointed the umbrella directly at his son and roared, "*Earthquake!*"

With a mighty crack the ground split right beneath Ches and he vanished. Zac ran to the edge of the fissure, but in the swirling dust he could see nothing. A sick feeling engulfed him as the voice of Dada, directed now at him, crawled under his skin, seeking his soul.

"You see, Boy? You can't escape. You followed me to this mountaintop and now you'll follow me anywhere. You belong to me. You proved it by getting me the umbrella. You're mine …"

That voice, droning on and on, was like a drug. Zac's mind worked furiously but all he could think of was an old nursery rhyme: "Sticks and stones may break my bones but words will never hurt me." Obviously that was wrong. Words were what hurt the most. Dada fired them like missiles.

"You thought you came up here to get back the umbrella," chanted the voice. "But what good is that? It won't change a thing between you and Porter. You'll never be his friend. You stole his most precious possession and he'll never forgive you …"

Beneath the verbal assault, Zac's mind kept dwelling on the little sticks-and-stones rhyme. It just wasn't true. Words—the real power was in words. And if Dada could use words, why couldn't he? Didn't Zac Sparks have a tongue? Couldn't he fire words like bullets, lob them like grenades? What might he say that could reach inside Dada and search out his weakness? Did Dada even have a weakness? What was it? Zac had no clue. All he could do was open his mouth and start talking.

"Listen to me, Dada! But why call you Dada? You're not my Dada. You're nobody's Dada. You weren't even a real father to your daughters. All you gave them was pain and fear. And now they're dead. Worse than dead …"

Words welled up from deep inside Zac, poured over his tongue like a river of fire.

"Oh yes, today your own children were eaten by worms. And the same will happen to you! Juicy, wriggling little worms and squishy maggots will burrow into the middle of your skull and nibble out your brains. You won't live forever. Today you die!"

Where did this come from? Zac himself felt the force of these words, and the man on the rock throne, despite being paralyzed, jumped as if electrified. The sudden movement was so alarming that Zac quit talking, giving Dada just enough time to recover.

Sinking back, his face red as flames, he bellowed, "*How dare you!*"

It was a real shout. The three words undid Zac's insides like a zipper. And Dada wasn't finished.

"*Edgerton, destroy that boy! Strike him dead with a thunderbolt!*"

Reverend Cholmondeley jabbed the umbrella at Zac and cried, "*Lightning!*" The umbrella lurched in his hand and a jagged yellow streak leapt out of the black clouds and rushed straight at Zachary Sparks.

Then all was darkness.

Chapter 36

Another Sky

Zac wasn't sure how long he remained in the dark. But gradually he became aware of a sound. Running water. At first he thought it was rain. Hard rain. Had the dark clouds over the mountain burst? However, the longer he listened, the more the rain was like water in a stream, rippling over rocks and swishing along reedy banks. It was a beautiful, clear sound, almost like music. Zac found it so soothing that his fear and tension began to melt away.

Having closed his eyes when the lightning struck, he opened them now and saw what he was hearing: a moving sheet of water, transparent as glass, shot through with skeins of silver and gold, blues and greens. The wondrous play of colors seemed perfectly synchronized with the music. Peering deeper into the watery window, his eyes met other, brighter colors: ruby, emerald, turquoise, sapphire. He realized he was seeing stones in the bed of a stream. Not ordinary stones, but gems, each one as pure and clear as the water itself. He had the impression he could have looked through the gems themselves and seen something else, and then more beyond that, layer after layer. But instead he looked up until he saw the whole river.

It was the most beautiful river ever—more beautiful than he'd imagined anything could be. Crystalline, gently winding, lined with luxuriant trees and brimming, burbling, sparkling with life. For a time Zac simply gazed, feeling perfectly tranquil, refreshed, washed clean, as though the river itself were flowing through him.

He sat up (he'd been lying on his side) and began to look around. Between him and the river lay an expanse of lawn whose color—a rich, blueish green—was at once restful and intriguing. Flowers dotted the grass, making their own delicate music as they stirred in the breeze, and the air was flecked with butterflies so bright the river stones might have taken flight. Farther off were rosebushes whose blooms seemed to sing their own lovely names: Peace, Gloriana, Paradise Gold, Heavenly Radiance.

Then he noticed the sky. Somehow it was different from the sky he had always known. Though intensely luminous, its radiance was gentle as twilight and seemed uniformly dispersed, as though emanating not from the sun but from within. Indeed everything—grass, trees, flowers, water—appeared lit from within and there were no shadows.

So enthralled was Zac that when he gazed across the lawn and saw a life-sized photograph of his mother—the same one that Esmeralda had burned up in the fire—he was scarcely surprised. He simply thought, *Of course she's here!*

Before his eyes the photograph began to move. A few strands of her long brown hair lifted; the roses around her stirred. As Zac stood and walked toward her, a deeper color suffused her cheeks, her head tilted slightly, her smile brightened.

Lightly he mounted the steps to the veranda of his old home and his mother reached out for his hand and motioned him into the chair beside her.

He had stepped into a scene that was exactly as in the photograph, but also different: richer, brighter, more vivid. His mother sat in the cane rocker and Zac in his favorite hanging basket chair, the one he loved to twirl in. But now he remained quite still, wanting only to drink deeply of this moment.

Giving his hand a squeeze, his mother said quietly, "Zachary, what's happened? Why are you here?"

"I was struck by lightning, Mom."

"My goodness! You, too? You weren't walking on the golf course, were you?"

"No. It's kind of a long story. Somebody threw a thunder-bolt at me."

"Oh! How thrilling!"

"Thrilling? I'm not sure. It was a bad man who did it."

"But now that you're here—isn't it wonderful?"

Again Zac looked around at the river, the soft trees, the teal grass. For the first time, off in the distance, he noticed what appeared to be a city, white and shining.

"Mom, where are we?"

Smiling, she replied, "I haven't explored, Zachary. I know I could. I can go anywhere I want. But so far I haven't wanted to. I've been very content right here. There's so much to think about, so much to see."

Had she answered his question? It didn't seem to matter because what she said was so beautiful. Her words, the very sound of her voice, rang with clarity and truth. Zac, too, felt perfectly content in this place.

"Still," she went on, "it may be time to go exploring. That city over there—it intrigues me."

Zac seemed to see the white, shining city through her eyes. She had a quality of simple openness that made him feel he could see into the depths of her heart.

"Do you think I should go, Zachary? To the city?"

"Why not?"

"Are you sure you don't mind?"

"Mind?"

Zac had to think about this. Though feelings were pure and immediate in that place, thinking seemed to come slowly. Before he could answer, his mother spoke again.

"May I tell you a story?"

"Yes, I'd like that."

"Do you recall those nights we used to sit up together on this veranda to watch thunder-and-lightning storms? Remember I used to say the thunder meant they were moving furniture upstairs?"

Yes, he remembered.

"One time we heard a particularly loud thunder crash, rumbling on and on, and you said that must be a big grand piano being rolled across a hardwood floor. We could hear all the strings vibrating like a thousand songs all at once, and you said the angels must play not harps but pianos. Remember?"

Oh yes! How they'd laughed about that and made up stories

about a whole orchestra in the sky. What talks they'd had out here on the veranda during those terrific, booming storms!

"Well, Zachary, one night I was out walking on the golf course in the rain. It was just an ordinary rain, not a thunderstorm. But suddenly, off in the distance I heard thunder. More than that"—leaning across and touching Zac's arm, she lowered her voice—"I heard music in it. It was so beautiful! I wasn't sure what the instrument was—not a piano but some instrument I'd never imagined. Like a voice, but richer, more magnificent. It played a song that was all about me. Furniture was being moved upstairs, and I knew it was being moved *for me.* I knew that a place was prepared for me. Imagine—a room in the sky! A bit like that penthouse we once stayed in by the ocean—remember?— where it felt like we could see for ever and ever?"

As she paused, there was the slightest movement of wind and all the flowers and leaves and grass blades chimed like little bells.

"Naturally I thought of you, Zachary. How could I leave you? But the thunder was calling me, singing to me, and before I knew it, it was right on top of me and the whole night lit up. That lightning—it happened so softly, so gently, like the little lamp on my bedside table being switched on. And the covers on the bed were turned down and the pillow fluffed, and there was a shelf of my favorite books and a picture of you on the wall. My own room up in the sky was all ready for me. And so I went."

In a moment of profound stillness, everything seemed to wait for Zac to respond. He didn't know what to say. It was a good story, and like all good stories it began to set something right inside him, as if some heavy furniture in his heart that had been out of place was being rearranged.

"Now," she went on, "I'm hearing the music again. Not the same, but different. Even more like a voice this time, or many voices, a great choir. They're calling to me from that city over there and I want to go. In fact there's someone I want to find there. Someone I hope to meet."

These words jarred a memory in Zac.

"Mom, the other night I dreamed that a strange man brought me my box of soldiers."

"Really? What did he look like?"

The man's face had been hazy. But all at once Zac saw him clearly and described him. He was slim, red-haired, dressed in a blue uniform with silver wings on the lapels …

"Why, Zachary," said his mother, "don't you know who that was?"

He did not. And then it came to him. Still, he asked, "Who?"

She beamed. "That was your father! Of course he'd be the one to bring you your soldiers—he was a soldier himself."

Zac was astonished. There'd been a photograph of his father on their mantel, right beside the vase of rose petals labeled ESSENCE OF SUMMERS PAST. In Zac's dream his father had looked the same as in that photo, yet Zac hadn't recognized him. His father was dead; he wasn't someone who moved and talked and did things—even in dreams. He'd never seemed quite real.

Now he was. This man only heard about in stories was no

longer a fairy tale but someone Zac had met, seen for himself, once in a dream and now again while talking to his mother. He couldn't get over it. Knowing his father—and knowing that his father had come to him—somehow changed things.

His mother said, "I want to go to the shining city to be with your father. I think it's time. Will you let me go?"

What? Why was she asking him?

"Can I come with you, Mom? Will you take me?"

The moment he said this, he knew it wasn't right. It wasn't his time to go to the city. It was right for her, not for him.

"The music calls me, Zachary. I hear your father's voice in it. I want to go. Where is your music calling you?"

Then he heard it. Not music, exactly, but a sound so enchanting that it seemed musical. A familiar sound, though he hadn't heard it often. It was the sound of the blue umbrella: the rich rustle of the canopy opening, like the murmur of a thousand wings, and the sliding of the golden ring up the smooth wooden shaft, then the squeak of the fabric as it tightened and the light, satisfying click of the spring finding its home.

The blue umbrella was calling to Zac. He could see it too—the deep, entrancing underside of the canopy, that silken circle the very color and texture of the sky. Not this sky—not the sky of this place where he sat with his mother. Another sky. Another sky was calling him.

"Yes, Mom," he said, "you can go to the city now. I want you to go."

She gave his hand another squeeze, and again he was plunged into darkness.

Chapter 37

The Red Umbrella

The next thing Zac knew, he was looking into the face of Sky Porter. Where had he come from? Sky was lying beside him on the ground, eyes closed. In the background rose the two tall spires of Wind Mountain.

Lifting himself on one elbow, Zac could now see the entire length of Sky's form. The man lay in a strange posture, sprawled, his arms and legs at odd angles. Tentatively Zac touched his shoulder, then shook him gently. There was no response.

"Sky. Sky. What's wrong?"

Zac heard the brittle cackle of laughter.

"Oh, how perfect! Far better than I could possibly have planned!"

Zac sprang to his feet and faced the source of the jeering voice: Dada. "What have you done to Sky?" he yelled.

"My dear boy," crooned Dada, "don't you understand? That lightning bolt was aimed at you, but that fool Porter stepped out and took it for you. And now he's dead! Oh happy day!"

Zac remembered something: Just before he'd lost consciousness, a figure had appeared beside him, blazing with light. Glancing again at Sky, his body tragically twisted, Zac

394

felt the dark weight of realization. But it was no time to grieve. Enraged, he balled his fists and rushed, yelling, straight at the figure on the rock. Faster than Ches had been, he got much closer; one more step and his knuckles would have plowed into the eggshell of that hateful old skull. But long, black arms caught him, stopped him, spun him round.

Reverend Cholmondeley.

Like a dark bird of prey the Reverend loomed over him. Struggling with all his might, Zac managed to land a few punches and kicks. But the Reverend, tough as an old tire, kept swatting him with the umbrella until finally, when Zac shrank back for a moment, the man plowed his fist full into the boy's stomach. Winded, Zac stumbled backward a step or two, and then the ground disappeared from under him. Blindly he flailed, seeking something, anything to grab onto. *Rope!* A piece of rope brushed his hands and he gripped it tight. The jolt nearly broke his arms, but he held on, swinging back and forth and finally coming to rest.

A roaring sound filled his ears and all around was dark. But looking up, he saw daylight, a circle of brightness laced with a network of black lines—boards, ropes, metal struts. Then the head of Reverend Cholmondeley came into view, peering down.

Zac realized he had fallen into the mine shaft. The noise was the roar of tornadoes and tidal waves thrashing far below. He would be down there himself were it not for the thin rope in his burning hands. Dangling just below the lip of the shaft, he clung to life.

"Good job, Edgerton!" cried Dada, his thin voice piercing even the din of winds and waters. "What a perfect end for the boy—right into the clutches of the weather he loves!"

Just when it seemed he could hang on no longer, Zac's toes located a narrow perch, enough to ease the pressure a little on his arms. As he pressed himself against the cold stone wall, Reverend Cholmondeley jerked on the rope, trying to make him let go.

"Come, Boy. You can't hang there forever."

"Perhaps he needs help, Edgerton," mused Dada. "Let's see. How about a little hot lava? A volcanic eruption? Not a big one, mind you, just enough to bubble up and tickle the boy's toes. Do it, Edgerton!"

Obedient to Dada's every command, Reverend Cholmondeley pointed the blue umbrella into the mouth of the mine and shouted, "Volcano!" From below came a deep rumbling sound like an immense beast clearing its throat. The whole mountain shook and Zac imagined molten lava spewing toward him. Too frightened to look down, he looked up and saw his one chance.

Reverend Cholmondeley, his gaunt frame trembling, was still pointing the umbrella down into the shaft. Its tip was just beyond Zac's reach, but propelled by adrenaline he shoved off hard from the narrow ledge, let go of the rope, and managed to catch hold of the furled canopy with both hands. Startled, the Reverend gave a mighty yank, managing only to pull Zac, like a big fish, all the way out of the mine. The two of them rolled on the ground, tugging the umbrella back and forth as the

Reverend yelled, "Let go, you little imp!" He bit the boy's hand but Zac held on and fought back savagely. In the background an eerie, keening sound began, something between a cry and a howl. Was it Dada?

"Helllllllllp! Helllllllllp!"

Riveted by his master's voice, Reverend Cholmondeley let go of the umbrella, jumped to his feet, and made a move to run to Dada. But in midstride he stopped and simply stared. Zac, too, glancing over his shoulder, went perfectly still and gaped in horror.

Down the mountain straight toward them flowed a bright, glowing, orange-gold stream of fiery magma. To Zac's surprise it issued not from the mineshaft but from the mountain peak, from between the two soaring spires. Heartsick for his friends trapped on the slopes below—whether alive or dead, he had no idea—what could he do? Nothing. With the burning torrent racing toward him, he took to his heels and scrambled sideways along the steep mountainside. When he paused to look back, he saw Reverend Cholmondeley down on his knees with hands lifted, apparently imploring heaven to stop the eruption. As if in answer, the lava flow, having first fanned out, narrowed to funnel through a rocky gully that led directly toward the mineshaft. Squarely in its path sat just one person, a figure utterly incapable of saving himself from the sizzling fate that, ironically, he had commanded.

Suddenly recalling that he had the blue umbrella, Zac lifted it and pointed—but too late. Already the lava was swarming around Dada on his rock throne, momentarily buoying him up so that he appeared to sit atop the blazing stream as though riding a dragon. In this exalted fashion, borne on a fiery chariot, he vanished down the mouth of the mine as the whole molten river poured down of top of him. All that remained of Dada—and that only for a second or two—was his voice, a thin, echoing shriek, fading and fading down the long shaft until suddenly, like a match extinguished, it ceased.

In shock Zac stared as the burning flow slowed to a smoking trickle. Gradually the ground stopped shaking; the eruption was over. Confined to the uppermost slope, the lava had touched no one except Dada. Even Reverend Cholmondeley, collapsed facedown in the dust, had escaped by inches.

The body of Sky Porter lay sprawled as before, limbs pitifully splayed. Running to him and kneeling down, Zac lifted one of the limp hands. Heavy, lifeless, it felt like a thing. Gently Zac slipped the smooth crook of the umbrella into Sky's hand and closed his fingers around it.

"Here, Sky," he whispered. "Here's your umbrella. I'm sorry I took it. I'm sorry for everything. It's all my fault. I'm so sorry."

He wanted to cry but could not. Even the blue umbrella, powerful as it was, could not help Sky now. He was beyond the weather of this world, carried beyond by a lightning bolt. Just like Zac's mother.

Had Zac really seen her, talked to her? Where? It didn't matter. He couldn't go back there. She was beyond reach. And now Sky was there too, beyond reach.

And the others—what about them? Looking around, Zac saw them—Iris, Pethybridge, Chelsea—all still frozen in the same postures to which Dada's cruel words had reduced them. Were they also dead? And what about Ches? Swallowed by the mountain, he was gone.

Alone. Zac Sparks had never felt so alone. In all his miserable time at Five Corners, he had never been so desolate. And it was all, entirely, his own fault. How many lives had been destroyed because of him?

Turning back to Sky and lightly touching the man's cheek, he whispered, "How I wish I could do things over. How I wish you could come back and make everything right again."

As though the sun had come out (though it hadn't), a warm brightness suffused the air. A hint of cool breeze stirred and to Zac's astonishment the man's eyelids fluttered open. Two flecks of cerulean blue flashed up at him like portals into another world. And starting at the very place where Zac's hand rested, color flowed into the face.

Sky Porter was alive! So amazed was Zac, so deeply relieved, that his pent-up tears began to flow. When Sky reached up to touch his glistening cheek, it felt like the sky itself caressing him.

"Hello, Zac," he said, smiling. "I see you accomplished what you came to do. Well done!"

"Well done?" Zac couldn't believe what he was hearing. Hardly able to see Sky through his tears, he muttered, "What do you mean?"

"Well, what's this in my hand?"

The reminder of the umbrella pricked Zac with shame. "Sky, this has all been my fault. I messed up so much. I never should have borrowed your umbrella."

"Why do you say that?"

"Don't you know what happened? I gave the umbrella to the Aunties. I still can't believe I did that. I'm so sorry, Sky. Why did you ever let me have it?"

"Why? Simple: I trusted you. And still do. When you trust someone, it's not because they won't ever fail you. It's because what you see in their heart is deeper than any failure."

Still doubtful, Zac looked away. Then he burst out, "But I thought you were dead!"

"Dead? Not quite. Though I could have been, without this."

Sky indicated an object in his other hand, something Zac had not noticed. For a split second it looked like a bloody sword. Then Zac realized it was another umbrella, a bright red one with a silver handle. Baffled, he asked, "Does that control the weather too?"

Sky laughed. "No, only one umbrella does that. This one is quite ordinary—except for one rather special feature. The tip, shaft, and handle are entirely made of one piece of metal."

Zac regarded him quizzically.

"Ever hear of a lightning rod? Lightning, you see, doesn't want to hurt anyone. What it wants is to travel harmlessly into the ground. For that, nothing works better than a length of conductive metal."

Zac was dumbfounded. "Are you saying the bolt intended for me passed through that umbrella instead?"

"Exactly."

"So that thing saved our lives?"

"Right. With Rutherford on the loose, I thought it might come in handy. In this case an ordinary umbrella turned out to be more powerful than my fancy blue one. Funny, isn't it?"

Sky's chuckle was so engaging that Zac, amazed as he was, joined in. Catching himself, he asked, "But how did you happen along just at that moment?"

Sky frowned. "I wish I'd come sooner. But when I learned of Rutherford's plans, I thought it best to make the storehouses under the mountain more secure. By the time I got here, Reverend Cholmondeley was just aiming the blue umbrella at you. I grabbed your hand and jabbed the red umbrella into the ground. The strike was enough to stun me, but that's all. How about you? Did you feel anything?"

"No, I just blacked out or something. I thought I was dead. And then …"

"Yes?"

"I saw my mother."

"Really? You must have had a vision."

"A vision? You mean it wasn't real?"

"Oh, it was real. A vision is more real than what we normally see."

Zac was bewildered. "So much has happened, Sky."

"Tell me."

Pointing to the pitifully stricken bodies of Chelsea, Iris,

and Pethybridge, Zac related the day's tragic events. Sky listened and looked on sorrowfully, but did not comment. Only on hearing of Dada's death did he show surprise. Looking off into the distance, his eyes moist, he responded, "So Rutherford is dead? Excuse me, Zac, but I've known him all my life."

After a respectful pause Zac said, "Well, I won't miss him. And nobody's going to miss that awful cane."

Zac then led Sky to the place where Ches had disappeared, but there was no sign of him. The crevice that had opened in the earth had closed.

"Sky, can you use the umbrella to open it?"

"It's not that easy, Zac. Major weather events can't simply be reversed."

"You mean Ches is gone?"

Sky looked troubled, but said nothing.

"And what about Chelsea and the others? Is there any hope for them?"

Chapter 38

A Keg of Glories

Crouching down to examine the body of Pethybridge, still lying in a crumpled heap, Sky said, "A curse has done this. But a curse, Zac, is only words. What did Rutherford say to him?"

Zac felt embarrassed. "He made fun of Pethybridge's name. And he called him … a bed wetter."

"I see. What would you say to someone who's ashamed about wetting the bed?"

Zac's face flushed. "Well, I'd tell him …"

"Tell Pethybridge. Speak to him."

So utterly still was Pethybridge, so deeply bewitched, that talking to him seemed like talking to the ground. Still, Zac tried.

"Pethybridge, that business about wetting the bed—don't let it get to you. Growing old so fast, and being sick, and having to live with those awful Aunties—it was really hard on you. Besides, lots of people are bed wetters. I—" Zac glanced at Sky. "I used to do it myself."

A tiny flicker passed over Pethybridge's face. His eyebrows lifted minutely, as if to say, "Really?"

"Yeah, it's true," pursued Zac. "But not anymore. I got over it and so will you."

Pethybridge's features seemed to relax a little, but there was no further sign of life.

Sky, leaning his face close to the victim's, whispered something. Then he winked at Zac and said, "That stuffy old name of his—I think he needs a new one, don't you? Let's see. How about Dick? Or maybe Harry?"

These suggestions elicited from Pethybridge a faint yet distinct scowl.

"What do you think, Zac? Have you a name for our friend?"

Zac said the first name that popped into his head. "How about Tom?"

This time the effect on Pethybridge was, if possible, even more dramatic than Dada's curse had been. Like someone who'd just won a million dollars, he not only revived but leaped to his feet like a jack-in-the-box.

"Tom? Tom?" he exclaimed. "I've always wanted to be Tom! How did you know?" Dancing with excitement, he threw his spindly arms around both Sky and Zac and hugged them hard. Then, stepping back, he examined himself all over. "Do you really think I look like a Tom?"

It was too funny. Zac and Sky had to laugh.

"Every inch a Tom," said Sky. "What thinkest thou, Zac?"

"Totally Tom-ish."

"Oh, thank you, thank you so much!" gushed Tom. "You don't know what this means to me. I feel like a new person. I *am* a new person! I'm Tom!" And to announce it to the world, he threw back his head and crowed like a rooster.

"Crow louder, Tom," urged Zac. "We have to wake up the others."

Next they turned their attention to the wilted form of Iris. Tom's crow must have done something, for the moment Sky took her by the hand, life flowed into her and she rose to her feet like a graceful dancer. Her face, however, remained drawn and vacant.

Whispering in Sky's ear, Zac reported what Dada had said to her. Then Sky said, "Iris, look at me. See this face of mine?"

From somewhere far away Iris peered, more and more intently, into the homely face of Sky Porter. As she looked, Zac saw her own face begin to change. Light came into her eyes as if an empty pool were filling with water.

"I'm no movie star," said Sky. "But tell me honestly: Do you find me ugly?"

Briskly Iris shook her head, then broke into such a smile that her whole face shone. Indeed in that moment a true beauty came upon her like a mantle, a blossoming into loveliness. It was as dramatic a change as her former transformation from the old Barber.

"Wow!" exclaimed both Tom and Zac.

"You're right, Iris," continued Sky, "I'm not ugly. And neither are you. You're a very beautiful girl."

Even to ten-year-old Zac there was no doubt now about Iris's gender. He felt a little strange when she gave him a hug.

Not far away stood Chelsea, still paralyzed, head and arms hanging limp as a rag doll. As they all gathered around her, Tom crowed again but to no effect. Finally Sky, laying one finger beneath her chin, gently raised her head. Then he lifted one of her arms and, again with one finger, wrote a word on her palm. Immediately Chelsea stood up straighter and the glow of life returned. But still her eyes stared vacantly.

"What else do you think she needs, Zac?" asked Sky.

Right away Zac knew. "The blue umbrella!" And as Sky gently settled the crook of the umbrella in her hand, Zac said, "Hey, Chelsea, haven't we had enough black clouds and lightning? How about some sun?"

Though her eyes brightened a little, the umbrella did not move.

"Sunshine is quite simple," said Sky. "All you have to do is hold the umbrella and smile."

Barely had Sky finished speaking when it happened—so quickly it was hard to say which came first: Did Chelsea's smile light up the sky, or did the sun come out and light up Chelsea?

"Oh my!" she exclaimed as the golden rays bathed her face. By now the afternoon was far advanced and a huge sun, low on the horizon, had slid down into the one narrow band of clear sky, igniting the entire ceiling of clouds with orange fire. For some time the five friends stood perfectly still, overcome now by a very different sort of spell, one cast by spectacular beauty.

"Nice job, Chelsea," said Zac.

"Have you ever seen anything so lovely?" she said.

"Only your smile," said Sky.

When Chelsea offered the umbrella back to Sky, he shook his head. "No, I feel silly carrying two umbrellas. Zac, would you take it for me?"

"No way!" Zac recoiled from the blue umbrella as if it had teeth. "I'm not touching that thing ever again."

Sky regarded him thoughtfully. "I understand how you feel. But look at it this way: You got the umbrella back for me, didn't you? And with Rutherford and his daughters dead, the world has been freed from a scourge. Just ask Tom and Iris if things have worked out well for them."

The two former senior citizens nodded vigorously.

"So you see, Zac, giving you the umbrella was a good thing. Don't you agree?"

Zac blushed and looked away. But Sky wouldn't leave it at that.

"I want you to answer me. Was I was right to trust you?"

Shuffling his feet, Zac murmured, "What about Ches?"

Chelsea had begun searching distractedly for her brother. Having not witnessed his disappearance, she had no idea what had happened. Gently Zac tried to explain, but she couldn't accept it and kept calling Ches's name.

And suddenly there he was! From behind a boulder, in precisely the place where the earth had swallowed him, Chesterton Cholmondeley came lumbering toward them. Covered in clumps of dirt and stones, he looked like a walking chunk of mountain.

"Ches!" cried his sister, throwing her arms around him. But he remained stiff and cold, even when all the children crowded around to welcome him and brush away the debris.

"What's wrong, Ches? Say something, please!" begged Chelsea.

"Keep talking," said Sky. "He loves the sound of your voice."

As Chelsea continued, Ches's face did soften some. But still he seemed far away, unreachable, and Chelsea grew frustrated.

"Ches," said Sky, "there's something I'd like you to see." He was pointing with the blue umbrella. "Will you come?"

About a hundred yards away was a promontory affording a spectacular view of the entire horizon. With Sky guiding him, Ches headed that way, shuffling his feet like an old man along a hospital corridor. The others followed until soon they were all remarking on how quickly the sun had burned off the western fog, leaving the town of Five Corners beautifully bathed in the golden rays of late afternoon. But this wasn't what Sky had in mind to show Ches. Instead he pointed eastward, where fog still clung to the valley as thick as wool on a sheep.

Suddenly Ches, seeing what Sky saw, stabbed his finger and cried, "Look! Look!"

Zac looked and caught his breath. The sun, directly behind them, was casting their enlarged shadows onto the fog bank directly below. Zac's shadow was surrounded by a glorious halo, beautifully colored, as if someone had taken a rainbow out of the sky and bent it into a circle all around him. Five other shadows were cast on the fog beside Zac's, but only his had the rainbow halo. He moved to the left, to the right, jumped up and down, did a little dance. Wherever he moved, the halo followed. The others, too, were jabbering and cavorting, but none more excitedly than Ches.

"Wow! I just read about this but never thought I'd see one. Usually you see them from airplanes, not from the ground …"

Zac couldn't understand why Ches was so elated, since the rainbow was around his shadow, not Ches's. Unwilling to spoil his friend's enthusiasm, Zac whispered his question to Iris.

"It's not around you, silly," she retorted. "It's around me!"

"Is not!" said Tom. "It's around me!"

"Hey, kids," laughed Sky, "no need to fight. You've all got your own halo, but only you can see it."

"What is it?" asked Iris. "Magic?"

"Nothing magic about it," said Ches. "It's a *glory:* a meteorological phenomenon caused by the sun's rays scattering in a cloud of small, uniform droplets."

"Try speaking English," said Tom.

"Ches is right," said Sky. "A glory is basically a mix of sunshine at your back and fog at your feet. This morning in the Weatherworks I opened a keg of glories."

"A *keg*?" echoed Tom. "That *must* be magic."

"No, only weather. But to see a glory, conditions have to be just right. I couldn't finish the job until Zac gave me back the blue umbrella."

Eyeing the umbrella with fresh admiration, the children then returned to enjoying their glories, waving their arms to make giant angel wings and generally behaving like kids with a new toy. In all the excitement they almost forgot the remarkable way the glory had revived Ches.

"Nice to have you back," said Zac. "What happened, anyway? We thought you were a goner."

"Down that piddly little crevice? Nah, I just crawled out. Luckily I made it just before she closed up. That's two brushes with death today. Getting a bit tiresome."

Zac asked Ches why the glory had had such an effect on him. It turned out that the junior meteorologist had recently graduated from nephology, the study of clouds, to rainbows and other optical phenomena.

"How can you study rainbows? What's to know?"

"Tons. You have no idea."

"For example?"

"Well, there are different types of rainbow: fogbow, moon-bow, hailbow …"

Zac's ears perked up. "Hailbow? What's that?"

"Just what it sounds like: a rainbow occurring not in rain but in hail. Extremely rare. They say it's almost colorless."

"That's right," said Zac. "I saw one."

"You did?" Ches sounded genuinely impressed.

"Yeah, the day of my mother's funeral. The whole sky was weird, all kinds of things going on at once. Almost like the weather was trying to tell me something."

Zac glanced at Sky. Was it possible, even back then, that Sky Porter had been communicating with him?

"I know what you mean," said Ches. "When I saw that glory, it was like a message just for me. I was looking at pictures of glories yesterday and wished I could see one. How could Sky know that, Zac?"

It came as a surprise to hear Ches call him Zac instead of Bud. Something about Ches had changed.

"Sky seems to know a lot of things," Zac reflected.

They were interrupted by a cry of distress from Chelsea, who had discovered her father lying on the ground near the mine shaft. Kneeling beside him, she cradled his head, spoke to him, stroked his hair. Finally her small face looked up imploringly at Sky. "What's wrong with him? Can you help?"

Sky frowned but said nothing. Together they turned Reverend Cholmondeley onto his back. Even in the golden glow of the sun, his long face looked ashen.

"I wish I could pour the sunshine into him!" lamented Chelsea.

"Perhaps you will, my dear," said Sky.

Ches regarded his father curiously, but without comment. He did help to hoist the Reverend into Dada's wheelchair, where he sat stiffly, surprisingly upright, his haggard eyes wide open like those of a stuffed animal in a museum.

Studying him, Zac asked Sky, "Why couldn't anyone stand up to Dada? It was like he mesmerized people."

"He did. Between the cane's power and the blue umbrella, none of you stood a chance up here."

"His voice was so creepy—the way it got right inside you."

"Yes, that's a form of sorcery."

"Eldy's voice does that too," reflected Zac.

"And how does that make you feel?" asked Sky.

Zac thought for some time before replying, "Dada's voice always pushed me where I didn't want to go. But Eldy's is like an invitation to what I really want—even if I don't know what that is."

"Well put," said Sky.

As they all assembled to make their way back down the mountain, Sky returned to his earlier question. "Now answer me, Zac. Was I right to trust you with the blue umbrella?"

When Zac still hesitated, Sky said, "Let me put it this way: Are you trustworthy? Answer yes or no."

Somehow, like a shaft of sunlight that finds its way into a dark forest, the rephrased question touched Zac's heart. With simple clarity he saw that even though he'd made mistakes and done wrong, still he could be trusted.

"Yes," he answered, "I am trustworthy."

"And can you say the same for me?"

Even more than the first question, this one caught Zac off guard. But looking up into those clear blue eyes and at that wise and merry face, he had not a trace of doubt that yes, he could trust this man. He could trust him more than anyone in the world.

"I do trust you, Sky," he said. "And from now on I always will."

"Thank you. I'm honored."

As if receiving a golden crown, Zac accepted Sky's offer of the blue umbrella. Again he was amazed at its lightness, a lightness instantly communicated from his hand to his heart so that a tension he'd felt for weeks lifted. It almost seemed as if years fell away from him.

"It's awfully warm for December twenty-third," commented Sky. "Shouldn't we do something about that?" When Zac went to hand back the umbrella, Sky stopped him. "No, you do it."

"Me? How?"

"How do you think? The umbrella works like a third hand, a natural extension of your thoughts."

Zac thought hard. He thought about lowering the temperature but nothing happened.

"You have to learn to think like the weather," said Sky. "This is important, Zac. You need to start somewhere if you're going to be my apprentice."

"Your *what*?"

"I've been looking for someone to pass on the trade to. Would you like the job?"

Zac was too astounded to speak.

"You need a home and a family. I mentioned it to Dad and we'd both love to have you to live with us. In fact I've already prepared a room for you upstairs in the Weatherworks. What do you say?"

Zac couldn't say anything. All he could do was throw his arms around Sky, bury his face in the flannel shirt, and let the tears come.

"Will you adopt me?" he managed to whisper.

"With your permission. And the old men will adopt you too. You'll have more grandfathers than you can shake a stick at. But right now there's work to be done. We can't have Christmas in this heat wave."

Christmas? As if a silver bell had rung, Zac recalled his mother's (or was it O's?) instruction: "I want you to have a merry Christmas." At the time this had seemed utterly impossible, but now, all by itself, it was coming true.

Suddenly Zac knew what to do. Pointing the umbrella

toward the northeast, where the clouds were darkest, he made a circular, stirring motion with the tip, just as he'd seen Sky do in the wind bins of the Weatherworks. At once a light breeze arose and began to dissipate Dada's oppressive heat.

"Good for you, Zac," said Sky. "That just happens to be the right direction to bring snow today."

As the breeze blew, the mountain began to sing. Funneling between the two peaks, the wind made the sweetest of sounds, rising and falling in an exquisite melody that seemed almost familiar. For a while everyone stopped to listen, and in the enchantment of the strange music, they remembered things they'd never known.

Chapter 39

Merry Christmas

As the whole company proceeded down the mountain, the wind picked up, the temperature dropped, and the song from the peak grew ever more intense and joyous. By now the sun had set and a beautiful twilight glow suffused the air. Colored lights were winking on in the town and the five intersecting roads twinkled like the rays of a star. With every step Zac felt himself traveling deeper into Christmas.

On approaching Porter's Store, they heard another sound of singing—high, thin, trembling voices spilling faintly into the street. Enthralled, and enticed by Sky's offer of hot chocolate, they entered to discover the old men—Abe, Sam, Joe, Ike, Dan, and Eli—gathered around the blazing Christmas tree, lifting their voices in a carol. The music seemed to blend with the natural aromas of the store: cheese and apples, nutmeg and peppermint, coffee, leather, old wood. Eli played the fiddle, Abe strummed a guitar, and Eldy was there too, not singing but tooting on a pennywhistle, and not standing upright but bent over, his bald head gleaming in the light of a hundred candles that glimmered along counters and shelves. And somewhere in the background was another voice lovelier than all the rest, distinct yet seamlessly blended, embroidering the most beautiful harmonies and descants like golden threads through the old men's homespun sounds. Zac knew this other voice—it was O—but though he peered all around he saw no sign of O herself. Her music seemed to come from nowhere, yet was everywhere, as though a part of each person.

For the first time since coming to Five Corners, all sense of Zac's separateness fled and he felt completely at one with these people. Late in the evening Sky took him upstairs to show him his new room, which could not have been more perfect. Entered through a secret door behind the wind bins, it seemed like the room he had always wanted—a room he had almost (if not consciously) foreseen. It was in fact the room Sky himself had had as a boy. The pleasantly sloped ceiling, as in Sky's office, reminded Zac of his old clubhouse. And of course there was a skylight, plus a dormer window that looked directly across the street to his old window at the Aunties' place, still boarded up, behind which lay the scene of so much torment. *What a short distance*, he thought, *but how far I had to travel to get here.*

"I wish I'd trusted you sooner, Sky."

"Things take as long as they take, Zac."

He was asleep before he knew it, and when he awoke and came downstairs, old Sam greeted him with, "Well, if it isn't Rip Van Zackle."

"Can't be," said Dan. "Hair's too short."

"We were afraid you'd sleep right through Christmas," said Eli.

It was Christmas Eve and already dark out. Zac had been

so tired, he'd slept the clock around. Ches and Chelsea and Tom and Iris were all there, and the old men were obviously tickled to have the store full of children.

"Can't have Christmas without kids," said Abe.

"Be like Valentine's without hearts," said Joe.

Then Zac had a thought. "Sky," he whispered, "what would happen if we gave some of Eldy's flowers to the old men? Could we all be children together?"

"I'm afraid not, Zac. These old men really are old. To try to change that would rob them of real life."

Noticing that Chelsea seemed uncharacteristically somber, Zac approached her shyly and asked, "You okay?"

Without looking up, she answered, "I wish my dad was here."

"How is he?"

"Still the same. He lies in bed perfectly still like he's fast asleep, but his eyes are wide open."

"At least he's still alive."

"Barely." Then Chelsea looked up. "I'm sorry, Zac. I know you miss your parents. And I know, in a way, my dad's been gone for a long time. But even Sky isn't sure if he'll recover and—"

Just then Iris walked by, looking more radiantly happy than anyone Zac had ever seen. There flashed in his mind the image of the hairy, tubby old Barber, repulsive as a troll, face pinched with age, bitterness, secret shame. What a transformation!

Chelsea must have thought the same, for she smiled, her black eyes sparkled, and she said, "Maybe the story's not over yet."

And so Christmas Eve was celebrated in Porter's General Store, with songs and stories and games and even dancing. All night long they carried on until the first light of day crept like a letter through the mail slot and turned the big black mirrors at the front of the store back into windows. It was Christmas morning and, delighted to discover it had snowed overnight, everyone went outside to romp and play and to greet the sunrise with Sky—a happy ritual that took Zac right back to his first morning in Five Corners and to his first unforgettable sight of the man who would, amazingly, become his adoptive father. Then, as now, the whole town had been transformed overnight, dressed like a bride in purest white so that it reminded Zac of the shining city his mother had yearned to go to. He wondered if she had found his father.

He wanted to talk to Sky about all this, but already everyone was trooping over to the Cholmondeleys' for breakfast. Mary, despite her husband having what Ches described as "a long winter's nap," wore a Santa hat and appeared happier than anyone could remember. Having laid in supplies from Porter's, she prepared a delicious breakfast of eggs and sausages and French toast, which Zac deftly sculpted into a snowman with yokes for eyes and sausage bits for buttons. It was the first proper meal that had ever been served in that dining room and Mary brought out her best china and silverware and even candelabra.

"Mom, what good are candles in broad daylight?" scoffed Ches.

"Candles are like smiles, Chesterton," she answered. "Always appropriate."

Ches frowned but didn't argue. Later, just as everyone was backing away from the table, Mary announced dessert.

"Dessert for *breakfast*?" cried a chorus of children.

"Of course," she replied. "It's Christmas." And then she carried out a platter of hot-from-the-oven pies, including Zac's all-time favorite, strawberry-rhubarb. Though this had been his own mother's specialty, even before the first bite melted in his mouth, he knew it would be just as good as hers. And it was.

"Zac, you're always welcome here," said Mary. "I love to cook and I have a lot of years to make up for. And Tom and Iris—please stay with us as long as you wish. I know Sky plans to trace your relatives, but until then consider this your home."

Tom and Iris, mouths filled with pie, offered no protest.

After breakfast they all went to church. Upon entering St. Heldred and All Angles, Sky strolled among the pews whistling softly to himself. He appeared extraordinarily happy and Zac asked what he was thinking.

"It's just so good to be here," Sky replied. "Though I've lived in Five Corners all my life, I've never been inside the church."

"Really? Why not?"

"Well, let's just say Dad and I were uninvited. It's a long story that has to do with O. I'll tell it to you sometime, not today."

Reverend Cholmondeley, of course, was not available to lead a service, but Mary played carols on the pump organ and after a while Sky began telling stories—not from the pulpit but just sitting on the wooden floor with everyone gathered around. He talked of everything from the blue umbrella to his own childhood, and he even gave a eulogy for his former neighbors, the Henbothers. Zac was amazed to think that the Aunties had once been little girls who snuck into Porter's Store to snitch candy!

How long they sat there in St. Heldred's listening to Sky, Zac couldn't say. He knew only that he was spellbound. And afterwards the day was still young and the sun still shone brilliantly as the children came spilling outside eager to make snowballs. Unfortunately it was too cold for sticky snow, so instead they made snow angels and then they all romped back to Porter's beneath the blue umbrella sky.

The rest of that Christmas was one big party in the store. As word got out, neighbors began dropping in for a look-see. It was, indeed, as though a spell had broken over the whole town, drawing people to Porter's who had not set foot there for years. At first they tended to stand apart wearing guarded looks, doubtless still worried that at any moment the notorious ghost of Porter's Store (or worse, the Aunties!) might jump out at them. But for most—though not all—suspicions soon melted in the genuine warmth of the gathering, amidst the sharing of punch and eggnog, shortbreads and peppermint candy.

"A toast to Porter's General Store!" someone would cry, and all glasses would rise.

"A toast to Mr. Porter!"

"A toast to Eldy!"

"A toast to Christmas!"

And of course there were gifts. Sky pulled things off the shelves to hand out, and soon everyone was doing the same, which Sky did not mind at all.

"That's what this store is for," he said.

Zac, for his part, ate more sugar than ever in his life and was soon laughing crazily, racing about playing tag, even dancing on the counters. Sugar or no, he would have been the life of the party, he was so happy. He felt like a spring, tightly coiled for weeks, finally released to go *boing*! The old men, too, were in fine form and with every joke they had Zac practically rolling on the floor.

"Hey, Zac, what do Santa's reindeer eat for breakfast?"

"Dunno."

"Frosted flakes!"

Then Sky was at his side, saying, "Come upstairs, Zac. You have a special present to open."

On the way they collected Ches and Chelsea, and the four of them mounted the stairs into the Weatherworks. It was completely quiet; no noise at all came from the party below. Once again, though it was obvious they were indoors, Zac had the curious sense of being outside. The upper room was much too large, it seemed, to be contained in this or any other building. The enormous barrels and bins and boxes of weather lined the walls like giant trees in an ancient grove, silent, waiting, as though never before seen by human eyes, never once disturbed in aeons of time.

"So this is the place," said Ches. "It's really real."

Zac resisted the urge to say I told you so.

"Almost feels like I've been here before," continued Ches, "in a dream or something. I'm sorry I didn't believe you, Zac."

Sky led the children to the giant white cardboard boxes that held different kinds of snow. Handing the blue umbrella to Chelsea, he said, "I thought it might be fun for each of you to choose the kind of snow you'd like for one day of the Christmas holidays."

"Even a blizzard?" asked Ches.

"I love a good blizzard myself," said Sky. "Chelsea? What'll it be?"

"Ooh, it's like choosing a flavor of ice cream," she said, pacing before the big boxes. She stopped before one whose label read SOFT & DREAMY. "I want a whole day of the biggest flakes I've ever seen, drifting down slowly and endlessly like feathers."

"A lovely choice," said Sky. Then he got Chelsea to write on the snow box, invisibly with the umbrella's tip, the date when she wanted the soft and dreamy snow.

Next it was Ches's turn. Cradling the umbrella gingerly in his arms, he ran his hand reverently again and again over the smooth blue fabric and the satisfying crook of the handle. When he was ready, he selected not a blizzard but a day of thin flakes floating lazily out of a cottony, gray sky.

"I just like that sort of mood," he said.

As for Zac, he went straight to the label that read WET & STICKY. "So we can build forts!" he cried.

"And snowmen!" said Chelsea.

"And have snowball fights!" added Ches.

Though Sky himself did not make a selection, Zac noticed him wave the umbrella before a perfectly round glass globe labeled MOONLIGHT. Not until later that night did Zac discover the reason for this. The party over, he lay in his room with Sky seated on the edge of the bed. They'd been talking for some time—the sort of dreamy talk that happens when hearts are so full they start to spill over.

"Sky, I don't understand what happened those two times I met my mother. Is she still alive, somehow, or isn't she? I mean, she's not here, right?"

"Depends what you mean by here. Is here Five Corners? Or is here *here* ...?" Sky touched Zac lightly in the center of his chest. As if he were a pool, Zac felt the touch rippling peacefully throughout his body.

"That city she went to, to find my father—is that a real place?"

"Of course."

Gazing out the window into the snowy night, Zac could almost see the place now. But not quite.

Eventually he said, "That was some trick you pulled with the red umbrella."

"We're just lucky it worked," said Sky.

"What do you mean?"

"Well, I had the umbrella in my left hand. Fortunately the lightning struck my left shoulder and traveled down that arm into the ground. If it had happened to strike my right shoulder, that would have been a different story."

"How so?"

"Then I would have been killed. Lightning can enter one side of the body and pass harmlessly through that same side. But if it crosses the heart, it's lights out."

Gently Sky squeezed Zac's shoulder, said a quiet good night, and was gone.

Zac lay in bed pondering. Who was this man who had not only adopted him as a son but was willing to die for him? Who was this who could summon clouds or paint a glory? Being close to such a person was like seeing the wind, talking to rain, holding hands with sunshine—or with lightning.

Outside it was snowing again—tiny silver flakes flowing past the window, so many they were like molecules of air made visible. There must have been a break in the clouds because just then a bright shaft of moonlight pierced the falling snow. It was a wonderful touch that reminded Zac of the first Christmas present he remembered receiving from his mother: a snow globe full of tiny glittering flakes whirling over a tiny town.

Zac was amazed, realizing that Sky had produced this effect especially for him. Through the window now he saw the moon itself, hanging fat and silvery as a Christmas ornament in the one cloudless patch. So far away it was, yet its light reached right into his room, and with it came a question: If Sky could make the moon shine, then did he control the moon itself, and the sun, and the planets and stars and … everything?

Zac's mind stopped there. Such thoughts were too big and he was too tired, and too happy, to think anymore. With a last glance into the vast, white, mysterious Christmas night snowing past his window, he closed his eyes and slept.

Have you entered the storehouses of the snow,
or seen where the hail is piled?
Do you know the place where lightning is launched,
or where the winds are scattered over the earth?
Who has the wisdom to count the clouds?
Who can tip over the water jars of the heavens?
Does the rain have a father?
Is there a womb for the dew?
—Job 38

... a little more ...

When a delightful concert comes to an end,

the orchestra might offer an encore.

When a fine meal comes to an end,

it's always nice to savor a bit of dessert.

When a great story comes to an end,

we think you may want to linger.

And so, we offer ...

AfterWords—just a little something more after you

have finished a David C. Cook novel.

We invite you to stay awhile in the story.

Thanks for reading!

Turn the page for ...

- **An Interview with Mike Mason**
- **Glossary**
- **Acknowledgments**

An Interview with Mike Mason

Where did you get your inspiration for The Blue Umbrella?

I live at the top of a hill. At the bottom of the hill, a couple of
blocks down, is the real Porter's Store. A few years ago I awoke
in the middle of the night to a flash of insight. I recalled that
when I was a little boy, many years ago and many miles away, I
also lived at the top of a hill and at the bottom was an old store.
How interesting! With this strange convergence of my present
and past lives, the whole geography of a children's fantasy novel
flowed into my mind. I could set the story right in my own
neighborhood! But it would really be the neighborhood of my
childhood, which is the deepest source of all writerly inspiration.

There was also a third old store, Foster's, which I knew as a
young man living in a small prairie town. Old Mr. Foster was
always talking about the weather and he even made up little
poems about it. In winter he might say:

> *Snow, snow, the lovely snow,*
> *You step on a bit and down you go.*

Or on a rainy day he'd say:

> *Sun, sun, the beautiful sun,*
> *It never shines, the son-of-a-gun!*

Listening to Mr. Foster recite his silly poems, one day my imagination got to wondering what might *really* be going on in that store …

Which character is most like you?

There is quite a bit of me in Zac Sparks—in two ways. Firstly, as a little boy I was very active and excitable and I got into a fair amount of trouble. I used to climb on top of the piano and shout, "Jump, Mommy, jump!" and from wherever she was in the house my mother would have to come running to catch me. And I once pushed the neighborhood bully off a high stone wall into a big tub of water! I picture Zac, under normal circumstances, as being like that.

This story, however, does not take place under normal circumstances. Zac's mother has died and he's been plunged into a dark situation, so for most of the book he struggles with grief, shock, fear, and confusion. This changes him. While he still has "sparks" of mischief and excitability, on the whole his behavior is much subdued, his natural character repressed. Interestingly I think this side of him reflects, to some extent, my adult self. Life has a lot of hard experiences that can knock you sideways. At some level aren't adults trying to get back to the fully alive children they once were?

So yes, I identify with Zac. But to say which character is *most* like me, I have to admit it's Ches. I like Ches a lot—so much that I decided to write book two in the series from Ches's point of view. Talk about repressed! Due to his background he has so many problems. But precisely because of that, he has a great journey to make from darkness to light.

Who is your favorite character?

Chelsea! I love her because she is the one who has most retained her childlikeness. Through her connection with Eldy, she has resisted all pressure to conform to the evil that has Five Corners in its grip. Book three in the series will be from Chelsea's point of view and I can hardly wait to write it!

This story seems to be an allegory. Did you start out intending to write an allegory or did it just happen?

For years I'd written nonfiction books with a message, and I was tired of that. I had nothing more to *tell* anyone; instead I just wanted to tell a good story. I had just turned fifty and I realized that fiction is what I'd really wanted to write all along. Somehow I'd gotten away from that, and it was time to return to my original dream.

So with *The Blue Umbrella* I set out with no message in mind, no allegory, just a story. As I went along, I myself was very surprised at the spiritual depth that developed. But I don't think this makes my book an allegory, so much as a work of literature with an allegorical dimension. An allegory tends to feel wooden because there is a clear one-to-one correspondence between all the elements of the story and some other reality. An allegory is so linked to what it represents that it cannot really stand on its own, whereas a good literary story, while it always points beyond itself, is fully alive in its own right.

Did you know how* The Blue Umbrella *would turn out? Were you surprised by any of the plot twists or characters?

At the outset I had a vague idea of the ending, which turned out to be completely different! Other than that, all I had were a few key scenes, places I wanted to get to. And I emphasize the word *places*. Books begin in different ways—sometimes with a character, sometimes with a bit of plot or setting. *The Blue Umbrella* is very much a novel of *setting*. From the beginning what was most vivid in my mind was the place: Porter's General Store at the five corners. Especially vivid was the all-important second story of Porter's. I've never actually been there (in the real store, I mean), but I did have a chance to visit the upper story of another old building down the street, while it was being renovated. This was a former service station that was being turned into, of all things, a chocolate factory! When the owner took me upstairs, I saw this huge room that looked like a dance hall, with a beautiful hardwood floor and no pillars, illuminated in the most extraordinary way by late-afternoon light. The building had one-hundred-foot beams, which meant (obviously) they were cut from trees at least a hundred feet tall. You don't see that anymore. My visit to that upper room was the inspiration for the Weatherworks.

Because I began my book with a setting, and not much else, the plot and characters came as a complete surprise as I wrote. I kept trying to make an outline but this didn't seem to work for me. In fact I discovered that I didn't really know how to tell a story, how to keep a plot moving over the long haul of a novel. Finding myself in the midst of a very steep learning curve, eventually I took a course that turned out to be exactly what I needed. The course was called *Story*, taught by Robert McKee—really a screenwriting course but wonderful for novelists, too. I can't recommend it highly enough. (McKee also has a book by the same title.)

What is your favorite type of weather and why?

I love thunder and lightning and wind. It goes back to my childhood when (just like Zac) I used to stay up with my mother late at night to watch storms. As it happens, the place where I live now (on the West Coast) doesn't have much electrical activity, but we do get a lot of rain. There's nothing I like better than an all-day rain. It's great writing weather! When the sun shines, it feels like a person should be outside enjoying it. But I'd rather have a good excuse to stay indoors and read and write.

When did you decide to be a writer?

I've wanted to be a writer since I was eleven years old. In grade 7 I had a great teacher who taught a form of creative writing that she called *Intensive Writing*. It was really a sneaky way of getting us to write poetry. From the moment I discovered that I could simply look at something (such as a spider spinning a web; I think that was my first topic) and write about it—and not just *about it* but *my feelings about it*—from that point I never looked back. I grew up in a family where deep feelings were repressed, never talked about, and so the idea that I could explore my feelings in writing was revolutionary to me. It seemed totally radical, and still does. Writing is a way of bringing one's inner life out into the open, and so bridging the two, and this is the most world-changing act a person can do. We all have these secret lives that we ourselves, often, are hardly aware of. To transform secrets into words and share them with others is truth.

In my pursuit of writing as a career, I made many mistakes. I've made even more in living my life. But somehow one thing I got right, both in writing and in life, was that, if I was going to be a writer, it meant not focusing on anything else. It meant not having any other career. It meant believing firmly enough in my artistic vision that, as long as I followed it faithfully, everything would work out. And it has. During my twenties I did a lot of odd jobs to support my writing—everything from library work to farming to garbage collecting. But for the last twenty-five years I've done nothing but write full time. And I love it!

Are you a disciplined writer or do you just write when you feel like it?

Yes! I write every day, five days a week, and usually I feel like it. I wake up in the morning thinking, "Oh boy, I get to write today!"

Having said that, I normally don't start until about 3:00 p.m., and then I write for three or four hours. Any longer and I soon get burned out. I start late in the day because, if I started any earlier, I would just keep going and become a workaholic. That's how much I love writing. So for me, the only way to have a life is to have it during the first part of the day. I also need time for planning, thinking, reading, handling the business end of writing, and just staring out the window or listening to music. Writing requires a lot of "nothing" time for mulling and daydreaming. Without that, creativity doesn't happen.

If I occasionally come to my writing desk and don't feel like writing, I just do it anyway, like being on a hike and putting one foot in front of another even if I'm worn out. It's like priming a pump: Pour in a few words, crank the handle a few times, and soon the stream is flowing. If I don't know where to start, I start where I *want* to. I try to identify one phrase or sentence or image that I find really intriguing, even if it's just a fragment and doesn't seem to be what I *should* be doing. Writing is fundamentally about writing what I *want*, not what I should. Otherwise it stops being fun.

What is your favorite novel?

My favorite books these days are children's books. I began reading them ten years ago, in preparation for writing my own, and it was a great revelation to read these stories as an adult. Children's literature allows an author to be idealistic in a way that modern adult literature does not. There are happy endings, heroic characters, a clear battle between good and evil, and portals leading to other worlds—all things that reflect, I believe, the deepest truths of life.

I love *The Lord of the Rings, The Chronicles of Narnia,* and some other classics. But right now I believe we're in a new golden age of children's literature, and I'm very excited about some books that have appeared more recently. For example, there's *Harry Potter* (of course!), Kenneth Oppel's *Airborn* series, and many others.

My favorite novel of all time is Mark Twain's *Huckleberry Finn*—full of page after page of pure, gorgeous, totally absorbing storytelling. Stevenson's *Treasure Island* is like that too; you get so deeply lost in the story you don't even notice you're turning pages. Another of my favorites is Jules Verne's *Twenty Thousand Leagues Under the Sea*—partly because I recall so vividly reading it as a boy, probably right around the time I began thinking of being a writer. I have a photograph of myself reading this book, which I think was the one that first opened my eyes to the imaginative possibilities of other worlds.

What is the main thing you hope readers remember from this story?

Weather: how it looks and feels, and how it suggests something much more than meets the eye. I want readers to remember Zac in his room at the Aunties' house, listening to the wind as it moves tree branches against his windowpane like someone tapping to be let in.

Have you ever wondered why weather is the number one topic of conversation? It seems like the smallest sort of small talk, but I think weather is really a very BIG topic. This is obvious in our own time, when the world is heading for climate disaster and everyone's talking about it. But even just normal chitchat about weather is, I believe, far more significant than it appears. I think it's a safe way for people to acknowledge something very important. We all have a deep yearning to discuss the big questions in life (such as "Why are we here?" and "What's it all about?"), but often we cannot talk freely because there are so many different beliefs and it just gets really awkward. Weather, however, is something right in our faces that both deeply affects us and that we can all agree on. It's perfectly obvious if it's raining or snowing or the sun is shining, and it's also perfectly obvious that such magnificent phenomena reflect a greater reality. Weather is the ultimate metaphor.

Glossary

These definitions are adapted from Websters-Online-Dictionary.org, Merriam-Webster.com/Dictionary, and Dictionary.Reference.com. Please check the dictionaries themselves for correct pronunciation.

albino	An animal or person with a condition that causes white hair, pink eyes, and milky skin.
alchemy	A combination of chemistry and philosophy, practiced in medieval times, that tried to change common metals into gold, find a single cure for all diseases, and discover a way to live forever.
ambrosial	Extremely pleasing to taste or smell; heavenly.
anemometer	An instrument used to measure the speed of wind.
apparatus	Equipment used for a specific task.
apparition	An unusual sight; a ghostlike figure.
aria	A complicated song, sung by a single voice and accompanied by other instruments.
atheist	A person who believes God does not exist.
aural	Having a distinct quality or atmosphere, like light or energy, radiating from within.
beatific	Giving bliss or extreme happiness.
balletic	Graceful and dancelike.
barometers	Instruments used to measure the pressure of the atmosphere.
behemoth	Something of monstrous size, power, or appearance.

blithe	Happy and lighthearted.
bludgeoning	Hitting heavily with a club or similar object.
brollies	Umbrellas.
bulbous	Round and bulging, like a bulb.
bumbershoot	An umbrella.
burgeoning	Growing and multiplying, like a plant sending off new shoots.
cannibalized	Having used part of one thing to feed or develop something else, such as one human eating another's flesh.
cavernous	Huge and winding; resembling a cave or cavern.
cavorting	Leaping and dancing wildly.
chinchilla	Made from the extremely soft fur of the chinchilla, a pearly-gray, squirrel-like animal from South America.
cirrostratus	A type of cloud found at high altitudes; very thin and made partly of ice crystals.
clandestinely	With secrecy or the attempt to keep something hidden.
coiffures	Arrangements of women's hair.
coloratura	A singer, usually a soprano, who specializes in a complicated style of opera music with many runs and trills.
conjecturing	Guessing or deducing a conclusion that may or may not be correct.
convection	A weather condition that occurs when atmospheric conditions move upward.
convivial	Enjoying the pleasures of good company.

after words

convoluted	Rolled or twisted together.
corroboration	Evidence or confirmation that something is true.
cumulonimbus	A type of cloud also called a thunderhead; has large, dense towers that stretch to high altitudes.
cumulus	A type of cloud that resembles a puffy pile or heap.
decrepitude	Deterioration; loss of strength or energy because of old age.
demurred	Made an objection.
dew point	The temperature at which dew starts forming.
diaphanous	Thin, gauzy, almost transparent.
diminutive	Having a small size or stature.
dirigible	A steerable balloon; an airship.
divulged	Shared a secret.
dodecahedron	A three-dimensional geometric shape with twelve faces or sides.
ebullient	Energetic; free, lively, and unrestrained.
effervescence	Having the trait of giving off bubbles.
eminence	A person who has high rank; someone prominent and worthy of respect.
encumbered	Burdened or hampered by a heavy load.
enigmas	Mysteries; things that are impossible to understand or explain.
ensconced	Settled, established.
erratic	Having no appearance of regularity or pattern; random
escargots	French for snails that have been prepared to be eaten.

expunging	Deleting, erasing, wiping away.
flabbergasted	Overwhelmed by astonishment, shock, or surprise.
fulminating	Suddenly and intensely exploding with a loud noise.
funereal	Suitable for the graveside or burial.
gamut	A complete range or series.
gargantuan	Huge, gigantic.
garrulous	Uninterestingly talkative.
grotesquely	With the quality of being distorted into absurdity or ugliness.
guffawed	Burst out in hearty laughter.
harangue	A ranting speech or lecture.
hors d'oeuvres	Appetizers; small, savory dishes served before the main meal.
hove	Rose; became raised.
hucksterism	Peddling, selling.
hygrometers	Instruments used to measure the water-vapor content of the atmosphere.
hyperventilations	Quick, uncontrolled gasps of breath.
imbecile	Fool, idiot.
imbued	Filled completely, saturated.
incarnations	Something, such as an idea or concept, appearing in human form.
indecorous	Improper, violating good manners.
isobars	A line drawn on a weather chart that connects points at which the barometric pressure is the same.

kilopascals	The measurement unit for air pressure.
lambent	Softly bright or radiant.
lamé	Shiny fabric for clothing.
languidness	Feeling of droopiness or sluggishness from exhaustion; desiring no quick movement.
limpid	Clear, serene, and untroubled.
lurid	Horrifying, revolting.
macabre	Being a reminder of death or of something gruesome.
magnanimous	Showing nobility or generosity.
malarkey	Nonsense.
many-faceted	Having many faces or surfaces.
mawkish	Sickly, childishly sentimental.
meticulous	Having extreme attention paid to details.
mimeographed	Copied using a system of pressing ink through a stencil.
nephology	The study of clouds.
nephoscope	An instrument that shows the speed and direction of cloud motion.
nimbostratus	A type of cloud that appears shapeless and dark gray; a lower-altitude rain cloud.
oblong	Oval-shaped.
officiousness	Dutiful volunteering of one's services, whether or not they are requested.
orotund	Proud, pompous.
ovoid	Egg-shaped.
pachyderm	An elephant.
pallid	Pale and lacking in color.

palpable	Touchable.
paraphernalia	Collection of various items or accessories.
pâté de foie gras	A French delicacy; a spread made from fat goose liver and usually a specific, expensive mushroom called a truffle.
patina	An appearance or aura belonging to something that has grown beautiful with age.
pedantry	Narrow-mindedness; formal, unimaginative use of knowledge.
phosphorescent	Still showing light, even after the source of the light has stopped.
pinioning	Binding the arms.
plaintive	Sad; expressing sorrow or suffering.
porticoed	Having a porch or a walkway with a roof supported by columns.
preponderance	A great number; a majority.
prerogatives	Privileges deserved because of having a certain position or job.
preternatural	Abnormal; supernatural.
prodigious	Amazing because of its size or amount.
promontory	A rocky, elevated cliff or plateau that overlooks a low area.
propriety	Appropriate behavior; good manners.
psychrometer	An instrument used to determine the humidity of the atmosphere.
raucous	Unpleasantly loud, harsh, or disorderly.
robustness	Display of health and strength.
sacrilegious	Violating something sacred; irreverent.

séance	A ritual meeting where people seek communication with spirits or ghosts.
sequestered	Set apart; secluded, placed alone.
skinflint	Miser; someone who would do anything to save or gain money.
sonorous	Full and imposing in sound.
sotto voce	Soft; in undertones.
spasmodic	Having fits of sudden violence, intensity.
specter	A visible spirit or ghost.
stratus	A type of cloud that has a gray horizontal layer and is found at lower altitudes.
succumbed	Gave in; collapsed under pressure.
suffused	Washed; spread over and through like fluid or light.
supernal	Heavenly; coming from on high.
taboo	Socially unacceptable; forbidden.
terrazzo	A polished, mosaic flooring made from bits of marble set in cement.
tome	A thick book; a volume in a series.
trepidation	Nervous, trembling fear and agitation.
unctuously	Too smooth; too sweet; excessively smooth.
vellum	Young animal skin treated so that it could be written on.
verboten	Forbidden; prohibited.
vileness	Being offensive, unpleasant, and repulsive.
visage	The face.
vortex	A whirling mass with a powerful, drawing current.